What I love about this writing group is that every author is a talented individual in their own right, but the genius is in how each of their individual – and sometimes very different – stories is magically woven together to create a single, whole, utterly compelling, many-faceted plot. It is so clever: brilliant!

Mimi Harker OBE

With a canny approach to writing a collaborative anthology, Buckinghamshire group Just Write create a seamless fictional world in Spilling the Beans, *in which each member contributes stories set in the same location and time, '...a day in the life of a coffee shop' and introduced each other's characters in the background to give the book a cohesion and consistency rarely found in group anthologies.*

Writing Magazine, July 2015

Another professional-level selection from last year's Anthology Award winners Just Write, Delayed Reaction *is testament to the value of producing anthology pieces to order. The book itself is of the highest standard, well-designed, with individual title pages for each story, a reader-friendly layout and attractive cover, all coming together to create an appealing package that is already into its second print run.*

Writing Magazine, July 2016

Delayed Reaction, *a modern-day* Canterbury Tales, *sweeps you along like an express train with its absorbing stories on current themes. The characters not only have their moment in the spotlight but are also cleverly woven into supporting roles throughout the book. I was so hooked in I was sorry to reach my destination. It was first class – I want a season ticket. Bring on the next collection.*

Barbara Fisher, journalist and columnist

SHAKESPEARE STREET

Ordinary lives...
extraordinary tales

In support of
The Hospice
of st francis

·SHAKESPEARE STREET·

Different times...

different lives...

different stories...

SHORT STORIES BY JUST WRITE

Self-published by Just Write, Amersham

First published in Great Britain 2017

ISBN 978-0-9931222-4-8

Design and artwork by Graham Blundell and Stuart Tennant.

Printed and bound in Great Britain.

A proportion of the proceeds from the sale of each book will be donated to The Hospice of St Francis in Berkhamsted.
(Registered charity number: 80825)

Acknowledgements

Just Write's thanks go to Chas Burton for his cover design and illustrations, to Melissa Scott-Miller for giving us permission to use two of her paintings on the front and back covers (inside and out) and on the title pages, and to Graham Blundell for preparing all the artwork. All of this work was done under the direction of Just Write member Stuart Tennant, to whom we are very grateful.

The texts were tirelessly edited by Lesley Close and proofread by Janet Mears.

Thanks are also due to the many anonymous test readers whose input improved the stories immensely.

Above all, the authors would like to thank Nicki Kelland, whose organisational skills and endless patience were vital to the task of producing this book.

About The Hospice of St Francis

The Hospice of St Francis provides free care and support when it matters most for around 2,000 people a year across West Herts and South Bucks, who are living with a life-limiting illness. It also supports their families, carers and those close to them.

Its professional multi-disciplinary team offers support from diagnosis, with care tailored to each individual's needs, helping patients to improve and maintain their quality of life – be that at home, at its health and wellbeing Spring Centre or in one of its 14 beds.

It also works closely with local hospitals and nursing homes to support patients and share best practice.

The Hospice is a registered charity, which receives less than 20% of its over £5million annual running costs from the NHS, relying on voluntary donations from the local community for the remainder.

In a year when it is celebrating the 10th anniversary of moving to its purpose-built premises in Spring Garden Lane, Berkhamsted, all monies raised through the sale of this book will help it to continue its vital work.

The Hospice
of st francis

www.stfrancis.org.uk

Case Study: *A positive ending...*

Philip and Jemma Crane were just five years into their marriage, enjoying family life with their two-year-old son Charlie, when out of the blue, in November 2015, Philip, 49, was diagnosed with terminal stomach cancer. He was given twelve months to live with treatment, and two to four months without it.

Both Philip and Jemma were apprehensive about receiving help from a hospice, but Jemma, 37, explains: "The impact of losing Philip has been huge – nothing else could have been so life-changing. But the all-round support we received as a family from The Hospice of St Francis – before, during and since Philip's death – has been invaluable. I can honestly say that our experience has totally changed our perceptions of what a hospice does.

"It's a really positive place which gave us valuable time together as a family – time for Charlie to play on the grass with his toy lawn mower; time to share hot meals in the dining room; time to watch Tottenham games on the telly over a take-away and a beer, and time for Charlie and I to be helped to deal with our loss in the right way – times that I will never forget."

This book is dedicated to David James Matthews 1991–2016

In Just Write's previous books, David told the story of his two-year battle with bone cancer. His tremendous courage inspired us to donate over £1,000 from the proceeds of our sales to the Royal Marsden Cancer Charity. When we published *Delayed Reaction* in 2015, David was in remission. Tragically, the cancer returned and David died in St Wilfrid's Hospice, Eastbourne, in September 2016, just four days after marrying his partner, Emily. Just Write is proud to dedicate this third collection of short stories to the memory of a brave, delightful young man.

INTRODUCTION

If you are reading this you have probably bought the book, so thank you! To date, Just Write has donated over £1,000 from the proceeds of book sales to The Royal Marsden Cancer Charity. A percentage of the proceeds from sales of this book will be donated to The Hospice of St Francis in Berkhamsted. This charity, which is local to us, has supported many terminally ill people of all ages as well as their relatives, including a member of our group.

Shakespeare Street is the third volume of short-stories-to-a-theme produced by Amersham-based writing group Just Write. The group first met in 2013, when Sally Norton started a writing class of the same name, and our mutual love of writing proved to be the foundation of a group with friendship at its heart. In addition we discovered that, between us, there was a broad spectrum of writing, editing and publishing experience.

We decided to put all this to good use by collaborating on our first book but, instead of following the traditional route of many anthologies in which the authors put together a collection of their best work, we decided to approach the book as more of a novel-with-ten-authors by creating a set of new stories. The result was an integrated story in which the characters moved in and out of one another's lives. The whole process was a huge learning curve, with communication and co-operation being the key to our success.

In that first book, *Spilling the Beans,* we took readers inside the lives of customers and staff in a coffee shop where they could eavesdrop on conversations and watch relationships unfold or finish. We were tremendously proud that this book won *Writing Magazine*'s Anthology Competition for 2014.

Our next book, *Delayed Reaction,* was a runner-up in the same competition the following year. In this collection, we reserved a seat for each reader on a stationary train where a series of dramas unfolded as a result of the delay.

While *Delayed Reaction* was in production, Nicki and Carol joined Sally's class. We invited them to join Just Write in January 2016 just as we were starting to discuss our next project, *Shakespeare Street,* the book you are holding in your hands.

The stories in this volume were inspired by the Shakespeare quote each author chose, quotes which appear at the start of each story. Unlike *Delayed Reaction,* there was only one rule governing the writing: that all the tales had to be set – in part, at least – in *Shakespeare Street.* They could be of any genre and the action could take place at any time since the late 1700s when the first of our invented houses were built in our fictional north London street. In this book we invite you to walk with us along that street, to take a look through the curtains and to peer into darkened hallways. As you do so, you will take a journey through time.

But we must detain you no further. Come with us into Shakespeare Street, and enjoy the walk.

Contents

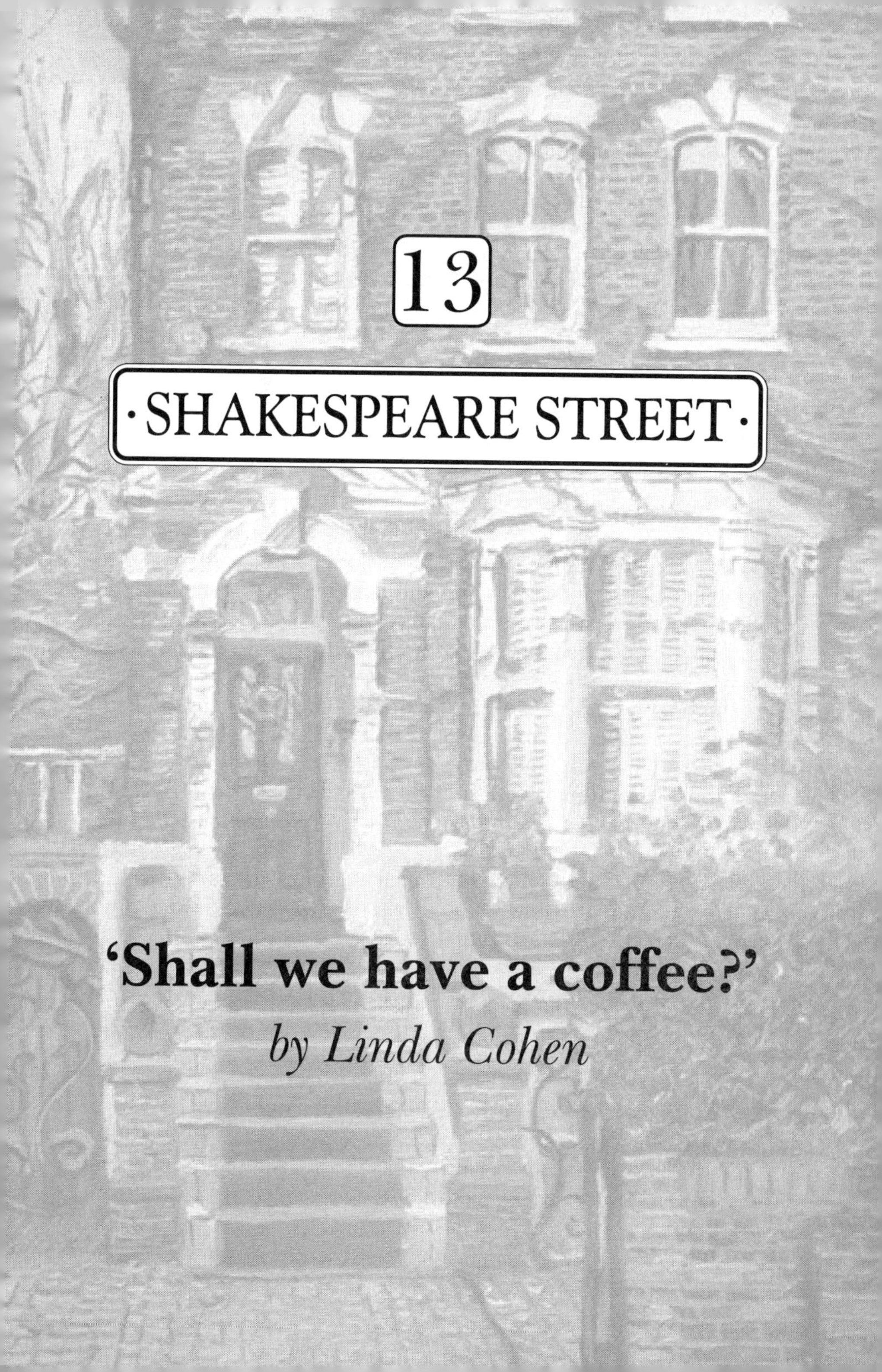

13

SHAKESPEARE STREET

'Shall we have a coffee?'

by Linda Cohen

I would not wish any companion in the world but you

The Tempest, Act 3, Scene 1

Emma's heart sank as she drew up outside the house. Re-reading the estate agent's ad she groaned inwardly. 'Desirable area, good family-sized house, needs some attention. Extremely good value, close to schools and shops.'

The line 'Needs some attention' is certainly true, she thought as she peered up at the peeling paintwork and cracked window frames. *Oh well, I might as well go in. I'm here now.*

Ringing the bell, she waited while whoever was inside could be heard shouting down the phone. 'Of course I'm bloody well trying to sell it. I can't help it if the place is a dump. You should've paid more attention to it while you were here instead of running around the country, sleeping with whoever you fancied . . . I've got to go, somebody is here.'

A dishevelled man opened the door, running his hands through his hair. 'Sorry about that,' he said. 'I was on the phone.' He stepped aside, allowing Emma to come in.

'Yes. I heard,' she said.

His eyes were strained and he was barefoot. Emma felt sorry for him. An air of despondency clung to him, giving him the appearance of a broken man.

'Hi, I'm Jake,' he said.

'Oh. Emma. Emma Hart,' she said. 'I've been sent by Hardwicke and Sons, the estate agents.'

'Excuse the mess,' Jake said. 'Meant to get up a bit earlier and clear up, but you know how it is.'

Emma smiled. She certainly did know how it was, the effort of putting on a brave face, showing your home to a stranger, trying to impress them with the extra lighting, or the fitted bathroom cupboard, or yet another power point, and knowing in your heart that the whole place needed to be gutted to ever resemble a loving home for anyone.

Emma smiled again. 'Please don't worry. I won't take up much of your time. I'll just have a quick look round then get out of your way.'

'Oh, don't rush on my behalf,' ventured Jake. 'I've nothing to do, nowhere to go. Take as long as you like.' He swept some half-eaten pizza and yesterday's newspapers out of the way while he gestured to her to carry on.

'I'll let you look round on your own. You don't need me following you around. You can get more of a feel of a place if you look at it without the owner breathing down your neck.'

Jake smiled and Emma was grateful to him. 'Thank you. Thank you so much. Where shall I start?'

'How about the garden?' suggested Jake. 'I've always been happiest in the garden.'

He pointed to the French doors and they both stepped outside.

Emma gasped; she hadn't been expecting that. A long lawn swept down to the end, with flower borders on either side brimming with stocks, lupins, hollyhocks and roses. A little water feature spouted merrily away and an apple tree was laden with fruit. 'It's enchanting,' said Emma.

'Thank you,' Jake replied. 'It's my life's work. I love it. To be honest it kept me sane while . . . ' His voice trailed off, and Emma noted the look of pain that shot across his face. She gazed around the garden, in awe at the beauty of it all.

'Do you do it all yourself?' she asked.

'Yup,' said Jake. 'Every moment I can when I'm not working, which to be honest is practically most of the time now.' He gave a laboured laugh, and Emma felt sad for this man who obviously had toiled long and hard out here and was now having to give it all up.

'It's what I do,' he said, 'gardening. I'm actually a landscape gardener, or I was before my business went bust.'

'Oh,' said Emma. 'I'm sorry to hear that. But no wonder your garden is so fantastic.'

'Wish some of my clients felt that way,' said Jake bitterly, 'or at least paid their bills. That would have been a help.'

Emma found herself once again feeling so sorry for this man, and she didn't really know what else to say. 'Well, I'll just take a look around inside now if you don't mind,' she said, trying to lighten the mood a bit.

'I was just about to make myself a coffee,' said Jake. 'Would you like one?'

'That would be lovely. Thanks.' Emma had rushed from her shift at the hospital without any breakfast to see the house. The estate agent told her it wouldn't hang around. *A real bargain,* he'd said, *and a queue of people lining up to see it.* He suggested she should act quickly if she wanted a chance of buying it.

Gordon was pushing her to leave the flat. He wanted her out so he could get on with his new life with Erica. He was putting so much pressure on her that some days she felt she would burst with the anguish, disappointment and sadness of her situation.

How could Gordon do this to their son? She was tired of trying to hide her sadness from four-year-old Bobby. One day he would have to know – he'd have to be told that his father had cast them aside, telling her he didn't love her anymore, that he had grown tired of their life together, that he needed to move on, to have a more exciting woman by his side as he climbed up the career ladder in his City job. He had said that he needed a more sophisticated woman, one who could entertain his clients, provide amazing dinner parties at the drop of a hat and talk intellectually to the crowd he moved with.

That last bit really hurt Emma. After a twelve-hour shift at the hospital it was hard to put a boiled egg on the table for herself and Bobby once she had picked him up from the childminder, let alone cook for a dinner party for six – or more – of Gordon's friends. The unfairness of the situation made tears prick behind her eyes, and she fought hard to pull herself together.

Conversations she and Gordon had had played over and over in her mind. The night she confronted him when she found him hunched over his mobile once more in the garden – that was the night she realised he had been having an affair with Erica. 'Actually, you are right,' he said. 'I never meant to hurt you but I am in love with Erica, and I have been for eighteen months now. We really tried, Emma, but I do love her.' He had tried to placate Emma by saying 'Of course I love you as well, but we have grown apart over the years and I think it would be better if we separated.'

Emma remembered reeling from the pain of it all. Her first thought was for their little boy. How would he cope without his daddy being there? Then she felt intense anger for the waste of it all, for the fact that Gordon could push them both aside and let this stranger come in and take over their lives.

Suddenly from downstairs she heard Jake's voice. 'Coffee's on the table when you are ready.' Emma pulled herself back from her thoughts and tried to concentrate on looking round the house. Wiping a small tear that had escaped from her eyes she gazed around the second bedroom, wondering whether Bobby would be happy in this room. She imagined him with his Peppa Pig posters on the wall and his little train set on the window sill, and she could almost see him there. Yes it was scruffy, but nothing a bit of paint wouldn't sort out. She ran down the stairs to join Jake in the kitchen. She would look at the rest of the house after her coffee.

Jake had put her coffee on the scrubbed pine kitchen table, and even put a plate of biscuits out with it. She smiled her thanks at him, and then immediately felt awkward. Should she sit, or stand? What do you do, two strangers standing together but each with their own agenda? And if she got too friendly with this man how awkward would it be if she wanted to make an offer on the house – if she liked it? She decided to stand. Jake offered her a biscuit but she declined, even though she really wanted one. *Best not to get too familiar,* she thought, *but a cup of coffee won't harm.* Besides, she felt faint from her long shift and a lack of food and drink.

Emma gulped the coffee down, while Jake stood on the other side of the table. 'So, have you sold your property?' Jake casually enquired.

'Oh, I don't need to,' said Emma. 'My partner is buying me out of my share. I just need somewhere for me and my son to call home for now.' Too much information, she thought. *Why did I tell him that?*

Jake looked at her. 'Oh I'm sorry. It sounds like we have a similar situation, except that I'm being kicked out rather than bought out.' He smiled an engaging smile, and Emma found herself warming to this man.

'Oh, I'm sorry too,' said Emma. 'Not much fun is it?'

'Fun it isn't,' said Jake. 'Still . . . the sooner I am out of here the better it will be, though I will miss the garden,' he said thoughtfully.

'Well, I'll carry on with the tour then, if you don't mind,' said Emma.

'No, you go ahead. Don't mind me.' With that he sat down at his computer and stared at the screen. Emma couldn't help noticing it was a list of properties. Just like her, he was trying to find another suitable home.

Emma climbed the stairs again, and peered into the bathroom. *What a mess,* she thought, although she smiled at the little yellow plastic duck sitting on the unit. *Funny, he doesn't look like the plastic duck sort.*

His bedroom looked as though it belonged to a student or a teenager and Emma couldn't help smiling to herself. There were clothes everywhere and piles of books on the floor. She glanced at some of the titles. Most of them seemed to be about history and there were lots of travel books. She wondered about him for a while. These books obviously reflected his interests, together with gardening of course.

The house really was in a state, and she wondered whether she would ever have the energy – or the money – to put it right. She wandered down to the lounge where she was surprised to see a grand piano. She gazed around the room, which had obviously been rather lovely at some point. She knew that this house needed a proper family living in it to become the home she would want.

'Thank you so much,' she said, 'for letting me have a look round. It's really nice but, to be honest, I think there is too much work to do before I could be comfortable here.' She hoped she hadn't hurt him.

'Oh I agree,' he said. 'It needs a bundle spending on it.'

Emma laughed. 'You aren't supposed to say that,' she said. 'You're supposed to be trying to sell it to me.'

'Well, I'm realistic,' Jake answered. 'It was going to be the perfect house, the perfect home. We had so many plans, my ex and I.'

Emma didn't know what to say. Once again she found herself feeling so sorry for this engaging man. He was so honest, and the hurt he felt was palpable. She wished she could make it better for him.

'I'm sure you'll find a buyer soon,' said Emma, trying to find something to say to comfort him. 'The agent told me you have loads of people queuing up to see the house.'

'He said *what?'* asked Jake. 'No-one's been for two weeks. I've had it on the market for nine months and I've dropped the price twice, but still no-one's interested. Still, that's estate agents for you. Don't they know people have eyes in their head, and can see for themselves what a dump it truly is?'

They stared at each other for a moment. Jake hadn't meant to say that, and Emma was shocked at his honesty. They both burst out laughing at the same time.

'Well,' said Emma, reaching out to shake his hand. 'Thank you so much for showing me the dump. I'll let the agent know.'

'It's nice to have met you,' said Jake. 'Good luck with your search. I hope you find what you're looking for.' He showed Emma to the door.

'Hope you find a buyer soon,' she said.

'Oh some mug will go for it sometime,' he said. 'I just need someone with vision and a large paintbrush'. They laughed again as Emma stepped outside and he added, 'oh, and by the way, who would live at No.13? That's another thing against it!' He laughed. As she got into her car, Emma saw the curtains twitch in the house opposite and she wondered who lived there.

Emma found herself smiling all the way home. This was the first time she had felt anything but sad in months.

Life went on for Emma. She was working harder than ever. Gordon was getting more and more frustrated at the lack of what he called her *initiative* in trying to find a new home for herself and Bobby. He even offered to view a few houses with her but Emma knew that would be a disaster. He would definitely try to push her into buying the first one he saw just to make things happen, regardless of whether or not it would be suitable for her and Bobby. She found it strange how the man she had married had suddenly become a hardened stranger.

'You know Emma,' he had said, 'I will always have you and Bobby's best interests at heart. He is my son as well as yours, and I love him.'

Emma had baulked at this. Yes, she thought. You love him. As long as you don't have to get up in the night when he has a nightmare, or he's sick and you might have to take time off of work to help look after him. You love him when he's being cute, or just playing quietly. As long as he's the perfect child, you love him. She wondered how the immaculate Erica would cope when it was their weekend to have Bobby and he didn't fit into their criteria of eating at the best restaurants. Time would tell on that one.

Emma reflected on how she had somehow always known – but denied – that Erica and Gordon had feelings for each other. How at the office party he had been so attentive to Erica, making sure her glass was always full. How he had laughed at Erica's jokes far longer than anyone else had. How he had praised her constantly as being the best PA he had ever had. Emma had noticed their glances towards each other when they thought no-one else was looking. It was probably inevitable, Emma thought. This was probably always going to happen, but she didn't have the energy to fight for her marriage anymore.

It had still come as a complete surprise when Gordon said he would make sure that she and Bobby had a house, not a flat. 'Bobby will need a garden as he gets older,' he had said. 'You know, somewhere for him to play football with his friends.' Emma had smiled to herself. Of course she knew this was her incentive to hurry out of their flat so he could move Erica in, but nevertheless it was definitely a result as far as Emma was concerned. She hadn't reckoned on having a garden, so at least some good had come out of their car crash of a marriage.

Over the next few weeks Emma's thoughts occasionally went back to the man at 13 Shakespeare Street. She found herself wondering how he was, whether he had had any luck in selling the house and, most importantly, whether he had tidied it up a bit. She wondered whether or not the house was sold, and how he was doing. *Strange,* she thought, *how you can meet someone for just a little while yet at odd times of the day they suddenly sprang into your mind.*

* * *

The phone started ringing, and Emma ran to answer it. 'Good morning Mrs Evans,' said a cheerful voice on the other end of the phone. 'And how are you today?' Emma recognised the really irritating man who worked at Hardwicke and Sons.

'Oh, hi,' she answered.

'Are you still looking for a property?' he asked her.

She felt like saying 'Well of course I am, you idiot! Everything you've shown me has been a disaster,' but she managed to keep her cool. Instead she answered, politely, 'Yes. I'm still looking.'

The estate agent started his usual patter. 'Well, you are in luck. Now I know you've already seen 13 Shakespeare Street but just today the gentleman who lives there has made an enormous reduction. Not only that, but he has done it up as well. So now it's not just £50,000 less than when you looked at it last time, but it has also been painted and spruced up. If I may say so, it looks a million dollars now.'

Emma sighed. 'Thank you,' she said, 'but I really don't think that is the house for me.'

'Now, now, Mrs Evans,' the irritating man carried on. 'You can't let an opportunity like this pass you by. What have you got to lose just by checking out what he's done to it?'

Emma sighed again. *Oh well, there's nothing else on the horizon,* she thought. *Maybe it would be worth another look just for the garden alone.* She hadn't been able to get the garden out of her mind, and a tiny part of her just wondered how Jake was doing. *What harm could it do?*

'Alright,' she said. 'Make me another appointment. I can go tomorrow at 4:15, if that's OK with the owner.'

'Will do,' he replied, speaking hastily in case she changed her mind, 'and I know you will just love it this time.'

Throughout the next day Emma found herself looking forward

to her appointment. As a nurse, she was on her feet nearly all day but somehow this day she didn't feel as tired as usual when the working day drew to a close. She had arranged for a friend to pick Bobby up from the childminder and, as she got ready to leave work, she noticed she took just a little bit longer to comb her hair and she put on fresh lipstick. *What am I like?* she thought.

This time as she approached the door of 13 Shakespeare Street she could hear beautiful piano music coming from behind it. She listened enraptured. Did he have a CD on? Surely that couldn't be him playing? Yet he did have a piano. She remembered being surprised by it but thought maybe it had belonged to his ex-wife. She rang the bell, the music stopped and she heard footsteps echoing down the hall.

As he opened the door Emma found herself smiling at the lovely face looking back at her.

'Well, hello again,' he said. 'I see the villains at Hardwicke and Sons have hijacked you into seeing this old place again. Come in, come in. I think you will see a bit of a change this time,' he said, 'at least I hope you will.'

As Emma stepped into the hall she experienced a vague feeling of homecoming. *This is where I belong,* Emma thought. It certainly had changed – the wallpaper was colourful and there were lovely lights hanging from the ceiling and walls. The house felt familiar, comfortable, welcoming and so cosy. 'It's beautiful,' she gasped. 'What have you done?'

'What I've done,' said Jake, 'is to stop feeling sorry for myself. I got off my backside, tidied the house up and did some decorating instead of just sitting slumped in a chair the whole time. I think you'll like what I've done. At least, I hope you do. Anyway, I would welcome your opinion on it. It's always good to have a woman's point of view. Of course, it still needs some curtains and a few homely touches but, on the whole, I've more or less finished it now.'

Emma looked from room to room, loving everything he had done. He had certainly been busy.

'It's wonderful,' she said. 'I love it.' She glanced outside to the garden, and once again it captivated her.

'It's funny,' said Jake. 'After you left last time I thought about what you said about making a home for you and your son, and I realised this wasn't a home. It was a shrine to a long-dead marriage. I know it sounds strange, but the whole time I was doing it up I was thinking what it would mean to someone like you if you moved in here. It actually gave me the incentive to do the work. And I couldn't help thinking about the Polish chap at number 37. It must have been so hard for him, coming over here without his family. Yet there he is, every day, painting and decorating for the chap who owns the house. He seems so self-contained and so happy in what he's doing. I thought, *If he can do it,* I *can do it,* and I did.' Jake grinned with delight at what was his obvious pride.

'Please don't feel pressured or anything,' he laughed. 'I didn't mean to sound like I was forcing you into buying it. In fact, quite a few people are coming back for second viewings. What I meant was that you made me realise that there you are, desperately needing a new home, and here I am with that very home but just sitting here, letting it fall into disrepair through my lack of care and despondency, and I could actually do something about it.'

He paused for breath, but spoke again before Emma could respond. 'And the best thing is that I've realised I love painting and decorating. Several people I know asked me to help them re-decorate their homes, and they've recommended me to other people. So now I'm going into business as a painter and decorator as well as a landscape gardener!'

'Wow,' said Emma. 'That's brilliant. Is there no end to your talent?'

'Oh, there's definitely an end to my talent,' he replied, laughing. 'More importantly is there a beginning?'

Emma looked at him. There was a light in his eyes that hadn't been there before. He looked so much better, stronger somehow, and she realised that it was probably six months since she had last viewed the house. Six months in which she herself had grown stronger, more able to make decisions and to stand on her own two feet. She supposed that was what people meant when they said that things happened *in the fullness of time*. Both she and Jake had moved on from the people they were to the people they had become. How wonderful that feeling was, and she was pleased for the progress both of them had made.

She realised that she and Gordon had been living as strangers side by side for far too long. She knew it would be such a relief to get away, to start again somewhere new. She'd be able to stop living a lie, at last.

'Would you like a coffee?' Jake asked.

'I'd love one,' Emma replied.

This time when Jake put out the coffee and the biscuits they both sat at the table, completely at ease with each other. 'So what do you think,' Jake asked. 'What do you think of the *dump* now?' He looked so proud, and so pleased with himself, that Emma found herself overcome with emotion.

'I really love it,' she replied. 'And I know Bobby will love it too. Please may I have it?'

Jake smiled his open easy smile. 'I couldn't think of a nicer person to take it off my hands,' he replied.

'Then let's shake on it,' said Emma. 'I'll call the agent straight away.'

'Call him from here, if you like,' said Jake. 'That's if you don't think I'm being too pushy . . . '

So Emma called Hardwicke and Sons and told them she loved it. She hated having to put up with the irritating agent telling her there were *lots of people after it* and she would have to *pay the full price to get it* and she would have to *move very quickly* if she was lucky enough to get it. Emma felt herself getting frantic in case someone else was able to snatch it away from her.

As she put the phone down, she saw Jake was watching her carefully. 'You OK?' he asked.

Emma sighed. 'He told me there are lots of people after it now, and if I don't move quickly I could lose it,' she told him, despondently.

Jake looked at her. 'I'm the one who says who will have it, not him. It's in my hands, not his.'

Emma smiled with relief. 'I can't believe it,' she said. 'Have I just found a home?'

'I'll get things moving as quickly as possible,' she said. 'Have you found somewhere to go?'

Jake sighed. 'Not yet, but I will. I'm only renting this time. There's only me – oh, and my piano of course.'

'And your yellow plastic duck,' interrupted Emma laughing. 'Don't forget your yellow duck.' They smiled gently at each other. 'You need to find a home for him as well,' said Emma.

'You're right,' said Jake. 'It's not his fault he's a victim of a broken home, but Rodney is tough.'

'Rodney,' said Emma, smiling. 'That's a nice name for a duck.'

'Thank you,' said Jake. 'Yes, I thought so . . . I can go anywhere,' he told her sadly. 'Well, at least, anywhere they will let a piano in – and a duck of course. I can't let go of my piano. It belonged to my late mother and she loved it. I can never hear Rachmaninoff without thinking of her, sitting at the piano with a faraway look in her eyes, and playing so beautifully.'

Emma looked across the table, and felt her heart breaking for this lovely man. Standing up, she hurriedly gathered her stuff together, feeling guilty about her excitement. 'I'll get things moving as quickly as I can,' she repeated.

Once again they wished each other luck, just as they had done before when she had viewed the house in its sorry state. How things could turn around, Emma thought, in just a few short months. 13 Shakespeare Street was going to be her home. It had had a makeover and she couldn't wait to move in, but her heart ached for Jake. Where would he go, what would he do? She wondered to herself why she cared so much about this stranger.

* * *

At last the great day dawned. Bobby was beside himself with excitement. He had been promised a desk for his new room. She noticed that Gordon didn't seem even a little bit sad. In fact he looked like he couldn't wait to see the back of them. She tried not to feel hurt, tried to look forward to the adventure before her, but of course it was hard.

Collecting the keys from the agent she made her way to the house. Once inside Bobby raced from room to room, loving it all. When he saw the garden he just couldn't wait to run outside.

Emma appreciated that Jake had left it so clean and so tidy, even putting a bottle of red wine on the kitchen window sill for her. Attached to it was a note.

Dear Emma,

I wish you and your son great happiness in your new home.

I am so sorry that I haven't been able to take the piano, but you know how it is in rented properties. No one seems to have room for it, much to my sadness. So much for all my talk about never leaving it behind!

I just wondered whether you and your son would like to have it. If not, I will certainly get rid of it for you. Just call me on 07........ if you really don't want it. In the meantime, please accept my apologies for lumbering you with it.

Also, could you please take care of Rodney as the landlady of my new rental said 'Definitely no ducks'.

All best wishes for the future,

Jake

Emma smiled to herself. He had left a little piece of himself behind. Who knew, but perhaps she would call him and invite him round, just to show him how she had carried on his good work of making 13 Shakespeare Street in to a beautiful home. The thought of seeing him again filled her with a warmth she couldn't quite believe. Yes – this time she would be the one making the coffee.

It must have been so hard for him to leave his piano behind with all its memories, not to mention abandoning his wonderful garden. The very least Emma could do was invite him back. She owed it to him for being so kind to her. The more she thought about seeing him again, the more she felt it was the right thing to do. Finding her *Forever Home* may just have led to something else, but only time would let Emma find that out. Anyway, Rodney needed to be part of a family again.

52 SHAKESPEARE STREET

A heart to love

by Liz Losty

A heart to love, and in that heart, Courage, to make's love known

Macbeth, Act 2, Scene 3

Where do you want this one, love? He was oblivious to the line of sweat running down the side of his face. It trickled slowly across his neck and got caught up in the grey, curly chest hair creeping out of the top of his stained vest. Libby watched it settle and sit there glistening like a greasy dew drop. She looked away in disgust, her stomach turned by the sour smell of sweat coming from him.

'It's marked *Main Bedroom* on the box, so best to put it there.' She fixed a brittle smile on her face to disguise the sharpness of her tone. The man tut-tutted and muttered under his breath as he braced the large cardboard box against his chest and started a slow, lumbering ascent of the stairs.

'Libby, do you know where this goes?' Rob appeared in the hallway, holding a similar sized box with another *Main Bedroom* sticker on the side.

'Really Rob? Is it really that hard to read the labels I spent all day designing and printing out? Or is it just easier to keep annoying me?'

'Alright, calm down! For goodness sake, Libby, we're all trying to help.' Rob brushed past her without another word, puffing under the weight of the box then he too lumbered up the stairs, his shoulder braced against the wall for support as he struggled under the weight of the heavy cardboard box.

Must be my interior design books in that one, Libby mused as she turned back into the kitchen, deciding that if she was out of sight they would just have to get on with it. She walked over to the large box labelled *Tea and Coffee* and started to unpack the mugs, tea bags, biscuits and instant coffee she had boxed up in their old flat the day before. Luckily, she had thought ahead and put the kettle in there too, as well as some teaspoons and sugar. She filled the kettle and plugged it into the nearest socket on the countertop. She knew she would want to wipe out every cupboard and drawer with disinfectant and a clean cloth, marking the territory and making it hers, before she properly unpacked any of her things in the kitchen. She stood leaning against the kitchen door frame, waiting for the kettle to boil.

Another removal man walked into the hallway and straight up the stairs without asking her where the box should go. He didn't smile at her either. They'd obviously picked up on her irritation and decided to leave her to it. Libby didn't care much for their grumpy attitude and decided this was a good time to get five minutes away from all of them.

'I'm just going to the corner shop to get some fresh milk,' she shouted upstairs. She didn't wait for a reply, nor did she bother to close the front door after herself. They were going to be in and out for hours yet, unloading the lorry. She'd seen a small express supermarket just down the road, on the corner. She breathed a sigh of relief at leaving the upheaval behind her, and decided to take her time. She walked slowly, enjoying the sun on her face, pulling at her loose T-shirt to get some fresh air around her body.

It was a hot July day, perfect for a trip to the beach or the park or for drinking a glass of chilled wine with a salad over a catch-up with the girls.

But she had no regrets about how she was spending her day. After years of scrimping and saving and day-dreaming and planning, they had finally managed to sell their upstairs flat and buy a house. Their first house, a whole house that would be all theirs.

It needed a lot of work, but that didn't bother them. It gave them the leverage to knock the price down, it was their dream project. Libby still couldn't quite believe they had been able to get the house she had dreamed of, with period features like corniced ceilings and oak floorboards under a stained, threadbare carpet. It was a solid old terraced London house in an 'up and coming area'. It was perfect, and she could never imagine wanting to move house again. As she walked slowly down the street towards the shops, she casually glanced into the front window of each house she passed.

Some of the houses were run down with flaking paint on the front doors and broken tiles in the porch, a buyer's dream just crying out for money and modernising. That was how she and Rob could afford to buy on this street. The yellowing net curtains in some front windows contrasted sharply with the modern, white wooden shutters in others. Libby mentally ticked off the houses that had been 'done' to her standard and resolved to get know those neighbours first.

The express supermarket was small but well-stocked. She wandered up and down the narrow aisles, making a mental note of what they had for future reference. She was pleased to see chilled wine and beer in a noisily humming fridge. They may not be her usual upmarket brands, but they would definitely come in handy for impromptu girls' nights and when friendly neighbours popped in.

She grabbed some milk and another packet of chocolate digestives, paying with the loose coins in her jeans pocket. She gave the shop assistant a broad smile and thought about introducing herself, but he was making more eye contact with his mobile phone than he was with her. Annoyed at his disinterest in her, she took her change and receipt without as much as a thank you.

She walked out of the shop and stood at the street corner for a moment, taking in the view. Pinching herself, she walked slowly back home. Inspired by the work done to the homes she admired further down the street, she was planning the changes she would make to their house. She looked closely at each front door as she passed, checking out each letter box and each front room, the bright sunlight of the day making it hard to pick out the shadowy details of other homes and other lives through the windows.

Arriving at her new home she glanced at the house next door, trying to peer in through the sitting room window to see what changes they had made. She gave a little jump of surprise when she realised there was an elderly man in the sitting room looking straight back at her. He was seated in a large wing-backed armchair, a newspaper resting on his lap, and he was staring at her with frank, open interest. She felt a little self-conscious, embarrassed to have been caught snooping. Unsure what the protocol was in situations like this and, not knowing how to manage the social gaffe she had committed, she feigned confidence and raised her arm to wave at him in acknowledgement. He smiled and nodded, then resumed reading his paper. She waited a moment, still unsure what to do. It felt like she had been dismissed so she hurried back into the safety of her house, her territory.

The back of the removal lorry was almost empty, so she decided it was as good a time as any for them to be allowed a tea break. Making six mugs of tea and splashing milk into all of them, she stirred sugar into three of the drinks then loaded the mugs and biscuits on to a tray. Walking carefully down the hallway, she checked for stray boxes and trip hazards that were out to snare her. She could hear voices outside so she carried the tray on to the street and around to the back of the lorry.

Three of the men were inside debating how to unload the huge, wood-framed bed her parents had bought them as wedding present.

'Tea? Those mugs have sugar in them,' she gestured with her head and held the tray out to the men. 'Help yourselves to biscuits,' she smiled, hoping it would be a peace offering for her scratchiness earlier.

'Thanks love. Nice one! Just in time for us to have a five-minute break.' The foreman smiled at her and the other two curtly nodded their thanks. She hated being called *love,* she grumbled to Rob when she took the last mug up to him.

'They're not doing it to offend you. It's just their way. They're good guys.' Rob picked up his tea and grabbed the last biscuit. 'Have you any idea how physical their job is lugging stuff from A to B, up and down stairs, packing and unpacking? I'm knackered and fed up with it and it's my stuff! And I've only spent two days packing and unpacking. I wouldn't want to do their job for the world. It must be relentless.'

Rob wasn't admonishing her, just chatting, but Libby still felt a little shamefaced at her grouchiness earlier. She looked out the bedroom window and saw the men sitting in the shade on her low garden wall. Even that irritated her but, when she saw the older man take out a handkerchief and mop his head and neck, she relented, realising just how hot it was to be heaving one box after another from the lorry and up the stairs. She resolved to make them more tea in an hour or so and to end the day on a good note. *To be honest, I just want the job done and them gone,* she thought. *I just want to be alone with Rob and in peace for the first time in our very own house.*

She watched the removal men finish their tea and put the mugs out of harm's way on the wall. She sighed. 'OK Rob. It looks like the tea break's over. Back to work for the final push.' Just as she was about to turn away from the window, she saw the elderly gentleman she had waved at earlier. He was going out, closing the front door firmly behind him. He was wearing a pale linen suit with a blue open-necked shirt and a Panama hat. He had a walking stick that he seemed to use more for effect than purpose. Shutting the garden gate behind him he walked off towards the corner shop but, instead of going in, he turned and crossed the road before disappearing round the corner. Libby watched him with interest, wondering who he was and who he had been. His dapper dress sense, fresh linen suit and self-assured manner spoke of someone who had an interesting history.

'I met our new neighbour by the way, the elderly man next door,' Libby said over her shoulder, still watching out of the window in case he reappeared.

'Did you? What's he called? And aren't we the new neighbours?' Rob chided gently. He had opened another box and was unpacking the bedside lights.

'I didn't get his name. Actually when I said I *met* him, I just waved at him and he smiled back.' Libby realised it sounded a bit hollow. 'He did seem nice, so dapper the way he dresses. I wonder what he used to do before he retired?'

'Didn't Mrs Marshall say the neighbour on one side works in the City and the other is a retired architect? It must be him. He must be the retired architect.'

'Of course, yes. That must be him. I forgot her mentioning that. Gosh, he could be useful to us if we need any ideas or free advice for the house. I must go around and introduce myself. Maybe we could invite him in for a drink in a day or two when we are settled. I know he's old but he might be of some use.'

It was a few days before Libby thought of him again. It had taken longer than she expected to get settled, even to get unpacked, and the lack of order was making her more irritable by the day.

She didn't even want to unpack all the boxes, reasoning that she would only have to repack them when the building work got underway. But Rob kept her grounded, reminding her that they had used every penny just to get through the front door. It would take a year or two of constant saving before they could even afford to think about what building work they would do.

In the end she had to slow down and curb her enthusiasm as there was no money in the pot to give it an outlet. She relaxed a little, realising the renovations would be a long-term plan, and took to making the best of what they already had. She explored the neighbourhood and treated herself to the occasional shopping trip for new towels or wine glasses, small spends to keep her dreams of a house makeover alive.

It was only when she was on her way to see friends for lunch, a few weeks after they moved in, that she saw her elderly neighbour again. She was bundling out of her front door, absent-mindedly searching her handbag to check she had her phone with her, as he arrived home.

'Good afternoon.' She looked up from her bag, not realising he had been standing watching her.

She smiled, a little shyly, surprised by the unexpected meeting. She looked up at him, realising that he was much taller than she had thought. Once again he was elegantly dressed, this time in a light summer suit with a shirt and bow tie that would have looked ridiculous on a younger man but was effortlessly stylish on him. His face was tanned, simply through spending many summers on this earth. His clear blue eyes had an unflinching directness, which would have unnerved her, if his smile hadn't been so warm and filled with the natural confidence that comes with age.

'Oh, hello. I'm sorry, we haven't met properly yet. I'm Libby, Libby Morecroft. My husband Rob and I have just moved in next door. Well, a couple of weeks ago.' She extended her hand over the brick wall separating their front paths.

'How do you do, Libby? My name is Phillip, Phillip Chambers.' His voice was quiet but confident and, as he reached over to shake her hand, she was surprised to find his skin was warm and dry and there was a strength in his handshake that belied his advancing years. Letting go of her hand, he smiled as he opened the front door. 'It was a pleasure to meet you, Libby. Have a good day.' And with a small nod he went into his hallway and closed the door behind him with a soft click.

Libby stood on the path for a moment, slightly confused. He was very polite and yet she felt slightly rejected by him. He didn't ask anything about her or how they were settling in. She didn't even get the chance to invite him to come round for a drink or a cup of tea. She had assumed he would be delighted at the opportunity to meet his new, younger neighbours. But, now that she thought about it, he did seem to get out and about quite ably. Maybe he wasn't the lonely old man she had presumed him to be?

Later that evening, after Rob had come home exhausted from another day in the office and a stifling tube ride, they changed into their painting clothes and started on the main bedroom. It had become their nightly routine to do an hour or two of painting together and, much as Libby was enthusiastic, it was Rob who had the skills needed to ensure the job was done as professionally as possible. The bedroom had previously been painted a pale insipid pink, a nothing colour that reminded her of old ladies' skin. They had spent a fortune on a couple of cans of pale grey paint that seemed to justify their own expense by having a ridiculous name.

Rob had gawped at the price and laughed at the name. '*Sea Storm Slate?* What the hell does that mean? It could be anywhere between blue, green and slate grey. I'm none the wiser. Who thinks up these stupid names?'

But Libby had persisted and they both agreed, now that two walls were painted, that this grey had been the right choice. It made the skirting boards whiter and seemed to bring out the features of the room, making the walls look further apart and the room seem larger.

'See? I told you it was a great colour. Grey is very calming, you know,' Libby announced, secretly relieved that they hadn't squandered a fortune on a colour they couldn't live with. They kept going until they had finished the entire room. By then it was after ten and even the chip shop had closed.

'I'm too tired to cook. Shall I just pop to the corner and pick up a pizza and a bottle of wine?' Libby said.

'Sure. You do that and I'll clean up here. In fact, don't bother with the wine unless you fancy some. I'm exhausted and I have to be in work for eight tomorrow.' Rob stood up, stretched and yawned, managing to wipe a smudge of paint across his face as he rubbed his eyes. 'When I've tidied up, I'll hop in the shower.'

Libby grabbed her purse and slipped out into the warm night air, rubbing her eyes as she walked slowly down to the shop. It was a good thing she was between contracts and that they were in agreement about her taking the summer off, putting all her efforts into getting the house sorted out. She loved doing it and already had a tick list as long as her arm, but it could be a bit lonely every day with Rob gone so early and only the radio for company. She longed for her friends to pop over or to get a few lunch invites so she could go out. But, at the height of summer, nearly everyone they knew was away. She had roped her brother Ben into helping when he got back from Greece. He had reluctantly agreed to spend one weekend painting and doing furniture assembly as long as his partner James didn't object. Libby had suggested that James could always come over and help, but Ben had batted that one away.

'He doesn't like DIY. He's the only person I know who's paid to have the self-assembly wardrobe he bought assembled by a carpenter,' Ben laughed.

But Ben kept his word and he and James did come over to help out. Ben got stuck into the jobs straight away but James, true to Ben's prediction, was no help. He spent the morning exclaiming at the state of the place, took an inordinate amount of time shopping for a few ingredients for lunch, then gossiped with Ben, Rob and Libby all afternoon while they slogged their way through painting the back bedroom. Ben more than compensated for James's lack of industry and Rob and Libby knew that they came as a pair. If you wanted Ben's time, you had to have James's company. And he was good fun. His wicked sense of humour and gossip meant the radio stayed off and James stayed on.

After that weekend the days dragged on but Libby kept going by herself. She was working her way through her to-do list, rewriting it every morning and ticking things off every night.

The day all the woodwork in the bedroom was finally finished she decided, even though it was only four, that she was done for the day. She was exhausted and didn't have the energy to start on the next job. Rob would probably be glad of a night off too. Though he was too kind to complain, she knew how exhausted he was after doing a full day at work. Then having to come home and do another four hours of painting, decorating and sanding. Libby texted him.

Main bedroom finished. Let's have a night off and go out for dinner. I'm exhausted and so are you. x

She went downstairs and made a cup of tea then, deciding she needed some air, went to the front door and opened it, looking up and down the street to see if anyone was passing. The soft summer breeze was a welcome relief from the smell of paint. She let out a long sigh of exhaustion mixed with boredom and sat down on the front step, resting her back against the warm brick of the porch. She closed her eyes and angled her face to the sun that was creeping overhead towards the back of the house.

'How are you getting on?'

She blinked and shielded her eyes from the sun, looking around to see where the voice was coming from. Phillip, their neighbour, was smiling at her with a look of patrician bemusement. She felt like a child caught bunking off school. She jumped up quickly, splashing some of her tea down her jeans, so she pretended she had finished it and flung the dregs over the rose bush. Her hands moved reflexively to smooth down her hair, and straighten her T shirt. 'Oh, fine thank you. I was just having a quick break.'

'Don't let me disturb you. It looks like you and your husband have been very hard at work. I hope it's going well?'

'Would you like to come in, to see what we're doing?' Libby offered 'Nothing too dramatic, just new colours and so on. We plan to modernise the house so we'll be putting in a new kitchen and bathroom but don't worry, we're not knocking anything down.' She realised she was rushing her words but something in her wanted to hold on to him, to engage him so he wouldn't leave. There was something fascinating about the confidence and knowing wisdom that seemed to emanate from his eyes, his way of carrying himself, his air of independence.

'Well I can pop in for five minutes if you have time?' he offered. Libby could hardly contain her enthusiasm. She didn't know if it was the thought of having some company to break the loneliness of the day, or the fact that she was finally getting some of his attention.

'Yes, do. Please come in. Watch the step and let me move some of the paint cans out of the way.' And so Phillip came into her house and she showed him round each room, gushing about her plans and what she hoped to do. He smiled warmly at her enthusiasm and nodded frequently. She wasn't sure if he was agreeing with her or just acknowledging what she was saying, but she felt strangely pleased and proud to have got his attention.

He declined the offer of tea or wine and did not reciprocate with an invitation into his home, but Libby felt she had achieved a small breakthrough. She proudly recounted the story to Rob that evening. 'Did he give you any ideas on what we could do with the place?' Rob asked.

'Well, no. But I didn't ask him. I didn't want to seem pushy,' Libby replied. But when she thought about it, she knew it hadn't really occurred to her to ask him for advice. She was just happy to have made the breakthrough of speaking to him.

Libby got into the routine of the street, nodding at the postman who didn't appear until ten and waving at the neighbour opposite who seemed to have some sort of mothers and babies meeting at her house every Wednesday. Friday was bin day in the neighbourhood and, as Libby lugged the heavy wheelie bin to the pavement one week, she turned to see Phillip doing the same. He was finding it difficult as he had his walking stick in one hand and was trying to drag the large black bin with the other.

'Please, Phillip, let me help you.' She moved towards him to take the bin, concerned that he may trip or fall, but she quickly sensed his hesitancy. 'I can manage, thank you Libby.' He seemed slightly irritated, but she wasn't sure if it was with her or the bin.

'I'm wearing my old scruffs and you have a beautiful suit on Phillip. You don't want to get dirty,' she explained, giving him the excuse he needed to preserve his dignity and independence. He smiled in defeat and relinquished the bin for her to drag on to the street for collection. 'There, all done, not a problem. Can I put it back for you once it's been emptied?' she offered. But Phillip held his hand up in protest.

'No need. But thank you,' he answered decisively. He walked slowly back to his front door and was gone.

For the first time, Libby had felt some insight into what it means to age, to lose physical ability, strength and independence while retaining a sense of self, dignity and worth. Phillip seemed so confident and able, but his body could no longer keep up with his mind. And with that small gesture of help from Libby, and her gentle acknowledgement of Phillip's need to be independent and able, their true friendship was born. It was to be one of the strongest and most influential friendships of Libby's life.

There was no longer any shyness or hesitancy on Libby's part when she bumped into Phillip, and their door-way chats became longer and less formal, moving from the safe topics of the weather and the joys of DIY to a genuine interest in each other's lives and wellbeing.

A few weeks later she felt confident and comfortable enough to invite Phillip for an evening drink to meet Rob and, when that went well, she invited him to join them for Sunday lunch. Libby fussed as if they were expecting royalty. She ensured Phillip had the best of the dining chairs to sit on and lunch was served on the wedding china that, as far as Rob could remember, was still meant to be in boxes in the attic.

In turn, they were invited into Phillip's house for morning coffee. When they arrived, the coffee was already made and an occasional table was set with small Italian espresso cups and saucers as well as a plate of delicately sugared continental biscuits.

Libby glanced around Phillip's sitting room, curious but trying not to appear overtly so. She took in the heavy oak furniture, rich wool carpet, architectural paintings artfully arranged on one wall and the silver photo frames displayed on the mantelpiece. She got up and walked over to study the people in the photographs more closely.

'Do you mind if I look, Phillip? These are beautiful photos.' She didn't want to smudge the polished frames so she stood with her hands behind her back, leaning forward to stare intently at each in turn. One showed Phillip looking perhaps a few years younger. He was in the centre of the photo, surrounded by family members but there was no woman standing beside him. Where was his wife? Libby wondered if she had perhaps died young. She was slowly sensing where the boundaries lay with Phillip and already knew not to ask too many intrusive questions for fear of endangering the burgeoning friendship.

Further along the mantelpiece she saw a black and white portrait photograph of a man in uniform, perhaps taken in the 1940s. He was handsome, with a strong profile. Her mother would have said he had a film star's looks. He was smiling openly into the camera, his face full of youth and confidence. And then it dawned on Libby 'Oh my goodness Phillip, is that you? Were you in the army? You look like a film star!'

Phillip sat in his armchair and smiled. 'Yes, that was me. Not the army, of course. I was in the RAF, a gunner in the Second World War. I joined up in 1942 when I was 20 and saw full active service in the last years of the war.'

Rob was suddenly interested too. 'Really? That's amazing. I am sure you have some stories to tell. I had to do World War II as part of my 'A' levels. The airmen were so young, and so many lives were lost. Were you on active operations? Which ones, any major battles?' Phillip smiled good-naturedly and held his hand up to stop the rush of questions.

'I was lucky. I survived and so many didn't. It was a bad time, looking back. 1945 was the last year of the war. At the time we didn't know how much longer it was going to drag on, the unbearable loss of life, the cruelty, the deprivation. But the idea was to break the Germans and to finally bring the war to an end. And, of course, that's what happened. The Germans eventually had no choice but to surrender. The campaigns against them were relentless and I was involved in some of them. Dresden. That was one of my final missions.'

He paused, looking at both of them to gauge their reaction, realising by their politely interested expressions that the Second World War was no more than a piece of history to them.

'Yes . . . We studied Dresden as part of our course work.' Rob hesitated, choosing his words carefully for fear of offending Phillip. 'I suppose the campaign achieved its aim. It did finally break the Germans.' He remembered the heated debates he had had with classmates. The morals and ethics of World War II, or rather the lack of them, humanity as a whole debased and brought to the gates of hell. Probably not a safe topic for morning coffee with an elderly ex-serviceman.

Sensing the same feeling, Phillip brought the conversation to a close. 'There has been so much debate about it since. People forget the devastation the Germans brought to London, Coventry, Belfast. The whole country was scarred by what they did. Still, it's all in the past now. Would you like some more coffee?'

Libby, still standing by the mantelpiece, sensed the need to move the conversation on to safer ground. 'And who are the people in this photo? Is this your family?'

Phillip smiled warmly as he looked at the photo Libby was pointing to. 'Yes. That's my son James with his wife, Catherine, and my two grandchildren Ben and Olivia. And, on the other side, my daughter Caroline with her husband, Sam, and their twins Tom and Emily.'

She was desperate to ask about his wife, to complete her mental picture of his place in the world. Phillip was watching her, and almost as though he could read her mind, he answered. 'Their mother, Grace, and I were divorced when they were still young and, sadly, she passed away some years back.'

'That's a shame. I'm sorry to hear that. And did you ever remarry? Were you ever tempted to try again, Phillip?' There was a heavy pause before Phillip answered, and Libby felt a small flush of embarrassment creep up her face. Rob shot her a warning look for overstepping the mark.

'No . . . No, I wasn't tempted to marry again. Would you like some more coffee, Libby?' Phillip held up the coffee pot and Libby returned to her chair. And, with that, the subjects of war and loss were dropped and the conversation moved on to the safer ground of the DIY projects they were undertaking and the weather. And, even though she felt she had crossed an invisible line, Libby also felt that somehow Phillip seemed to understand her gaucheness and forgive her for it. He smiled at her and tutted sympathetically at the amount of work she had taken on and the frustrations of choosing the right colours and fittings for the house.

Over the summer and into late September they kept up their regular chats over coffee or the occasional lunch and Libby found she was looking forward to each meeting with Phillip. His world was so different from hers, his interests so distant from her own, that she realised she had a lot to learn from him. So, while he was occasionally happy to offer insight into the pros and cons of their renovation plans, more often than not Libby found herself more interested in hearing about Phillip's life than talking about her own.

He happily shared stories of some of the building projects he had worked on, how he had retrained as an architect after the war and the huge opportunities for redevelopment and rebuilding that the destruction and despair of London had provided. He had been heavily involved in restoring much of London's infrastructure and had spent time with such interesting people. His anecdotes were all the more funny for the dry and witty delivery he gave them.

Even the nicknames of some of the characters he had rubbed shoulders with made her laugh. 'Really? You actually worked with a man called Bunny? That couldn't be his real name, was it?' she laughed. 'It sounds like something out of a Wodehouse novel!'

'Oh but he was, my dear!' Phillip chuckled. 'Bunny and his pal, Ponsonby, ran the most dubious of finance companies. No-one quite knew where they got the funds from. Some people just seemed to have money after the war. They appeared to have endless pots of cash to invest in building projects, but also a long list of creditors. It was their charm and sheer effrontery that got them so far. In the end, inevitably, they went bust. They owed me over five hundred pounds – complete scoundrels but so charming with it. Then there was Foxy Norton, he was well named. And Buffy . . . Gosh when I think back to the people I knew then, such characters, all gone now. But they were fun times and all the more so because we had survived the war and knew what that freedom meant.'

'What about you, Phillip. Did you have a nickname then? I'm sure you did. Something fun, cheeky?' Libby joked. 'What could it have been? I know, I bet they all called you Pip back then. It's a very English nickname.' Libby was laughing and had turned to pick up her phone which had just beeped with a text. She was unaware of the change in the atmosphere and it was only when she looked up from her phone that she realised something was wrong.

'Phillip, what's up? Are you alright? What is it?'

He looked stricken, distant. Libby searched her mind for what it could be. 'What is it? Have I said something wrong? Gosh was it the name? Was it asking you if you had been called Pip? I'm so sorry, I didn't mean to offend you!' Phillip's face flickered with emotion and his eyes appeared to film over with tears.

'Oh God, Phillip. What is it? What have I done? I'm so sorry.' She didn't know what else to say and her panicked words sounded gauche, filling the silence and only making it worse.

Eventually Phillip turned back to look at her. 'No, it's not your fault. It's just that I haven't heard that name in years. In fact, I haven't been called it in years. You just reminded me of someone I used to know. An old friend, a very dear friend from a long time ago. He called me Pip. In fact, he was the only person I allowed to call me that name apart from my mother. He and I fought together during the war. We were in the same flight squadron. He died, shot down. It was tragic, heart-breaking.' Phillip broke off and looked at the window, his eyes fixed on some distant memory. The depth of sadness emanating from him seemed to fill the room with stillness.

For once, Libby knew to say nothing, to sit quietly and wait. Eventually, Phillip reached into his trouser pocket and pulled out a freshly laundered handkerchief, quickly dabbing his eyes then clearing his throat before turning back to face Libby. He forced a smile, but his usual confidence and vigour had been replaced by a fog of sadness. It was almost palpable.

'He was so young. He meant a lot to me and it was so cruel. We didn't know it then but the war was on the turn. We were finally winning and you could sense the change. A few more months and we would have been safe. With fewer battles in the sky, it was down to the ground troops. But it just wasn't to be.' He looked down at his hands and Libby felt compelled to move towards him. She knelt on the carpet beside his armchair and rested her hand gently on his arm.

'Who was he Phillip? Your best friend? Someone from home?'

Phillip smiled sadly and looked at her. 'No.' He hesitated, appearing to choose his next words carefully then, having arrived at a decision within himself, he sighed and continued. 'He was my first love, Libby. In fact he was the love of my life.' He watched her face, waiting for her reaction. But she didn't recoil or jump up, or scream and shout obscenities as Grace had done all those years ago, when he had finally plucked up the courage to tell her the truth.

Libby didn't move. Her hand continued to rest on his arm, her face impassive as her mind was processing what Phillip had just told her. Libby felt a flicker of puzzlement pass over her face and looked away for a moment. Then, resolving the question in her mind, she turned back to ask him with naïve frankness, 'Phillip, you're gay? Are you saying you're gay? But you were married, you had a wife and family. I don't understand. I didn't realise you were gay.'

'Nor did I, not until I met him. I grew up in a nice middle class family. I was a typical grammar school boy, living in a quiet market town. Father ran a small architectural practice and Mother was a housewife. I had even met Grace by then. We had been together since we were sixteen and our parents were close friends. We were young, of course, but there was talk of marriage after the war was over. Naturally, my parents hoped the war would be over before I was old enough to sign up but I joined the RAF and saw active service. It was harrowing, nerve-wracking, life-changing. You never knew when your number was up, whether you would ever see your family again. It wasn't just the fear of losing one's own life on flying missions. There was the constant threat of German bombardments. Some chaps came back from successful operations, high on life, feeling that they had cheated death and done their duty, only to return home to find their family had been killed in a German raid.

'We lived every day as though it was our last, as for so many it was. They counted us out on each mission and counted us in as we limped back to base. The numbers rarely tallied. And in many ways you couldn't think about it or you would lose your nerve. They kept morale up on the base with parties, dances and such. But only those who ran the same risks as you knew how it felt to get up every morning and dread the briefing, the mission, the risks. I could never decide which were the worst, broad daylight or night-time sorties, always knowing it could be your last.

'We jollied each other along with bluff confidence, stiff upper lip and all that. But we were only young. Nowadays most of us would have still been at school or college and going to parties at the weekend, not fighting each day as though it was our last. I suppose that sense of urgency, immediacy, the unknown made us reckless, even fearless. I was in with a good bunch of chaps. We bonded well as a pack, of course. There were many in-jokes and black humour that kept us going, and we got up to all sorts of japes on our nights off. And yes, we lost some good men even in the first few months I was there but you didn't focus on that. You couldn't dwell on that but, if you did, it was only to strengthen your resolve, your nerve.

'And then I met Edward. He joined our crew a few months after me in 1942. He was handsome, brown eyes, dark blond hair, strong, confident, a great sportsman. Now he *did* have the film star looks, Libby. He had played cricket and rugby for his school and county. He had a very different upbringing to me, a very wealthy family, boarding school, holidays in France, something we take for granted nowadays. He could tell a joke that made you laugh till you cried. The girls on base were all in love with him of course. It just took me a little longer to realise I was, too.

'I'd never thought about a man that way before. My path was all mapped out for me. Once the war was over I would return home, study architecture, pass my exams, join my father's business, marry Grace, have children, carry on the family name, the family business. I suppose I did do some of what was expected of me in the end, but none of it was my choice.

'After the war, after what I had lost, I didn't really care much what I did. I was happy to be steered by my parents, by Grace...' Phillip faltered when he mentioned her name again, his shame and sadness heavy but unspoken.

'Something happened to me when I met Edward. I didn't even realise I was falling in love with him. I just knew I loved being with him. We just clicked, I suppose you could say. He was funny, confident and he had a way with him that made it so easy to be in his company.

'We became firm friends quite quickly, but that was how it was during the war. There was such an immediacy, an urgency to living, being alive. I didn't realise the path I was on, and I don't think he really did either. I remember the first time I felt what was happening. I was in the officers' mess, reading the newspaper, when he came in. He chatted to some of the others then joined me. He asked me to pass the paper over when I had finished so I did and, just for a brief moment, our fingertips touched and the moment held as if forever. It felt like an electric current had fired between our fingertips. I looked up and he was just gazing at me. There was something in that look, a connection so fleeting that I felt certain I must have imagined it. And yet, afterwards, I couldn't stop thinking about it and what it meant.

'A few nights later a gang of us went to the local town, just for a change of scene. We all drank too much, sang too much and joked too loudly. Eventually the landlord got fed up with us, called time and sent us on our way. We all staggered along the long country road back to base. Somehow Edward and I got further behind the others until they were out of sight, and so were we. His hand reached out across the darkness to touch mine, and we stopped. We just stopped walking and I turned to look at him. There was nothing more to be said. It was the first time we kissed, and that was it. I was lost.

'It was so different to what I had experienced before, so unexpected and yet all-consuming, knowing. I felt like I had come home. It felt so *right.* You always hear people talking about their first kiss, their first love, like they were the same thing. But my first kiss was with Grace and my first love, I suppose looking back my *only* love, was Edward. Nothing ever came close to that again. That feeling, that depth, that love . . .' Phillip broke off and looked down at Libby, almost as if he had only just realised he was talking out loud, sharing his deepest feelings and memories. 'I'm sorry Libby, I don't know what's come over me. I haven't talked about this in years. I didn't mean to embarrass you.' He started to move out of his chair.

'Don't be embarrassed, Phillip,' said Libby, looking up at his sad face with genuine concern. 'There's nothing to be embarrassed about. My brother Ben is gay. He's in a long-term relationship with a lovely guy called James. They've moved in together, they're even thinking about getting married next summer.'

Phillip sat back down, intrigued. 'Married? It's amazing how times have changed. And your parents aren't upset? Your family?'

'No, not at all, they just wanted Ben to happy, to be with someone he loves and who loves him. Was it really so bad in your day Phillip? I mean people have always been gay. Surely it wasn't that bad?'

Libby looked up at him, her hand still resting gently on his arm. She was stunned by his revelations and the shared intimacy of his life long ago, as well as the regret in his voice. If only he had been born in a different time, in the last forty-five years rather than eighty-five years ago, how different his life would have been. It gave her the courage to go on and ask more. She felt almost overwhelmed by the emotion in his voice. 'Did you love Grace? Did she ever know?' she asked gently.

'I did love Grace, of course I did, but I wasn't in love with her. I suppose, looking back on it, we were more like brother and sister. Well, that's how it was for me but maybe not for Grace. I did my best. I tried to love her the way she wanted to be loved, to make her happy, but there was no spark, no passion, no true intimacy, because there was a huge lie at the very centre of our marriage. I thought if we had children she'd be happy. But she always knew something was wrong. At first, she put it down to the war. So many men came back changed, depressed, traumatised. I suppose it was easier for me to allow her to think that, and it was true in many ways. I don't think I ever got over the trauma of losing him. Then, as time went on, her patience ran out and she thought I was having an affair. She started to get more hysterical, snappy, angry. It was worse after the children were born. One night we'd been out to a local hotel for dinner with friends and we drank too much, as usual. It was a habit we had fallen into. I suppose it had become our coping mechanism. She had been brittle, snappy, all evening and it made the atmosphere uncomfortable for our friends. We'd stopped being much fun as dinner companions and invitations were dropping off as people distanced themselves from the unpleasantness.

'I had been absent, remote. Looking back, I was grieving for the man I loved and a bereavement I wasn't allowed to feel. I realise now she sensed it more, the distance. That's what upset her the most. We got home and then the inevitable argument started. Thank God, the children were at her mother's, so they didn't hear any of it. The accusations started again, the sniping, the goading. "Who is it? Who is she? Why won't you tell me?" On and on she went. She just wouldn't let it go. I told her there was no-one else, that she was imagining it. Then she started to fire out random accusations, naming family friends, accusing me of having an affair with Margaret, our next door neighbour, even Pamela, who was my secretary at the time. She was so angry, so hell-bent, she said she would march to Margaret's house there and then and ask her to her face. She kept going on and on, asking the same question. "Tell me who she is?"

'I snapped. I'd had enough of the accusations and the lying and her caustic bitterness and I just snapped. I told her there was no "she" and there was no secret affair. That I had loved someone during the war, when I was away from her, and his name was Edward. For a moment I almost felt a sense of relief, finally saying it out loud, saying his name out loud, finally shutting her up and stopping the constant bombardment. But the relief was only fleeting.

'God, I'll never forget the look of shock and disgust on her face. She collapsed into a chair as though I had punched her. She was stricken, ashen. She couldn't speak for what seemed like ages and, when she eventually did, the filth that came out of her mouth...' Phillip broke off, wincing at the memory of the words spoken in anger then, now left unsaid. He couldn't bear to repeat them, not because of the words themselves but because he knew they did not come from Grace but from a well of grief inside her that had erupted and spewed out all her deepest fears and pain. It wasn't her fault, it was his.

Phillip looked into the distance, his mind no longer in the sitting room of his home in 2010, but in the bedroom of the house he and Grace had shared in 1952. Grace's shocked deathly white face, her eyes red from crying, her body bent with pain that was beyond physical. He closed his eyes to banish the image and opened them again to bring himself back to the present day. There was a quiet stillness in the room. The late summer sun had started to set and the room was falling into shadows and darkness. Libby didn't want to move or turn on a light, sensing it would be an intrusion which could break the delicate thread of Edward's confession. That was what it felt like. She sensed the hesitation and pain with which he connected to old memories and touched the hurt that had long been buried in the deepest part of his heart.

She shifted slightly to one side as she knelt on the floor beside Edward. He no longer appeared tall and elegant but broken and bereft. His grief was palpable, his shoulders sagged and his head was bowed. His hand moved to his cover his eyes and, for a moment, Libby thought he was going to break down. But the moment and the memories passed. He sighed and rubbed his eyes, then straightened up and turned to look at Libby, trying to gauge her reaction to all that he had revealed.

'It wasn't Grace's fault, none of it. She deserved so much more than I was able to give her. I almost drove her to madness with the not knowing, not understanding why there was a distance between us. It was wrong of me to marry, I know that now. I just didn't have the courage to say so then.'

Libby's voice was as soft as the darkness. 'I'm sure it must have been a real shock to her when she finally discovered the truth. I can understand that. Did she have any idea at all? Did she ever find out more? Did you . . . I don't know how to ask this, but did you have other men, other lovers when you were married? Was that what she sensed, what she was guessing at?' Libby asked the question as gently as she could, knowing it was none of her business but somehow feeling that the whole truth had to be known.

'What? No! No, I would never have done that to Grace, despite what she thought of me. I did respect her and I never betrayed her once we were married. But I suppose the deception I committed was the most hurtful of all. In my heart I loved somebody else and I always had, even before I had married her. He was my first love and I realised I could never love Grace in the same way. I should never have married her.

'I realised that what I'd had with Edward, what I'd felt for him, made my feelings for Grace seem shallow and distant. I think that was the most hurtful aspect of all to her, that I loved somebody else with a passion and depth I could never feel for her. And for that somebody else to have been a man, well . . . And of course in those days it was illegal. The repercussions were huge. If Edward and I had been discovered, the disgrace on us, our squadron, our families, the shame. It was unthinkable. We would have been court-martialled, imprisoned. I am sure you've read what happened to homosexuals, how they were treated. It wouldn't have mattered that Edward and I had put our lives on the line for King and country, that we were honourable men defending our nation, that we fought with courage and bravery every day. None of that would have been taken into account if we had been discovered. We would have been treated as criminals, perverts, a danger to the free society we were trying to protect and defend. But not once did we talk about the risks we were taking and neither of us regretted any of it. Yes we took risks, stupid risks on reflection, but thankfully we never got caught. We could go out on the town, drink in the pub just like any other men on leave, go up to London, stay in hotels there. As long as we were discreet, which we were, we would never be found out. And we never were.' Phillip smiled sadly, as in his mind he revisited those moments, those risks.

'So what actually happened, how did Edward die, was it in battle? How did you find out?' Libby asked. And somehow, even as soon as she had asked the question, she knew it was the most intimate of all.

'We were all on active service, at an airbase just north of London. Edward and I were each owed a day's leave and managed to get the same day off. We went up to London, the West End, had a pub lunch, saw a film. Nothing extraordinary, nothing that would draw attention to ourselves. We just wanted to be with each other. The day after we returned to base a number of us were scrambled to go on a raid against some German weapon sites. Hitting those sites helped reduce the attacks on British towns and cities and, as I later discovered, this was part of the end-game in the war effort.

'My crew was one of the first back. We waited, and the next plane came in when I was on my way to a debrief with my crew. Afterwards, when I was in the mess hut, one of the others came in. Even before he spoke I could tell it was bad news. We had lost one of our planes, shot down. I didn't even hear the rest of what he said. My heart was ice and I felt sick to the pit of my stomach. I just knew. Somehow, I just knew. Then word came back to confirm. The plane had been shot down, there were no survivors and Edward was one of crew. Someone got a bottle out, we toasted the men we'd lost and everyone sat in shocked silence, thinking the same thing. *It could have been me.*

'Apart from me that is. I wished it *had* been me. I made my excuses and left quickly. I walked back to my quarters and bolted my door. Curling up on the floor, I silently raged at the pain, the loss. It was unbearable. I truly wanted to die there and then. I wanted to scream and rage against the world, the Germans, the Gods, the cruelty of it all. But I couldn't. I couldn't make a sound and risk being heard. I grabbed a pillow to bury my face and smother my cries. And that's when I found it, hidden under my pillow. An old anthology of Shakespeare's greatest plays. On the fly leaf was a simple inscription: *To Phillip. Best wishes, Edward.* I knew he couldn't have written more. If he had and anyone found it, well . . . But I was completely thrown. I didn't know when he had bought it, but it must have been when we had gone up to London the day before. We had visited a couple of bookshops and Edward said I was a Philistine because I didn't like Shakespeare. He said there was so much to learn about life and love from his works.

'Then I realised there was a bookmark, just a blank slip of paper with a small sketch of a heart and a pair of angel's wings drawn on it. I knew his hand straightaway. I opened the book at the page it was marking and there it was, a quote from Macbeth, underlined in pencil. *A heart to love, and in that heart, Courage, to make's love known.*

'I was undone. That was his last message to me. I couldn't tell anyone how I felt or show my pain, or share it with any of my crew or friends on base, for they would have known, instinctively. They would have known. So the pain went deep inside me and stayed there, locked away from the world. I wouldn't even go to the service they had for him. I couldn't trust myself. I didn't know if I could keep the pain in check so I stayed away, made excuses. The others came to resent me, thought I was a cold fish, distant, unfeeling. They never quite trusted me after that, but by then I didn't care what anyone else thought or felt about me. Everyone was glad when the war ended, but my biggest fear was *What now?* And there was no other avenue open to me, other than to go home, marry Grace, do my architecture training and have children. So that's how it went. I went through the motions of life without feeling the emotions.'

'And what about your children?' Libby asked. 'Did you feel differently when they were born? You all look very happy in that beautiful photo in the silver frame. Did they ever know about Edward or what happened?'

'No. I never told them and, to her credit, Grace didn't either. We eventually got divorced, quietly and civilly, and she still let me be part of their lives. She remarried and was happy, I think. I suppose we both reached an understanding of each other's pain and we loved the children more than we resented each other. Grace stayed on in the family house and I moved up to London. I got a flat and the business prospered. I was able to provide well for the children and Grace kept my secret. I did have other relationships after the divorce. My last partner, Tony, and I were together for fifteen years but we never lived together. In a funny way, he felt the same as Grace. He often complained there was a part of me he couldn't reach, part of me that was locked away. I realised he was right, but no-one can mend a broken heart. It can only heal itself, and mine never could.'

'Did your children eventually find out you were gay? I suppose they know now do they?' Libby knew Phillip was tiring but she wanted to bring the story to the present day, to know how it ended.

'I never really told them. All families have their secrets, don't they? I suppose they may have guessed but they never asked and I never told. I didn't feel the need. And I had a very busy and full life, what with my architectural practice, bridge club and, of course, I have always loved travelling. I suppose I became comfortable in my own company and didn't feel the need to share my time and my world.' And with that Phillip turned to Libby and smiled, realising the irony of his remark after all they had discussed.

Libby smiled and rubbed his arm affectionately. He put his hand on top of hers. 'I'm tired now Libby. Would you mind if we called it a day? I think I need to be alone with my thoughts.'

'Of course, Phillip. I'll leave you in peace. And you have my word that I won't disclose anything you have told me to anyone else. It is your story and yours alone to tell.' With that she kissed him gently on the cheek and left him sitting alone in his chair with his thoughts and his memories.

Letting herself out, Libby stood and looked up at the clear night sky for a few moments. She listened to the thrum of distant traffic that echoed the vibrant, busy and thriving city of London. It could all have been so different, and probably so much worse, she thought, if not for the men who had fought so bravely, especially those who had given their lives.

Rob looked up from his laptop as Libby let herself back into the house. 'You were at Phillip's a long time. Chatting about paint colours and counter tops again?' She didn't reply, just walked over to stand behind him, leaning down to wrap her arms around him and kissing him gently before resting her cheek against his. He took both her hands in his and kissed each in turn.

'I love you,' she said, simply and quietly.

'And I, you.' Rob shut the computer and pulled Libby round to sit on his lap. And there they stayed for a long time, wrapped in each other's arms, in loving and peaceful silence.

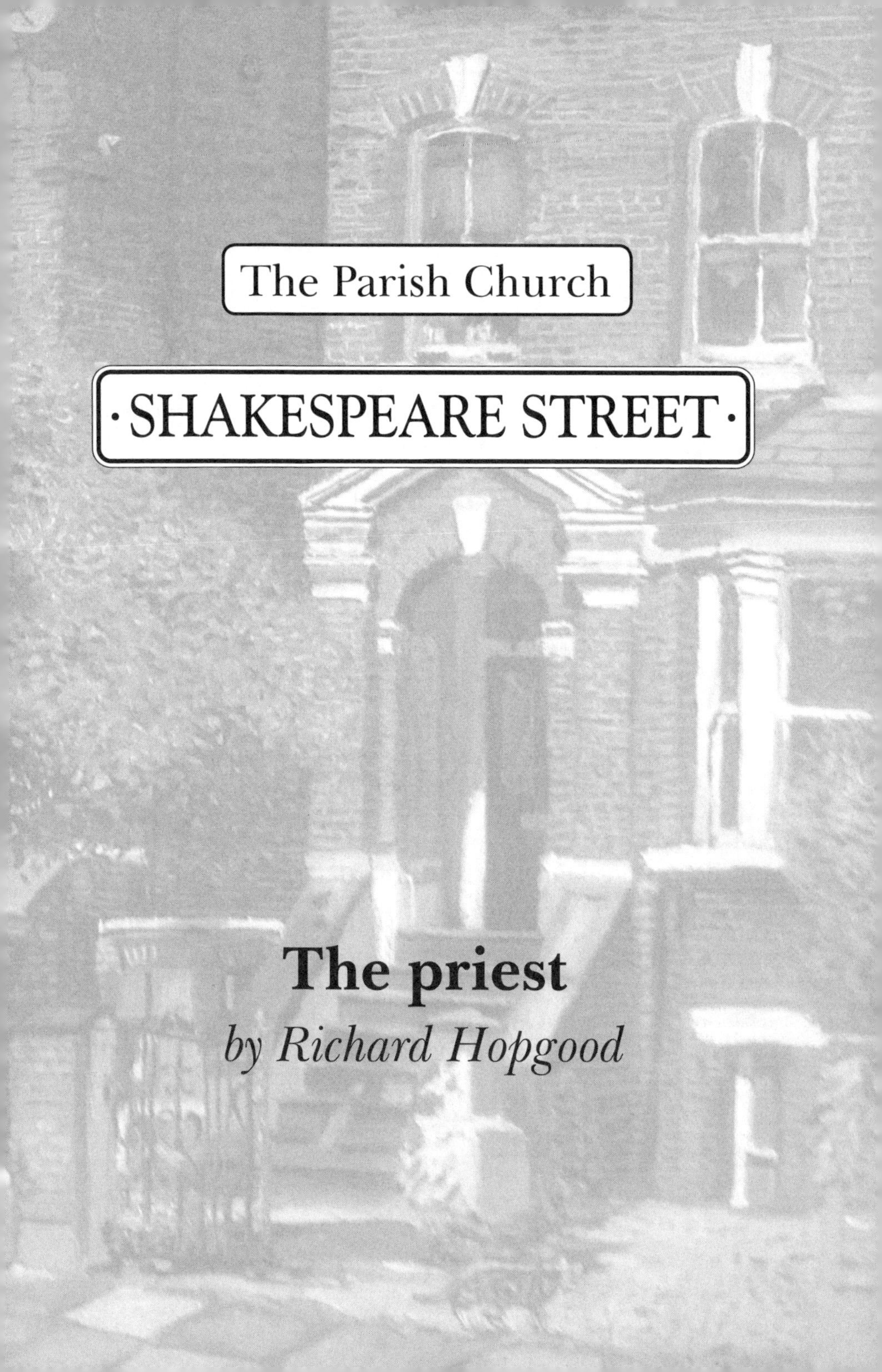

The Parish Church

·SHAKESPEARE STREET·

The priest

by Richard Hopgood

Bare ruined choirs, where late the sweet birds sang

Sonnet 73

Where did it begin, this descent from a complacent happiness to the twin peaks of ecstasy and despair? Well, like most beginnings, with a quite ordinary meeting at the beginning of extraordinary times.

It was the first year of the war. Hitherto secluded in a theological college in the Oxfordshire countryside, the principal had called me to his study, told me it was time to test my faith in an urban ministry, and thrust a train ticket to Paddington into my hand. Three hours later, after a journey of interminable delays in a blacked-out train, I arrived at my destination.

'They're great people but you have to understand what they are going through. We're on the front line here . . .'

We were sitting in a crowded café in Paddington Station, alongside a platform where a long phalanx of children was being briskly loaded on to the train. A crowd of women waved and wailed on the other side of the barrier. We couldn't hear them through the deafening racket of whistles, clanking and hissing and the slamming of train doors, but their faces said it all. In the café, soldiers lounged on their kitbags and I felt incongruous in my dark suit and dog collar. My companion, Chapman, was a stocky priest with bright blue eyes set in a pugnacious red face. Dressed in mufti – a loud checked jacket and creased tie – he cheerfully ignored the swearing all around us as he shovelled another sugar into his tea and pointed the spoon at the children.

'There, you see. They hate sending their children away. Some say it's worse than the bombs.'

'Surely not,' I said. 'They must sleep more easily knowing their children are safe.'

'What makes you think they sleep?'

I don't think Chapman thought much of me. He was off in a week to train as an army chaplain and I was to replace him in his north London parish. He had been there for five years, his second incumbency after a spell in Halifax among the mills, and said he wanted to be with the men. I didn't tell him I was a pacifist. We were very different, and I found it hard to take it all in as he told me about the parish, the church and the various clubs he ran.

He shook my hand firmly, as if he was testing my grip, and gave me a set of keys for the church, hall and vicarage. He was travelling north the next day to see his parents before reporting for training in Reading.

'Good luck,' he said. 'Look after your flock and they will look after you.' He paused, looked at the soldiers eating their sandwiches, and added, 'And one other piece of advice. Never refuse their hospitality.'

After which, with a cheery wave, he strode through the crowds to the steps down to the underground.

* * *

It's spring, but you wouldn't know it around here apart from the odd daffodil in a front garden and the blossom on a stunted cherry tree in the churchyard. People say that front gardens were full of crocuses and narcissi in pre-war springs, before rationing was introduced and every scrap of earth was planted with vegetable and salad seeds.

I've forbidden them to dig up the churchyard, for now at least, and most of them seem to understand. 'I want Mum and Dad pushing up daisies, not bleeding potatoes,' a lady in a green hat tartly observed. In any case, the wardens warned me that the churchyard is *fuller than people know* as a result of various contagions and epidemics which decimated the population a hundred or so years ago and the dead had to be buried on top of each other. 'They won't thank us when they dig up bones with their carrots.'

'No, doubtless they won't,' I agreed whilst wishing that people here would employ a higher reasoning, such as the fact the churchyard is consecrated ground and not to be treated like a makeshift allotment.

I miss my old life now that the evenings are getting longer. Darkness is a great equalizer, but the sunshine lays bare the sheer shabbiness of life here, the dirt and rubbish and smoke, the stench of fried onions coming out of a hundred kitchen windows every evening, the way in which nature is suffocated or emaciated. Above my old college was a woodland which stretched over a hill. In March it was bordered with daffodils and, in May, it was carpeted with bluebells which glowed in a haze in the shafts of light from the setting sun. How could you not believe in God with such beauty? But here, well . . . This felt like an alien creation. And at night, when the stars failed to appear and were hidden by cloud, or fog or the smoke of all the chimneys, I felt as if I had been expelled from Eden and imprisoned in this London street.

* * *

The 7th of March was a Thursday, and my first midweek Eucharist. On Sunday morning I had extolled the virtues of this quiet communion service amidst the bustle and busyness of the working week. Fred, an asthmatic veteran of the print trade, and his son Raymond were robed as the two servers. Fred's wife Betty, who did the flowers when there were any to be had, was in the front row dressed in a brown woollen coat which smelled of tobacco and cheap perfume. A pew behind were two women in headscarves who whispered to each other and seemed to be sharing a joke. I wondered whether they were making humorous comparisons between me and my predecessor, who prided himself on his speed and brevity. Near the back of the church, on either side of the aisle, were two younger women. One, who was wearing a stylish green velvet coat, crossed herself and bobbed her head at every mention of the Lord or the Virgin Mary and the other, a short, petite woman with her hair in a bun, had a very small child perched beside her.

I remember I preached that day on a line from the Lord's Prayer, *And lead us not into temptation but deliver us from evil.* I said that God would be faithful but could not turn aside the evil of man, just as He had not saved Jesus from the agony of the cross. I was addressing myself as much as my flock, and my resentment that God had taken me from the tranquillity of the Oxfordshire countryside to this vale of tears in Islington. But I was also trying to rationalise the suffering of the local people, now and to come, in enduring not only the threat of death and destruction from the skies but also the enforced absence of husbands and brothers and evacuated children. I didn't want them to blame God, or me as His apologist. He was all-powerful, but had ceded control so that man could choose between good and evil. And if some men chose evil, well look what happened to Cain.

After the service, the taller woman at the back remained praying as the congregation left. I went to the vestry to take off my cassock and to have a few words with Raymond, the second server, who had forgotten to ring the bell when I raised the chalice of wine. Perhaps I was a bit sharper than I should have been but all these little rituals are suffused with meaning. I explained this to Raymond as patiently as I could, but he seemed too anxious to understand. After he left, I went to the altar and muttered a prayer for the living and the dead. I thought of my older brother who had been blown to bits at the end of the Great War, over twenty years ago, and of my mother who still grieved for him intensely.

I was vaguely conscious of some movement behind me, and when I turned round, the tall woman was standing in the aisle, her hands folded in front of her.

'Father, I need to speak to you, if you can spare me some minutes.' She spoke with a German accent, which surprised me as most Germans in London had just been rounded up and taken to the Isle of Man. Her face was pale, with heavy lips and an aquiline nose. Her green eyes seemed unnaturally large, as if she had thyroid problems. She looked tired and careworn, which was not unusual during those terrible days. I put her in her early thirties, although she could have been younger.

I invited her back to the vicarage and brewed a pot of strong tea which she drank without milk. 'I am Anna Schneider,' she said, shaking my hand earnestly. 'A refugee from Austria. My parents sent me here when Dollfuss was murdered. They are communists.'

I nodded, waiting for her to go on. There had been a few German protestants at theological college, very serious minded, who regarded Hitler as the anti-Christ. They were, I'm ashamed to say, derided by some of my fellow ordinands as politically extreme and theologically illiberal. But the press in those days really was quite sympathetic to the Nazis, especially after the Olympics.

'I am not a communist,' she added, 'but the Nazis do not distinguish between the politics of the parents and the children.' She pursed her lips.

'And where are your parents now?'

'I have not heard from them since the Anschluss.'

'Do you not have friends who can tell you?'

She sighed. 'You do not understand, Father. Life is very dangerous in Graz if you have any connections to the communists. They open the mail of anybody they think is suspect. A letter from me, or to me, could land them in a camp.'

I realised her parents were more than likely in a camp already, if indeed they were still alive. I had read enough about the brutality of the Nazi camps to guess the likely consequences. 'Where do you live?'

'At number 47. I have a room with Mrs MacLennan.'

'I know Mrs MacLennan, but not very well.' Jean MacLennan was a wiry Glaswegian, not a regular churchgoer. Her three small children had all been evacuated and were now living somewhere in the Chilterns. Her husband, whom I had never met, was a merchant seaman. I had exchanged no more than a few words with Jean, whose expression did not encourage conversation. I imagined she must feel very lonely in an empty house and that she would be pleased to have Anna's company.

Anna was silent for a little while, as if trying to translate her thoughts into English. The tension in her face suggested a more immediate anxiety overlaying her deeper fears.

'I am scared,' she said, without feeling. 'The people here

suspect me, even Mrs MacLennan. They think I might be a German spy. Somebody in the shop yesterday, who had not seen me, said I might be somehow signalling to the Luftwaffe to guide them to their targets.'

'I'm very sorry. You must not take any notice. People think all sorts of strange things when they are frightened. I'm sure they don't mean any harm.'

She looked hurt. I realised I must sound rather trite, as if one could simply ignore the hostile murmurings of the locals. I tried to imagine what it might be like in her shoes, in a foreign country at war with your homeland, without friends or family. As a non-local I knew how hard it was to be accepted, even as a priest.

She spoke again. 'Maybe if I work for you, and people see that you trust me, they will trust me. After all, you can see into people's souls.'

I shrugged. 'I am not God. I see only what people choose to reveal. And I don't know whether the people trust me enough to translate that trust to you. I'm quite new here myself.'

'Please, Father, I feel so lonely. I even wish sometimes I was back in Graz. At least I have some friends and relations there, if they are still free.' She sat in silence as tears slid down her gaunt cheeks and she twisted her hands together. I felt very sorry for her.

'Listen,' I said. 'We already have a parish secretary and the PCC will not vote me the funds to take on an extra pair of hands, but I could do with a cook once or twice a week if you don't mind helping out. I can maybe afford a few shillings a week, at least for the time being.'

'Thank you Father. Thank you. Thank you! When would you like me to start?'

We settled on the following Tuesday, when I would be alone. I did not entertain often – it wasn't easy to get the food to do so – but I thought I should sample Anna's cooking before making the arrangement more public. I wasn't at all sure how it would go down.

* * *

Doreen, the other woman at the back of the church at that midweek communion, asked to see me after morning prayers the following Sunday. We'd had two air raid warnings the previous evening and the sky to the south had been a dazzling show of search lights peering into the heavens, followed by anti-aircraft fire and the flames of explosions as the Luftwaffe pounded the docks. There had been no damage in Islington, but people looked shocked and tense the next day. How long would this go on for? And when would the bombs start landing nearer to home?

'Some people are finding it hard to get to the shelters. We wondered whether you could open the crypt. Be a lot less cramped for people, and . . . '

She stopped talking as I involuntarily frowned. The crypt was dark, dank, poorly lit and full of all sorts of junk from Lord knew when. 'It wouldn't be suitable without putting in some heating and lighting. And there's an awful lot to clear out.'

'Well, I'm sure the church can afford that. Surely it's the Christian thing to do?' She looked me in the eye as if daring me to disagree.

'It is,' I conceded. 'I just want to make sure we do it properly. I'll talk to the wardens.'

'We need to get a move on. The bombers won't wait until we are ready.'

As we talked, a small queue of church members was forming behind her, waiting to have a word and no doubt listening intently to our little exchange. I realised this was my first test.

'Don't worry, Doreen. We'll open as soon as the authorities say we can – tomorrow, if possible.'

As it happened, there was a lull in the bombing over the next few days. Hitler had made a speech which offered peace whilst threatening annihilation if we refused. People read the headlines and wondered whether the war might be a short one after all. The authorities clearly thought otherwise as electric heaters and extra lights were installed along with a generator to keep things going if the power supply failed. The dusty old pews, curtains and theatrical props were replaced by chairs and bedding, and a camping stove was rigged up to enable tea and coffee to be brewed. The following week the siren sounded again and half the population of Shakespeare Street, most of whom I'd never seen before, poured down the steps and settled themselves for the evening. We were in business.

Doreen was a regular in the crypt, making tea, comforting the old people and finding new games to distract the children who seemed alternatively terrified and curious about what was going on outside. Quite a few families brought their dogs, and one woman even brought her parrot in its cage.

Over the next few weeks, the bombing raids happened night after night. Shakespeare Street escaped any direct damage but you didn't have to walk far to see collapsed houses and holes in the road or witness the strange intimacy of people's domestic lives revealed in exposed interiors where bedrooms were missing a wall and toilet cisterns hung in mid air. Dogs howled and shivered as they sensed the vibration of the planes, long before we could hear them and rats flickered around the bomb sites. The people who worked in local factories and shops looked exhausted each morning after working as ARPs and volunteer firemen and nurses during the night. We all said to each other *This cannot go on. We will go mad or die of exhaustion.* But it became our new normality, one in which we could not quite conceive of the tranquil world which had existed before the war.

Every evening I went down to the crypt and it became very crowded as people became more and more scared. I now knew most of the street's residents by sight, although I was never good at remembering names. To begin with, many people ignored me. They didn't know how to address me and I had never been introduced to them. Furthermore, I lacked the natural gregariousness of my predecessor who had known instinctively how to talk to people without talking down to them. I found myself tongue-tied, uttering feeble platitudes about seeing it through and hoping they were comfortable. They sensed all this and responded with their own meaningless phrases. But all that was about to change.

Late one evening, there was a sudden hammering at the

door and the sound of shouting in the street. I thought it was probably another drunk fresh from the pub. We were already crammed to the rafters and I was about to shout back that we were full and he should try the shelter in Stony Street when Doreen, who was closer to the door, beckoned me over.

'Number 42 is down. The firemen are asking for a priest.'

I seized my bag of holy oils and slipped outside. There stood a man with a smoke-blackened face, blood seeping from one hand. 'It's the O'Neill family,' he said. I started to walk behind him, the wavering beam of his torch picking up every mote of dust in the choking air. 'The daughter is very bad,' he added.

'I know the family, they're good people,' a woman's voice whispered. 'I hope to God it's not Aileen, it will kill her Mammy.' I had not realised Doreen had followed me out of the crypt and I was relieved she was there. I had visited the living in hospital and comforted the bereaved, but never like this.

It had been very dark near the church but I could see flames further down the street, where the bomb had struck. We had not heard or felt it in the crypt, perhaps because we were too close to get the full force of the shock waves. Firemen were training a hose on the smoking building, but the water main must have gone because the water pressure was very weak. An ARP warden in his white hat was keeping passers-by away, in so far as he could see them. Thieves and pilferers were a fact of life, and they often appeared at bomb sites before the firemen. You could tell them by the scarves they wore over their mouths and the caps pulled low over their eyes. According to the locals, they came from Hackney and Finsbury.

As we got closer there was a smell of charred burning wood overlain with a choking cloud of hot dust. I gulped and wondered how anybody had survived. When we got to the house, we could see that the roof had caved in and half of the front and back walls had been blown out. A double bed teetered over the edge of the first floor, its torn eiderdown draped over the remains of the front window. The front door had splintered and half opened.

'I hope you've some holy water. They're Catholics,' Doreen whispered as we picked our way across the debris in the front garden. When we squeezed through the door, we found Mrs O'Neill crouched over her daughter. Aileen lay motionless on the floor with blood seeping from her ears while her mother sobbed quietly. Doreen bent down and felt the girl's pulse for some while, then put her ear to her chest.

'Her pulse is very weak.' She turned to Mrs O'Neill, who had not moved, and squeezed her hand. An ambulance had been called, and I wondered whether we should simply wait rather than act as if death was inevitable.

'Go on then. Do your stuff,' Doreen said quietly in my ear. At this, Mrs O'Neill sobbed more loudly.

I motioned the ARP man over and asked him to shine his torch on my prayer book. I knew the words well enough but, in the intensity of the moment, I was not sure I could accurately call them to mind. And so we began, with me intoning the prayers, the pulverized air shaking with the vibrations of another wave of bombers thousands of feet above us, and this little girl lying there, soundlessly, before us.

As I anointed Aileen's head, cradled in Doreen's arms, her eyes opened and she gave a low moan. There was a moment of stillness which seemed to separate us, for a few seconds, from the chaos and noise around us, a tiny door of silence before life resumed. Mrs O'Neill, her head resting on her daughter's tummy, cried more loudly and I continued to the end of the prayers and the blessing.

'She's gone,' Doreen said. 'The poor darling.'

The ARP warden turned away and went back to his guard duties. After a little while an ambulance arrived and Doreen and I walked back to the crypt.

'I'd best not say anything. Mrs O'Neill will want some time alone to grieve in private,' I said.

'No, you must tell them. She'll need everyone's support, and Aileen was one of our own.'

So I told the people sheltering in the crypt. There was a good deal of shock, and some anger. The death and destruction which were being visited on other parts of London had arrived in Shakespeare Street. Aileen was the first child to die in our street, but she would not be the last.

The immediate aftermath involved one of those ecclesiastical spats which mystify the general public. I informed Father Murphy, the local Catholic priest, that I had given the last rites to Aileen.

'And what might those rites have been?' he asked, spikily.

I explained that time had been short and that I had been called, unaware of the religious allegiance of the O'Neills until I had arrived at the house.

'Your predecessor would have known, and anybody would have told you if you had bothered to ask.'

I reminded him that I was relatively new to the parish and apologised for my ignorance, but that only seemed to increase his anger. Poor Aileen would not be in the arms of Jesus, he said sternly, if the last rites were invalid. At this I exploded and we had a good set to. Then, just when I thought we might come to blows, he smiled.

'Well, it sounds as if you did the best you could. God, in his infinite mercy, will understand.'

With which he invited me down to the local Irish pub for a pint of Guinness and introduced me to some of his flock, retelling the story of what I had done as if it had never been the subject of a row between us. It broke the ice with a lot of people in the community and I began to feel accepted for the first time.

It also marked the start of my friendship with Doreen. She made a point of inviting me round to her house for a cup of tea and a scone, and told me a little of her life. She had four children, three of whom had been evacuated first to Reading and then out to a village north of the Chilterns where they were lodged with a farmer's wife. Doreen missed them terribly and was upset that they were ten miles from the nearest railway station.

'I'd like to think I could pop up to see them in an emergency, but it's too far to walk from the station at the other end and I couldn't afford a taxi if they even *have* such a thing in the sticks.'

Her husband, Wilf, had gone over to France with the British Expeditionary Force and had not returned. His unit had stayed outside Dunkirk to slow the advance of the Germans but nobody seemed to know what had happened to it. On Doreen's mantelpiece was a photo of a saturnine-looking man with thick black hair, a strong chin and a piercing gaze, a handsome man. They had met at a dance. Like most of the local men, Wilf was not religious but he did not object to his wife attending church and, indeed, regarded it as a kind of superstitious insurance against mishaps and disasters.

'He always tells me to say a prayer for him. Well of course I did, but now, when I don't know whether he's dead or alive...' Her voice trailed off.

After we prayed together for Wilf and for her absent children, she brightened up and we fell to talking about the crypt. It was comfortable enough, although the two toilets were hardly adequate, but Doreen felt people needed something more than shelter.

'People get bored. You want to be taken out of yourself, not sit there having the same old conversations and wondering whether another wave of bombers will come.'

Some families played cards and word games, but we both thought it would be good if something could be done which joined people together.

'Why don't we form a choir?' Doreen asked. 'We could move the piano down there. Jesse can play and lead on the popular stuff, and Cyril could do the churchy stuff. And either of them could do stuff for the kids.'

'We could call it the People's Choir,' I suggested.

She pulled a face. 'That sounds a bit Soviet. We need something more obvious.'

And so the Crypt Choir was born. We advertised for singers in the local churches and pubs, and gathered a pool of pianists to allow for people's work and volunteering commitments. Ellen Cox, who taught music at the local junior school, volunteered to conduct. We practised on Tuesdays and Fridays, straight after work, and gave our first concert after a few weeks. Switching from *Abide with Me* to pub songs and Vera Lynn's latest was not easy for some of our more churchy members, but everybody entered into the swing of it. When the planes droned overhead and the bombs began to fall, there was something electrifying about all of us singing together and defying everything outside which Hitler had sent to destroy us.

The fact that the choir was much more than just a church choir also helped. I was thrilled, and so was Doreen. After our first concert 'away' she sent me an apple pie. Underneath the cloth covering it was a little note. *Everybody is saying how the choir has raised their spirits. Thank you for helping it happen – our joint project. Your friend Doreen.'*

Those were intense times. People went to work not knowing whether their office would still be there when they arrived, or whether their home would be intact when they returned. The postman became a bringer of grim tidings as well as good, and was observed closely as he worked his way down the street for signs of the former. The newspapers contained stories of 'sexual immorality' in the London parks, as young men and women threw caution to the wind and lived for the moment. Rationing had created a thriving black market via which almost anything could be had for a price. The local villains who had somehow escaped conscription had a field day. But moral disorder aside, the danger and – let's be honest – the excitement lent an extraordinary edginess to the ordinary business of living, and it impassioned relationships. It was like one of those days when the light alternates between storm clouds and sudden floods of sunshine. The greyness seemed to have been washed out of our lives, and we were left with extremes of joy and despair.

* * *

Anna proved to be an able cook, producing decent meals from the most unpromising ingredients with a touch of Austrian style from time to time. To begin with, I ate alone while she stayed in the kitchen. I could feel her listening to me eat. I have a thing about the noise of people eating, having spent my childhood being castigated by my father for every gulp and inelegant swallow. Being listened to by somebody who was out of sight felt even worse so I asked her either to sit in the lounge, out of earshot, or come and eat with me, which she did. Disconcertingly, she was a very noisy eater but maybe that was sheer hunger.

Mrs MacLennan kept a sparse kitchen.

So, twice a week, we lunched together. Parish callers raised an eyebrow but that wasn't my problem. She spoke of her childhood, her father's work for the Party, which kept him away most evenings, and the activities of the local stormtroopers who sounded like a uniformed version of our London gangs. She loved the outdoor life in Austria, skiing and ice skating in the winter and hiking in the summer. At home she had felt her mother's anxiety and sensed her parents' struggle to survive after the failure of the banks wiped out their meagre savings. At school, where children knew the politics of most families, she stuck with her friends and some tough boys from communist families to avoid being picked on. But, in the mountains, all her worries were left behind. Here in London, she felt claustrophobic – something we had in common. I promised to take her out to the English countryside if the bombing eased off.

Sometimes we fell to talking of religion. Anna was a Catholic, like most Austrians (even Hitler), and had developed an intense piety as though God really was present in the wine and bread of Mass and the Virgin Mary might at any moment weep tears of sorrow from the plaster eyes with which she gazed upon the cross. Anna told me she found my services 'nice' but lacking in holy mystery. I didn't know whether this was as a result of my own uninspired performance or simply the traditional reserve of the English and Anglicanism. We'd had some ordinands for whom the mystery of God brought an other-dimensional sensuousness to their spirituality. For them, the liturgy was a kind of magic spell in which the minutiae – down to the rubrics of their actions – were essential to the integrity and efficacy of the whole. I had leant that way for a while in my late teens as it lent a romanticism to religion which corresponded to my longing to fall in love, but then it faded. I half-envied Anna.

Now that she was eating a little better, some of the gauntness in her face disappeared and her features softened. She sometimes wore makeup and a hint of perfume. She even smiled occasionally and, although she was still regarded with suspicion by some of them, many of my parishioners began to chat to her during air raids. At church she kept herself apart, but nobody seemed offended. I got her to help occasionally with a little secretarial work, for which I could not pay her but which she seemed glad to do.

To my relief nobody questioned Anna's occasional presence in the vicarage, at least not to me. Mrs MacLennan now had more lodgers including Mrs O'Neill, Aileen's mother, and, as I was spooning up some rather watery custard which Anna had prepared one lunchtime, she told me that Mrs MacLennan had said she might need Anna to share a room if Mrs O'Neill's son was allowed to return from Chesham to support his grieving mother.

'I wondered, Father, whether I might move into your spare room. I do not think it would be a good idea for me to share a room with a young boy.'

I hesitated. The Archdeacon, on his last visit, had told me of the loneliness of women in the absence of their husbands and of the need for clergy to be on their guard against attentions which might have a 'carnal intention'. This was different, he had explained, from the platonic obsessions of middle aged spinsters which had traditionally afflicted unmarried clergy. Anna sometimes made me feel uneasy.

'Of course if you need your room for other purposes, I can look elsewhere,' Anna added. There was an edge of hurt in her voice. I agreed that she could move in. The following week, Mrs O'Neill told me that young Ronnie was being allowed back and, a few days later, Anna appeared at my door with all her worldly possessions in a small battered suitcase. She became my first lodger. It seemed a sensible arrangement.

* * *

Life moved on. The choir thrived. The Blitz waxed and waned. Other cities suffered. Buses and carts moved through scenes of devastation, travelling on novel routes up side streets and through previously undisturbed squares and mews as the economic life of the nation staggered on. Imported fruit was becoming a rarity as merchant shipping struggled to get through and the dock workers toiled to unload the cargoes before they rotted. People fantasized about eating fresh oranges and bananas. Life before the war now shimmered with all the things we had taken for granted. The news from Europe was unremittingly grim. Hitler had made short work of Poland and France, and now had his armies poised to cross the Channel. Where was God, people asked, in all this?

I didn't even try to answer that question. The bible was full of disasters and warnings of worse to follow when the Israelites forgot their God. Sometimes I wondered whether the boot was on the other foot and God simply forgot about the Israelites for a time, leaving them to their fate while He created other worlds and galaxies as he spoke to other forms of life trillions of light years away where, for all we knew, cataclysmic conflicts were raging which would make our wars look tiny. Somehow God seemed real and tangible in church and in the cheerful chaos of the crypt, in the small lives of the here and now, but remote from the stage of world history. At least, I could not discern Him there.

One winter's day, when the vicarage felt like an ice box, I had a visit from Doreen. She had a friend with a car who had got hold of some petrol. He was willing to lend her the car to see her children, if she could find someone to drive it. I had not driven for quite a while and wondered why Doreen's friend was unwilling to drive her, but one look at her imploring eyes persuaded me to agree. It would be good to get out of London.

So, on a bright December morning, we picked the car up outside the Arsenal football stadium and proceeded, rather jerkily at first as I got used to the clutch.

'Who would have imagined you and me driving into the country in a private car?' Doreen giggled. She was in a skittish, excitable mood and had a sparkle I'd not see before.

'Who indeed,' I said, slowing down to let an army lorry cross in front. The soldiers in the back of it waved and wolf whistled and seemed to find something funny in the two of us. Maybe it was the dog collar.

Doreen had dressed up for her children and she looked different, younger. She was wearing a blue head scarf, a pair of leather gloves and a brown woollen coat, a sensible outfit as there was no heating in the car to speak of.

'I haven't been out of London since we took the family hop picking one year. Right old laugh that was.' She smiled and put her hand on my wrist. 'You know, Father, I'm really grateful for you taking me today. You don't know how much it means to me.'

The soft pressure of her hand startled me. Not the gesture but the touch, the warmth. She squeezed my wrist then removed her hand. We were both silent for a while. It felt hard to say anything without acknowledging what had happened, but I did not know how to do that without making either more or less of it than was justified. I knew it was probably no more than a mark of friendship and, professionally, I hoped that was what it was. She didn't even use my Christian name, so how could it be more than that? But something in her touch, in those few seconds, electrified me. I felt an emotional charge had passed between us.

After a while, we resumed talking – about the scenery and the streets of undamaged houses interspersed, here and there, with broken windows, missing roof tiles and, in one case, a caved-in roof. But the scale of damage grew less and less as we moved towards the outskirts of London.

Life was different here from Islington. Maybe it had always been different. But there was a feeling of order, prosperity and calm. If the Germans ever invaded, they would find plenty of fine houses out here to billet their officers and nurse their wounded – and maybe, in some of the wooded parks, a suitably discreet location for a prison camp. In Poland, it had been reported that lots of clergy had been arrested. The very normality unsettled me.

Finally the outer London suburbs petered out, giving way initially to shabby countryside full of corrugated iron sheds, concrete prefabs and tethered horses grazing at the side of the road, indifferent to the lorries whining by. Then the landscape settled into a rhythm of tilled fields, hedgerows, woodlands, farm buildings and electricity pylons, a worked, ordered geography, undulating in the steep ridges of the Chilterns and the lower hills north of Aylesbury. Doreen had dozed for a while, woke with a start, and lit a cigarette.

'Do you smoke?' she asked above the clatter of the engine.

'I wouldn't say no to a drag.'

She took the cigarette from her mouth and placed it in my own. I could taste her lipstick on the filter. When I handed the cigarette back she puffed furiously on it, so much so that I had to wind down the window to let out some of the smoke.

'Sorry. I don't know why but I'm feeling a bit nervous. I'm half-wondering if the kids will recognise me.'

'Don't be ridiculous,' I said. 'They'll be all over you. It must be hard for them to understand why you've been separated.'

She frowned and fell silent, remaining quiet until we drew into the village where they were billeted.

'Here, stop for a few moments would you? I want to look my best.' She pulled a tiny mirror out of her handbag, brushed her hair and put on some fresh lipstick.

'How do I look?' she asked, turning towards me and tilting her head to one side while pursing her lips.

'Beautiful,' I said.

'I'm not asking whether you fancy me, Father. Do I look smart?'

I blushed, and nodded. She laughed. 'Only joking!'

We stopped at the post office to ask for directions then drove to the farm where Beryl and Tom were staying with the Appleby family. The farmhouse was down a muddy track, some way off the main road. It was a biggish red brick house with a slate roof. Two lines of washing were flapping in the breeze as we arrived. A large Alsatian started barking as I opened the farm gate. Almost immediately a middle aged woman in an apron appeared at the front door. With one hand she waved at Doreen before the other hand gestured the dog back into the house.

The plan was for me to make the introductions and then leave Doreen to spend a couple of hours with the children, after which I would return to pick her up and drive her back to London. The children were at school when we arrived but they would be back at lunchtime and had been granted permission to stay home after lunch.

When I returned two hours later, after mooching around the local church and drinking half a pint of bitter very slowly in the local pub, I found a strained atmosphere. Doreen was sitting on the sofa with Beryl and Tom beside her. Beryl, a seven year old, was snuggled up close to her mum. Tom was wriggling restlessly, anxious to get out and play. Mrs Appleby, I learned later, had told Doreen how the children had needed 'feeding up' and how Beryl had wet the bed for the first two weeks, which she intimated was the result of a lack of manners rather than a surfeit of misery. She had also explained how she was endeavouring to wean the children off 'common expressions', which I assumed was either their London slang or the odd swear word. Either way, Doreen felt patronised and put down. She told Mrs Appleby she would be asking the authorities if she could have the children back home as soon as possible. Mrs Appleby said she expected more gratitude and told Doreen she only had the children's best interests at heart.

When it was time to go, Beryl clung to Doreen's leg as she got up and would not release her grip until Doreen told her quite sharply that she had to leave. Tom seemed relieved that he could return to his outdoor pursuits. Mrs Appleby folded her arms and stood by the kitchen door, glaring at us as we walked down the garden path.

As we drove away into the greyness of a cold afternoon, Doreen wound down the window to look back then sobbed. Little Beryl was waving plaintively. Tom was nowhere to be seen. She seemed to feel shattered rather than restored by the brief reunion. After a while, when we were clear of the village and heading for the main road south, she asked me to stop the car in a lay-by.

'I can see her game,' she snorted. 'She hasn't got any kids of her own so she's decided to keep hold of mine and turn them against me.' I thought this was a bit harsh on Mrs Appleby, who seemed to me insensitive rather than hard hearted and I was stupid enough to say so.

That only threw fat on the flames. 'So you think she's a better mother than me, do you? Just because she's got more food in the larder and a house big enough to give them a bedroom each and God knows what else. And teach them the Queen's English while she's at it.'

I protested my innocence and said I was sure Doreen was the best of mothers and, more to the point, she was the children's real mother and not just a stand-in.

She lit a cigarette and sat in silence, smoking sullenly. Her eye make-up had run and her lipstick had smeared. She blew her nose, then dabbed a handkerchief at the corners of her eyes. They were glittering with tears. I leant over and put an arm around her, and she lay her head against my shoulder and began to shake. I clasped her more firmly, and she raised her head towards me. I kissed. We kissed. Not for more than a moment, but a moment that was long enough to taste the salt of her tears on her upper lip and to feel a fleeting vivid connection before we both drew back. The moment passed, I raised my head, gazed blankly at the road and, after a little while, drew my arm away.

'We'd best be starting back,' I said. 'We need to be home before it gets dark.'

Her head was resting on my shoulder but she did not move. I felt her breath becoming more measured and regular on my neck. She had fallen asleep. I started the car, but the engine did not seem to waken her. I put the car into gear and drove off through a world that was shades of grey. As the landscape drifted by I thought of all those Hollywood films in which a couple are in a car, cocooned from the world outside as it dissolves into a wavering unreality while the rain pours down and the windscreen wipers go back and forth, back and forth. Here, in wartime England, it was not rain but snow which floated out of the sky, first a few flakes, and then thickening. I turned on the wipers and they squeaked until the glass grew wet, when they swished to and fro. I feared we might lose our way but I fell into a trance-like focus that disallowed any distraction from the time which absorbed us and held us together.

After a while Doreen stirred and sat up. 'Where are we? I must have fallen asleep.'

The spell was broken. We spoke as if nothing had happened, about the weather, the journey, the life to which we were returning, the difficulty of keeping warm on the coal rations which had been introduced. When we got to Highbury, I let her out by the underground station. She disappeared into the building with a brief wave and I went off to park the car where we had collected it. I was disappointed we could not complete our journey together but I needed the time to reflect on what had happened. I played and replayed the moment of the kiss, trying to decipher what it might mean – for her . . . and for me.

* * *

I did not see Doreen for a few days. There was a lull in the bombing and no air raid warnings, so we did not have to open the crypt and she did not appear at the midweek communion. Over lunch afterwards, I told Anna that I had taken Doreen to see her children.

'You did not think about our trip to the country?' Anna's voice betrayed her disappointment. I explained that the car had been lent by a friend of Doreen's for that purpose alone, and it was Doreen's only chance as the house where the children were billeted was so far from the station.

Anna pulled a face, and I sensed she was jealous – not of the missed chance to see the country but of my being with Doreen. I changed the subject to lighten her mood, but she showed no interest and disappeared into the kitchen to do the washing up before returning to her room. I wondered whether, intuitively, she sensed that something had happened between Doreen and me, but dismissed the idea as paranoia.

At theological college the most handsome tutor, by tradition, had to give the annual lecture on *Dangerous Women.* It was presented as an after-dinner speech during the final week of the summer term and was advertised as a humorous party piece with some serious intent. The speaker was elected by popular vote and, in my year, was a muscular bespectacled giant who was famed for his brutality on the rugger field where he strode around the pitch with opposition players hanging on to him like baby monkeys until he swatted them into the mud. He was also a thoughtful tutor in pastoral studies.

'You are about to enter a world where you will be the equivalent of the court eunuch. To the men you will be sexless, half man half spirit. To the women, especially but not exclusively older spinsters, you will seem to offer temptation without risk, an object of innocent flirtation and private fantasy. However modestly and prudently you comport yourself, at some point, with someone, you will stand accused of indiscretion. So plan, dear ordinands, not how you can avoid such an outcome but how you will deal with it when it happens.'

This sage advice was followed by a series of Wodehousian anecdotes which we found funnier and funnier as we sank into our cups. I guess what most of us took away was a story or two we could repeat as party pieces in the right company, but not much else. I had forgotten the anecdotes, but now found myself brooding on the image of the court eunuch. I wondered whether, for Doreen, I was simply that, a half man who could be touched inconsequentially and kissed without sin. Or whether it was the indiscretion for which I might have to face an accuser.

In the following week my thoughts often turned to Doreen. I glimpsed her in the congregation on Sunday, but after the service a matriarch buttonholed me and Doreen slipped past without a word. Had I offended her? Did she think I had taken advantage of her distress? Or was she being distant to protect both of us from gossip? Perhaps her silence was intended to emphasise that what had happened was an accident, a momentary impulse which had no relevance for the future. All the while, I felt oppressed by Anna's constant attention. She came to every service, looked up at me with a soulful gaze as she took communion and was a watching presence in the house. In the evening, if I was in my study, I would hear her footsteps in the corridor followed by a kind of sigh, somewhere between longing and disappointment. One afternoon, when I returned from visiting a parishioner, I went straight to my study. I could sense, somehow, that she had been in there. My diary had been moved and one of the drawers was slightly ajar. I wondered whether she had been checking whether I had visited Doreen.

As it happened, Doreen herself broke the stalemate between us. She posted a note through the door asking if I could drop by to see her. I went round but she was not in and a neighbour said she had got a job in a local factory manufacturing aeroplane propellers. When I returned at four, she opened the door before I had a chance to knock and ushered me inside.

She looked different. More tired, more careworn, but also more self possessed than when I had last seen her. 'It's Wilf,' she said. 'There's still no word. I need some certainty.'

I tried to reassure her. 'If he's a POW, it can take months for letters to get through. Mrs Garlick heard from her son last Monday that he's been in a German prison camp for the last six months. The Germans wouldn't let any letters through until there was a negotiated protocol.'

'It's funny,' she said. 'I always thought that I'd know whether he was alive or dead. A sixth sense, you know, like twins. I certainly know whether my children are happy or not. But with Wilf it's as if he's in a kind of limbo, neither dead nor alive. I mean, I don't even know whether I'm still married, do I?'

'No, but you don't know you're not married, nor will you till you get definite news one way or the other.'

She pulled a face. I don't think it was what she wanted to hear. 'I wish you hadn't kissed me,' she said, and looked me in the eye. 'Not because I didn't want you to. I needed you to. But where does it leave me with God?'

She took my hand across the dining table. It felt like a gesture of consolation. I did not know what to answer. 'I can't explain it,' I said. 'It felt right in the moment. We all need affection, and you were very upset.'

'But you're a priest. And I've a husband, or had one.'

'Maybe I shouldn't have done it,' I said. 'But I can't find it in myself to regret it.'

We were both silent for a while. The whistling kettle provided a welcome distraction and she made a pot of weak tea. 'I baked a cake,' she said, 'to have in for when you called round.' She handed me a slice of sponge cake. It had been dusted with real icing sugar, shining white. I closed my eyes and smelled its sweetness. 'It's real,' she reassured me. 'I found it at the back of the cupboard.' I wanted to say she should have kept it back for Christmas, for the children, but of course there was only little Jimmy and he was too young to enjoy it.

'It's a real treat, but I don't deserve it.'

'Oh yes you do,' she replied, fluttering her eyes.

That was probably the moment I fell in love with Doreen. Not because of the cake, of course not, nice though it was. There was a certain reckless honesty about her, so different from my innate caution. Her feelings were not always obvious and I was still unsure quite how – or as what – she regarded me. But if her feelings were sometimes masked they were never entirely hidden. She didn't want to block out the light and, in the near apocalyptic menace of those days, a little human warmth went a long way. God knew that, I thought. He was the still small voice, not the howl of a hurricane; the burning bush, not the volcano.

We parted without an embrace, let alone a kiss. But, for me at least, things had moved to a different level. When I walked back to the vicarage through the darkness, the stars that glittered in the heavens seemed like a vision of another dimension just revealed to me.

* * *

It was now the Christmas season and, although Christmas trees and toys were in short supply and turkeys virtually extinct, people still yearned for the old songs and shows. There were rumours that the evacuated children might be allowed home for Christmas week. For a few days the mothers of Shakespeare Street sparkled with expectation as they set about decorating their homes and hoarding sweet rations for the big return. Alas, the Government decided that there was too much risk of children not wanting to go back to the country, or being secreted by their parents. They were probably right, but morale dropped like a stone.

We had to do something and Ellen, the Crypt Choir-mistress, decided we should have a grand concert on Christmas Eve. It was to be in the church and we would tackle the first part of Bach's *Christmas Oratorio* followed by some carols and a few pub songs to encourage the non-churchgoers to come along. Advertisements were put up in all the local churches and pubs as well as the butchers' shops, where people had plenty of time to read as they queued. Choir members pooled their ration cards to enable sandwiches, jellies and cakes to be laid on, and the pubs donated some beer and lemonade. Rehearsals started in earnest and, long into the night, the church resounded with snatches of song, passages in unison and solo voices, and the crisp commands of the diminutive Miss Cox, who stood on a chair occasionally so she could see what the basses were up to in the back row.

I sang with the tenors occasionally to make up the numbers, but I much preferred to observe from the sidelines. Like all rehearsals, the early stages were fractious, fragmented and painful. Many of the singers could not read music so had to learn by ear and others persisted in coming in at the wrong time or reading the wrong line. But things slowly came together, thanks to Ellen's dogged perseverance and the presence of a few really good singers whom others could follow. Doreen and Anna sang among the contraltos but I tried not to look at them too often.

In the crypt we had found an old crib which we put out, complete with hay and a manger from the milkman's yard. As the last week of Advent approached, we were all set. We prayed for a cloudy night to deter the bombers, and mild weather so we did not freeze in the church. On the 21st of December, the shortest day of the year, with the church lit only by candles in the sanctuary, I crept in and sat on a back pew to listen to the choir rehearsing. It started a little raggedly when the tenors missed their cue, so Ellen made them stop and start again. But then something happened. It was as if the dust was wiped away from an optic and a glowing glory revealed. The harmonies and counterpoint of Bach flowed, complicated but easy, and the music in turn evoked the birth of Jesus, the fear and the mystery, the strangeness and familiarity, the tentative new light within an old darkness. I looked at Doreen on the end of the row, knowing she could not see me, and the magic of the music fused for a moment with my love for her. I was moved, without quite understanding why. Then the old carols sounded out their peculiar mixture of pathos and joy and finally, as a rousing finale, a few pub songs. Then it was at an end, and I stole out before Ellen could prick the bubble with her critique. If the choir performed even half as well on Christmas Eve, the audience were in for a rare treat.

The 23rd of December dawned cold and sunny. The forecast was for a clear frosty night but with the possibility of rain or snow on Christmas Eve. I remember thinking, *Well, that's good. Better to have clear weather tonight than tomorrow.*

I was busy during the day, visiting parishioners who had lost their homes and attending a meeting of the local clergy. All of them looked as exhausted as I felt. Some of the clergy were old enough to have ministered during the Great War, and remembered the aerial bombing towards its end. The Blitz, they agreed, was of a totally different order and, despite the newspaper stories about the British stiff upper lip and cockney cheerfulness, many of their people were nearing the end of their tether and wondered whether the time had come to negotiate. As we prayed I wondered how near some of us clergy were to the abyss.

The air raid sirens sounded as I was walking home. I felt too tired to hurry – and indeed nobody around me seemed able or willing to quicken their pace. The crypt shelter had yet to be opened when there was a whistling noise, an ear splitting crash and an explosion. The shock waves knocked me to the ground and I felt as if I was spinning like a top before blackness overcame me. Then I saw pinpricks of light which, as I opened my eyes wider, I realised were flames. Somebody was looming over me, their hands cradling my head. I heard voices, far above me and muffled as if in another room, then the feeble ringing of the fire engine bells. Then nothing.

When I came to, I was in a hospital bed with a bandage covering my eyes. My body felt like a collection of disconnected outposts. Consciousness came and went. I thought I heard the voices of my mother and my dead brother, of Doreen, and my predecessor Chapman and of Mrs O'Neill's dead daughter whose name I could not remember. I wondered whether I should be giving the last rites to anybody, but I could not find my case of the oils. When I picked up my prayer book the words swam in and out of my vision, the letters like shoals of tiny black fish. If I was dying, I was not frightened. I had already spoken to the dead, if not in words. I looked forward to seeing my brother James and telling my mother how he was. Then sadness overcame me as I thought of all the people I would leave behind, even the people of Shakespeare Street who had been so suspicious, even Anna with all her troubles.

I could have died many times but I didn't. When I was finally able to reconnect with the world and the present, it was to wake up to the lugubrious features of the Archdeacon. Had he, I wondered, come to speak to me about Doreen? But no, it was to tell me that I had lost a leg and possibly the sight of one eye, and that the church had been bombed.

'Who else was hurt? Was anyone killed?' I asked.

He did not answer immediately. I could feel his gaze upon my face, and knew he was deciding whether to tell me now or later.

'I'm afraid so,' he said after a long pause. 'Raymond, your assistant sacristan, was killed. He must have been in the church preparing for a service. And the music teacher, Miss Cox, died of her wounds two days ago. She was just outside the church, and took the full force of the blast.'

I was silent as I tried to absorb the news. 'And the choir?' I asked.

'No other reports of anybody hurt or missing. I gather they were due to meet for a final rehearsal, so it's lucky the bomb didn't fall a bit later.'

'Not lucky for me,' I said, and began to sob. *Well, you really are half a man now,* a voice said within me, disfigured. *Nobody will love you now.*

The Archdeacon did not stay long. He disapproved of clergy 'emoting', whatever the circumstances, and probably felt I should have kept my feelings in check. I brooded about Raymond and Ellen. It was the end of the church, and the choir. Maybe the building would be replaced one day, in an unimaginable future when war had given way to peace, or maybe not. Maybe the people would be sick of the church and clergy and of God, this all-powerful God who could part the Red Sea and raise His son from the dead but would not prevent the death of the innocents, just as He had not after the birth of Christ.

I was angry with God too. I didn't deserve this. The people didn't deserve this. Suffering like this was not ennobling, but degrading. I wished I were dead. For a while I refused all visitors. Doreen tried to come a few times and then desisted. Anna ignored the ward sister and simply marched up to my bed, but I turned my back on her. Eventually, when I was well enough to be transferred, I was sent up to a hotel in the Lake District which had been turned into a convalescent home. And there I met people whose injuries, both physical and spiritual, were far worse than mine and I slowly came out of my own personal desert and rejoined the living.

It's a long time ago now. I stuck at the priesting business for ten more years, until my mother died and I felt free finally to do what I wanted. I lost my belief in God, and then re-found it – but not the God of the established church. The trouble, I decided, was not that God was remote from people's suffering but that he was too immersed in it. He suffered with and in them. Whether they found Him in their own suffering, I could not tell. He did not seem present in mine, but then I was probably looking in the wrong place.

And Doreen? She wrote to me when I was convalescing, a lovely affectionate letter. She had heard at last from Wilf who was in a POW camp in northern Germany. Her children were back with her. She was enjoying her job but missed the church, and me, the crypt shelter and the choir.

Everyone wants to see you again, she wrote. *We all loved you in our own rough and ready way. Do please come and see us.* I wished she had said 'I' rather than 'we', but Wilf would, God willing, be returning to her. I had no right to her love. Even if I could not stop loving her.

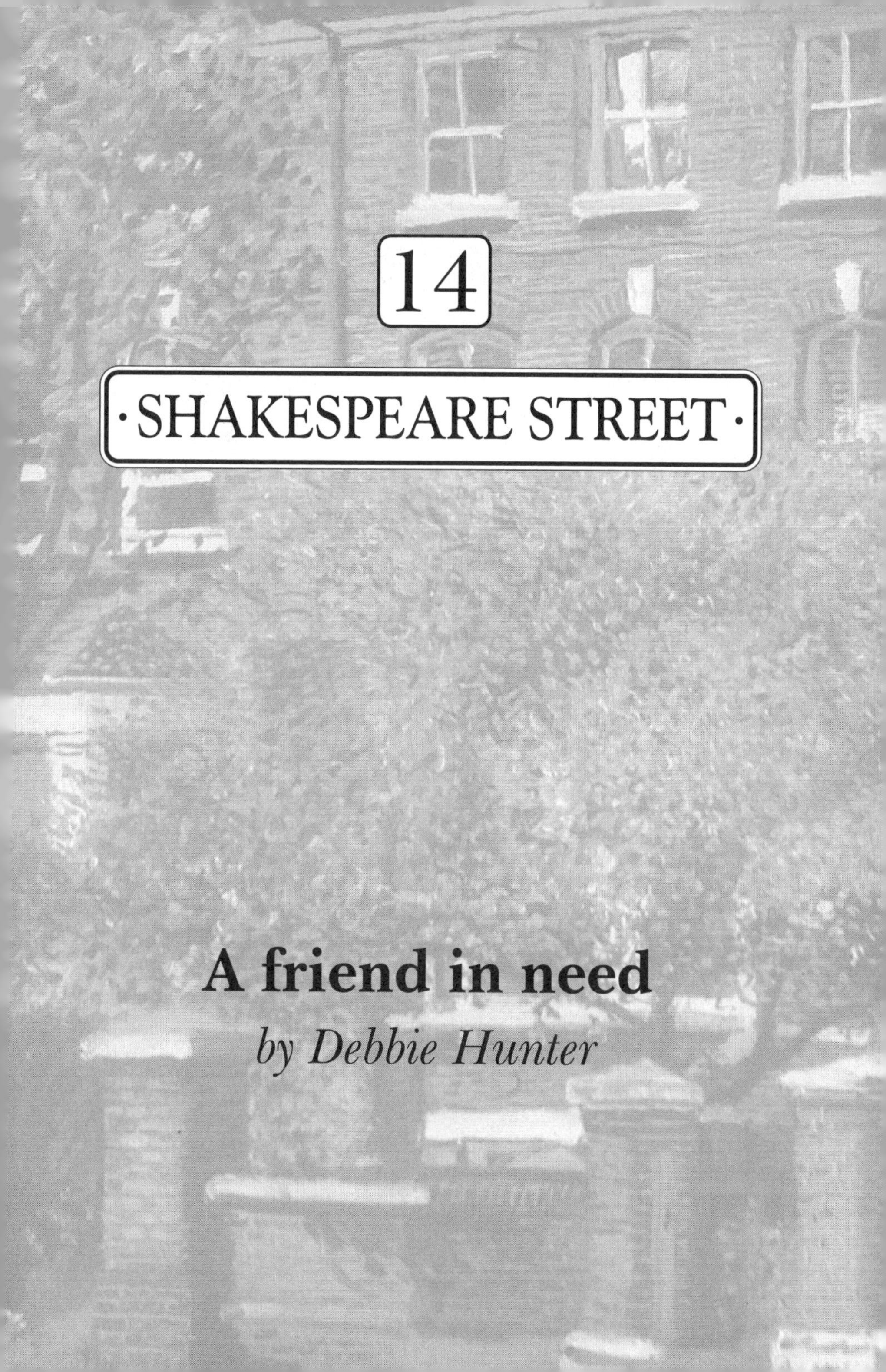

14 SHAKESPEARE STREET

A friend in need

by Debbie Hunter

If you poison us, do we not die? And if you wrong us, shall we not revenge?

Merchant of Venice, Act 3, Scene 1

You were having a laugh on that day, weren't you Fate, when you brought those two together? Sometimes two people should never meet.

* * *

Things seemed to change gear when Auntie Lil was around. One of life's joyriders, she left destruction and skid marks in her wake.

You wouldn't think it to look at her. Short in stature and hair resembling a Brillo pad, she cut a crazy picture as she stood on my doorstep – think fortune teller crossed with Napoleon. Her beady eyes, though small, missed nothing and her aquiline nose could sniff out a challenge a mile away. Trepidation snaked around my body as I went to greet her.

'Hold this a minute,' she said, ignoring my greeting and thrusting a tapestry-decorated portmanteau into my hands. She pursed her lips as a feather from the boa swathing her neck brushed against her mouth. The beads on the scarlet scarf wound around her head rattled as she turned away from me, saying, 'I'll just get the rest of my stuff from the taxi.'

The rest of her stuff? How long is she staying?

My feet had felt the weight of my heart a few days ago when she rang to invite herself to stay while her house was being 'refurbished', as she grandly put it. 'Can't stand the smell of paint,' she had declared. 'It'll only be for a couple of days.' As with Bonaparte it was difficult to argue with Lil.

She strode towards a car parked a little way down the street, her ankle-length skirt flapping and lifting as she walked to reveal a pair of Doc Martens. The taxi driver, whose puzzled expression no doubt mirrored my own, attempted to help Lil unload her belongings but she pushed him away. 'I can manage,' she said, piling boxes, baskets and bottles on to the pavement. I watched in mounting horror as she extricated a wire structure which was wedged in the back. She hooked her fingers into the loop at the top and marched back to my doorstep with her bounty. I peered into the birdcage and a beady eye peered back. Lil's avian clone and I regarded each other with equal suspicion. Not only were we expected to put up with Lil but Henry, her African grey parrot and companion, was to be our unwelcome house guest too.

Lil placed the bird cage on the doorstep and went back to the taxi for the rest of her belongings.

'How long's she here for?' Joe's rasping stage whisper revealed his stifled panic. 'I thought you said it was only a couple of days.'

'I don't know,' I replied as I pushed past him, carrying the cage into the house. 'Not long, I hope.'

'Me too,' he said. 'She's seen off four husbands already – I don't want to be the fifth.' He shot me a warning look. My usually calm and collected husband morphed into a threatened species whenever Lil was near.

'They were *her* husbands,' I started to explain, 'not other people's,' but I was talking to myself. Joe had taken flight.

'Daylight robbery what those taxis charge these days,' said Lil, scattering boxes and baskets around her. 'And he wanted to charge extra for Henry. Not paying that, I told him. Fancy charging for a bird. I sent him off with a flea in his ear.'

Probably got that from Henry. I picked up some of Lil's belongings and followed her into the house.

'So this is the new abode then?' she asked, swivelling her head from side to side to take in our new dwelling.

She surveyed the hallway and peered into the kitchen, then walked into the sitting room, sizing up the house like a prospective buyer. She stopped and lifted her head as if sniffing the air.

'A ghost,' she pronounced. 'You've got a ghost.'

'Oh Lil, give it a rest,' I pleaded. 'Every place I've lived in you've told me there was a ghost.'

'Well, there certainly is in this one,' Lil replied. 'A woman, and not a good one either. I can sense her.' Lil gave a shiver, setting beads and feathers bouncing.

Anxious to change the subject I picked up the bird cage. 'Let me show you your room,' I said in a voice intended to sound welcoming. My ears disagreed. I led Lil and Henry to the 'guest room', a tiny room at the back of the house just big enough for a bed – and a bird cage. 'I'll let you sort yourself out,' I said, ushering them in and closing the door.

'Cup of tea please!' Lil's shout was echoed by Henry. 'Cup of tea, cup of tea.' I groaned inwardly. It had started already. One of Lil's many quirks was her need to be in reach of the teapot at all times. And she never made tea for herself either. 'My dear,' she once said in a voice pitched to affect wisdom, 'a kitchen can only ever be one woman's domain.' So, I was to be tea-girl on constant duty, and not teabags in mugs either. Oh no, only the best leaves from China would do for Lil, preferably brewed and served in bone china.

Still no sign of Joe.

I made the tea, carefully placing fragile teacups and a teapot on my one and only tray. I hoped Lil would think they were family heirlooms and not guess I had purchased them the day before from the local charity shop. Why I felt the need to impress Lil I do not know but her invisible cloak of authority was impossible to disobey.

It was a chilly day and I was glad of the warmth of the fire when I took the tray into the sitting room. As I closed the curtains I noticed dark clouds gathering in the sky.

'The tea's ready,' I called to Lil.

A waft of cedar and cinnamon with a hint of cheroot filled the air as Lil made a grand entrance, Henry clinging to her forearm like a bemused escort. I blinked. The skirt had been exchanged for a dragon-infested kimono and the Doc Martens for slippers which would have brought joy to Aladdin's heart. Lil's feet were adorned with mules whose sharply curved points were aimed at her ankles. Mythical monsters exhaling silky flames draped themselves around her body and on her head a bright green turban was not quite tight enough to stop wispy, wiry curls escaping to form a frame around her face.

'That's better,' she said, settling herself on to the sofa. She took the teacup from me and delicately placed it on her lap. 'I feel more myself now. And how are you settling in darling?'

I was about to thank her for asking when I realised the question was not aimed at my well-being. Henry, perched on the edge of my new sofa, let out a little squawk as his claws embedded patterns in the fabric. He closed his eyes as Lil gently massaged his head. Massaging was not what I would have liked to do to his head.

Lil loved to talk and soon she was regaling me with aspects of her life involving husbands past. My mother's brother had been number two or three, I'm not sure which. Between sips of tea I was treated to 'life according to Lil'. It was certainly colourful and she approached challenges with her own unique flair and originality. From what I could untangle she always emerged the victor where marital disagreements were involved.

'Did I tell you about the horseradish?' she asked, not waiting for my answer. 'I think it was Jack, or it might have been Claude, I can't remember now, but anyway I'd cooked a lovely dinner for him – roast beef, yorkies, roast potatoes, gravy, you know, the lot – and when he went to eat it he didn't say anything about how tasty it was, or thank me for going to all this trouble. Oh no, all he said was "Where's the horseradish?" Horseradish! Jolly lucky he's being fed at all, I thought. Anyway the next time I went shopping I bought horseradish. Dear Lord did I buy horseradish. That night when Jack – Claude whichever – got home and went to put on his slippers, there was a jar of horseradish in them. He opened the cupboard to get out a beer and there was a jar of horseradish. Went to bed that night and there was a jar of horseradish under the pillow.' Lil's cup rattled and the tea slopped dangerously as she laughed at the memory. 'But that wasn't the best part.' She put down the cup, wiping a tear from her face. 'When he went to clean his teeth that night, there was horseradish. Who says you can't put toothpaste back in the tube! Oh I did laugh!' Tears of merriment oozed from her small eyes. 'I think he was the one who took to the drink . . . or was that Harry?'

Still smiling she picked up the cup and finished her tea. Suddenly the expression on her face changed from glee to gloom. 'There's trouble ahead,' she announced, swirling the cup and peering at the leaves in the bottom. 'A storm.'

'You're right,' I said. 'It's pouring out there.'

'I didn't mean the weather.' She pushed her teacup towards me. 'Is there more tea?'

'I'll make a fresh pot,' I said, picking up the teapot and taking it to the kitchen.

I was waiting for the kettle to boil when I heard the doorbell. 'Someone at the door,' called out Lil, unnecessarily.

I opened the door to see a bedraggled figure standing on the porch. Drops of water fell from her soaked hair on to her saturated blouse and her thin skirt clung to her legs. Mascara streaked down her face, forming black tracks from her eyes to her mouth.

'Alison! Come inside, quickly,' I urged, pulling her in to the hallway. 'You're absolutely drenched. Why on earth are you out in this weather – and dressed like that?'

She lifted her head and looked at me. It wasn't only the rain drawing patterns on her face; her eyes and cheeks were full of tears.

'Whatever is the matter?' I asked.

'It's Toby,' she cried, putting her wet head on my shoulder. She seemed unaware of her saturated state. 'He's left me. He just walked out and left . . . He's moved in with Karen.' She leaned against me, loud sobs muffled against my neck, the dampness from her clothes seeping into mine.

'How did you get here?' I asked, looking along the street for her car.

'I walked,' she snuffled.

No wonder she was so wet, it was nearly two miles from her flat to Shakespeare Street. 'Come on, Alison,' I said. 'Let's get you dry.'

I led the wet figure to the sitting room. 'This is Alison,' I said to Lil. 'She was my neighbour at our last place, before we moved here. She's . . . she's having a bit of a problem.' The last word was mouthed to Lil. 'Husband, Toby, has left her,' I continued as quietly as I could.

Lil rose from the sofa, a smile of welcome on her face as if Alison had been her expected guest. Hand outstretched she glided majestically across the room. 'Lillianne du Bois. Dee-lated to meet you.' Poor sodden Alison didn't know whether to shake the hand, kiss it or curtsey, and alarm spread across her tear-streaked face.

'Come and sit by the fire, Alison,' I said, rescuing her from Lil's attempts at grandeur. *Lillianne du Bois, what was that all about? She was Lil Woods as far as I knew.*

'This is my Auntie Lil,' I explained 'She's staying with me for a couple of days. Take off those wet shoes. I'll get you a towel and some tea.'

I went to the kitchen, my thoughts tumbling around Alison's situation. There had been clues that she and Toby were having problems, like his hints that twenty years of marriage was long enough and it was time to explore pastures new. To Alison's sorrow, this exploration had involved the assistance of Karen, a young work colleague. But Alison had hoped it would all blow over.

I never understood what Alison had seen in Toby, or what any woman could really. Joe and I had been on pleasant enough terms in a neighbourly way but I can't say Alison and Toby were friends of choice. Joe made a point of getting along with them as Toby would occasionally send work Joe's way. Often they'd meet at the local pub, or discuss business at Toby's office.

Alison always seemed a bit pathetic to me, needy and eager to please. She'd latched on to me as soon as we met, as if I was the sister she never had. She wanted to go shopping together, or to the cinema, all the while entrusting me with her woes and insecurities. And as for Toby – well, to be truthful, he was a bore whose only topics of conversation were his stamp collection and his badminton prowess. Shelves piled with dusty stamp albums and displays of badminton trophies lined the walls of their flat. Toby's boasts of his ownership of rare stamps impressed me not one bit but Joe told me that some of the stamps were in pristine condition. Being unused and unmarked apparently made the stamps extremely valuable. 'He looks on them as an investment,' explained Joe. 'He wants to sell them one day to keep himself in luxury in his old age.' Still bored me to tears, though.

Alison kept in touch after Joe and I had moved to Shakespeare Street but only because she wanted to carry on pouring her troubles into my sympathetic ear. She would phone at inconvenient times and regale me with the latest marital problem, long tearful calls about how much she hated Toby, how much she hated Karen, how much she hated life in general.

I commiserated as best I could and took time to listen to her woes. After a while I ran out of the words she wanted to hear. I longed to shake her and say 'Listen to yourself – just get a grip.' It wouldn't have made any difference. I suspect she enjoyed playing the wronged wife.

Now Toby had walked out and here she was in my house. What on earth was I going to do?

* * *

I took the freshly brewed tea to the sitting room and found Alison warming her bare feet next to the fire, pouring out her woes to Lil. So pathetic was her sob story that even Henry looked mournful.

Lil listened to Alison with the utmost sympathy and patience. She and Henry played the perfect confidantes; heads on one side, precise eye contact, tut-tut murmurs in tune with the tinkling of tea cups. Alison was relishing it. I'd had enough of this, having heard it all before. We hadn't long moved into Shakespeare Street and I had plenty of chores to do. I decided to leave them to it and went to get on with some unpacking.

Big mistake! I should have known better.

It was with a degree of apprehension that I went back to the sitting room an hour or so later. Cautiously opening the door I expected to find the room strewn with tissues, tea leaves and tears and I was completely taken aback by the scene which greeted me. Lil and Alison were sitting side-by-side on the sofa, teacups had been exchanged for wine glasses and Henry was inspecting the dregs at the bottom of a bottle of Chenin Blanc. Pink-cheeked Alison, no longer drenched, was laughing. Instead of the expected sobs and sympathy, the room glowed with warmth and cheeriness. Alison, Lil and Henry had become the greatest of spirited chums, it seemed.

'Why haven't I met your Auntie before?' Alison asked me as I entered the room. Her whole face had come alive. 'She's just wonderful.' Lil and Henry nodded in agreement.

'Gosh, have I been here *that* long?' said Alison, checking her watch. 'I really ought to be going now.' She enveloped Lil in a warm hug. 'It's been so great talking to you.' Releasing Lil she screwed up one side of her face, now clear of mascara streaks, and gave her a sort of wink. 'I've got a lot of tidying up to do,' she said with a chuckle.

Auntie Lil waved her wineglass at Alison with a chummy toast-like gesture. I regarded Lil with newfound admiration. In one hour she had succeeded in cheering up Alison. I hadn't been able to do that in months.

'How are you going to get home?' I asked. 'It's getting dark.'

'Don't worry. I'll get a taxi.' She gave me a brief hug. 'Thank you so much. So loved meeting your Auntie,' she said, still with a big smile on her face.

Such a different person to the one I had opened the door to. I watched her go, no longer a forlorn female but a purposeful woman, striding down the road with her head held high. What had happened to the Alison who wavered through life without any direction? Now she walked like a woman with a mission. And what was that she was doing? Was she skipping?

* * *

Lil and Henry graced us with their presence for a week. I say 'graced' but Joe would probably have described it as 'disgraced'.

He was barely around during that week and used every possible excuse to be away from the house, especially after he witnessed Lil attempting to exorcise the 'ghost'. 'I walked into the room and there she was, swaying this incense-burner type thing, muttering to herself and dancing around. The smell was awful.' A flicker of panic spread across Joe's face as he recalled the incident. 'Couldn't get out of there fast enough.'

'I'll have a word,' I promised.

'Please do,' he said, 'or the ghost won't be the only thing to be exorcised.'

I tackled her later that evening. 'Lil . . . You don't honestly think there's a ghost here, do you? I mean, really, in this day and age, a ghost . . . You've got to be kidding.'

Lil looked at me as if I was the batty one. 'Of course there's a ghost,' she said. 'A miserable, meddlesome hag. And do you know,' she leaned towards me, her voice lowered to a conspiratorial whisper, 'she makes people do things they wouldn't normally do.' She sat back, her mouth a tight line, her eyes wide open.

'Oh really,' I said, exasperated.

'You need to get rid of her,' said Lil. 'I've been trying – '

'Yes, I know you have,' I said. 'That's what I want to talk to you about.'

'– I've been trying all sorts of things.' She ignored my interruption. 'I've tried the salt and rice method – that didn't work. I've tried dousing the room with garlic and cabbage water . . . '

That accounts for the smell.

'I think stronger methods may be necessary,' she sighed. 'I'll have a word with Henry.'

She's really lost it now, I thought. *I do hope she goes home soon.*

My wish was granted two days later when she announced that she knew I'd be upset but it was time to move back into her house. I assured her I'd get over it and helped to gather up her belongings. Joe had reappeared and wasted no time in calling a taxi. Henry was perched impatiently in his cage, muttering to himself about cups of tea. He had started to moult and feathers lined the bottom of the cage.

'I've been thinking about it. Your ghost, I mean,' Lil said as I peered out of the window hoping to see the taxi arrive. 'I don't like to leave you here with her still going strong. I'm afraid she'll meddle in your marriage. Let me try one more thing.'

'Oh don't worry Lil,' I said, but Lil was not to be discouraged. She opened Henry's cage and picked up a large feather. Henry looked intrigued. Joe looked worried.

Closing her eyes and lowering her head, she breathed in and out deeply. Her arms were limp by her side, the feather loosely held in her hand. She stood like that for a few seconds, her chest rising and falling, before she slowly raised her head and arms.

'Be gone,' she intoned. 'Be gone from this house. Seek forgiveness elsewhere.'

Is that it? I thought. Has she finished? But no, there was more to come. Joe looked on in horror.

'I give you this quill. Use it to expunge your guilt.' She waved the feather in the air. 'Examine your woes and repent. Do this so you may journey to the next level.'

Lil opened her eyes and blinked, looking around her as if she had just awoken from a deep sleep. She sniffed the air.

'She's gone now,' she said. Joe's relief was palpable as a hoot announced the taxi's arrival . . . and Lil's departure.

* * *

It took a while for things to get back to normal but eventually the house became more settled, as if it too had been unnerved by Lil and Henry. I didn't hear anything more about Alison's situation until one evening, some weeks later, after Joe came home from work. I knew by the way the door banged behind him that things were not right.

'You OK?' I asked as I watched his briefcase bounce on the floor and his discarded jacket slide to join it.

'No. No, I'm not. I'm definitely not OK. In fact I'm furious. What's for dinner?' Whatever was bothering Joe certainly hadn't affected his appetite.

'Roast chicken,' I replied 'It's just about ready to carve.'

'Good,' he said. 'I'm starving.'

He marched into the kitchen, selected a knife and a sharpener from the drawer and surveyed the cooked chicken.

'I bumped into Toby in the pub today,' he said. 'I almost didn't recognise him.'

'Really? How's he getting on?' I asked. 'Is he still with the girlfriend?'

'No, not any more.' Joe pulled the knife back and forth against the sharpener with more force than was required.

'Back with Alison, then?' I asked.

'There's no chance of him getting back with Alison – not after what that bitch did.'

Bitch? Did he really say that? Gentle Joe who never swore?

'Why, what did she do?' I'd heard of unease creeping up on people; it was galloping over me.

'What didn't she do, more likely,' Joe said. 'Toby's a ruined man

– a shadow of his former self. I've never felt so sorry for anyone. He was distraught.'

'What happened? What do you mean?' A voice which didn't sound like mine came out of my mouth. It was stilted, as if I was reading a script.

Joe looked at me oddly, then explained. Toby had been surprised when, having taken his leaving so badly, Alison appeared to have a sudden change of heart. She had been refusing all contact with Toby so he was amazed when she phoned out of the blue and offered to send his belongings over. Apparently she was very courteous and even managed a little joke about how awful she must have been to him. Toby told Joe he'd felt a bit stunned after all that had happened but was pleased Alison had come to her senses. She appeared civil and understanding about the situation so he gave her Karen's address.

Parcels soon started to arrive at the flat, all carefully wrapped in brown paper and addressed to Karen. A couple of parcels came on the first day and, being unaware of the sender, Karen ripped off the paper only to find an assortment of humdrum items including pens, rubber bands and shuttlecocks. As promised, Alison was sending all of Toby's belongings. Every single thing. Taking the torn and crumpled packaging to the recycling bin, Karen reflected on how petty Toby's wife was being. And each day after that, more parcels arrived. Even the paperclips Toby had kept on his desk and the contents of his waste paper basket had been packed, sealed and carefully despatched. To begin with the postman found it amusing but, after delivering dozens of parcels in a few days, he became quite irate. Eventually the flow of parcels slowed down until one day the relieved postman delivered just one bulky package, this time addressed to Toby.

'Not more rubbish, please,' Karen beseeched.

'No this is different,' Toby had replied. 'These are my stamp albums.'

The joy he felt at the prospect of being reunited with his precious collection soon turned to anguish. The pages of the albums were bare, blank, empty, leaving only hinge marks to show where once his treasured stamps had been fastidiously displayed.

With trembling hands Toby gathered up the creased brown paper in which the albums had been wrapped. Despite his tormented state the philatelist in him couldn't help noticing that an unusual number of stamps had been used. He took a closer look at the profusion of low-denomination stamps and saw that the middle rows were slightly raised. The Queen's profile curled up in a sneer as Toby carefully prised the stamps away from the paper. He told Joe he felt sick as he peeled off the stamps to reveal his rare treasures underneath, marred and mutilated. He thought of all the previous parcels. 'When was the paper recycling collected?' he asked Karen, his voice choked with apprehension.

'Yesterday,' she replied.

* * *

'So that's what happened to poor old Toby,' said Joe. 'I've never seen anyone in such a state. His wife's a cunning hag, his girlfriend's turned him out and his life savings are ruined. Apparently he's become so depressed that he's on the verge of losing his job.' He thrust the knife into the chicken as if the poor bird had been an accomplice to Toby's demise. 'I know you could say a lot of it was his own fault, but really, give a guy a chance. It makes my blood boil how this woman has walked all over him.'

My heart felt as if it was taking a trip on a treadmill.

'You alright?' He peered at me. 'Why have you gone so pale?'

'I'm thinking about Toby,' I lied, watching as the carcass became more and more mangled. The usual surgeon-like precision Joe took with carving was replaced by manic butchery. I passed him a serving plate. 'He was never really my favourite person but no-one deserves that.'

'Well I would never have believed it of Alison,' Joe went on. 'Didn't know she had it in her to be so vindictive.'

He placed jagged portions of poultry on the serving plate, hacked-about pieces of innocent bird which looked pathetic and unappetising.

'Couldn't have been her idea, about the stamps I mean,' he said. He stopped hacking at the chicken and ran his finger along the knife, testing the sharpness of the blade. 'I'd like to get my hands on whoever put her up to it.'

I surveyed the sorry sight of the remains of the mutilated bird and the revengeful look in my husband's eyes – and prayed he would never find out.

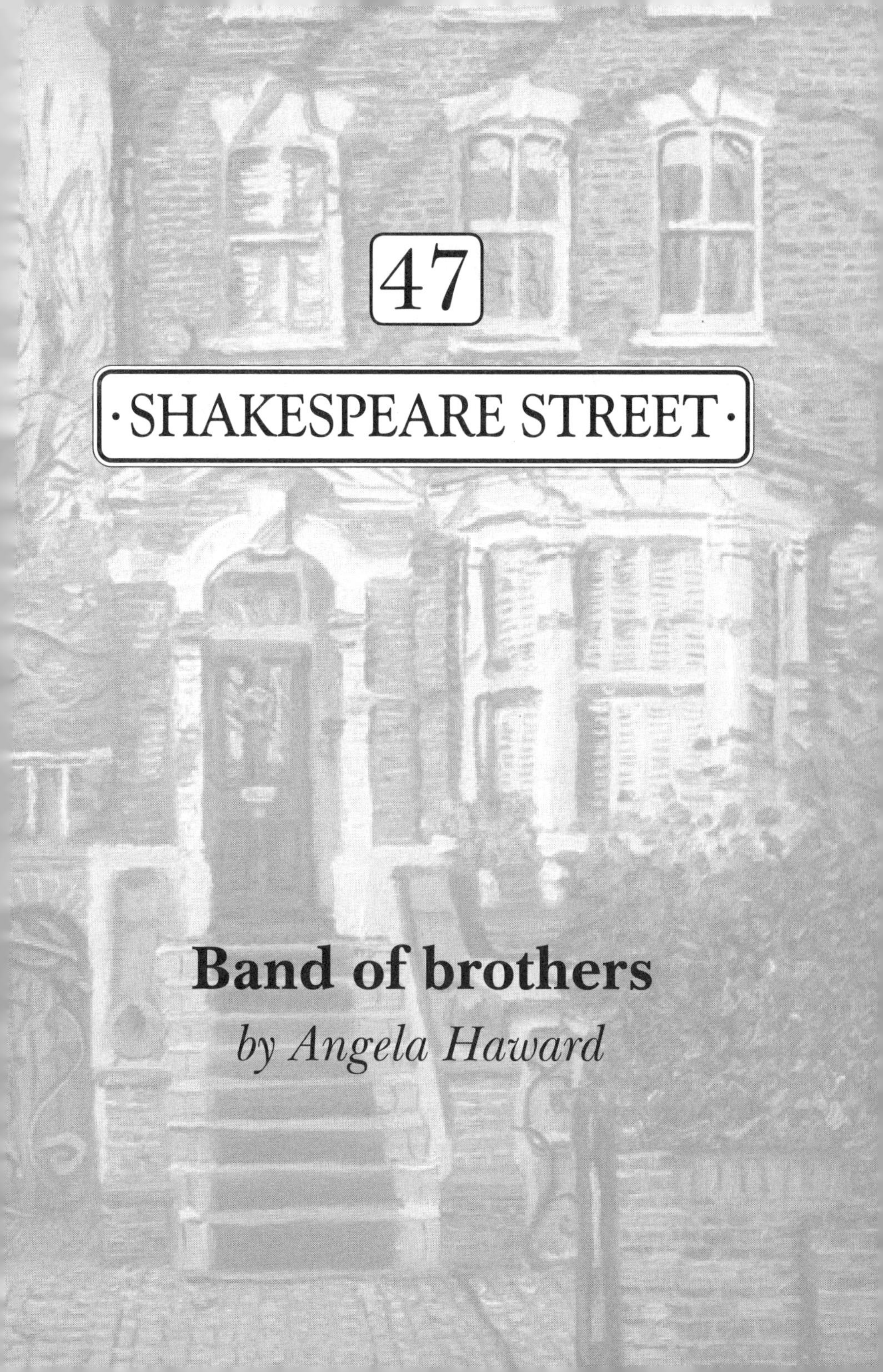

47 · SHAKESPEARE STREET ·

Band of brothers

by Angela Haward

We few, we happy few, we band of brothers, For he today that sheds his blood with me Shall be my brother

Henry V Act 4 Scene 3

The hallway hadn't changed in six years. Red quarry tiles led straight to the kitchen, clashing with the dingy brown of the walls and dado rail. The stair carpet was still the trip hazard which had catapulted Mrs Morris down five steps on to her face in 1913. The lingering odour of boiled cabbage seemed to have impregnated the very bricks and mortar of the place.

'Well, I suppose you'd better come in then, Mr Forrester. I don't want to let the heat out.'

'Thanks.' Henry Forrester wondered where this heat was supposed to be. The draught from the back of the house all but whistled along in its eagerness to escape through the front.

'You'll know the way. Your old room's taken, so it'll be the box room on the second floor.' Henry had hoped for a warmer welcome – goodness knows why. Mrs Morris's pragmatic approach to room rental wasn't going to change just because he was back from the war. 'You did your duty, Mr Forrester. Life goes on. Rent's three and six a week, payable on Sunday night. Same rules – no women in the room, no pets, no singing.'

Henry had always wondered about the ban on singing. The night after a trip to see Florrie Ford at an Islington music hall, he'd been humming *The Old Bull and Bush* as he waited for his dinner, and the force with which she'd slammed the plate in front of him had sent the gravy all down his shirt front.

He started to drag his kit bag up the stairs, treading carefully because of the carpet and missing stair rods. 'What happened to the others, then?'

Henry paused and looked down on her as she stood in the hall, arms akimbo. He opened his mouth to reply but nothing came out, so he turned away, making his way up to the tiny room which looked out on to Shakespeare Street. He stood at the window, staring unseeing at a woman who was braving the elements to collect steaming horse manure dropped by the rag-and-bone man's old nag. The motor car hadn't penetrated this part of London in any great numbers yet, though Henry had seen plenty of them milling around the city streets near Charing Cross. Mrs Morris's question still echoed up the stairwell behind him. What happened to the others? He couldn't even begin to tell her.

He had to watch his head because of the eaves, especially as he sat on the bed. The springs groaned beneath the worn flock of the mattress, and he determined to spend his first earnings on a new one. The only other furniture in the room was a mahogany tallboy whose mid-Victorian solidity made a mockery of the broken oak wardrobe on the other wall. This had been Reggie's room.

So, Henry was back. Would he ever be able to pick up the stitches of his life again? Kitchener had snatched him and his fellow tenants from a threadbare normality and flung them, mind, body and spirit, into the bottom chamber of hell. As he sat on the bed he remembered the last time he had been in that room. The war was still in its early months and young men were champing at the bit to answer Kitchener's summons. Reggie had been standing in the window. It was the only part of the room where he could fully extend to his six foot two inches.

'There are fellows up north joining Pals battalions, you know.'

'You think we should do that, then?'

'Course we should. The four of us, we're gonna wipe that smirk off Kaiser Bill's face, arrogant bastard.'

The tableau was shattered as Mrs Morris's strident voice cut through the twilight.

'Mr Forrester – have you gone deaf? Your dinner's ready in the kitchen.'

Henry pushed away the shadows and descended to the ground floor, following the smell of overcooked liver and bacon. His fellow lodgers were already seated and he gave them a perfunctory nod before taking the fourth chair. Mrs Morris slapped slices of rubbery offal on each plate, followed, with equal aggression, by soggy cabbage and a couple of boiled potatoes before covering the meal with the brown water which passed for gravy. Henry's eyes flicked round the table but, instead of the faces of three strangers, he saw only Reggie, Jack and Arthur, all arguing with him about the benefits of enlisting together. They had been just four mates together, different backgrounds, different personalities, same outlook on life and the same aspirations for the future.

Arthur's widowed mother had wept as he set off for London like Dick Whittington seeking his fortune. He hadn't made one, but he was beginning to make ends meet as an apprentice at the new telephone exchange. Reggie's father was a diplomat and life abroad was something with which Reggie was very familiar. He was starting at the bottom as a clerk in the Foreign Office, but he had aspirations. His gung-ho approach to life made every discussion that little bit brighter, funnier, and more controversial. Jack hailed from a long line of lawyers and was articled to a solicitor's office in Islington, an appointment in which Papa had had more than a little influence. Although he didn't really enjoy the menial nature of the work, Jack was mature enough to know that the only way was up. And Henry? Well, Henry had come to London when his mother died. With his only remaining parent gone, and with no-one left to advise him otherwise, he got a clerical job in a shipping office and concentrated on replacing family with friends.

So, of course, when all three of his best mates urged him to take the King's shilling, he had caved in, as always, and Queen Victoria's Rifles were four recruits better off.

'Johnson, put your effing foot on that ladder. It's an order, soldier.'

Arthur didn't move. Henry and Jack were right behind him. True to form, Reggie had already disappeared over the top. Their feet sank into the quagmire of the trench floor after the late June rain and their senses were assaulted by the smells, sounds and sights of the inferno above them.

'Get up that ladder, Johnson, or you're a dead man.' Henry heard the underlying terror in the junior officer's command and knew this was no empty threat. His own body shook so violently he could barely hold the rifle – but it was certain death for Arthur or a chance of survival up there. He glanced back at Jack and they took an arm each, forcing Arthur up the ladder ahead of them.

'Mr Forrester, I don't spend the afternoon getting your dinner for you to just push it round in circles, you know.'

Henry jumped. The other three diners were looking at him over their empty plates, eyes variously exhibiting curiosity, irritation and pity.

'Sorry, Mrs Morris – I . . . It's been a long day. I'll do better tomorrow.'

'Yes, well make sure you do.'

Mrs Morris swept his plate away and turned her back, her stance oozing offended dignity as Henry excused himeself and retreated to the stairs, assaulted by memories. Maybe he shouldn't have come back here.

In the attic bedroom once more he tried to move back into the present, unpacking the kitbag and stowing his few possessions, concentrating on the prosaic. Top drawer, socks and underwear; second drawer, shirts and ties; third drawer . . . the lining paper was ripped. Henry dragged it out, determined to replace it the next day – and as he did so, his eye was caught by writing on the underside of the ripped sheet. Taking it to the window, Henry looked more closely but it was difficult to read in the fading light and had obviously been written in haste. The hand was familiar though – he'd seen it often enough before the war – it was Reggie's distinctive spidery scrawl.

'Where the bloody hell's Reggie?' Henry had to shout across Arthur's bent head to make his voice heard above the cacophony around them. They were walking forward as best they could, their heads down, their movements hampered by Arthur. He was still hanging between them, his feet moving like a puppet. Jack didn't reply and his eyes glazed over, staring at the barely visible enemy wire 300 yards away, strung as it was with the remains of soldiers who had reached but not taken their objective. Gommecourt might as well be in another continent as half a mile away.

Reggie. They never found him. He didn't make it back to the trench. And nor did Arthur. The gamble didn't pay off. Strung between them, the little clerk took a direct hit in the head. Devastated, suffused with guilt and with the officers urging them forwards they had to leave him there, in no man's land, lying face down in the mud and ordure. Just another casualty of that most inglorious day.

The bombardment was ceaseless. All rest days were cancelled until the men were on their knees. After two weeks Henry took a bullet in the shoulder. His clavicle was shattered, but penetrating the searing pain was relief that he would be sent behind the line. The wound dressed, he went round all the huts in the field hospital searching ruined faces for some semblance of Reggie. He even visited the morgue. Eventually, Reggie's name appeared on the list of missing, presumed dead, and that's what his parents were told.

There was no time to brood. The battle had just begun. Henry returned to the front to sit in a dugout and was ordered to ghost-write letters of condolence from the Captain to the wives and mothers of the fallen, men at whose sides he had eaten and slept for months, men with whom he had laughed and cried, but who had died without him. It was worse than going over the top. Fear had become a familiar foe. Emotional torment on behalf of people he had never met was unsolvable and unbearable. Then, finally, after six weeks, he could handle a rifle and mount a bayonet – and he was back up there.

The light was fading. Henry knew the rule that forbade lighting the gas lamp until it was completely dark, but the note had been scrawled using a blunt pencil and he couldn't quite make out what it said. It was probably just a bit of scribble, a reminder that he had been there. But Henry had to make sure. He stood at the window, watching as the sun disappeared behind the houses opposite and their Georgian façades merged into the gloom. The lamplighters never got to Shakespeare Street until after eight o'clock at this time of year. A child was kicking a pig's bladder stuffed with newspaper down the middle of the road, heading for home. Two women walked past the house and crossed over to go into number 44. Henry recognised one of them as young Phoebe Prior from number 37. She'd been a schoolgirl when they left for the front. Now she was quite the young lady. Henry continued to watch them as the other woman glanced up at number 47, but she wouldn't have seen him standing there in the dark. The murmur of their voices made the road seem like an unbridgeable canyon between him and normality.

When you're busy with your life, night can pounce like a black jaguar, but when you're waiting, it arrives with the timidity of a field mouse. Henry stilled his mind, as he had when listening for the next order to charge. The street was silent for a while, waiting with him, until a lone man approached the house. A pronounced limp hindered his progress and he had a walking stick in his right hand. He was enveloped in a greatcoat with a trilby hat pulled well down against the wind. From inside his own quietness, Henry watched him without thought or feeling. The man was peering at the house numbers as he made his painful way along the street. Henry could almost hear him muttering '53, 51, 49, 47' – and then he stopped.

1917 The Huns were skulking behind the Hindenburg Line. The Allies threw every resource into driving them out and the QVRs were battling to their last breath. Henry often wished his last breath would come, dust-free and pure. It didn't. Instead, he and Jack fought on, loading, reloading, taking breaks behind the lines, sleeping with any willing French woman, or girl, begging fags off their mates or stealing them from the dead. They didn't talk about Arthur or Reggie, as if the names alone were the key which would unlock their own darkest fears. Day after endless day they endured the onslaught, until Jack clambered out of a trench one evening, when the guns were silent – except for one. The explosion all but blew his leg off and Jack screamed for the stretcher bearers to finish the job then and there as they carried him away. For a second time, Henry tried to find out what had happened to his friend, but, once again, no one seemed to know. One thing was certain, even if he survived, his war was over. Henry felt a certain perverse envy as he struggled on, fighting for yards of land which were promptly wrenched back. Would it never end?

The man in the street appeared to rake his eyes over the front of the house, his hand resting briefly on the gate. Another demobbed soldier looking for a room. Another traumatised beggar failing to rebuild a shattered life. Then he stumbled on down the street, meeting the lamplighters as they came the other way.

Henry lit the gas lamp in his room. It was fixed to the wall, so he tried not to stand in his own shadow as he peered at the scratched note which appeared to be a series of numbers followed by a few words.

6 4 1 9 5 1 5 0 7 9 0 1 2 7 4 for I love you sweetheart only so remember when you're lonely when the fields are white with daisies I'll return

The note had clearly scribbled in great haste. He must have written this before he left to enlist. Hell's bells, Reggie! Why be so tricky? What's with those numbers? The words were familiar, but Henry's head was thumping. Maybe he should turn in and try again tomorrow – after he had pounded the pavements in search of paid work.

Later, lying awkwardly on the apology for a mattress, his mind began to drift. He was standing in a field of daisies, waiting for something and he didn't know what it was. In the corner of his eye, he saw a figure approaching, scarring the purity of the white field as he limped towards Henry, his right arm outstretched in supplication – or accusation. He woke sweating with a pounding heart. Sleep taunted him for the rest of the night.

* * *

'Five bob a week, clock in at eight sharp, half an hour for lunch, day ends at six. No overtime. At least you're not one of them cripples that came back from the war. I need someone in one piece to do this job. I'd have sent you on your way sharpish if you'd had bits missing.'

Henry was floored by the antipathy in the supervisor's tone as he talked of the wounded veterans. He couldn't afford to say no, though. It was good money and clerking was what he knew. He'd just keep his head down and get on with it. 'Thank you, Sir. Should I start tomorrow?'

'Always good to start at the beginning of the week – helps with the wages. Monday next, then. Don't forget, eight o'clock sharp.' The man turned away from the desk to speak to a colleague. The interview was obviously over.

Henry was stunned. It hadn't been as difficult as he'd expected.

At least he'd be able to pay Mrs Morris the rent. Might even manage to put a bit by. He went into the small café up the road from the import company which had taken him on. Having ordered tea and a Bath bun, he pulled out the scrap of paper from his pocket and looked again at the string of numbers and the verse. This time, he recognised the song immediately because it was an old Florrie Ford number. He'd heard her sing it several times in person. Reggie had been a fan too and they'd often gone to hear her together. Henry sipped his tea and tried to climb inside Reggie's mind. You might write down lyrics that meant something to you, or because you liked the tune. Maybe the verse reminded him of someone special, or a significant moment in his life. But with any of these, why write them underneath the lining paper? It was like some sort of secret game, something he used to play with his brother when they were nippers. Who did Reggie think would see it? Or was it a note to himself, a reminder? Too many imponderables here.

'May I join you?'

Henry hadn't heard the door open, hadn't seen the young lady come in, hesitate and then walk towards him. He glanced around at the other tables and saw that there were at least two spare. This young lady clearly wanted to sit with him. As he thrust the paper back into his pocket, he looked at her more closely. She seemed familiar.

'Yes, of course.' Then chivalry kicked in. 'Can I order you a tea?'

'Oh – well, that's very kind of you. I wouldn't want to impose.' The girl had an accent he recognised. It took him right back to those sordid, smoky nights behind the lines where any willing French woman was better than none when it might be a final opportunity to find such comfort.

'It's no trouble, really.' Henry wasn't used to being singled out by women. When he was out with the lads before the war, it had been Reggie, with his height and easy smile, or Jack with his intense dark eyes and promise of hidden depths, who drew the female eye first.

There was an intensity in the young woman's face which was faintly disturbing. Henry realised where he had seen her before. She was the girl from the street last night, the one who had looked up at the house while Phoebe Prior chatted on. He ordered the tea and waited, smiling encouragingly in an attempt to allay her obvious anxiety.

She leaned forward across the table, her shoulders hunched and a heavy fringe of hair threatening to hide her deep brown eyes. 'I am looking for Reggie.'

Henry was speechless for a second. Then, 'Reggie? I'm sorry – I have no idea where he is. We fought together until the Somme – then he disappeared. He was listed as missing, presumed dead.'

'He's not dead.'

Henry's face registered confusion rapidly followed by disbelief. 'He's not? Have you seen him, then?'

'Not since before the Armistice. But I met him in Holland and I got to know him – quite well.' She glanced away, a slight blush rising from her neck. 'I have to meet him here, in London. We have a sort of pact. And I really need you to help me.'

'Me?' Henry remained incredulous. 'But I have no idea at all who you are, and I've heard nothing from Reggie since 1916. If he's alive, why wouldn't he get in touch with you?'

The girl's blush deepened and her fists clenched. 'I will try and explain. My name is Martine Lamont – from Ypres. And you? You are Henry?'

Henry nodded.

'You look as Reggie described. He said you had wise eyes, and you have. He told me that if I came to London in the spring I would find you. He thought, if you had survived the war, you would come back to Shakespeare Street. I believe your parents are dead so you wouldn't have anywhere else to go? And he said he had left me a message there. It is hidden in his room, in a drawer. He didn't think he could come back to the street himself as he would be watched.'

Henry was still suspicious of the girl. 'Why would he leave you a hidden message? If he told you where to find it, why didn't he just tell you what it said?'

'I can't tell you here. There are too many people who might be listening.' Martine's voice dropped to a whisper and her eyes flicked towards the other customers.

Henry pushed his half-full cup to one side and scraped his chair back, overcome by a sudden desire to get out of the café. What the hell was Reggie involved in? Why would he be watched? And why did he want to involve Henry? He had to think. Leaving sixpence on the table, he looked down at Martine.

'Come with me,' he said, brusquely. 'We'll take a walk somewhere quieter. I have a lot of questions and I need some answers before I decide if I should help you.'

Reggie lay in a shell hole trying to gauge the extent of his injuries. Mrs Morris's sharp voice seemed to emerge like a phantasm from the gunsmoke. 'Hot-headed, Mr Robinson, that's what you are. Rushing in and out without thinking – no good'll come of it, I'm telling you.' That was the day he'd run out of the door, late as ever, and left it wide open all day when Mrs Morris was visiting her sister. His present predicament was of a somewhat greater magnitude. He should have waited for the others, not flung himself willy-nilly into the fray with no-one to cover his back.

It was nightfall before the gunfire slowed and the stretcher bearers were able to reach Reggie – and it was another twenty-four hours before they finally found him a bed in the field hospital. But to save his right arm, half torn off by shrapnel, they needed to send him further into Allied territory. He lost two fingers, but he felt that was a small price to pay when he saw some of his fellow patients. His head wound took longer to heal, and by the time his faculties were restored to something approaching normal, the Battle of the Somme was all but over with only a few miles of land gained and nearly half a million soldiers dead, wounded or missing. The regiment had been re-posted further up the line and Reggie had no idea what had happened to Henry, Jack or Arthur.

When he was called in for an interview with the commanding officer, he imagined it would be to receive his order back to the front line.

'Ah, Sergeant Robinson – I have a proposition to put to you. You're something of a linguist, I believe?'

'Well . . . ' Reggie was nonplussed. 'I do speak Dutch, as a matter of fact, Sir. My mother came from Amsterdam originally and she spoke to us in Dutch when I was young. And Father was a diplomat in Germany until '06. We lived in Bonn, so I picked up German pretty well. It's been useful in the field when rounding up prisoners.'

'So you're tri-lingual?'

'I suppose so, Sir.'

'And you're familiar with Amsterdam?'

'Yes, Sir. From childhood.'

'We can use that, Robinson. And you've been noticed, you know, out there in the field.'

Reggie's six foot two inch frame stiffened to attention. What had he done now that he hadn't realised?

'How's that, Sir?'

'You're a bit hot-headed, but you've shown courage, leadership potential and a certain native cunning. We can use that too. There's a new branch of the service starting up and your skills and personality will be more useful to them than in the trenches. I'm sending you to the Netherlands.'

'Sir. And what will I be doing there, Sir?'

'You will be joining the Secret Service, Robinson. I hope that meets with your approval. You will leave for Amsterdam tomorrow morning. Go straight to Dam Square, to the Nieuwe Kerk and wait in the third pew from the front. You'll be in civvies. You'll find them on your bunk when you return to your quarters. Your contact in the Nieuwe Kerk will give you further instructions. And keep this *strictly* to yourself. Good luck, Sergeant.'

Reggie turned without hesitation and marched back to the ward, his mind in turmoil. So he was not going back to find his mates. He was no longer going to fight openly on the front line. He was going to fight in the shadows, with his brain rather than a rifle. He had lost control of his destiny.

Henry and Martine had reached the top of Shakespeare Street, but she had still not got to the point in her narrative where her path had crossed with Reggie's.

The scrap of paper with the string of numbers and the song fragment was burning a hole in Henry's pocket. It must be that note she was after, but Henry didn't feel he knew enough about her connection with his friend to share it with her.

'Look, I still don't know who you really are. We need to talk some more, but I have to get back now or I'll miss dinner and there'll be hell to pay. Mrs Morris goes to the market on Friday mornings. Why don't you watch for her to leave, then come round? The other lodgers will be at work and we'll have a good hour-and-a-half before she gets back.'

'Alright. Until tomorrow then.'

Henry watched Martine go into number 44 before unlocking

the door of his lodgings. He was immediately confronted by his formidable landlady. 'So you've met up with Madam from across the road, have you?' Henry didn't bother to reply. Mrs Morris had always been an inveterate curtain-twitcher. 'You want to watch your step with that one, you know.' Her tone was laden with melodramatic warning. 'Never did trust foreigners. They don't think the same as we do. She's knocked on the door twice, already – asking for Mr Robinson. I told her I hadn't seen him since 1915 and he was most likely dead, and sent her on her way.' And with a *harrumph,* she stomped off in the direction of the cabbage smell.

With its unseasonably low temperatures March 1919 had indeed come in like the proverbial lion and, by Friday 28th, the lion continued to rage while the longed-for lamb remained in hiding. Temperatures were more suited to January and Mrs Morris headed out suitably attired, as if in anticipation of a blizzard. Henry sat on the stairs, shivering in the draught. He had waited less than five minutes when a light knock sounded through the hall.

Henry didn't feel it would be appropriate to take Martine up to his room but the parlour was out of bounds. In the two years he had lived in the house before the war, none of the lodgers had ever seen past the closed door. He never saw Mrs Morris use it either. However, she was out and it was the only place in which to entertain a young lady. With some trepidation, Henry showed Martine into the room. It was spotless – it obviously got dusted when she was alone in the house. A motley collection of old fashioned armchairs jostled with a Victorian sideboard and table lamps which had seen better days.

Occasional tables were crowded with fading sepia photographs. With just a glance Henry could see they were all of the same young man at different stages of his development, from a toddler posing on a rocking horse to the fresh-faced soldier wearing a pith helmet as part of a tropical uniform.

Martine perched delicately on a chair to one side of the fireplace and waited in silence for Henry to initiate the conversation.

'So . . . we left Reggie in the Netherlands at the end of 1916. Do you know what happened to him after that? And where do you fit in?'

Reggie sat in a café on Spuistraat absent-mindedly stirring his coffee and waiting. He'd been doing the job for six months now, six months of sitting in back alleys and hanging around on obscure street corners. Waiting, always waiting. Eventually someone would turn up, stop for a chat and pass him a packet of cigarettes or a folded newspaper. Inside, there would be a piece of paper with details of German troop movements across the border in occupied Belgium. He would take them back to his room, encode them and tap the details into a transmitter. His predecessor had obviously been a talented carpenter and had created a barely detectable cavity hidden in the wardrobe. It wasn't hard, though it didn't do to become complacent and he was chafing at the bit for some action.

The summer of 1917 turned out to be wet and chilly, so he sat and watched yet more rain obscure the windows as his coffee cooled. Finally the door opened and a young woman walked in, spotting him instantly.

'Geodedag.' He recognised the French accent behind the word. Returning the greeting, he gestured to the seat opposite and leant across to give her the customary kisses used to greet friends. It was important they appeared to know one another. He ordered a coffee for her and they talked in English, in quiet voices. The café was empty, so the risk was low.

'You're late. Was there a problem?'

'Yes. They searched me at the border. Usually they just wave me through but the Kommandant has ordered a crackdown because they've realised there's a leak. Fortunately, as a midwife, I don't arouse too much suspicion – we're always popping back and forth across the border to deliver a child. The note's in my corset though, and I'm not sure how to get it out. Sorry.' She looked embarrassed.

'Ah . . . how about this for a plan? My room is at 43A Raadhuistraat, round the corner. You go up the stairs to the third floor and it's the room right opposite you. I'll leave in a minute and say goodbye in a big way. Give it fifteen minutes, then finish your coffee and make your way there. Make sure you're not followed and don't go in until the coast is completely clear. Do the SOS knock on the door and I'll know it's you.'

Reggie got up from the table, kissed the girl on both cheeks and left the café with a loud, 'Tot ziens.'

Henry struggled to reconcile this Reggie, full of secrets and subterfuge, with the impulsive youth of his memory. He urged Martine to go on. 'So that girl was you?' he asked.

'Of course,' she replied. 'I found the room and gave him the note. Then we sat and talked for hours, even though my orders were to return to the border after dark. We just . . . got on.' Her gaze slipped, momentarily, from Henry's face to the floor before she continued. 'After that, I volunteered for as many deliveries as possible just to see him again. Then, towards Christmas, I turned up at the meeting place, as arranged, and he wasn't there. I waited for two hours, but he didn't come and in the end I went to his room. It was locked and the light was out. I thought he had been transferred or his cover was blown. I was devastated.'

'Did you see him again after that?'

'Well, yes. In the end, I did. I'd kept up the deliveries, always hoping to see Reggie again but meeting a different contact each time. And finally, in February 1918, it *was* him. I can't tell you the relief I felt to know he was all right. He told me he'd been in England because he'd had to go to ground. He said he was being hunted and he knew it wouldn't end with the war. He seemed to believe his life was in danger. That's when he told me about the note he'd hidden here in case he didn't see me again. He was about to tell me the plan when we were . . . interrupted. So my only option to track him down was to come here and find the note.'

'This all sounds like another case for Sherlock Holmes or something. Are you sure you're not making it up?'

'Oh for goodness sake! Why would I do that? Have you heard of La Dame Blanche?'

'The White Lady? No, I haven't. But I'm sure you're about to enlighten me.'

'We were a spy network in Belgium – mostly women – watching the trains, monitoring the troop movements, second-guessing where the next enemy attack would come. There were 800 of us in the end, all working for the British and passing information to contacts across the Dutch border. I was just a tiny link in a chain which stretched across Europe, and so was Reggie. But each link was vital and carried its own risk. Many Germans died because of us. And Reggie was found out . . . '

The cold of a Dutch December eats into your bones, gnawing at your extremities and slowing your thinking. Reggie was standing on the corner of an alley in the red light district, waiting for yet another contact. He tried to blend in with the other overcoat-wearing men, furtively stalking the streets in search of satisfaction. A woman approached him, openly flirtatious.

'Fancy a good time, Mister?' She wasn't very original in her phraseology. She pressed herself against him and he felt her push a slip of paper into his palm. 'No? Oh well, suit yourself. Your loss.' And she was once more absorbed by the night.

Reggie slipped the paper into his pocket and started to walk towards the relative safety of the main street, but it was too late. His arms were grabbed from behind and he was dragged into a doorway. A hand came over his mouth and a voice hissed in German, 'Was haben Sie, Herr Robinson?' They knew his name.

Reggie was aware of his whole body tingling as adrenalin surged through him. His army training had been extended with a course in self-defence and he managed to jab a vicious elbow into his assailant's solar plexus. The pained gasp and momentary loss of grip was enough. Reggie wrenched himself free and within less than a second the small knife in his pocket was embedded in the man's chest. His assailant staggered back, his eyes registering a faint surprise before he fell. Reggie didn't wait to see if he was dead. Backing out into the passage, he glanced quickly to right and left as a tall man limped towards him from the doorway opposite. Reggie ran towards the city centre, where he could disappear more effectively. He knew he couldn't go back to his room but he had to contact his spymaster. He would have to vanish.

'So he killed a German spy? That's why he had to go back?'

'Yes – but it doesn't end there.'

Henry stiffened. He could hear a key turn in the front door. He'd forgotten the time. Mrs Morris was back from the market and he was sitting in her parlour, entertaining the despised 'foreigner' from over the road and breaking every rule in her book. For one wry moment he considered putting the final nail in his coffin by bursting into song, but thought better of it. Fortunately, he'd closed the door, so she wouldn't realise immediately that anything was amiss. He put a finger to his lips and gestured to Martine to keep quiet. Mrs Morris's footsteps clicked along the hall floor en route to the kitchen and Henry was about to heave a sigh and plan their escape, when the clicking stopped. His landlady was heading back up the hall. The door handle turned and, before he could take avoiding action, she was standing in the doorway, a look of utter horror and disbelief on her face.

Henry leapt to his feet. 'I'm so very sorry, Mrs Morris. We'll leave right now. Martine . . . Miss Lamont . . . '

'How dare you? How dare you open this door, Mr Forrester! This is my private space and you have invaded it. I told you I wouldn't have that woman in my house.'

'Mrs Morris, I can explain . . . '

'It's too late for you to explain, Mr Forrester, far too late. You can pack your bags. I want you out by tomorrow. How can I have you here if I can't trust you to keep a few simple rules?'

Henry said nothing. He was too embarrassed. Mrs Morris stood to one side while they edged past her. Martine astonished him by maintaining an almost glacial composure as she let herself out. Henry retreated to his room. Now what would he do? There was no contingency and Martine hadn't finished her story. She still didn't know about the message.

Downstairs, all was silent. Maybe he could have a word with Mrs Morris – grovel a bit and persuade her to rethink. He went down again, trying to avoid the creaking steps and torn areas of carpet. The door to the parlour was closed as before, but Henry could hear a stifled sobbing coming from inside. He couldn't imagine Mrs Morris in tears and his sense of mortification increased because he had been the cause of this uncharacteristic display of emotion.

By way of a poor apology, he decided to take the liberty of making her a cup of tea so he went to the kitchen. Tea in hand he approached the parlour once again, expecting to hear a renewal of his marching orders. Instead, there was silence so, with some trepidation, he opened the door. From where he stood in the hall he could see Mrs Morris, sitting on one of the overstuffed sofas and holding the photograph of the young soldier in tropical kit. She didn't look up.

'I'm so very sorry, Mrs Morris. I've brought you some tea . . . '

'This is my son, Mr Forrester. This is my boy. He used to entertain his young lady in here before . . . ' She choked back a sob. 'It was the bloody foreigners that did for him – over in Africa in 1901. I won't have foreigners in my house.'

'Please forgive me, Mrs Morris. Here's your tea. I'll go first thing.' Leaving the tea on a small table, Henry returned to his room. His head was once again in turmoil. Uppermost in his mind was Reggie's unfinished story and now he had to face imminent homelessness, just when he thought he was settled here. He went over to the window and looked across at number 44. Upstairs, a net curtain was pulled aside and he could make out Martine's face looking right back at him. She was beckoning. He hesitated for a moment, before deciding he had little to lose by going over. He could hardly fall any lower in Mrs Morris's estimation.

Martine was standing at the door by the time he arrived. She glanced up and down the street before ushering him into the parlour of her own lodgings. Her face looked pinched and a certain anxiety played round her eyes.

'Did you look for the note?' Her tone was surprisingly clipped and detached in the face of her involvement in Henry's eviction. Before he could respond, she seemed to collect herself and her face assumed its habitual expression of polite neutrality. 'I am so sorry, Henry. I am forgetting my manners. I should have brought you here in the first place. The rules are more relaxed. And I have had an idea that might help. I want to make it up to you anyway.' Henry waited for her to continue. 'There's an empty attic here. I think you can probably stay in there if we fix it up a bit. Just till you sort out something else. I already spoke to my landlady and explained you are a veteran newly returned from the front. She is happy to help out. She doesn't like Mrs Morris.'

Henry was once more overwhelmed. But it was a bit of a lifeline – and he didn't really have an alternative – so the next morning, he moved his kitbag over to number 44. The house had a far less utilitarian feel than Mrs Morris's lodging. Ornaments cluttered every available surface and the owner obviously had a penchant for chintz and tassels. Henry immediately felt very male and clumsy. Martine showed him up to an adequately appointed attic room and he deposited his kit bag before she ushered him into the parlour – clearly not out of bounds here. She even brought him a glass of beer before joining him with a muttered 'Prost...' Henry checked the glass on the way to his lips. A German toast felt inappropriate, to say the least, but then he reasoned that the expression was most likely a Flemish word as well.

'So, you were telling me about the German spy Reggie killed?'

'Yes, given the nature of our relationship, I knew Reggie would try to come back if only to see me. I was desperate to know he was safe . . . '

A Siberian wind swept across the polders into Amsterdam in February 1918. The Central Powers had an on-off Armistice agreement with Russia, but had yet to capitulate completely. Reggie knew he couldn't return to his old room in Raadhuistraat and that his presence in the city remained a high risk, but he needed to explain to Martine. He hid in an unlit recess off the main street and watched the café where he had met her several times in the autumn. He saw a man he recognised walk in and order a coffee before moving to a table out of sight. He'd never known the fellow's name – agents were careful with their identity. Within ten minutes, Martine appeared. Fifteen minutes later, she emerged, glancing around before hurrying away, head down against the cold. Reggie followed, catching up with her at the next junction and pulling her into a side street.

'Martine . . . ' His tone was urgent.

The expression of surprise and shock in her face disappeared in a moment and she grasped his arm.

'Reggie – where . . . ?'

Reggie interrupted her. 'I can't stop. I think I'm being followed again and they're probably looking for you too. I've been in London. I got back into 47 Shakespeare Street – never mind how – and . . . '

'Reggie – there's someone coming.'

Glancing further down the alley, Reggie could just distinguish a silhouette limping towards him. As they both turned back to the main road, he managed to say, 'I don't know how I'll get out of this, but if I do, I've left you a note in my room at number 47, in the tallboy. Look out for Henry when the war ends – he'll go back, I know it. The note tells you . . . '

He didn't finish. The man was gaining on them and they could hear his laboured breathing. They headed in opposite directions and, by the time their pursuer reached the top of the alley, they had disappeared.

'And that was it? You haven't seen him since?'

'No. It was obvious that it was too dangerous to continue. There was one border guard who seemed very suspicious of the number of babies being born across the line. My controller released me from my commitment and set me up with false papers. I moved to the backstreets of Ghent and worked there until the Armistice. Then, in January, I decided it was safe to come and wait for you – to find Reggie.'

Henry took a deep breath. 'Well, I have the note.'

'You found it?'

He pulled the tattered scrap of lining paper from his pocket and passed it to her. She took it to the window to study the hastily written scrawl. Her brow furrowed as she endeavoured to work out the significance of the words and the code.

'Why is it encoded?' Henry asked. 'Why does it not just tell you in plain English?'

'He said the danger would go on after the war, so I imagine he thought the house could be searched. He must have thought there was some danger from agencies other than the Germans. We should try and work this out.'

'I recognised the verse. It's from a well-known song by a musical hall artist. Reggie and I were both keen on her act.' Henry was glad he could contribute.

Martine hesitated before replying. 'I don't think the source of the verse is important. It's what it says. He told me the note was for me and he is making sure I know this is the one. We were sweethearts, like it says here. He knows if I have come to London I could be lonely and he's telling me he'll return, probably in the spring when the daisies are in flower. It's obvious when you look at it like that. That last time I saw him, I think he meant to tell me what was in the note, but he didn't have time.'

She was making Henry feel a little stupid now. Put like that, it was, indeed, obvious, especially in the light of his newfound knowledge. He wracked his brains over the numbers, determined to get there first.

'Do you think the numbers relate to letters of the alphabet?'

'Well, they could do, I suppose. We could try to work it out.'

Martine produced a notebook and pencil and they started to write down various permutations of letters with 4 being D, the fourth letter of the alphabet, then again with 4 as A, B, C, E, F and G and so on. Nothing made sense.

Henry was stumped. Martine's face was flushed and she looked irritated. Then her eyes widened. 'I think we should take the numbers at face value. Look at the first four digits – 6 4 1 9. What strikes you about them?'

'Nothing in particular.' Henry felt mildly frustrated that she seemed to be three steps ahead of him yet again.

'It could be a date. 6th of April 1919.' He saw immediately that this was a distinct possibility. But, if she was right, the 6th of April was the day after tomorrow. Whatever the note signified, they didn't have much time.

'Brilliant! Have you got any ideas about the other numbers, though?'

'Well, my guess would be that if 6th April is the date of his return then these numbers indicate where we can meet him. Grouped in pairs, they look like co-ordinates. Do you know anything about them? I learned a little in my training but it was very sketchy.'

Henry had done a bit of map reading at school and he trawled his distant memory of the calculation of co-ordinates. 'Do you have a map of London? I may be able to work it out from that.'

As a newcomer to the city, a map had been among her first purchases, and it took Henry about ten minutes to calculate that the location was in central London. The final digits took them precisely to the ancient cross outside Charing Cross station. They couldn't come up with a better interpretation and the jigsaw of words and numbers fitted this theory, so they decided to go with it. A slight fly in the ointment was that no time was indicated in the coding. They'd have to stay there all day. Roll on Sunday.

* * *

They caught an omnibus from Islington to central London. When it reached Trafalgar Square, Henry saw that the place was alive with people going about their business. They scurried along with purpose, their heads down against the bite of the early spring morning, glancing at one another from between hunched shoulders before moving apart. The Spanish 'flu pandemic still stalked the city, brought back from the trenches to murder in a single day those who had survived four years of war.

The omnibus set them down near Nelson's Column and Henry looked up at the Admiral, whose stony gaze embraced the spires and rooftops of London. He felt a momentary anger at this man on his ridiculous pedestal, a statue which not only glorified the Admiral himself but the wars he had fought. Henry had seen with his own eyes the reality of war, all that hope and patriotism buried deep in the filth of northern France.

But there were more important concerns on this auspicious day. After Reggie disappeared, Henry never really believed they would meet again and he was about to be proved wrong. He would witness the reunion of two lovers, which he himself had facilitated, and he would hear Martine's story from the principal character himself.

Henry was aware that crowds were best avoided so he and Martine turned into The Strand. Their collars were turned up against a light drizzle and, within moments, they could see the Charing Cross, a station of pilgrimage for generations and now dwarfed by the imposing railway station behind it. It looked as if they wouldn't have to wait all day after all. Amidst the scurrying crowds Henry saw a still figure, enveloped in a greatcoat and with a hat pulled down well over his eyes, standing at the base of the monument. Reggie was easily identified by his height. Henry's steps quickened but Martine didn't keep pace with him, so he paused and looked back with some impatience. She had seemed on edge all morning, which Henry had put down to anticipation or nerves which he expected would vanish as soon as she caught sight of her man. Now, though, she had stopped beside a small tea shop and her eyes revealed an indecision, almost a fear, which seemed inexplicable.

'Come on – he's there. Can't you see him?' Henry was frustrated.

'I just feel a bit nervous. Why don't you meet him? I'll come over when I have pulled myself together.'

Henry hesitated, in some confusion. 'Of course, if that's what you want. But I thought you were desperate to see him again . . . '

'Yes, I am, but I need a moment. Please go on.' She turned abruptly and disappeared into the tea shop, looking almost furtive, as if she was battling with a sudden desire to hide.

Henry was momentarily nonplussed, but he dismissed his concerns and turned back towards Charing Cross. Seeing Reggie, still standing there, he broke into a run.

'Reggie, old pal.'

'Henry!' As Reggie swamped his friend in a huge man-hug Henry registered the changes to his familiar face, the new lines and the now-anxious eyes. As they stepped back to take stock of one another, Reggie stared over Henry's shoulder. 'Are you on your own?' His voice sounded harsh somehow.

'No I'm not! Martine's in the café over there, Reggie. I'd never have understood that message without her. How about we go and join her and you can start explaining yourself?' Henry looked up at Reggie expecting to see excitement and enthusiasm and saw an inexplicable guardedness.

'Is she now? All right, but I'll go in first so make sure you stay behind me.' Reggie thrust his right hand deep into his coat pocket as he spoke. Henry put this surprising attitude down to nerves and a desire to see his lover's reaction, so was quite happy to follow on.

They crossed the street, and Reggie hesitated for a moment before opening the door of the tea shop. Henry trailed a yard or so in his wake. The aroma of newly baked cakes inside the door extended a welcome that was belied by the expression on the face of the girl they were looking for. She was seated at a table well away from the window, next to a rear door. Instead of the expression of delight and love he had anticipated Henry recognised tension and control, which was mirrored in the face of his friend. Martine stood up, one hand on the handle of the door. Reggie and Martine exchanged a long look and something indefinable passed between them. Each seemed to search for something in the eyes of the other. A couple of nearby customers glanced up from their teas with curiosity.

Like Reggie's hand, Martine's was also in her pocket but, as she went to remove it, there was a sudden, loud report. A red flower bloomed on her shoulder and there was a thud as a small revolver spun from her grasp, ending up under the chair from which she had risen. Time hung motionless for a moment before the room erupted. As Martine slumped to the floor, the formerly curious customers overturned tables and chairs in their haste to leave the shop, a young girl screamed and the waitress dropped a tray of cups on to the counter. Henry moved instinctively towards the prone woman, hands outstretched to lift her.

'Henry – no! Don't move!' The voice wasn't Reggie's. Reggie remained where he had been standing, his hand still in his pocket and his face shell-shocked. Henry was kneeling beside Martine, who seemed to be breathing although her eyes were closed. He looked up to identify who had issued the command. A man in a black greatcoat and battered trilby was limping across the room towards them, a drawn gun in his hand.

It was Jack.

* * *

The mangled fields around Hébuterne were just beginning to recover. Farmers were reclaiming their lost lands and every turn of the plough revealed some gruesome remnant of the most murderous battle of the Great War or of any war. Identity discs and bones were reverently collected and relatives of the missing received official notification of the truth they had prayed might be a lie. Those relatives would come alone or in family groups to pay their respects to the fallen in the new British Cemetery No 2. The portier watched them wander up and down the neat rows of stones until they stopped and stood, each lost in his own grief. In Plot 1 were the 101 original graves of those who fell on 1st July 1916 in that first futile push to take the village of Gommecourt.

On 6th April 1920, the *portier* directed three young men to a row of graves lying against the boundary wall of Plot 1. Beyond it stretched the barren landscape, still a sea of flattened mud. The men stopped at one or two of the graves, pointing and discussing the names on the stones. Finally, they huddled together in front of one near the end of the line, silently reading the inscription.

2741 RIFLEMAN A. J. JOHNSON
QUEEN VICTORIA'S RIFLES
1st JULY 1916 AGED 19

It seemed too little, somehow, to mark the end of a life, the snuffing out of a person when he was little more than a child. And this man-child was Arthur Johnson, fellow lodger, soldier, friend, blood brother, poor terrified Arthur, who had died in a moment surrounded by a symphony of death but supported by his mates.

They stood together but alone, each deep in his own memories – of the days of innocence at 47 Shakespeare Street, of the early battles fought side by side, of their separation and Arthur's death, and of the grim circumstances of their reunion just a year ago to the day. Amidst the serenity of the cemetery, the shock and drama of that morning seemed something that happened to someone else. But it wasn't.

Martine wasn't dead. Jack's aim was too good for that. As the ambulance arrived to remove her, handcuffed to a constable Jack had summoned from the street, Henry felt rather as if he had stepped into someone else's life. Jack was in control of the situation and Reggie – well, he sat slumped at a table, his head in his hands, while statements were taken and the café was put to rights.

Once back on the pavement, the three men looked wordlessly at one another. Henry was shocked and appalled by the horror he had witnessed in the last hour. He had seen countless men shot in cold blood, but not a woman – never a woman. He was the first to speak. 'What just happened there? For heaven's sake, I need some sort of explanation.'

'Shall we wait until we get off the street?' Jack replied. 'I think I'm the only one of us who has the whole picture. I know a quiet pub in Covent Garden.' They walked down The Strand together, each feeling there was both too much and too little to say.

Finally, seated in the half-darkness of The Duke of Wellington with pints to hand, the explanations began.

'Who are you, Jack? It *was* you in Amsterdam, wasn't it? What the hell was going on? I thought you were a German agent.' Reggie sounded confused and angry.

'I'm not that, old pal. I'm not that. I'm in Special Branch.'

'The police?' Henry was incredulous. This was the man he'd last seen carted off on a stretcher screaming in pain.

'I'd been invalided out of the army, hadn't I? So my old man pulled a few strings – I told you he was a top notch barrister before the war. He knew the Chief Inspector at Scotland Yard, and with the call-ups and everything they were desperate for police officers to manage things back home. Crimes don't stop because there's a war on.'

'But this was more than a handbag theft in Camden. This was espionage. How do the police get involved in that?'

'In 1918, they asked me to join Special Branch because there was an agent in Amsterdam who was passing false information about enemy troop movements to the military back home.'

'Oh God,' murmured Reggie. 'That was me. Only I had no idea at the time. I truly didn't. Martine was my contact and I was falling in love with her. It blinded me for far longer than it should have done, though I knew someone had betrayed me. After I last saw her in Amsterdam, I finally put two and two together. It could only have been her. It destroyed me for a while, I can tell you. I really thought she loved me too.' Reggie paused and passed a hand over his eyes.

Henry couldn't remain silent. 'She did love you, mate. I'm sure of it . . . and she was torn. I reckon her orders were to eliminate you, but, at the last minute, she couldn't do it. It's why she went into the tea shop, rather than face up to you.'

'Thanks, Henry. At least I wasn't totally duped, then. You know, when I came back here, I had no idea whether she had found you or the note I left at number 47 but I knew that, if she had, both our lives might be in danger. It was hard to believe she'd actually go through with killing me, but I couldn't take that chance.'

Jack resumed his story. 'I only knew you by your code name, so it wasn't until I saw the two of you together that I realised you were the agent in Amsterdam. My boss was convinced you had defected to the enemy, but I was one hundred per cent convinced you wouldn't do such a terrible thing. That meant the double agent *had* to be Mademoiselle Lamont. Her real name is Gretchen Schmidt, by the way, though she has a Belgian mother.'

Reggie managed a rueful grin. 'And I thought you were a German spymaster out to kill me. I saw you when those two louts attacked me. And then Martine and I ran away from you that time.'

'I couldn't keep up with this bloody leg. That second time I almost called out to you, but I didn't want to alert Martine to the fact that it was her I was after. The first time you saw me I wanted to talk to you, to warn you, but the louts got there first and I had to preserve my cover while she was still out there.'

Henry was listening open-mouthed. 'I saw you too, Jack, from the window of number 47 on the night I came back. You were looking at the houses and you nearly came in. I took you for some poor bloke with nowhere to go. But you haunted my dreams.'

'I had no idea you'd seen me,' Jack replied. 'I was about to knock, to see whether you or Reggie were back at the old place, but I thought better of it. Then, the next day, my boss had word that Gretchen Schmidt had been seen in Shakespeare Street and she'd be asking for Reggie. So I followed you into town on the omnibus. I was downstairs, away from the door. You want to look around you more, Henry, mate!'

'So every word Martine – or Gretchen – told me was a lie then?' Henry was astonished at her acting talent. 'I can't believe I didn't see through her, Reg.'

Reggie was knocking back his third pint. 'Best liar I ever met,' he muttered. 'I imagine some of what she told you was true, Henry, but she would have turned the crucial information on its head so she came out of it with her halo intact.'

'If you knew where she was, why didn't you just arrest her and avoid traumatising all those people in the tea shop?' Henry asked.

'We just needed that final piece of evidence. We wanted her to incriminate herself, so we used surveillance. I had no intention of shooting her in public but in the end there was no choice. My boss would call it a necessary evil.'

'Seems a bit harsh,' Henry commented. 'So what'll happen to her?' He probably knew the answer. They both looked at him, before Jack drew a finger across his throat. They sat in silence for a couple of minutes, Henry and Reggie contemplating their gullibility. All it had taken was a pretty face and a good line in flattery.

Henry, Reggie and Jack each clutched a bunch of early flowering poppies, plucked from the roadside near Hébuterne. They lay the blood-red blooms on Arthur's grave before turning away and walking together to the gate. The *portier* nodded as they passed. He'd seen many such faces in the last three years, grief-etched or empty. He watched them walk up the lane towards the village, a little band of brothers, linked by more than family, joined forever by common experience and suffering as well as by a trust which had truly been through the refiner's fire and emerged the other side, still polished and intact.

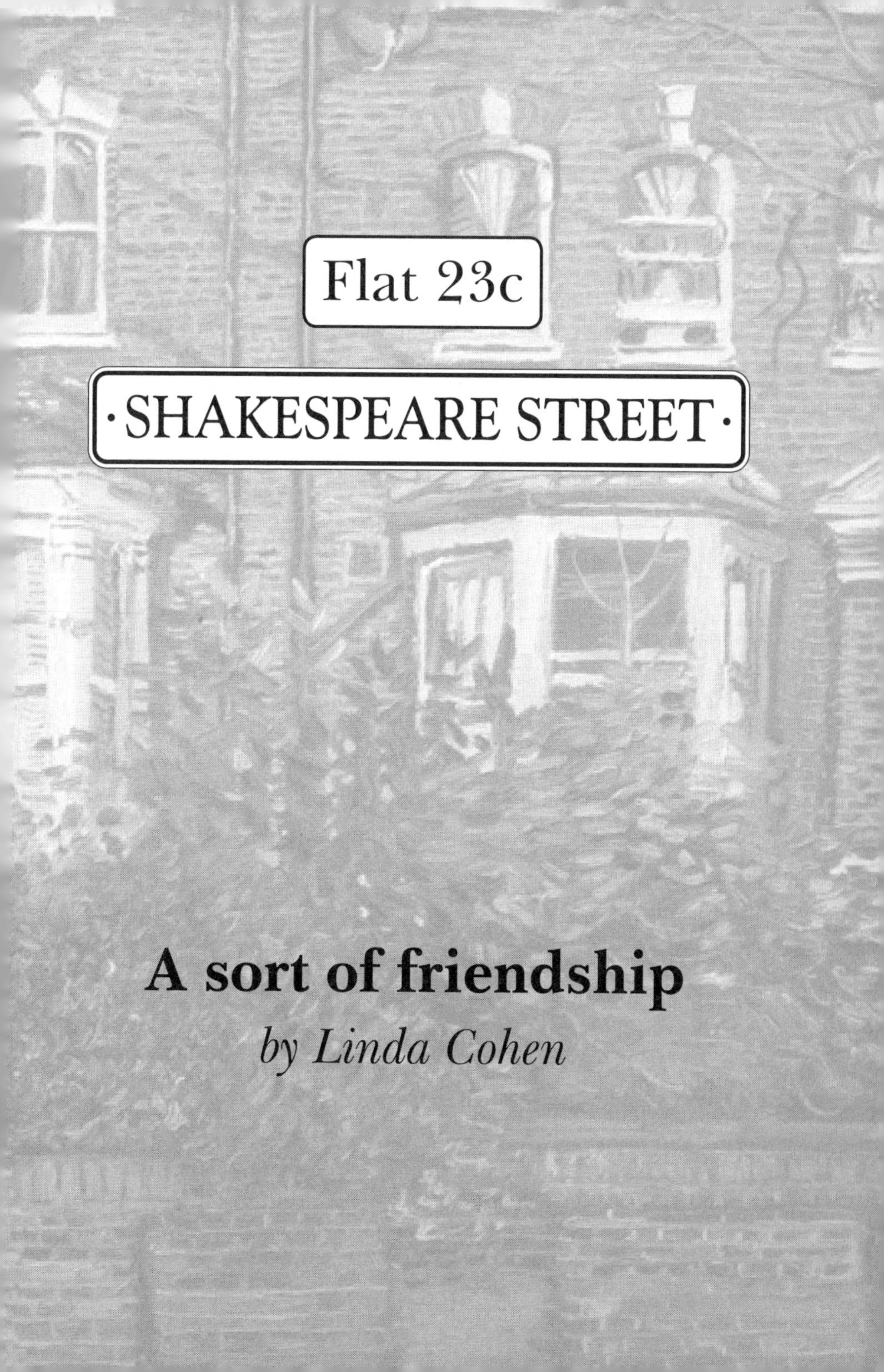

Flat 23c

·SHAKESPEARE STREET·

A sort of friendship

by Linda Cohen

The course of true love never did run smooth

A Midsummer Night's Dream, Act 1, Scene 1

Why can't you come for a drink tonight? You owe me. All the nights that you've been miserable and, even though it didn't suit me, I'd always come out when you needed me. I never let you down. You don't have to stay long, just an hour or so, just a quick drink. Please Si, I can't do this on my own.'

It was true, of course. Laura *was* there for him. When he lost his job, when his mother died unexpectedly, and all sorts of other times when things had gone wrong for him. But, in truth, Simon had more than paid back his dues.

He groaned. He really couldn't face the consequences of yet another of Laura's relationships going wrong. There would be the inevitable crying. That would go on for maybe half an hour or so and would be followed by a little hand wringing about how this time she really had thought he was The One. Then would come the swearing about why hadn't she been able to see what a plonker he was, everyone else had seen it but not her. That would last at least another half an hour before, eventually – oh bliss – he would be allowed to take her home. Probably, and not for the first time, he would put her to bed before creeping quietly out of her flat while the poor, inebriated Laura fell into a deep and troubled sleep.

'Just this once, then,' said Si. 'I can't keep doing this. It always feels as though it's me in the relationship with what'shisname. By the way, what was his name this time? Harold, Edgar, Walter?'

'You know perfectly well his name was Jonathon. Jonathon Mayers. And don't make me say it again. I never want to hear his name or see his face. I just want to forget I ever met him.'

Simon sighed on the end of the phone. How many times had he heard Laura say those words? She never meant it, of course. He knew she would have done anything to see Jonathon Mayers again. Wasn't he the love of her life just two weeks ago? Now he had told Laura that he was going to work in New York for two years and, because of the distance between them, he felt it was better to break up rather than to try to make a long distance relationship work. In his opinion, they *never* worked. To Laura this sounded like the feeble excuse it was – she knew many people who carried on long distance relationships. To Jonathon it was a good reason to end the relationship, something he had apparently wanted to do for some time.

Simon ached for Laura. He always felt this way when she was unhappy. No-one was unhappy like Laura. She sobbed, she threw herself around, she swore, she broke things, she shouted. Just being around her was absolutely exhausting, but Simon loved being around her so, once again, Friday night would see them sitting in the Dog and Duck with Laura beside herself with grief.

He got to the pub early, lining up two gin and tonics for her and a beer for himself, and sat at a side table watching the door and waiting for her to arrive. Laura always entered any room the same way, flinging the door open then coming in as a mass of flowing hair followed by a load of limbs that seemed uncoordinated before throwing herself into a chair. She would either be beaming with joy, if it had been a good day, or her eyes would be red-rimmed and desperate if she was sad.

'Exhausting,' Simon thought. 'Either way, it's exhausting,' but here he was ready to pick up the pieces all over again.

And sure enough, here she was. As she flew in through the door, heads turned to see what the disruption was. Why did she do that? Why couldn't she simply *come in* like anybody else? Simon knew that she didn't *mean* to draw attention to herself. She was just one of those people who couldn't help it, and that was another thing that he loved about her.

Simon and Laura had met at nursery school. He had been a very grown up three-and-a-half-year-old and she had been a very immature three-year-old who had screamed and screamed when her mother had left her at the school, sobbing bitterly at being abandoned and left to fend for herself. Simon had approached her and pushed a very bald and very ugly doll at her, which had made Laura cry even more. Quickly realising the error of his ways he had found some crayons and paper and, taking her hand, had gently guided her to the little chair next to his where he showed her how to draw a flower. Laura had promptly scribbled all over his flower but nevertheless the tears had stopped, and forever after she had tagged along after him wherever he went. Simon never complained. He loved having Laura there even when he was playing with the other children and he always looked to see if she was nearby because that was when he was happy, when Laura was nearby.

Yes, Simon had to admit it. He had been in love with Laura for probably twenty or more years now. It wasn't easy of course, loving Laura but not letting her know. Going through all the traumas with her, and helping her cope with every break up (of which there had been many).

For all these years he had pretended to be her best friend. Of course that was exactly what he was, but he wanted to be more than her best friend: he wanted to be The One, the perfect partner she kept thinking she had found. He wanted her to realise that The One she had been searching for all these years was right there under her nose. Because one thing was for sure: for Simon, Laura definitely was The One. If the only way he could be close to Laura was as her confidant and best friend, he would just have to accept this as his role in life.

However, Simon had a plan. He hadn't worked out the details yet, but the plan had formed in his mind just after her frantic phone call. He felt it was now time to disclose his feelings and, maybe, change the course of both their lives once and for all.

Many years ago, when Laura was twelve and he was thirteen,

they had gone to a party. Laura was with a boy whose name he couldn't remember and he was with his very first girlfriend, Alison Hardy. He really thought at the time, in the immature way thirteen-year-old boys think, that he *could* love Alison Hardy but Laura had been awful about her, really quite cruel in fact, which had surprised Simon. Alison was a pretty girl but Laura had ripped her apart, criticising her hair, her dress, the way she talked. Simon had been angry at the time but, being immature, had finished with Alison the very next day. After all, if his best friend had found so many faults in her she couldn't possibly be right for him.

Now, with the benefit of time, Simon realised that the reason Laura had been so critical was simply because she was afraid that Simon would have less time for her. This scenario had been played out each time Simon met someone. Instead of Laura welcoming the girls and wanting to be friends, she had found something wrong with all of them. It happened every time and, eventually, Simon didn't even bother introducing her to anyone anymore. Once when he challenged her about her behaviour she had said, 'In my eyes, Si, no-one is good enough for you.' This comment had kept him going for quite some time and he had allowed himself to wonder whether, unbeknown even to herself, Laura might – just might – have some feelings for him after all.

Laura swigged back her gin and tonic, gave an unladylike burp and focused on Simon. 'So, go on, tell me.'

'Tell you what?'

'Tell me I've done it again. Gone and made a fool of myself yet again.'

'You've gone and made a fool of yourself yet again,' said Simon.

'Oh Si, I know. Why didn't you stop me? Why didn't you tell me he was the most selfish, arrogant pig?'

'Why? Would you have listened?' asked Simon.

'I might have done,' Laura replied.

'You know bloody well that I would have been talking to the wall. You would have given me forty reasons why he was *just perfect*, and completely ignored me as usual.'

Laura looked up at him. 'Why are you shouting?'

'I'm not shouting, I'm just talking. Shouting is much louder, and if you go on like this I may just have to start shouting just to make you realise how ridiculous all this is.'

Laura looked crestfallen, started on her second gin and tonic, and suddenly started to giggle. 'Do you remember when you started shouting at me once before? When old whatisname stood me up after you'd told me he would, and I wouldn't believe you. And then I called you from somewhere near Brighton and you had to come and pick me up because I didn't know where the hell I was. And when you got there I was so drunk you had to carry me to the car and I was sick all over your new brown shoes.'

Simon shuddered. He remembered it well. He had been having a lovely evening with a girl called Carol, someone he felt he really could get close to, when Laura called. Simon had had to explain to Carol that a friend was in trouble and he had to go. Carol had not been happy, especially when she realised the friend was another girl. It had taken quite a while for him to extricate himself from Carol and she was still clinging to him as he got into the car.

He shrugged her off, saying he had to go, and watched her get smaller and smaller in his rear view mirror. He felt so guilty, and so angry with Laura. When he had phoned Carol to apologise the next night, she told him not to worry as she had met someone else that very night so he had actually done her a favour.

'I loved those shoes,' said Simon.

'I hated them,' said Laura. 'They looked like shoes a geography teacher would wear, all brogue-y and lace-upy. I did you a favour being sick over them. It was good you had to throw them away. No-one would have gone out with you wearing those shoes, anyway.'

They both looked at each other and burst out laughing. Whatever went on and however mad they got at each other, they always ended up laughing – well after a while at least.

Simon put down his beer glass and looked Laura straight in the eyes. 'So . . . where do you go from here?' he ventured. 'Are you having a rest from men, or are you going to save yourself for when Jonathon Meyers comes back from America. Or are you going to see who else is around?'

Laura gave a sigh. 'I'm not waiting around for that cretin, thank you very much. I don't really know what I ever saw in him,' she sniffed.

Simon smiled to himself. This *was* an improvement. By his reckoning he had saved himself at least fourteen days of aggravation as she seemed to have fast forwarded a few weeks and skipped a lot of the crying and heart-rending bits of the process. She seemed almost to have reached the concluding stage, the bit he liked best, when she was nearly over the now-despised individual and was beginning to move forward slowly.

'Only I was thinking,' said Simon, 'that there is something you have never tried and it just might be the answer for you.' Simon felt himself redden.

'Oh yeah, and what's that?' Laura was beginning to slur her words a bit, and Simon wondered if he wasn't about to take a bit of an advantage of her. The two gin and tonics were certainly doing their job, and she was about to embark on a third.

'Look Laura, we've been friends a long time haven't we?'

'We certainly have, my old pal, my old friend, my old darling. What would I do without you?' This was followed by another hiccup which made Laura pick up Simon's beer glass and drain it then wipe her mouth on her sleeve in a very unladylike way before, with great difficulty, she tried to focus on Simon's face.

'Well I was thinking,' said Simon. 'I'm single, you're single. How about you and I give it a try? You know, go out, have a few dates, see how we feel about each other, just generally, and no pressure, just . . . '

But Laura had collapsed in a heap face down on the table and Simon could not rouse her. 'Laura, come on. Wake up. I'll take you home.' He looked around while people tut-tutted, and looked disapprovingly at the pair.

Simon pulled Laura's chair away from the table, wound her arms around his neck and, as he had done on so many other nights, pulled her up and dragged her out of the pub door. As he left, a stag party at another table cheered.

'Wish you luck with that one tonight,' they heckled as he staggered past them bearing Laura's weight. As the door shut behind them, Simon could still hear the group cheering and whooping with pleasure and he felt anger welling up inside him. So many nights, so much wasted time. There had to be something he could do. This was just ridiculous.

After pouring Laura into the back of the car, where she fell into a deep sleep and started snoring quietly, Simon slowly drove back to Laura's flat. As he passed through the dark streets, a silent depression came over him and he made a decision. He simply would not go on like this any longer.

When he parked outside Laura's flat, Laura started to wake up. 'Where are we?' she asked.

'Where do you think? Back at your flat after another wasted evening, you collapsing in a heap and me picking up the pieces.'

'Oh Si, I'm sorry. I did it again, didn't I. How can you put up with me?'

'That's just it Laura, I can't. I've had enough of this. In future, sort out your own problems. It's just not funny anymore. You're not eighteen, not a kid any more. I don't think I want to know about your latest boyfriend and how it's all gone wrong *yet again*. I've got my own problems, and I've actually had enough of yours!'

There, he'd said it. He hadn't meant it to come out quite as brutally as that, but now it was out in the open. After all, how much longer could he carry on like this, loving her, while she was pining over some other man? No, this was it. He would simply put some space between them, let her get on with it herself, and not be so *available* all the time.

Laura was staring at him, silent tears pouring down her cheeks and obviously sobering up by the minute. She climbed out of the car without another word, looking suitably chastened, and started to walk towards her flat. Simon watched her go. When she got to the front door, she turned and started to walk back towards him. Simon just sat there, staring straight ahead and she opened the car door and got in next to him.

They sat there in silence for a while, and then Laura spoke. 'I'm sorry Si. I'm truly sorry. I know I'm a complete pain, and no-one would put up with me like you do. Please, I promise this will never happen again. In future when I'm in this state – but, no, I promise I will never be in this state again. I will never let another man in to my life to unsettle and destroy me. You will never have to see me like this from this moment on. I'm finished with all that romance rubbish, from now on it's just me and my mates having fun. No more of this *in love* nonsense. Just me hanging out with my best mate.'

Simon stared ahead. What to do now? His heart was aching for her. Should he disclose his feelings now or simply turn her out of the car and drive away, never letting her know how he felt? He just sat there, saying nothing, his mind a whirl of indecision.

Laura turned to him. 'Simon, say something, please. I know I've behaved abominably but hey, we're best friends and best friends can do this with each other.'

Simon turned abruptly towards her. 'Best friends, you say. Just best friends. OK Laura, well here's the deal. You may be best friends with me, but I don't feel that way about you. I would like to be your best friend, but unfortunately other feelings have got in the way and they have for a long time now. I love you Laura, I love you more than life itself. I've loved you forever really, even when you've been making a complete fool of yourself over all those unsuitable men. I can't bear the way you fall apart when your latest love affair is over. I can't bear the way I have to listen to all the details of how much you loved him. I can't bear any of it any longer so you will have to find yourself a new best friend.'

There, it was out. He had said it, not the way he had planned but at least he had said it. He realised in that moment that everything had changed. He had disclosed so much to her by revealing his innermost feelings, feelings he had kept inside for so many years. Did he feel better for it being out? It was too soon to know yet but at least he had been honest, not only with her but with himself.

They both sat, staring ahead, before Laura slowly turned towards him. The uneasy silence lay between them. 'Si, I had no idea. How amazing. I can't believe what you are saying. Do you mean it?'

Simon turned towards her. 'Of course I mean it, you idiot. Why would I say something like that and not mean it?'

'Well, why didn't you tell me before? Why did you let me make such a fool of myself with so many people, and not ever tell me how you felt?'

'Because I didn't want to frighten you off, and I didn't want to spoil our friendship. That's why.'

Simon and Laura just sat there, each afraid to move. Suddenly Laura turned towards him and reached up to touch his face, his dear face that had always meant the world to her. She couldn't believe what he had said. All those years of her longing to hear those words from Simon, *her* Simon, of trying not to let her best friend know how she really felt about him, of trying to feel the same way about other men while knowing that something was always going to be missing. How could they have wasted all this time? She could never have envisaged her life without him in it, and now it turned out that he felt the same about her.

They stayed in the car for ages, just sitting with Laura's head on Simon's shoulder and neither of them saying anything. Daylight was creeping over them by the time they decided to go indoors.

They gazed at each other, each seeing the other in a new light, as Laura opened the door to the welcoming flat which had been her refuge throughout her chaotic love life. Number 23c Shakespeare Street. Home – and a place that Simon had always thought of as his second home.

'Coming in?' she asked.

'You bet,' said Simon.

They held on to each other in the hall, each not able to let the other go. The wonder of the last few hours, when they had told each other exactly how they had felt for so many years, each not able to disclose their real feelings to the other until now. It was just unbelievable.

When they entered the lounge, Laura's answerphone was flashing. She pressed *Play* while holding Simon's hand.

'Hello Laura,' the machine chirped. 'It's Jonathon. Look, I've been thinking. I may have made a terrible mistake. I'm sorry Babe. I know I hurt you. How about we meet up, discuss things, maybe we could even think about you coming out to New York with me? I've missed you Laura. It was rash of me to say I wanted to finish it. Don't know what I was thinking of, my head was all over the place. Give me a call as soon as you get this message. I love you.'

Laura and Simon looked at each other. Simon could hardly

dare to breathe until she looked enquiringly at him.

'Jonathon?' she said, winding her arms around Simon's neck. 'Who on earth is Jonathon?' They both burst out laughing, and Laura pressed *Delete* on the answerphone.

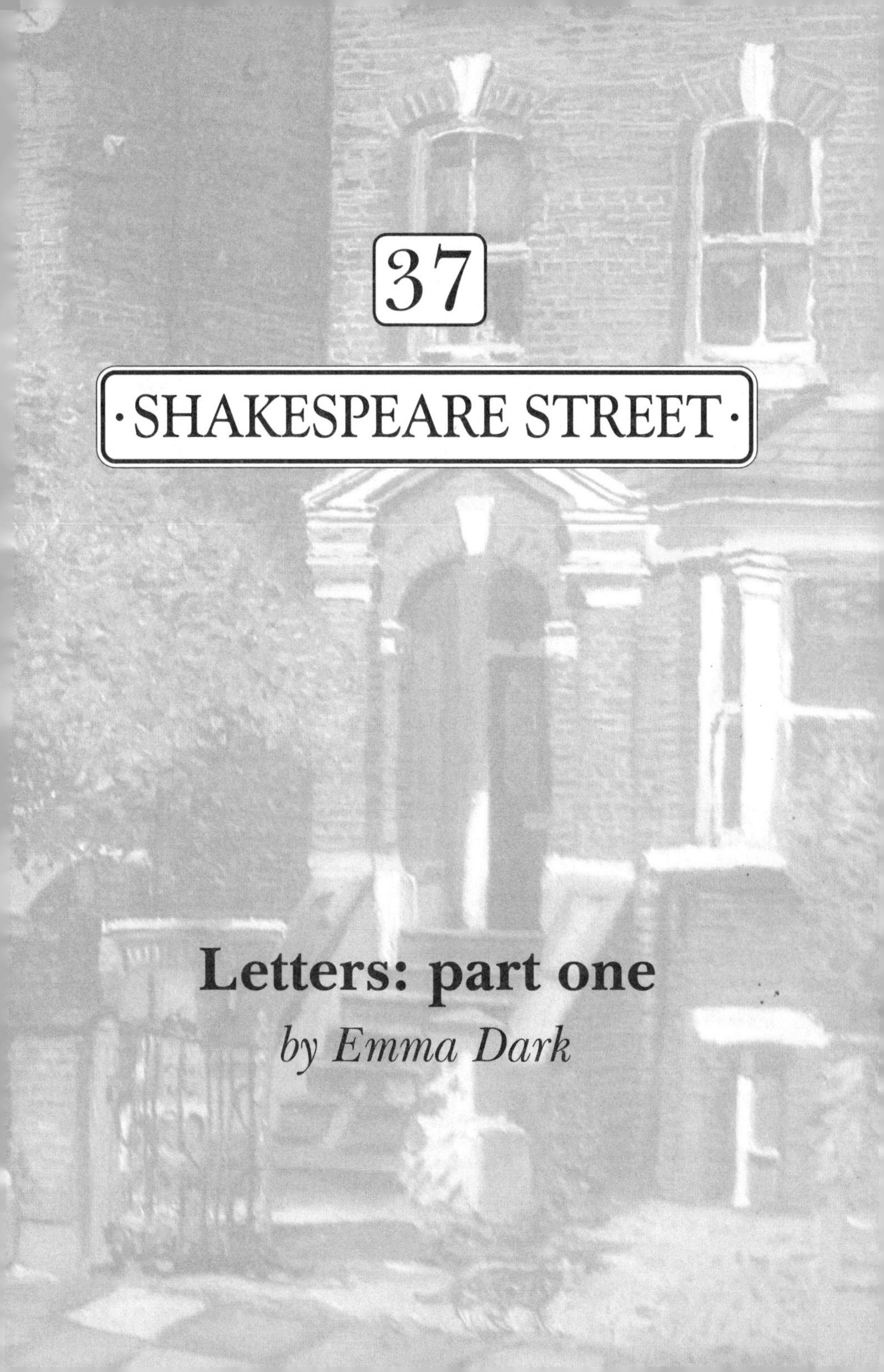

37 SHAKESPEARE STREET

Letters: part one

by Emma Dark

*Let me not to the marriage of true minds
Admit impediments. Love is not love
Which alters when it alteration finds,
Or bends with the remover to remove*

Sonnet 116.

Part 1

37 Shakespeare Street, London
4th September 1914

Dear Sir,

May I take the liberty of introducing myself. I am Miss Phoebe Prior, and I am writing to you from The North London Collegiate School for Young Ladies. I enclose a pair of woollen socks I have knitted for you, whomever you may be.

Our illustrious headmistress, Dr. Sophie Bryant, has instructed all the young ladies in the senior classes to spend their free time helping the war effort. Therefore, a group of us have joined together in this noble exercise and put aside our academic studies for one hour every day to knit warm socks for our gallant troops, especially those who are less fortunate than ourselves and do not have families to send them parcels. Some of us can only knit scarves, but I have moved on to socks.

My group are in our last year at school and most of us want to go on to college or university, if our parents will permit it. Although our headmistress believes in the broadest possible intellectual education for girls, rejecting the ridiculous idea that it is just for boys, she recognises its limitations and has introduced the study of home crafts. This includes knitting, and household management in case some of us get married in the future.

I certainly will not get married because I choose to pursue an academic career and, if possible, to become a teacher myself. I intend to go to the Cambridge Training College for Women. Our previous headmistresses, Miss Buss and Dr Bryant, were instrumental in founding the college.

I do hope that you are not shocked by my ambition to go to college, and that the socks fit.

Yours faithfully
Miss P Prior

Barracks, England
4th October 1914

Dear Miss Prior,

I am Edward Green, an infantry man in the British Expeditionary Force.

I was so surprised and truly delighted by your letter and parcel which was given to me by my CO. For quite a few weeks I have been watching the other chaps get letters and parcels from home, and I am ashamed to say I did feel a bit envious. But please do not think I have not had a respectable family. It is just that some unfortunate circumstance led us to poorer conditions than we would have liked, and led to the loss of my family. However, I have made a lot of pals in the regiment and after training we will soon be off to France to see some action I hope.

Thank you once again for the socks which fit perfectly, and are very warm and comfortable. I am very grateful to you. It made my day to receive your kind letter and parcel.

Yours sincerely,
Edward Green

P.S. I am not shocked by your ambition to go to college. Education is a fine thing. I wish I could have finished mine.

37 Shakespeare Street
3rd November 1914

Dear Mr Green,

I enclose a pair of gloves which I have knitted. I must admit I did find them more difficult than the socks and you will notice that I have made some errors, which I hope you will forgive.

Thank you for your kind words of encouragement for my plans to go to college. I have found that it is not very usual for people in general to encourage further education for women. My father is very critical of one of our neighbours, a Mr Roberts, who allowed his daughter Sybil to go to King's College for Women. Her mother, Mrs Dorothy Roberts, is in agreement with my father and said she regretted having to give way to her late husband on this issue because now Sybil would never find a husband. No man would want to marry a bluestocking she said. But I think Sybil is wonderful.

I understand that your regiment may have left for France but that you should all be home in a few months, by Christmas at the latest, so I hope you get the socks in time.

Yours sincerely
Miss P Prior

P.S. I am sorry to hear that you have no family so, as letters from home make such a difference to you, I shall write on a regular basis.

England
8th January 1915

Dear Miss Prior,

I apologise for the delay in thanking you for the gloves. They are quite the finest thing I have ever owned. My pals are teasing me a bit saying I have a sweetheart. Please do not think I am being presumptuous. I tell them they are from a fine young lady who is helping us chaps get through the war.

Just to let you know we have not shipped out yet, but should do any day now. We should be stationed near ███. The rumours are that no letters are going to be sent between England and France. I do hope that the rumours are not true as I so look forward to your kind letters.

We are really kept on our toes here and do not have a moment to spare, what with all the things we have to learn. We have learnt company drills and physical drills, semaphore and knot tying. We also do long jumping, route marching and a lot of parading so we are all exhausted in the evening.

Some of my pals were able to go to town on Saturday and post this for me. I could not go because I, and a few of the others, are under orders for overseas service now and we may ship out any minute. We are sent out in alphabetical order and Green is up next. We are now equipped, and we can't wait to get over there and sort it all out once and for all.

Please let me know how your studies are going. I wish I could have had a little more schooling myself, but I do not regret leaving to help provide for my family.

Again, thank you so much for the gloves. They are warm and fit well and I certainly cannot see any error in the stitches.

Yours most sincerely,
Edward Green

37 Shakespeare Street
14th February 1915

Dear Mr Green,

I hope this letter reaches you safely. I do not know if you have left for France yet. I do not know where you will be stationed in France because you may be aware that letters from troops are being censored. I shall continue to send letters to your regiment's address in England and hope they get to you.

I am sorry I have not been able to send you anything except this letter, but my present situation is not a happy one. My father has been made aware (thanks to my sister) that, prior to the war, I was a member of the Women's Social and Political Union. He has also been made aware that I attended some meetings held by Mrs Pankhurst and the funeral of Miss Davison. He has, therefore, given orders that I am to be locked in my room for a week and fed only bread and water to see how I would like prison. He has also said that, if I do not see sense in a week, he will withdraw me from my school because he thinks it is a bad influence on me. I cannot help but think this is very unjust, and I hate injustice.

I am not ashamed of supporting women's suffrage, and I am proud to be a member of the Women's Social and Political Union. The life and death of Miss Emily Davison has been an inspiration to me, and I only hope that I could show the same courage as her.

I hope you are well and that the war is not too awful for you all. You must write and tell me how you are getting on.

Yours sincerely,
Phoebe Prior

France
20th March 1915

Dear Miss Prior,

I am so sorry to hear about your present unhappy situation and I hope you and your father enjoy better relations very soon. It is not for me to comment further on this.

I have heard a little of the 'Votes for Women' campaign, but must admit to not knowing a great deal. However, if an educated young lady like yourself thinks it is a good idea, I am sure it is. I am not sure who Miss Davison is. Is she the lady who threw herself under the King's horse at the Epsom Derby?

You asked me to let you know how I am getting on. Well, the war is not too bad. At the moment we are stationed in ■■■■ France and I am staying in the very nice village of ■■■■.

I have been out in France a while now and am finding army life quite tolerable. The best thing is you make such good friends and you meet people from all walks of life, people you would not ordinarily come across. The food is not bad, and there is plenty of it. Of course, some of the chaps find the life much rougher than they were used to at home but they have obviously not experienced real poverty or the workhouse. Overall, I think I can say it is a fine thing for me.

Just to let you know what happened when we arrived. We were at ■■■■ Camp for a week where we were equipped. There were lots of drills and bayonet practice, which we all found to be a great laugh. The sleeping arrangements were a bit rough. We slept in what looked like a big barn and had a sack of straw as a mattress and a few blankets each, which were very itchy. The barn was about two miles from the camp. We had an early start in order to march down to the camp where we had to parade before the Brass. One of the captains would make sure we did an hour's drill before breakfast. We moved on after a week to ███ on ███. We were so tired after that journey that we went straight to our hut. No-one had thought to provide lights so we stumbled around in the dark trying to find our beds. We were pleased when morning came and we could see. When we got up we heard that we were to be inspected by the Sergeant Major. He is quite a stern sort of fellow with no sense of humour. For breakfast we had sausages. They were rather greasy and we only had forks to eat them with, no knives, so the sausages slipped all over the place. We all laughed, much to the disapproval of the Sergeant Major. If you know anyone who is coming, tell him to bring a knife.

We arrived finally at our destination about midday last Wednesday. Now I live ████████.

We are out in the country. I think this camp is about ███ miles from the firing line. We can hear the noise of the guns and see the star shells at night. They are quite beautiful, just like fireworks.

I have just been told we are to move up to the front tomorrow. So we will see some action at last, and I will have a chance to do my duty.

Yours sincerely,
Edward Green

37 Shakespeare Street
2nd May 1915

Dear Mr Green,

Thank you for your last letter.

I enclose some more socks for you as they are a lot easier to knit than gloves.

I am quite surprised to hear that you are not sure who Emily Davison is. She is indeed the lady who sacrificed herself for the cause of women's suffrage by throwing herself under Anmer, King George's racehorse, at the Epsom Derby on 4th June 1913. It was in all the newspapers and thousands of suffragettes accompanied her coffin, myself and Dr Bryant included. Also tens of thousands of people lined the streets of London to pay their respects, men as well as women.

Miss Davison has been an inspiration because she bravely protested by means of hunger strikes and, although she was force-fed 49 times, she persisted in her protests. She was an educated woman, and attended St Hugh's College, Oxford. Although she obtained first-class honours in her final exams she was not allowed to graduate because she was a woman.

With all this war nonsense going on the women's suffrage movement is suspended for the time being but, mark my words, we will not give in until we have votes for women.

From your last letter I gather that conditions do seem a bit rough. I suppose it is a bit like being in the Boy Scouts. Do you sit around a camp fire? I shall send you some literature on women's suffrage so you have something to read.

Yours sincerely
PP

France
September 1915

Dear Miss Prior,

The Hun is going to be given what for! We are going over the top tomorrow, and I hope to show them what we Tommies are made of. There will be a bit of danger I know, but I am good at ducking and diving. I am absolutely sure that I shall get through it all right, but even if I don't I shall rest content that I have not let my pals down and that I have done my duty – and one can't do more.

May I ask a favour from you? I hope it is not too much trouble but would you be kind enough to send me your photograph? I would so very much like to have something fine to look at instead of the mud and the rats. I must admit that the trenches and the noise have come as a bit of a shock, but hopefully this is only a very temporary situation and we will advance soon.

Thank you for your many letters and friendship. It has meant a great deal to me.

Edward Green

37 Shakespeare Street
10th December 1916

Dear Mr Green,

I have not heard from you for quite some time and I was just wondering if you are alright. I would be most grateful if you could just send me word that everything is indeed alright.

I must admit that I do enjoy writing these letters to you, and I hope you got the pamphlets I sent. It is not often that I can confide in a person about my political views, and my ambitions. Most people just laugh at me. My father has forbidden any talk of women's suffrage.

I will send you a photograph, but I must warn you that physically I am not much to look at. In fact I heard my father say to my mother that he was glad I might go into teaching because my marriage prospects were poor, being so unattractive and outspoken. Maybe he is coming around to my point of view, considering how many young men have been lost and that my path is academic rather than domestic. But, of course, he cannot bring himself to agree with me.

Please send word as soon as you can. I am feeling quite worried about you. There seems to be such a lot of really bad news about the war now.

Yours sincerely,
PP

France
31st December 1916

Dear Miss Prior,

I apologise for my long silence. I did not mean to distress you in any way. I am writing this whilst in my billets, a few miles behind the line. I must admit to feeling rather sad and downhearted at the moment because a couple of my friends bought it at Loos on the first day. So many have been killed or badly wounded around me. Who knows my number might be up next. But this letter is not to complain about my woes it is just that I could not bear parting without my heartfelt thanks for your innumerable kindnesses.

Because I have you to write to I have felt more like the other chaps who get letters and parcels from home. I have not felt alone because knowing there might be a letter from you makes the days bearable. Just knowing that life goes on in a fairly normal way somewhere is of great help.

I must tell you that ████ ████ ████████ ██████ ██████████ ██████████████████ ██████ ██████ ██████████.

Once more, before I close this rather depressing note, I must thank you again for the way you have remembered me. You never know, one day we may meet in person, but if not, I am sure I will see you in heaven, where I shall be able to thank you personally for everything.

Goodbye.

Edward Green

France 29th January 1917

Dear Miss Prior,

I write to inform you that Private Green has been wounded in action. He is soon to be sent home to recover from his wounds. He especially asked me to let you know, as I understand you are a special friend and he has no family. He also asked me to let you know where he will be convalescing and whether it would be convenient for you to visit him when he is sufficiently recovered. I will forward the details when more is known.

His unit went on a raid two days ago and I am told he was wounded when trying to rescue a fellow soldier, a very brave act, and he will be awarded a medal.

Yours sincerely,

Capt. C. P. Blake

37 Shakespeare Street
17th April 1917

Dear Mr Green,

I was so glad to hear that you are recovering, and of course I shall visit you in the convalescent home as soon as it is allowed.

Even although I feel as if I know you, I am quite nervous about meeting you. I hope you are not expecting some very attractive lady. I must warn you I am quite plain in appearance.

I shall bring you some books to read. You may have had enough of the pamphlets I sent you. Let me know what topics are of particular interest to you. I can read them to you if your wounds make it hard for you to hold a book at the moment. I shall also bring you some of the scones I have learnt to make. Although food is more scarce these days, Mother and Father believe we should support our troops as best we can.

Yours truly,
PP

Ealing Convalescent Home
27th April 1917

Dear Miss Prior,

I am writing on behalf of Private Green. He cannot hold a pen at the moment, but I can assure you that his condition will improve with time.

He asked me to let you know that he is interested in books on nature and horticulture.

He sends his regards to your family and thanks them for allowing the correspondence between you two, and also their kind invitation to him to visit when he is more recovered. He also thanks you for your letters and looks forward to meeting you.

Yours sincerely,
Nurse Olive

37 Shakespeare Street
5th August 1918

My dear Edward,

I often go and stand at the place, just a little way off from our front door in Shakespeare Street, where you asked me to marry you as you were taking your leave. I am sitting in my bedroom gazing at that small space now. Every morning my eyes keep wandering to that spot and I see you there. You must have been so shocked after you proposed when I, an unbeliever, took flight and ran down the street into the church without a word to you. You must have thought I had gone mad, and in a way I had. You see I was in such a turmoil of emotion I did not know what to do. I felt overwhelmed and I just ran. My path in life had always been so clear to me and it had not included marriage. I was in such a state anyway as you were leaving to go to war and then, in a few words, you turned my world upside down and I was just so stunned when you told me you loved me.

A few months ago, when you were still in the convalescent home, one of your nurses did tell me that you were sweet on me. I'm afraid at that time I didn't think anything of it, just that she was a silly romantic, and that the real reason you seemed to like me was that I was your only visitor and you were lonely. Also we did seem to understand each other so well and rub along in an easy fashion, but that was more down to you than me. I did enjoy our conversations. You are the most broad-minded person I have ever met, and you have a kind of intuitive intelligence that I lack. Despite your hard life you have a gentle, kind, positive attitude. You seem to know the right thing to say at the right time. You put people at their ease and make them laugh, something I have never been able to do. Even the soldiers who are in a very bad way smile when they see you. My sister describes me as a bluestocking prig with no sense of humour. She might be right. I wish I had some of your positive qualities. You are the only person who does not think my ideas on women's suffrage a silly childish thing, and that I was only a suffragette because I had no marriage prospects.

It was not until after you were wounded last year, and I got to know you in person in the convalescent home and asked you to tea in Shakespeare Street so often, that I realised how much I looked forward to seeing you. In fact, much to my astonishment, my whole family looked forward to your visits. Even my father, who is not the most companionable person, has taken a great liking to you. I have never heard him laugh so much as when he is in your company. I have to tell you that I am more fond of you than any other person I know. Although you made light of it, saying that you hoped your next job would not be pushing up the daisies, I dreaded the fact that you had to go back to your regiment.

I know I am saying 'fond' and you would like to hear 'love', but you see I am so confused. I don't really understand love, and it was never really on the cards for me. This really is a matter of head over heart or heart over head, and I do not know which is the most sensible course of action. I know that we are the very closest of friends and can discuss any topic in a compatible manner. I have never met anyone like you, but I have never thought whether it was love or not. Love and marriage had not figured in my future. I was the daughter who was not expected to get married, and this is how I have always thought of myself. Marriage is such a new idea to me, and my hope of going to college and teaching afterwards would have to be ended. I am not sure if I am ready to forsake this. I am sorry if this sounds selfish but it is the truth, and one thing I must have is the truth. I know you like me, but I never guessed that you love me.

However, having said all that, the other day my sister made a remark which led me to think that you had muddled me up with her. She is much prettier, and acts in a more conventional ladylike manner. I could not get the notion out of my head that by mistake you had asked me to marry you instead of her. This is silly, I know, but then I dreamed that you were trying to explain to me that it was all a misunderstanding and you did mean to ask her rather than me. When I woke up I was miserable and low all day. I felt heartbroken, and I am ashamed to say I was very cold towards my sister.

Edward, how can you be sure you love me? I can imagine how hard life can be without a family and home. I did notice how well you got on with my parents. Are you sure it is not just the lack of family affection that has led you to think you love me? Or could it be that this war has influenced you, and that when you asked me to marry you, you were just moved by your impending departure to that dreadful place?

Think how awful it would be if we made a terrible mistake, what could we do? We are very different you know. Not that I care in the least about class and position in society, but you might find it hard to live with an outspoken woman. I know I drive my father to such fury, but I cannot help myself.

When I went to bed last night I overheard Father tell Mother that the front you are going to is very dangerous, and this might be the last we see of you. I stood stock still, and could hardly breathe. When I heard this it started me thinking. What if you never came back and I never saw you again? There would be no one in my life.

I am so sorry to raise the possibility of you not coming back but it did make me realise that I do love you Edward, at least I think I do. I cannot bear the thought of never seeing you again. How can we know our love is real? Would we love each other if it was not for this war? How much do you love me Edward? Remember only the deepest most sacred love between a man and a woman can be a true marriage.

I should like to get to know you better but we can only do this by letter. When I can be quite sure of my own mind, and yours, I will promise to become your wife. Do not be afraid to tell me if you have changed your mind since we spoke on Shakespeare Street. We can go on being the best of friends, and continue our correspondence as if nothing had happened. I will be the same to you. I do not think I can live without you in my life now.

Goodbye, Edward, and remember I have the deepest affection for you.

Phoebe

France

20th September 1918

My dear Phoebe,

Please believe me that I had thought of nothing else before asking you to marry me. I was and am quite sure of my own feelings. I know it sounds like some romantic nonsense but from the moment I saw you I knew. I have never met anyone like you. The weeks we spent together, when I was at the convalescent home, and visiting your house convinced me that you are the most wonderful person I have ever met. I would never want you to change. You must continue your education, and go to college, and teach if that is what you want. I will wait for you as you are waiting for me. I love your determination and spirit. Why should we let the world tell us how to live? Look at what ████████ ██ ████████ ████████ ██████ Where has that got us in this terrible war?

I know I am not really good enough for you. My family was ruined by bad investments, and, I am ashamed to say, drink, which led us to the workhouse. You are an educated young lady with views of your own, and you are not afraid to express them. I think you are very brave, and I admire that. I have always been the sort of chap who just does what he is told, obeying orders without giving it too much thought, and even going ████ with the others, even when I know the orders are ████ █████, for the other chaps

I know I should not have sprung my proposal on you in such a clumsy way, and I am not surprised you ran, but at least you did not say no. I ought to have waited until this mess was over, and I could have courted you properly. I should have had a clearer impression of your feelings on the matter. And of course I should have asked your father for your hand, and bought you a ring. As it is, I have thrown you into turmoil and given you a shock. I should have been more considerate.

You asked me to be quite sure I was not influenced by my lack of a family, and being on the verge of leaving. I was not. I have admired you ever since I received your first letter. A romantic notion then maybe, that often happens to soldiers, and then dies out on meeting. Mine did not die. If anything it grew stronger. You are more than I expected.

You ask me how much I love you. All I can say is that I just love you with my whole being. You are the world to me, more important than the air I breathe, the ground I stand on and the blood in my veins. I suppose I might have been carried away a little by the fact that if

I had not told you how I felt then, I might never have got another chance. But please do not be swayed by any feelings of pity for me. I would not want our marriage to be based on anything other than the deepest love.

There is just one thing you must know. If I should not come home whole and able bodied, I would not expect to marry you. We would call it off. I would not dream of burdening you, and tying you to the life of an unpaid nurse. I could not bear that. That is why I think it best if I withdraw my proposal. At the moment I have nothing to offer you but the love of a poor man, and besides, I should not have asked you in the middle of the war. The best thing I can do for you is to ask you to forget my proposal for the time being, or at least until after the war when we know how things stand. Would you agree to that?

Love,

Edward

37 Shakespeare Street
9th October 1918

My dearest Edward,

In your last letter when you said we should forget your proposal until after the war it made me confront my feelings. Putting things off is the very last thing I want to do. I would marry you today if you were here. I should have followed my heart and said yes straight away. I think things over far too much. I cannot imagine going back to having no one with your sensibility to talk to. You are such a handsome man, but I don't care if you come back crippled. It would not make any difference to me.

So many people are suffering losses. There is not one married woman in the street who is not wearing black for a husband, son or brother.

Just to let you know there is a big ████████ ██████ ██████ ███ I am intending to ██████ ██████ Trafalgar Square.

Now we all know the real and horrible dangers you face every single minute, and the way you have to live in those trenches, I feel thoroughly ashamed of myself thinking I was hard done by. I was so caught up in women's suffrage that I was blind to how the soldiers on both sides are suffering. A rightful cause can do this to a person, make them blind to what is in front of them. I have never known hunger or cold, danger or dire poverty as you have. I have a warm bed to sleep in every night. You call me brave, but it is you who is more courageous than I could ever be. Can you ever forgive me for being so self centred and thinking my path in life was of the slightest importance compared to your love? You have improved my character beyond measure. I have tried to become a better more considerate person. I will live in a prison of anxiety until you are home.

I see now that there is nothing greater than the love between a man and a woman. It would be an honour to be your wife. Please take the greatest care of yourself but let me stress again that no alteration in your physical appearance would make me love you less. Just come back safe into my arms in any form.

With all my heartfelt love,

Phoebe

France

20th October 1918

My Darling Phoebe,

I now understand why some of the chaps used to call me lucky because I had no one at home who would grieve for me. We all know why the late Lord Kitchener only wanted to recruit unmarried chaps as soldiers. Of course things have changed now but he must have realised, although he was not married himself, that many a man feared death not because they were cowards but because they would leave their beloved wives alone in this brutal world. Now you have agreed to marry me I feel death would cheat me of being the happiest of men. When I see the shells and bullets whistling by and finding their targets, I can only think of the poor families left behind. My life means more to me because of you, so I will take extra care.

Good night my darling. Longing and hoping this madness will end soon and I can kiss you for the first time,

Your Edward

France
2nd November 1918

My Darling Phoebe,

Please, whatever you do, do not show this letter to anyone. In fact it would be better if you burn it after reading it. It must not been see by anyone in authority. It contains things I should not say and you should not hear, but you once told me that you valued the truth so here it is. I am not sending this letter through the usual channels but with a friend who is getting out of here, lucky chap. It will dodge the censors.

As you know my first baptism of fire at Loos was horrific. We all tried to make light of it for the folks at home but the truth is now I am surrounded by chaps who have lost the will to go on and most are mad with what they call shell shock. A huge shell dropped a couple of yards off the parapet last night. The chaps who were closer bought it, God help them, but at least it was quick. The ones who were a little further off got the worst of it. Limbs were flying everywhere. We could hear them screaming all night and there was nothing we could do.

I think you are strong enough to hear this, so I will let you know that we have no more fighting spirit left. The truth is no one has any patriotism any more. We have seen too much slaughter to believe we are anything more than cannon fodder. The Generals don't care if we live or die and are willing to sacrifice us all for a few yards of useless mud. Who cares one jot if Germany or us have this or that bit of mud? It is covered in our blood anyway. Now that's the honest truth. Any man who has been here will tell you the same.

They shoot men at dawn, you know. I heard there was one poor chap this morning. He was not a coward, just a scared child. I can't say more on this. It is too upsetting for me to even think about. His poor family.

My darling, I wanted to protect you from this terrible knowledge but the hope of the men now is that if enough people like you know the real truth about the war they will demonstrate and revolt and force the government to stop this mad slaughter on any terms. So if you can rally your women and march, my darling, do it for all of us and for justice and peace. Surely this is why you were made the way you are? I love you for it.

Just one more thing. The only reason that keeps me here is the thought of you at home in dear old Shakespeare Street. You who love and trust me to do my bit to keep you safe. So I will do my duty, despite what I think, but not for God, King and Country but for love of you. How I wish I could hold you and kiss you just once. I have purpose now because of you. I would be happy to die for you.

Au revoir, my own little one. May you be kept in safe hands till the storm's over.

With all my heart's deepest love,

Your own loving Edward

France
6th November 1918

Dear Miss Prior,

I regret very much to inform you that your fiancé Pte. E. Green, No. 23762 of this Company is missing in action and presumed killed on the night of the 4th instant. Death would have been instantaneous and without any suffering if he was involved.

The Company was taking part in an attack and your fiancé's unit was supporting a gun team, which was advancing against the enemy. Because of their bravery the attack was successful, and all guns reached and established in new positions. Later in the night the enemy shelled our lines and one shell fell on your fiancé's unit, wounding a comrade. I am sorry to tell you that none of the other men could be identified. It was impossible to get their remains away and they lie together in a soldiers' grave where they fell.

The C.O. and I, and all the Company, deeply sympathise with you in your loss.

Your fiancé always did his duty and now has given his life for his country. We all honour him, and I trust you will feel some consolation in remembering this.

His effects will reach you via the base in due course.

In true sympathy,

Capt. C. P. Blake

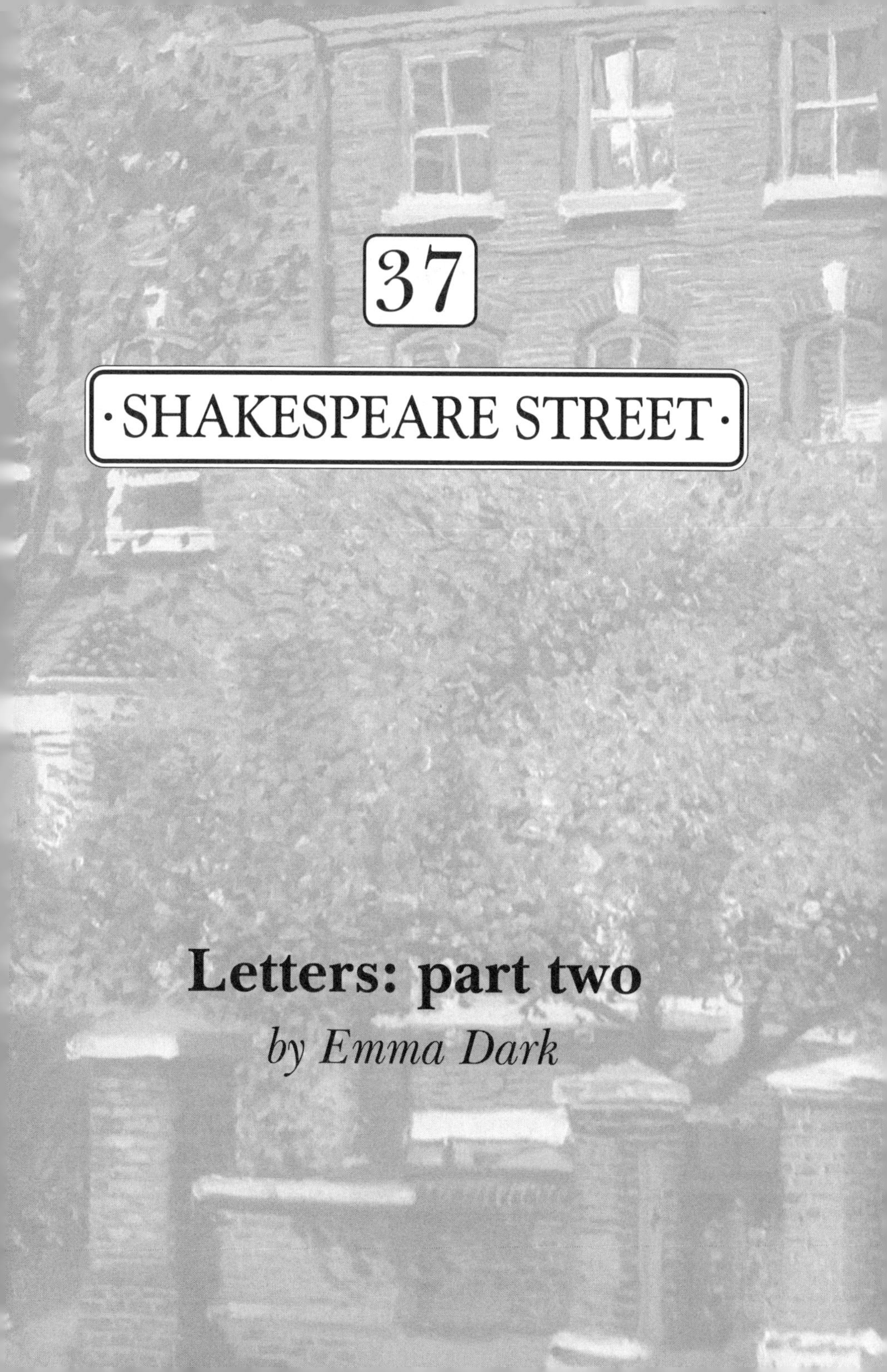

37 · SHAKESPEARE STREET ·

Letters: part two

by Emma Dark

Let me not to the marriage of true minds
Admit impediments. Love is not love
Which alters when it alteration finds,
Or bends with the remover to remove

Sonnet 116.

Part 2

'Dariusz, don't you miss your wife and child?'

'Oh Ted. It's hard for me to talk about.'

'But you've been here, how many months now?'

'Four.'

'That's a long time to be away from your family.'

As Ted shuffled off he said, over his shoulder, 'absence makes the heart grow fonder.'

'I wish it did Ted, but I'm not sure. For me yes, but I'm not sure about my wife.'

Dariusz's phone buzzed with a text from his wife, Karolina.

Can you get home for Christmas? K
Don't know yet, will let you know as soon Bartek lets me know. D
Tomasz will miss you. K
I am doing everything I can. Send him my love. D
But no love for me? K
Of course there is. D x

Ted watched as Dariusz responded to the text.

'That's amazing,' he said. 'In my day we had nothing like that, just letters, and if you phoned overseas you had to shout. But I won't hold you up. I don't want to get you into trouble with Bartek again.'

With a big yawn Ted headed off into his living room, and lowered himself gingerly into the old arm chair in front of his brand new fifty-inch television. His last television had lasted over twenty years but eventually they no longer made the parts to fix it. *This new telly is great,* he thought. *I can actually see everything clearly.*

'Dariusz, can you just show me how this telly remote thing works again?'

Dariusz had been waiting for this summons, and smiled.

'Coming, Ted. See this symbol here? This is the *On* button.'

'Why the hell don't they just put *On* on the *On* button like they used to?'

'I think it is because not everyone speaks English, so it's a universal symbol.'

'Well you speak English very well, better than some of us natives. What other languages do you speak?'

'My native Polish of course, Russian, German and English. A little French and Italian too, but not so well.'

'Golly! You are a clever chap, too clever to be a decorator. What else can you do?'

'Not much, but I suppose maths was my favourite subject at school. I wanted to do something using it, but it never happened. I just got a job doing bookkeeping.'

'Look on the bright side. See how fit you're getting doing all this manual work? You don't need to go to the gym now, do you? Look at those muscles! No-one would kick sand in *your* face.'

Dariusz did not really understand the reference to sand and kicking, but decided not to ask. After he had once again shown Ted how the arrow buttons worked, he went back to scraping layers of paper off the walls in the hall. On top were the panels, stripes and flowers of the 1990s, then the orange and brown swirls of the of 1970s and eventually a William Morris, which might have been the original. *This is a lovely old house* Dariusz thought. *It managed to escape most of the modernisation of 1960s and 70s.*

'Dariusz, quick! *Homes Under the Hammer* is on again. Do you want to watch it with me to get some more ideas?'

'I think we have seen that one Ted. It's a repeat.'

'Oh really? I don't remember. Never mind, they make all the houses look the same. You know, beige with nothing in them. What's it called? Minimalist? I'll just rest my eyes for a few minutes then, Dariusz. Don't work too hard now lad, and have a cup of tea when you want.'

'Thanks, Ted.'

Dariusz hardly needed a break. Ted had forgotten that they had just had tea.

At first the unaccustomed physical work of labouring and decorating had been hard but, over the months, his body had strengthened and now he found the work soothing. He liked to be exhausted at night so that his mind stopped his endless questioning about whether he had done the right thing. *Maybe Karolina was right?* he thought. *She said I think about things too much. I am too slow at making decisions and I let opportunities pass me by. That's why I have ended up doing this, and for Bartek of all people.*

He thought how decisions troubled him in a way that his academic studies never had. Real life was messy, weighing one course of action against another. Changing his mind and changing it again until he came to an impasse was exhausting. He had loved school. Mathematical problems had a right or wrong answer – there was no middle ground. Such an easy, ordered way of thinking. Music, maths and languages came easy to him. Karolina had said it was his strength and his weakness. She often said that she had to be the practical one, that he lived in his head. It was true that he would spend hours with his books but not one moment talking to her. Did he even love her, she often asked. The fact was that, if Karolina had not made the decision to get married, he would never have summoned up the courage to ask her. He had loved her for years. He just didn't know how to tell her, and now he had left her for four months to come here to make some money. Was it the right thing to do? He felt so alone, and missed Karolina and Tomasz. Ted burst in on his thoughts.

'Dariusz. Shall we have another cup of tea?'

'We just had one Ted.'

'Ah, then it must be coffee time. Go and put the kettle on.'

'OK, Ted.'

'And bring the biscuits!'

Ted stared at Dariusz as he carried in the coffee and biscuits.

'You've got that worried look again Dariusz. What's up?'

'I was just thinking you are right. Four months is a long time to be away from my family, and I was wondering whether I have done the right thing coming here. I sometimes feel as bad as I did on my first day in England, just before I met you.'

'Well get it off your chest, lad, and tell me about it. I'm a good listener, you know.'

'Where shall I start?'

'When you arrived, of course.'

'I was the last to step off the bus at London's Victoria Coach Station. If I could have stayed on that bus and let it take me home again, I would have. I remember thinking *These wheels have touched the ground where I grew up. There might be mud and gravel from home. Maybe I could just touch the wheels?* Silly I know, Ted, but that's the truth.'

Ted listened. He nodded, slowly.

Dariusz continued. 'On the bus I had felt drowsy and cocooned, kind of safe, so when we arrived it felt like a shock. I had not wanted to leave Poland. Poland is so beautiful, full of forests. I dream about the forests a lot. I should not tell you this, but I certainly did not want to work for my brother-in-law Bartek.'

'Don't blame you there, lad. He's got no time to chat. He just wants to move on to the next job, to make more money.'

'You must think I am weak, Ted. I know being homesick is not manly, but I had never travelled much before. The only thing that kept me from getting back on that bus was that I had made a pact with my son to be brave for each other, and I was not going to let him down. Also, I want to make something of myself for Karolina. That's why I do everything, really, to make her happy. I want her to be proud of me.'

'Of course she is proud of you. You left your home to make your fortune didn't you? That's brave. I never left home.'

'Maybe not make a *fortune*, but enough. Anyway once off the bus I just stood with my bag my hand, not really knowing what to do. It felt like it was the worst day of my life. Bartek should have been there, but he wasn't. I texted Karolina immediately. Look I'll show you the text.'

'Oh yes, show me these text things, but I'm not sure if my eyes are up to it so just read them to me.'

Bartek's not here.
He will be there soon. Don't be a worrier. You are stronger and more able than you think.

'See, I told you. Your wife thinks you're strong.'

'I'm not sure about that, Ted. When I couldn't find Bartek I started to panic. It was planned that he was going to meet me off the bus, but where? The plans that seemed easy at home suddenly seemed so vague. You see, at home it is easy. I come from a small village and we have only one bus stop. You just wait there until the person comes, but at Victoria there were so many buses pulling in and out . . . I thought he would not find me. I said to myself *This is impossible, this is stupid. I should not have come. Nothing ever goes right for me.* I started to pace around the bus station. After twenty minutes I got so nervous I could hardly breathe, my chest felt so tight. I texted Karolina again, see here.'

He is still not here.
So call him. Calm down.

'And then this man and woman who had been watching me came over. They were smiling at me and they spoke in Polish. "Do you want work? Somewhere to stay?" they said.'

'So what happened then?' asked Ted.

'Bartek arrived, but I was so embarrassed because he yelled at the couple at the top of his voice. "Get the hell away!", he said.'

'Why did he do that? Weren't they just trying to help?'

'He said not. He said, "They are scum" and he said it right in front of them.'

'Really?'

'Yes. I was so confused. I was speechless. I was very relieved that Bartek had arrived but shocked at the way he had spoken to those people. Then he explained that they were looking for slave labour. "Listen to me," he said. "You have to be so careful, they are not what they seem." Maybe he was right.'

'We don't have slaves here. This is England.'

'Oh Ted, I'm afraid we do. It is well hidden, and takes many different forms. With so much war and poverty in the world, terrible people are taking advantage. They lure people here with the promise of good jobs and then pay them nothing. It is terrible.'

'Well someone should do something about it. They should call the police and report these people.'

'People are trying. Remember we watched that programme last night about human trafficking?'

'I think I nodded off, I thought it was about people stuck in traffic. Anyway what happened to you next?'

'Bartek led me out of the bus station with his arm around me like I was some little child. This really irritated me. I was still embarrassed. He said, "Don't look so worried. I'm here now. Tell me, how is Karolina and little Tomasz ?" He was not really interested. He did not let me speak. He just went on and said, "I have a great job for you, something even you can do. You will soon be sending so much money home that even my sister will stop nagging you. It is a good life here but you must be careful. It's a shame you waited so long to come, and just as they have decided to kick us all out after the Brexit vote last night, but that's you all over isn't it?" I think he guessed he had upset me so he then said, "Come, we will start with a full English breakfast." He was trying to be nice but everything he said made me feel worse.

'I texted Karolina, but I did not tell her about the bad people. Here are the other texts, Ted.'

He's arrived.
I told you!

'You don't say much in these text things do you?'

'No. Texts are usually short. I must get back to work now, Ted.'

'No! Have a longer break. Tell me about Bartek.' Ted lowered his head and looked around before saying, in a whisper, 'Don't tell him, but I'm not that keen on him. You're much more to my liking, not pushy. He is just after a quick buck.'

'I know, Ted, but I must not criticise. I do *try* to like him because in many ways he is a very good man. He gave me a chance here. But I do know what you mean. Now he is successful in England with his own building firm he might seem very proud.'

'*Full of himself,* we would say.'

'OK, full of himself. Also I know when he thinks he is being funny it may sound cruel but he doesn't mean it. He hasn't always been like this. At school he was not treated well. He was seen as the slow one. He was going to work in his father's small building company as a labourer because that was all he could do, but that was where he learnt the skills which led to him to start his business in England. He was one of the first to come over here. I think that was brave.'

'Well, that shouldn't worry you. You're here now.'

'Yes, but you see at school I was thought to be the one who would be successful. People said I was clever and academic and destined to become something, maybe a teacher or university professor. I could even have got a government job. In a small village a steady job is much valued. I had hoped this would impress Karolina and maybe it did, but I have let her down. I am quite useless.'

Dariusz realised he had been talking for some time, and he noticed that Ted's eyes were starting to close and his head was nodding. Dariusz did not mind. Ted was an old man but also a very kind man. After a few minutes, when he knew Ted was asleep, Dariusz gently took the cup from his hand and carefully covered him with a throw.

When he returned to scraping the wall, his thoughts got even darker. He remembered how, when he was still in Poland, Karolina would often talk about how much money her brother was sending home from England and that her sister-in-law was going to move to England to be with her husband who loved and appreciated her so much. Dariusz could only focus on the part about the money, and he felt such a failure.

There had been a silence between Dariusz and Karolina for months. When they had talked, it had been very painful and Karolina threatened to leave Dariusz and take Tomasz to live with her father. *Maybe they would be better without me?* He had often repeated the worst of their conversations over and over in his head. 'You would not notice if I left. Maybe you never loved me. If I did leave you, could just stick your head in those books in peace,' she had said, more than once.

In desperation, Dariusz had decided he must do *something*. Karolina must be disappointed that his bright career had not materialized. That must be why she seemed so unhappy. If he could work hard and give her a better life, maybe she would realise how much he loved her. He had made the decision to come to England and work for Bartek but he did not mention it to Karolina until after he had bought the ticket. When he did tell her he was stunned by her reaction. She fell silent, and then said, 'You just don't understand, do you?' She left the room and they had not really spoken since. Had he missed the point?

To cheer himself up he thought about when he first met Ted, in June. Dariusz had to smile. He remembered everything about that day. Bartek had taken him to Ted's house. They were installing a downstairs bathroom in what used to be a utility room. The job involved fitting various aids to help Ted, who lived alone, get around. Dariusz was to help with the redecoration and general labouring.

Bartek had carefully explained that, in England, he was called Barry rather than Bartek. 'The English always like to change your name to something they can pronounce,' he had said. 'So we will call you Darren.' But Ted had ruined that plan almost as soon as they met.

Ted greeted Dariusz with a big smile.

'My name is Ted. I was telling Barry that I have lived here all my life. This was my grandparents' house. They bought it in 1899 when there was still a bit of countryside around the place, and they loved Shakespeare Street. It has seen its fair share of ups and downs over the years, mind you. Parts of the street are still a bit shabby but I think the area is on the up again, so I must improve my house too. I never want to leave. Having a downstairs bathroom and making the dining room into my bedroom will keep social services off my back for a while. There is plenty of room to eat in the kitchen . . . What's your name, and have you had any breakfast?'

Bartek had been starting to fidget.

'Dariusz, my name is Dariusz but you can call me Darren if you wish.'

'No, Dariusz is fine. Polish is it? I knew a chap called Dariusz in the war. The second one, that is. He was a Polish airman, came to help out in 1940. He stayed with us for a while in this house. Great chap, but didn't last long I'm afraid. Very few of them did. There's a very smart dapper fellow up the road I know was a pilot, but he doesn't talk about the war. He keeps himself to himself.'

'Were you in the war?'

'Yes. Just caught the end of it. RAF, but not a flyer. I was lucky. I was a parachute instructor. I taught the chaps how to jump out of them not fly them. Do you want a cup of tea?'

Bartek interrupted, saying 'We have to get on now. No time for tea.'

Dariusz had to smile again as he remembered that, over the weeks Ted had insisted on making Dariusz and Bartek a cup of tea when they arrived. It took him ages and, although he didn't appear to notice that Bartek got irritated, he always gave Dariusz a conspiratorial wink.

'Dariusz, don't encourage him or we will never get out of here,' Bartek had mumbled.

'He is lonely, and I don't mind,' Dariusz had replied.

* * *

By August, when the conversion job was coming to an end, Ted decided he needed the whole of the downstairs redecorated and asked Dariusz to do it. Dariusz half-suspected Ted just wanted the company and he was worried that Bartek would not allow it, but Bartek was appeased when Ted did not argue over the price.

Bartek was not needed for the decoration so he was happy to let Dariusz do the work on his own. To start with he would drop in from time to time to check on progress and to give advice, but those visits became less and less frequent. The fact was that both Bartek and Dariusz were relieved not to spend so much time together. When Ted suggested that Dariusz should move out of Bartek's house and move in with him to save time on commuting, Dariusz and Bartek readily agreed.

When Dariusz moved in, Ted insisted he take the huge master bedroom on the first floor. Entering the room was like taking a step back in time, with heavy dark wooden furniture, an original wash stand with jug and bowl, a feather mattress which swallowed him every night and, best of all, a real fireplace that worked. Ted had made himself very snug in his dining-room-now-bedroom, installing one of those motorised beds which sat its occupant up at the touch of a button. At night Dariusz could hear the motor whirring as Ted played with it, going up and down, and he would smile to himself.

Ted and Dariusz fell into a comfortable routine. They would start their days with breakfast, tea and a chat. Ted loved to talk about his past. 'I remember the past better than whatever it was that I did an hour ago,' he would say.

One morning he told Dariusz how his grandparents made the upstairs attic rooms into a small apartment for his mother and father after the First World War.

'My father was Private Edward Green. He won quite a few medals in the Great War. This was my mother's parents' house. Prior, they were called. It was quite usual in those days for generations to live together. Not many people could afford houses, a bit like today,' he said.

'Did they all get along?' asked Dariusz.

'Oh yes, my grandparents were so delighted that my mother actually found herself a husband after the Great War that they welcomed him with open arms. In fact, I think they liked my father better than my mother in the end. He would often intervene, acting as the peacemaker between my mother and my grandfather. He would get them both to laugh at themselves. I think he was why my grandparents converted the rooms upstairs for them. Mind you, before the war my mother's parents were very middle class, snobby sort of people but after the war, with so few men around, they would probably have let my mother marry a dustman. My aunt, Mum's sister, the pretty one, never did find a husband. She became a secretary and went off to America. Maybe she had better luck there, but we lost touch.

After breakfast Dariusz would work for two hours, then Ted would call for coffee and biscuits. After a bit more work, Dariusz would often go to the local supermarket to get sandwiches for lunch. And at the end of the day they would take it in turn to cook. Ted got quite fond of Polish food. After dinner they would play an ongoing game of chess, which was often interrupted by a text from Karolina.

What about Christmas?
I don't know yet.
So you are just going to leave us here waiting?
No. I will let you know soon.
Thanks very much!

Dariusz was brought back to the present with a jolt when Ted shouted from the living room, 'Dariusz shall we have a spot of lunch? My turn to make it. I'll make egg sandwiches. Would you mind just putting the eggs on and buttering a bit of bread. Oh, and then could you pop to the shop and get some salad cream. I will have it all ready when you get back.'

'Yes, will do Ted. Anything else you need?'

'Yes. Let's have sausage and mash for dinner, so can you pick up some sausages?'

'Yes, Ted.'

When Dariusz got back from the shop Ted called out, 'Shall we have sardines on toast for lunch?'

'I thought we could have egg sandwiches. Is that alright?'

'Great. Let's have fish and chips for dinner, my treat.'

'Oh, I picked up some sausages at the shop, so is sausage and mash OK for dinner?'

'Even better. You must have read my mind.'

After dinner that night Ted said to Dariusz, 'Every time you text your wife you frown. Why is that?'

'She wants to know what is happening about Christmas. I don't know yet. It will depend on Bartek letting me go.'

'Oh sod Bartek! Tell her to come here. It will be easy, you can move into the attic apartment. You could even do it up for me, that would be a great favour. It would be lovely to have a family here for Christmas again. Stay as long as you like. Even forever, I don't mind. I don't have a family to worry about. Anyway, why do you have to work for Bartek? With your qualifications you could teach here. The country is crying out for maths teachers. And they'll pay you to learn, you know.'

'You're too kind, Ted. Could you really put up with a young child here?'

'Of course I could. This huge old house should be a family home, not just for one old git like me.'

'I don't know. My wife and I are so different, nothing in common. There is an atmosphere. Maybe we should not have married. I can't seem to make her happy. I would love it if she and Tomasz came here, but I don't want to be a nuisance to you.'

'I would love the company. I think lots of people have very happy marriages, even if they have nothing in common.'

'Well, maybe. But not us. She is quick and decisive, and very able, and I am not. She wants reassurance all the time, to be told I love her, and I am no good at that stuff.'

'Have you tried?'

'Tried?'

'Yes, you know like the song. *Try a little tenderness.*' Ted started to sing then stopped and said, 'Try courting her.'

'It might be too late.'

'No, it's never too late. Look at me. I might be approaching my tenth decade but if some gorgeous old lady crossed my path I'd give it a go.'

'Were you ever married?'

Ted hesitated. His eyes misted a little and then he said, 'I got close once, but a bomb dropped by the church in the last war. She died of her wounds. I was at home on leave when it happened. She was on her way to a choir rehearsal, and we were going to meet afterwards.'

'I am so sorry Ted. That must have been terrible for you.'

'It was. I tried to put my head in the gas oven when I found out she had been killed, but my mother pulled me out. She told me she had tried the same thing when she thought my father had been killed in the First World War. He hadn't been of course, and it turned out to be an administrative blunder. There were three chaps called Green in his unit – they were sent out in alphabetical order, you see – and, several weeks after getting the official letter saying he was dead, he turned up on the doorstep. When my mother told me about it . . . Well, that was the only time I saw her cry. I remember she said, "If you kill yourself, you are just helping the Nazis. Live for her and do all the things she would have wanted you to do. Don't let those evil people take another life." So I lived, and I have never regretted it.'

'And you never found anyone else?'

'Well I'd found my girl, my one and only, hadn't I? My dad used to say *When we Greens fall in love, it's forever.* Just because she didn't live, didn't mean my love didn't last. I used to talk to her up at the cemetery when I could get there. Later on I used to take one of those cassette player things and play her favourite music, and carols at Christmas. She was musical, and so talented. No-one else ever measured up, you see.'

Ted paused, then continued. 'But I'm still looking, there's life in the old dog yet. Anyway, it's been years now so I don't dwell on it. I've had a happy life on the whole. But enough about me. Look at you! You are young and more than half way there – you already have a wife and son. You're a lucky man. Don't lose it. You should give it a go, too.'

'I would not know how. I don't even know what she likes. I told you, we are so different.'

'My parents were very different too, but they fell in love.'

'How is that possible?'

'I told you it was during the First World War, but they really got to know each other by letter. They didn't actually spend a lot to time together before he proposed. He was home on leave after being wounded and, just before he took his leave to go back, he popped the question just by the front doorstep here. My mother told me the story. She said the only regret she ever had in her life was that the letters they wrote to each other during the war went missing. She blamed her sister at the time, but we never really knew what happened to them.'

'Did you ever find them?'

'No. She was sure she kept them in a little box and the box is still in her study upstairs, in the attic apartment. Every day she would look in that box just in case they had turned up, and we would tease her about it.'

'Did you help her to look for them?'

'Yes, but not in her study. It is a cold room and it used to give me the creeps, so I never went in there. My mother was the only person who would go in. *Got a ghost,* my dad would say, but Mum didn't believe in any of that hocus pocus. No ghost could have frightened her anyway. She was strong, a headmistress of her own school eventually. She was the main breadwinner in our house, and it wasn't the done thing for a woman to wear the trousers in those days. Most people would have tut-tutted, but my father admired her for it.

'Did he mind?'

'Not in the least. He did not have much education himself so valued it for others. He made sure I went to university after the Second World War. I became a teacher, and taught history. I loved it. I loved being with the kids. I did not want to become a headmaster though, too much confrontation. I think I took after my father more than my mother. He was a very gentle sort. He acted as the caretaker of her school. Although her school was run on progressive lines, the children were always a little afraid of my mother but they loved my father.'

'Why were they so different?'

'Well, my mother was an educated, intellectual type, all for women's lib, etc. She was one of the first suffragettes and went to a college in Cambridge. If there was a cause, she would join it. I can't tell you how many marches she went on . . . Aldermaston, Anti-Apartheid, Women's Lib, of course, and I think Gay Rights was the last. She knew Bertrand Russell, and we had tea with him once. She could hold her own, even in a discussion with him. She liked to speak in public and rouse a crowd, and she liked a good fight.'

'And your father?'

'He'd had enough fighting in the Great War. He had been badly injured, and was scarred down one side of his body. His face was OK but he rarely took his shirt off. His scars were quite difficult to look at until you got used to them, but that made no difference to my mother. She loved and cared for him. My father adored my mother. Throughout their married life he always treated her like a lady, even though she was a women's libber. Whenever she entered the room he would stand up, and whenever she left the room he would rush to open the door for her. Mum would half-smile. Dad was a real gentleman.'

'So what did your father do?'

'My father liked nothing more than to make things grow. He provided almost all the vegetables and fruit for the school from his allotment. He was quiet. We became vegetarian for a while. He did not want anything killed.'

'So, your mother was strong and your father weak? That sounds like me and Karolina.'

'Not really. My mother did have a gentle side, but we were the only ones who saw it. When my father had bad dreams, she would hold him and read to him. Sometimes I would climb in bed with them and listen. And sometimes we would all fall asleep together in their bed, another thing that was not supposed to be done in my time. My father was not weak, though. He had been a brave soldier, and he was decorated. In fact, he was the only one who could stand up to my mother and let me tell you that took some courage. I know they loved each other very much and I wish I had seen the letters so I could tell you what they told each other. These text things you send are pretty clinical, don't you think? Why don't you try writing a proper letter to Karolina? A proper love letter, like my parents used to.'

'I don't know if I could, Ted.'

'Tell you what, why don't you go and get my mother's box from the attic apartment. *Let's look inside,* as my mother would say, *just in case*.'

Dariusz went to the attic. He was expecting a small dingy

apartment but it was huge, with lots of light from the skylights. *It feels cheerful, and it is not cold in here,* he thought. It contained a kitchen, bathroom and living room and there were three bedrooms. It was mostly empty of furniture and it was all in need of a good clean and a lick of paint, but there was nothing really wrong with it. *One of the bedrooms must be her study,* he thought. He tried each door in turn then came across a bedroom with a desk and some bookshelves. It seemed a bit colder than the other rooms and a wooden box stood on the desk, as Ted had explained. Dariusz carried it down stairs.

'Open the box or take the money,' said Ted with a smile. Dariusz looked confused, and Ted tried to explain. 'It was television game show I used to watch with my dad, way before your time. Dad would shout "Take the money!" and I would shout "Open the box!" Mum would shake her head but we loved it. *Take Your Pick,* it was called.' Seeing Dariusz's continuing bewilderment, Ted gave up trying. 'Never mind, let's see what's inside *this* box.'

Ted started to undo the latch, but the hinges were stiff and Ted's fingers were not very strong. It took him some time to get the box open and, when the lid finally – and suddenly – gave way, dust flew everywhere and started him coughing. 'Well I never,' he wheezed. 'I don't believe it. Look at this! How did they get here? Mum looked for these for years. I'm almost speechless. How can they just appear after all these years?'

Dariusz looked in the box and there, tied in a classic pink ribbon, lay a pile of letters which were obviously years old. 'Do you think those are the letters?'

'Must be. Mum told me they were in a pink ribbon and, if I ever found them, I should take them to her immediately. It's too late to take them to her, so there is only one way to find out. Open one.'

Dariusz looked doubtful. He could not decide whether they should read them. It seemed such an intrusion. 'Maybe she wanted to keep them private. Maybe they weren't missing but she just didn't want anyone to see them. Do you think we really should read them?'

'Of course we should. She often talked about them. She wanted to show me. Dariusz, I think this must be a sign that you are meant to read them. Otherwise why would they materialise after all these years? Go on read them to me, my eyes aren't up to it. You might learn a few things about love letters. And then, my lad, you are going to sit right here and write the first proper love letter of your life.'

* * *

37 Shakespeare Street
11th November 2016

My darling Karolina,

I have never written to you before. I have never even really spoken of my feelings for you in a proper manner. I just assumed you knew how I felt, which was very wrong of me. I know this letter will come as a big surprise to you.

You know I am no good at showing my feelings, but please believe me when I say it is not because I do not have the deepest love for you. It is because when I look at you I become tongue tied. I am that nervous school boy again who is afraid he will say the stupid thing, and ruin everything. I have done that so often in the past.

Karolina, you are the most important person in my life. You are more to me than the air I breathe and the blood in my veins. I miss you so much. I have your photo with me all the time, the one where your hair is blowing off your face. You look like a goddess. I see your beautiful smile in the photo and I want to touch you, stroke you hair, breathe in your perfume, hold you, and kiss you.

I was stunned, and the happiest of men, when you let me know I could ask you to marry me. You are the most beautiful woman in the world, full of laughter and fun, and I adore you. I love your zest for life, your ability to make decisions and organise our life together with Tomasz. You do it so well, so naturally, and I have taken too much of a back seat and left you to get on with it. I see that now, and I am so sorry. I must have driven you mad with my dithering. I hated leaving Poland. I did not explain things well. I hated leaving because I was leaving you and Tomasz, leaving my beloved wife and life with you. I love you so much, you give my life purpose and meaning. I am nothing without you.

I have to tell you I am now living with a wonderful old man called Ted. He has asked me to invite you and Tomasz to his home for Christmas. He said you can stay as long as you like and he has even hinted that he would like us to make our home with him, but we will see. He is helping me apply for teaching jobs here. He has quite a few contacts, having been a teacher once himself. I am already giving private maths lessons, and you would not believe the pay! There is a private school near here, and they are interested in me teaching maths. The pay is very good, and Tomasz could go there.

You have given me so much. You have given me Tomasz, and I have let you down in so many ways. I have not been a brave soldier for you in life. I have not shown you every day that I am not really alive without you. I shall tell you every day from now on what you mean to me. Please give me a second chance to be a better husband, the one you deserve. I have not achieved the things in life I hoped to. I have not given you the home and security you need. But here in England, in this Shakespeare Street, I hope to put this right.

Loving you so much,

Dariusz

* * *

'What are you grinning at Dariusz? Is that a letter the postman just gave you?'

'Yes Ted, and we have two special guests arriving for Christmas.'

'I'll put the kettle on.'

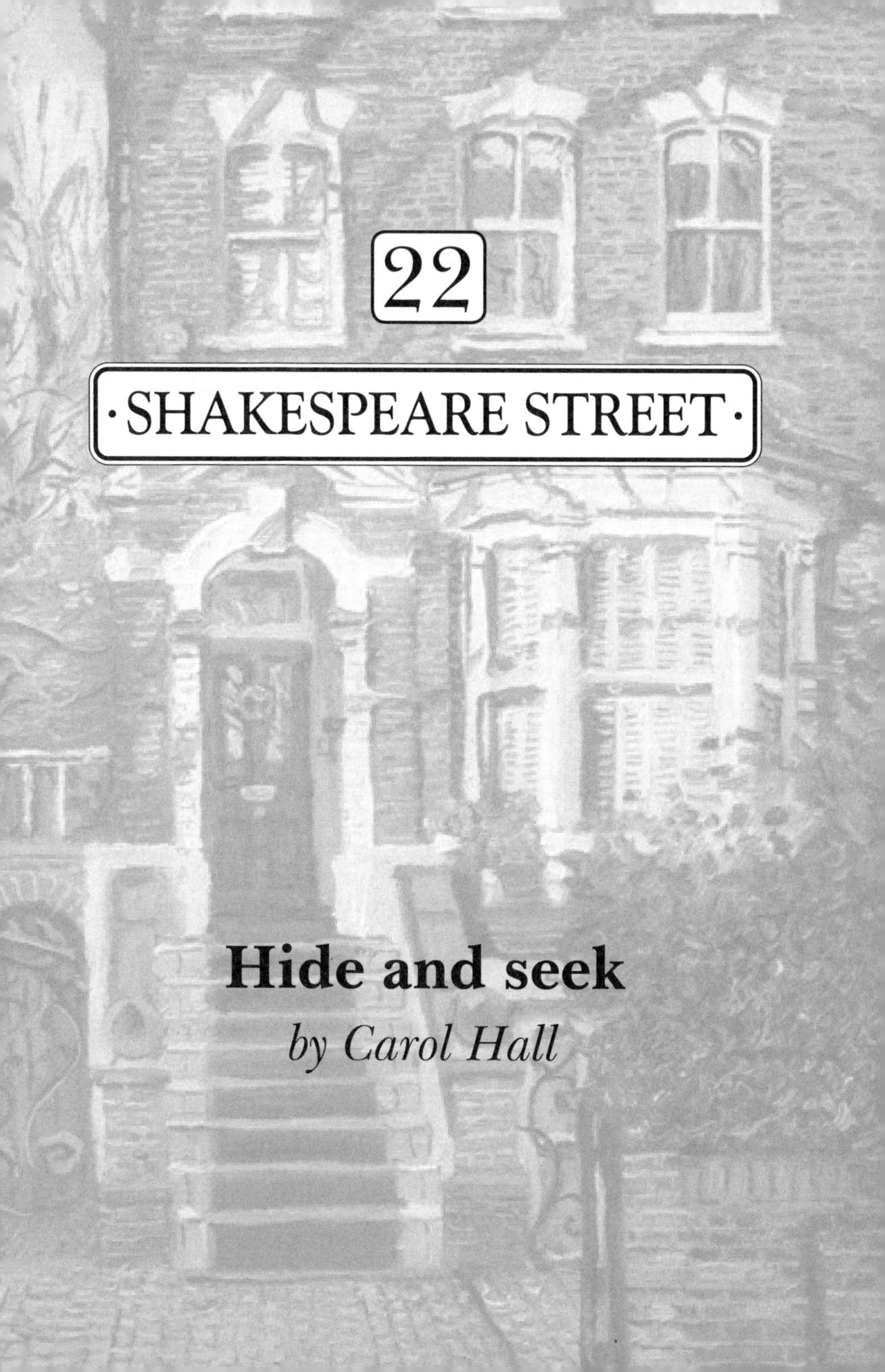

22

·SHAKESPEARE STREET·

Hide and seek

by Carol Hall

I pray you, do not fall in love with me,
For I am falser than vows made in wine

As You Like It, Act 3, Scene 5

Roger forced a smile as the flash bulbs went off, temporarily blinding him.

'Just one more please, Mr Wells,' the reporter yelled, 'and then we're finished.'

As his workmates queued to slap him on the back or shake his hand, all Roger wanted to do was to slip quietly away. He was tired. His night shift had ended two hours ago but his boss had insisted on calling in the local papers to report on the night's heroic events.

Roger didn't feel like a hero. All he'd done was to foil a burglary. *Isn't that what security guards are paid to do?* he thought.

'But Roger,' his boss had pleaded when Roger begged him not to make a fuss. 'You didn't just prevent a burglary. You actually caught the villain and handed him over to the police. Stopped us losing thousands of pounds worth of computers. And anyway, it's good publicity for Fox's Engineering. Getting our name in the papers can only ever be good for business.'

In the end, Roger had relented. It was only the local press after all. Hardly anyone would read the story and, in any case, he was fairly new to these parts and no-one would recognise him. He considered not even telling his wife although he would have to find some excuse for leaving work late, so he relented and gave her a quick call.

'My hero!' she cried, flinging her arms around his neck when he finally arrived home. 'I've told all the neighbours about you. Margaret next door was positively green with envy when I told her you'd be appearing in *The Herald*. You'll be the toast of Shakespeare Street when the paper comes out on Friday! I'm thinking we should have a party to celebrate.'

'It was nothing, Liz,' said Roger, wearily. 'Don't make a fuss. He was only a kid, not much older than James.'

It was the first time Roger had mentioned James, his son, since he and Liz had married nearly two years ago. Roger had fallen quickly for Liz. He was lonely. After his first marriage fell apart three years ago he had moved thirty miles from rural Hertfordshire to start a new life, leaving the fourteen-year-old James with his mother, Natalie. He had chosen London because he thought the sprawl of the city would allow him to blend into the background, to disappear.

He had met Natalie, when he was twenty-five. She was his first serious girlfriend. He had initially been attracted to her because she was so different to him. She was loud and forthright, feisty and afraid of no-one. He was quiet, conventional and avoided confrontation like the plague. He liked a quiet life and was happy to let Natalie do all the fighting.

He didn't have much success with girls in his teens. He was too gawky and painfully shy. But Natalie had liked the way he was, finding him different to the other boys; quieter and more sensitive. Some of her friends thought he was boring but at least he didn't get drunk and treat her badly, as some of their boyfriends did.

They had married two years later and Natalie moved into the tiny cottage that he had been renting.

Their marriage had started off well and they were both overjoyed when their son was born just after their first wedding anniversary. Natalie gave up her job at the local garden centre to look after him and Roger took on extra shifts at the distribution warehouse where he worked as a foreman to help provide for them all.

They had both wanted more children but, try as they might, it just never happened. Roger resigned himself to the possibility that there would never be a brother or sister for James, but Natalie started to feel resentful. Roger could still remember the day she had looked at him after yet another month had passed without a pregnancy, her eyes full of blame.

'This isn't working,' she had said with resignation. She meant getting pregnant, but he wondered from the look on her face if she was really referring to something much deeper.

Roger threw himself into his job but the rot had set into his marriage. Natalie began to pick fault with him, first in private and then in public.

'Roger's useless at DIY, aren't you, Roger?' she would quip, not even waiting for him to answer before she moved on to another insult. She would do it in front of their friends, making everyone squirm. She would even do it in front of James, causing him to blush and slope off into another room, embarrassed for his dad. Roger hated her for doing that. Her strength of character, which he had once loved, was now being used against him.

He had occasionally contemplated leaving her, but he couldn't bear the thought of losing contact with his little boy. So he plodded on, absorbing the knocks and insults from Natalie and trying to be a good father to James.

And then, one day, it had all changed.

It was James's fourteenth birthday and Natalie had decided that they should go out for a celebratory meal at the local pub. She invited two of her girlfriends, whom she had known since they had all stood as young mums outside the school gates, plus their husbands and their teenage children who were mostly James's classmates. Natalie had booked a long table in the centre of the pub's best dining room. The women took up the middle section of the table, gossiping loudly. They were flanked on one side by the kids, communicating in teenage-speak punctuated by guffaws of laughter, and on the other by the men, who were quietly getting to know each other.

'Hey, Roger,' one of the husbands said, putting down his knife and fork and leaning across the table. 'Do you play snooker?'

'Well . . . ' Roger replied, cautiously. 'I used to play as a teenager, but-'

'Great!' interrupted the man, whose name Roger had already forgotten. 'Why don't you join me and my mates for a game on Friday night?' He put his arm around the other man's shoulder. 'We're both hopeless amateurs but we have a great laugh, don't we?'

'We sure do,' he replied. 'Especially after a few drinks.'

'Well, OK then. I'd love to,' said Roger, sitting back in his chair and draining his pint of shandy. The thought of an evening of freedom away from Natalie was appealing.

Later on, the waiter put the bill down on the table.

'I'll get this,' said Roger, snatching up the long slip of paper and reaching into his jacket pocket for his wallet.

It wasn't there.

'Damn!' he said, patting down his trouser pockets. 'I've left my wallet at home. I'll have to nip back to get it.'

Natalie's face flushed a deep red as she pushed back her chair and stood up to vent her fury.

'For goodness' sake, Roger,' she had screamed. 'Can't you be trusted to do anything right? I've organised everything; all you had to do was remember to bring your wallet. You're absolutely useless!'

'Whoa, steady on, Natalie,' said one of the husbands. 'It's not a capital offence. We can sort it out.'

'There wouldn't have to be any *sorting it out* if he wasn't such a total waste of space,' she snapped. 'I gave him one thing to do – one thing – and he's failed spectacularly!'

Roger said nothing. He glared at his wife, willing her to shut up and sit down, but she wasn't looking at him. She wasn't looking at anyone.

The table was silent. The kids all slid out their smartphones and stared intently at them. James looked like he might cry. The men picked imaginary crumbs off the tablecloth while the women shifted uncomfortably in their seats and shot mortified looks at each other. A hush had fallen on the restaurant. Everyone was embarrassed. Everyone except Natalie. She took a long drink from her wine glass then slapped it down onto the table before reaching in to her bag for her own credit card, which she threw like a Frisbee in Roger's direction.

Roger was utterly humiliated. Arguing with Natalie in the restaurant would have been considered very bad form, especially by the women present. And he didn't want to make things even worse for James, who was supposed to be enjoying his birthday party. So he quietly paid the bill, catching James's eye across the table while he waited for the receipt. James had that look which is peculiar to boys of his age who are no longer children but are not yet men either. He still loved and depended on his mother, but he didn't understand her. Why was she so horrible to his dad? And, whilst he didn't want to see his dad shout at his mum, he couldn't bear his dad's emasculation either.

Roger's heart ached for his son.

Most men would have started a blazing row once they were safely inside the car but Roger drove home in silence, ignoring Natalie's continued sniping. When they got home, he went straight to bed. He needed to think. The party had broken up as soon as the bill was paid, the men gently and wordlessly slapping Roger on the back as he left the restaurant with his head down, only raising it briefly to mouth an apology to the now stony-faced landlord.

Next morning he got ready for work and left the house, exactly as usual. He didn't make it to the factory, though. Instead, he drove to the supermarket, parked in a secluded corner and rang his boss to say he was sick. He then waited until the time Natalie usually left for work and drove home again. He let himself into the house and sprinted up the stairs. Lifting a rucksack down from the top of the wardrobe, he quickly but calmly packed some clothes and toiletries. As he left the bedroom he picked up a small framed photograph of his son and, after staring at it for a few seconds, stuffed it in his already bulging bag. After one final hesitation at the foot of the stairs, he walked out of the front door for the last time.

He had thought about leaving a note, but didn't know what to say. Something inside him had snapped and he just wanted to escape, to start again on his own.

He had headed towards London, hoping he would be sucked up into the crowds where he could be himself, become invisible. He had found a cheap B&B, unpacked his few belongings and immediately began to look for work. It was difficult. Everyone wanted to know why he'd left his last job and no-one seemed to believe him when he said he simply wanted to start afresh after a divorce.

And he missed his son. He'd had no qualms about leaving Natalie – she obviously hated him – but he had had sleepless nights about abandoning James at such a difficult age.

After a few weeks in London, Roger finally found a job as a security guard. Although he was over-qualified, he took the job on the basis that it would tide him over until something better came along.

When he got his first month's wages he moved out of the B&B and into a tiny bedsit. The job was easy enough, but it was a solitary existence, pacing the offices and the shop floor of Fox's Engineering through the night.

The job gave him the time and space to think and, as time went by, he found himself increasingly preoccupied with thoughts of James. Had he joined forces with his mother in hating him, or was he pining for his father? Was he showing his unhappiness by rebelling or had he simply withdrawn into himself?

As he trudged up the stairs to bed after a particularly distressing night, Roger decided that he would make contact with his son. In his meal break during the following shift, he sat down and wrote a long letter to James. He tried his best to explain why he'd had to leave and that he still loved him dearly and hoped that he and his mum were doing OK. He pinned a cheque to the letter in an attempt to further salve his conscience, but he didn't include his new address. He couldn't face a confrontation, even with his beloved son.

He posted the letter on his way home from work the next morning. He had hoped that dropping it into the post box would somehow lift the burden of his guilt at abandoning his son but, if anything, it made him feel worse. James would never forgive him, he was sure, especially if Natalie had anything to do with it.

But he couldn't go back, he knew that. His marriage was dead and buried. He detested conflict – always had. Walking away was so much easier than all that fighting and unpleasantness.

After a few months, he started to visit a pub two or three times a week to satisfy his need for human contact. It was here that he met Liz, who was working behind the bar. She was around fifty, a little older and plumper than him, and she had a warm smile and an easy manner. He felt he could relax in her company. Despite initially wanting to be on his own, he felt lonely sleeping in his tiny bedsit during the day and working alone at night.

They began seeing each other and quickly realised that they were good together. Liz was a strong, confident woman who enjoyed the simple things in life, like spending an evening reading or listening to music. Roger loved the fact that she was content to just be with him and didn't demand to be taken out to fancy restaurants and theatres all the time, like Natalie had.

Liz didn't ask too many questions about his first marriage, which suited him. He told her that he and Natalie had grown apart and had eventually decided to call it a day. Liz had escaped a poor marriage herself and wanted to put the past behind her. She had no kids to worry about and she was eager for a fresh start. Roger loved her easy-going nature and her laid-back attitude to life. She loved Roger and cared for him and he felt happy and secure.

Liz owned a house about half a mile away in Shakespeare Street, which meant he could finally move out of the bedsit. The house was large and untidy and full of books and arty knick-knacks that Liz had collected over the years. He felt happy when he was in the house with Liz and put all thoughts of Natalie out of his mind.

Some months later, as they were sitting on her sofa one evening and nearing the end of a bottle of wine, she turned to him and said, simply, 'Shall we get married?' Roger's heart skipped a beat. He hadn't expected this.

'Married?' he said, taking a gulp from his wine glass to give himself time to think. 'What's brought this on? I thought we were happy the way things are?'

'We are happy, Roger,' she answered. 'That's why I think we should get married, make it official. We're both free agents, so why not?'

Roger swallowed the last of his wine and picked up the almost-empty bottle, shaking the dregs into his glass. He shuffled to the edge of the sofa and clasped his hands. Looking at the floor, he said, 'I love you, Liz, and I want to be with you always. I really do.' He turned to look at her. 'But I don't see why it's so important that we get married. I love the way things are now. Let's not spoil it.'

'Roger,' she said, gently unclasping his hands and taking them in hers. 'It's important to me because I want to do the right thing.

My last marriage was a sham – there was very little love or respect – and I was glad when it was over. I made a mess of it. With you, I have a chance to get it right, to make a go of it.'

'But we can still do that without getting married,' he reasoned.

'No, we can't,' she said, looking deep into his eyes. 'If we're going to make a commitment to each other, we have to go all the way. And that means marriage.'

She leaned forward and kissed him tenderly on the lips.

'I'm not going to argue with you, my darling,' he said after a pause. He let go of her hands and slapped his thighs. 'Let's get married!'

Roger watched Liz leap from the sofa and dance into the kitchen, emerging seconds later with a second bottle of wine to celebrate. He temporarily put his misgivings aside in the presence of such joy. He loved this woman.

A few weeks later, as they sat at the kitchen table one evening making their wedding plans, Liz had suggested that they invite James to the wedding. Roger wouldn't hear of it.

'He blames me for the break-up with his mum,' he told Liz. 'There's no way he would want to see me marrying someone else.'

'Just ask him,' she had implored. 'He can say no if he wants to. How old is he now? He's seventeen, isn't he? He's old enough to make his own decisions, Roger.'

'No!' he shouted, banging the table with such force that Liz had jumped. 'I don't care how old he is, I'm not asking him and that's that!'

'OK, OK!' said Liz, startled at his outburst. 'I just don't want you to do something you might regret.'

In fact Roger *didn't* know what his son felt about his leaving his marriage. He had written another letter to James soon after the first, but had again omitted his own address. He didn't want to face the music even with his own dear son. He had since resolved not to write any more letters because doing so reminded him what a weak, spineless excuse for a man he really was. The subject wasn't mentioned again and Roger and Liz married quietly and happily in the presence of Liz's parents and her sister and brother-in-law. Afterwards, they celebrated with a meal at a local hotel.

They led a quiet life. Liz continued working shifts at the pub and Roger worked long hours in his security job, never realising his dream to move to something more suited to his experience. He had at least achieved his aim to blend into the background, though, and he was happy with that.

And now, almost two years later, he was suddenly a local hero.

The story appeared in the local rag a few days later. Liz bought several copies so that she could send cuttings of the story to her friends and family. But Roger was nervous.

'I wish you wouldn't do that, Liz,' he said.

'What's the problem?' Liz kept asking him.

'You know I don't like fuss,' was his constant reply.

It was true. He could never understand why anyone would want to be famous and have their life become public property. He was gentle and sociable but he was only really happy when he was in the back row, out of sight, content to simply listen to the conversation around him.

Happily for Roger his fame was short-lived and, within a week, even his workmates had stopped slapping him on the back. He was glad to be able to fade into the background again.

Then one morning, as he was leaving work after an uneventful night-shift, he saw a lanky youth standing at the entrance to the car park. His hands were stuffed into the pockets of his hoody and he nervously scuffed at the ground with a trainer-clad foot. He reminded Roger of someone, but he couldn't quite place him.

As Roger approached, the youth withdrew his hands from his pockets and started walking towards him. 'Hello, Dad,' he said.

'James? What on earth . . . ?' Roger began to move towards his son, then thought better of it. 'How did you know I worked here?'

'Someone posted the story about the office burglary on Facebook and I recognised you straightaway. Dad, I . . . I've missed you, we both have. Why did you walk out on us like that?'

His voice was trembling and Roger felt a rush of love for his son that threatened to overwhelm him. The last time he had seen him, three years ago, he was a fourteen-year-old boy with a high-pitched voice and an innocent outlook on life. Now he was a man, mature enough to confront his father but still feeling the pain of his betrayal like a child.

'Son, I'm sorry for what I did but I had my reasons. It wasn't about you; it was about your mum and me.' Roger reached across the space between them and touched James's arm. 'I love you, son,' he said, his voice cracking. 'Did you get my letters?'

James nodded silently then stepped forward and flung his arms around his father's neck, clinging to him as the tears started to fall. Roger wrapped his arms around him and held him close until the sobbing subsided.

'I'm sorry, son,' he whispered.

James pulled away and stood up straight, wiping the tears from his eyes with the heels of his hands.

'Dad, I need to talk to you. Can I come and see you?'

Roger's body stiffened. 'James,' he said, backing away, a look of panic in his eyes. 'I can't talk to you, I can't see you, I . . . I'm so sorry.' He turned on his heels.

'But Dad, it's Mum.' He followed his father into the car park. 'She's met someone. She . . . She wants a divorce.'

James's words were lost on Roger as he bolted for his car. He put his foot down and sped away, almost knocking his son down in his desperation to get away. As much as he loved his son and hated himself for what he did to him, he wouldn't let James spoil things for him. Not now. He was happy with Liz and he couldn't ruin that. She didn't deserve it.

Roger stayed awake all day, too tormented to rest. He dragged himself to work that night, exhausted through lack of sleep and worry that his quiet, contented world was about to come crashing down around him.

By the time he arrived home the next morning, it was all he could do to climb the stairs and fall into bed. He slept heavily and woke only when Liz brought him a mug of tea late that afternoon.

'I had a phone call while you were asleep,' she said breezily, perching herself on the edge of the bed and handing him the tea. 'It was James!'

'What?' said Roger, jumping up and spilling scalding tea on his hand.

'Your son,' she repeated. 'He managed to track you down from the newspaper article. I can't believe you never gave him your address, Roger. Anyway, he sounds like a really lovely young man. We didn't talk for long but I've invited him over for dinner this evening, as it's your night off.'

'You've done what?' he said, slamming the mug down on the bedside table.

'Oh, don't make such a fuss, Roger. He's your son. I thought you'd be pleased to see him.'

She got up to go. Roger's heart was beating so violently he thought he might be sick. 'No rush to get up, love,' she said, plumping up his pillows and failing to notice his sudden pallor. 'He's not coming until six.'

Roger's body was rigid with fear, his hands and face covered in a growing slick of cold sweat. He took a gulp of air and tried to marshal his scattered thoughts.

Every atom in his body was preparing him to run. It would be so easy. All he had to do was to put on some clothes, grab a few essentials and walk out of the door. *Simple,* he thought, before addressing his thoughts to himself as if he was a stranger. *You did it before, remember? Walking out on Natalie was easy and you never regretted it, did you? You can do it again, can't you?*

But things were different this time. He loved Liz. It would kill him to leave the life he had built with her. But, if he stayed, he would have to admit that he was a liar and a cheat and she would never forgive him. She would stop loving him and he wouldn't blame her.

And then there was James. He already loathed himself for running away from him for a second time, yesterday. What sort of a father was he? What sort of a man was he? A coward, that's what.

Roger started to cry. He let his tears fall freely onto the pillow for a minute or two. Then, he made his decision.

Before he could change his mind he leapt out of bed and into the shower, washing himself vigorously as if to cleanse himself of his sins. He would go downstairs and confess to Liz. For the first time in his life he would face the consequences of his actions like a man.

Ten minutes later he crept into the kitchen, his head held high but his legs trembling. Liz hadn't heard him come downstairs and he stood and watched her for a moment as she mashed the potatoes for the shepherd's pie, innocently singing to herself.

Roger's mouth was so dry he wondered if he was capable of speech. For a second, he felt the urge to turn and run but, just at that moment, Liz turned around. She was startled to see him standing there.

'Oh!' she cried. 'You made me jump. I didn't hear you come in.'

'I'm sorry,' he croaked. 'I didn't mean to . . . Liz, I need to talk to you.'

'Fire away, love,' she said, smoothing buttery mash over the meat and vegetables. 'I'm all ears. Do you think James will eat this? Teenage boys will eat anything, I suppose.'

'Liz . . . '

'I've bought a sticky toffee pudding for afters. I hope he . . . '

'Liz! Sit down, please. I need to talk to you.'

'This sounds serious,' she said, sliding on to a chair opposite Roger. 'What is it?'

'It's James. I'm worried about how he'll take the news.'

'What news?'

'The news that we're married. He won't be expecting it.'

'Oh, Roger. Stop fretting. I'm not exactly a wicked stepmother, am I? He'll get used to me. Actually, I'm quite looking forward to getting to know him.'

'Liz,' said Roger, staring right into her eyes, his voice fading, 'the reason James isn't expecting us to be married is because . . . '

'What, Roger?'

'It's because . . . I'm still married to his mother.'

Liz paused, bringing her hands up to her temples.

'I don't understand, Roger. How can you still be married to Natalie? You told me you were divorced.'

'Actually, I didn't ever tell you that, Liz. I said that my marriage had broken down.'

'So you've been lying to me all this time?' The colour had drained from her face.

'Do you remember that I didn't want us to get married? I wanted us to stay as we were, but you insisted that we tie the knot.'

'Don't you dare blame me for this,' shouted Liz, finally losing her cool and banging the table with both hands, making the cutlery rattle. 'Don't you bloody dare!'

'I'm not blaming you, Liz, I'm-'

'Well, it sounds like blame to me! Why didn't you just tell me that you weren't divorced?'

'I know, I should have done, I was terrified of losing you, I . . . '

Liz took a sharp intake of breath, as if she had been struck by a sudden pain. She stood up, her hand covering her mouth.

'Roger, this means that we're not legally married, doesn't it?'

'Yes,' he whispered. 'I'm so sorry, you must hate my guts. I'll pack my bags and go.'

'Oh, no you won't!' she screamed. 'You'll bloody well stay here and face the music. You got us into this mess, so you can get us out of it.'

She flopped back down into her chair, her legs suddenly too weak to support her, and put her head in her hands. Roger reached over the table to touch her but she shrugged him off. There was a moment's silence, neither of them knowing what to do next.

'Liz, I'll have to go to the police. I may be sent to prison.'

'I know,' she said, raising her head. 'And you deserve it.'

She started to cry. Roger couldn't bear it.

'I'll put this right,' he said, pleading. 'I'll take my punishment. I'll divorce Natalie and then . . . '

'And then we'll get married,' she said, retrieving a tissue from her sleeve and blowing her nose. 'Properly.'

'Liz, I don't deserve you. I'm a pathetic excuse for a man. I –'

They were both startled by the sound of the front door bell.

'James!' they said, in unison.

They both jumped up from the table. Liz rubbed her hands over her face and through her hair while Roger straightened the cutlery in a symbolic attempt to disguise what had just happened.

'I'll explain everything,' said Roger, heading for the front door. 'Leave it to me. There'll be no more lies.'

James stood awkwardly on the doorstep, his hands clutching a cheap bunch of flowers. Roger's heart swelled.

'Come in, James. It's good to see you.'

'Is it?' said James. 'You ran away from me yesterday.'

'I know, I'm sorry. Come in and sit down and I'll explain everything.'

Liz was waiting in the kitchen, tidying things that didn't need tidying to give her hands something to do.

'James,' she said stretching out her arms to embrace him. 'It's so lovely to meet you at last. Come and sit down. Dinner won't be long.'

They made small talk, Liz getting up occasionally to check the oven or turn down the heat under the vegetables.

Roger shot her a look, willing her to shut up now so that he could begin his confession. She sat back in her chair.

'James,' he started, 'I need to explain . . . '

'Can I use your toilet?' James blurted out, pushing back his chair.

'Of course,' Liz said. 'It's on the left by the front door.'

Roger was holding his breath.

'He'll be OK,' Liz whispered, kindly. 'He's just feeling a bit awkward.'

Roger took a deep breath, preparing himself again for his revelation. Liz gave him a warm smile that he didn't feel he deserved, and they waited for James to return.

James stood in the doorway. He had something in his hands. Roger couldn't work out what it was but Liz knew straightaway and her hand flew to her mouth. It was the framed photograph of the two of them on their wedding day, smiling under a shower of confetti. It hung on the wall opposite the door to the toilet. James would have seen it as soon as he came out.

'Dad,' he said, the picture rattling in his hands. 'What's this? I don't understand.'

He looked like a lost little boy, not a strapping seventeenyear-old. Roger jumped up from his chair and grabbed James in a bear hug so tight that all Liz could think was that the glass in the photo frame, now wedged between them, might break and injure them.

'My boy, my boy,' Roger sobbed, refusing to release him from his arms. They stood there for a moment longer, Roger unashamedly releasing all his pent-up guilt and sorrow and James's face a picture of confusion.

'Sit down, son, please.'

James obeyed and Roger poured out his confession, pausing only to blow his nose or clear his throat. James sat motionless, his face betraying nothing. When his father had finished, he slowly stood up, looked his father in the eye and said, 'I never want to see you again. I'll give Mum your address so that she can start the divorce proceedings but I never want to see you again. Do you understand?'

He turned to go. Roger leapt from his chair so violently that it fell backwards, crashing on to the tiled floor. He grabbed his son's arm.

'No, James. No!' he cried, clinging to his son as he tried to get away. 'Don't be like me. Don't run away from problems. I've done that all my life and it's got me nowhere. All I've done is lie and cheat and hurt people. Please don't be like me, son, I beg you. Nothing good will come of it.'

James paused for a second to consider his options and Roger seized the opportunity to continue his plea.

'You're a man now, son,' he said quietly, relaxing his grip on James's arm. 'Be a proper man, not a gutless idiot like me. Watch how I'm going to change, to put all this right, and *then* make up your mind about me. This woman,' he said, turning to point at Liz. 'This wonderful woman has just had her life turned upside down by me, but *she's* willing to stand by me as long as I put right all my mistakes. All I'm asking is that you do the same for me. Do you think you can do that, son?'

James put the photograph on the table and stood behind the chair, tears running down his cheeks and dripping off his chin.

'Mum deserves an explanation and a proper apology,' he said, gripping the chair back for support. 'She cried for months after you abandoned her, Dad. You have no idea how much grief you caused. The very least she deserves is a meeting with you.'

'Anything, James, I'll do anything to make this right. You've been a good boy, looking after your mum. I'll-'

'Why don't you have something to eat with us?' Liz interrupted, gently. 'Then your father will drive you home and talk to your mum.'

The room fell silent, Roger and Liz willing James to acquiesce.

Eventually, he pulled back his chair and lowered himself into it, his face expressionless.

'I'm doing this for Mum, not you,' he said, staring straight at his father.

Roger smiled at his boy. It was a start.

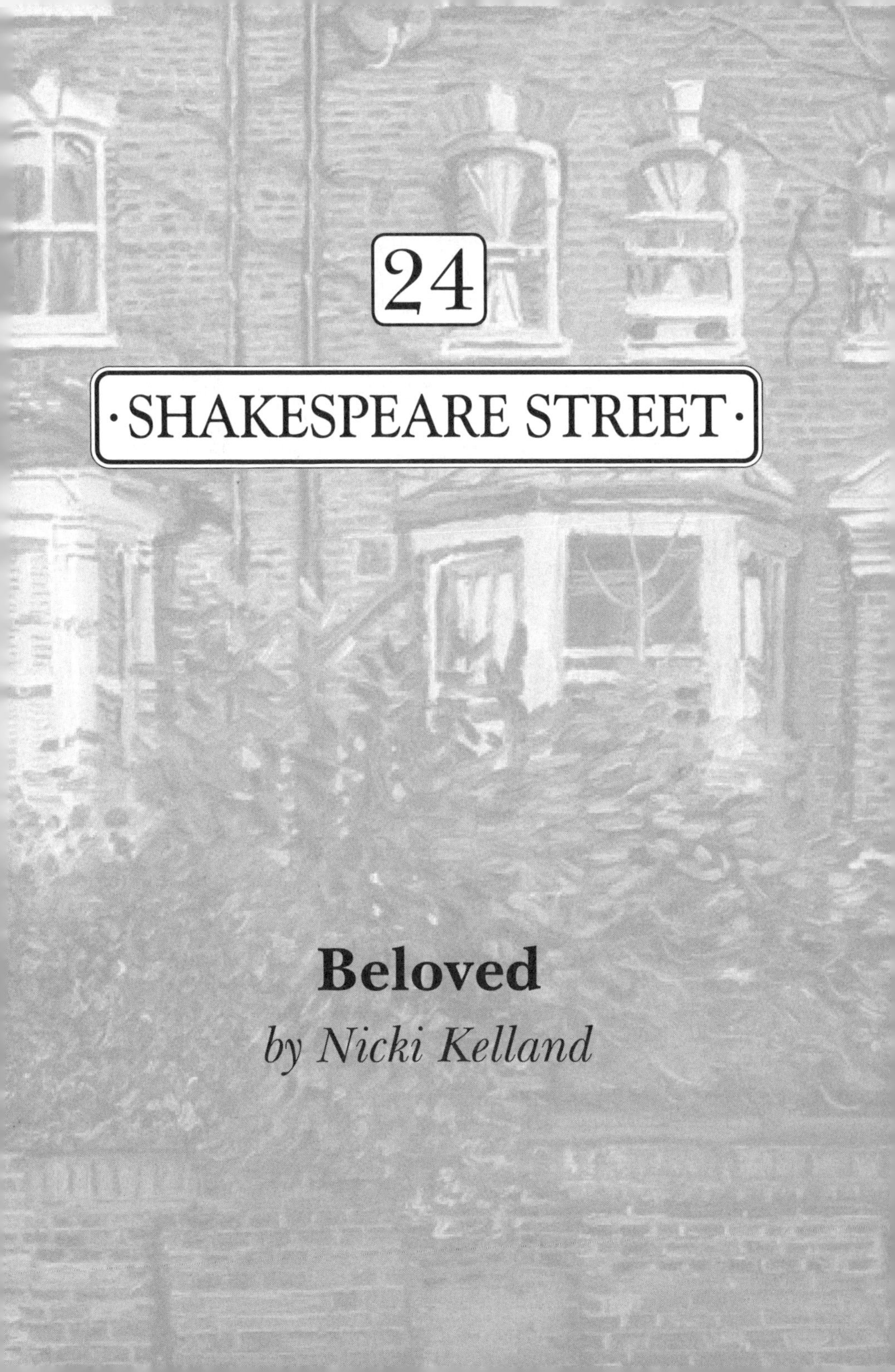

24 · SHAKESPEARE STREET ·

Beloved

by Nicki Kelland

By the pricking of my thumbs
something wicked this way comes.

Macbeth, Act 4, Scene 1

Daily News

20 August 2003
By Alison Bryan

'I knew you were there and I will find you again. You can't hide from me, not again you won't!'

This was the chilling response of the infamous 'Kitchen Killer', Patrick Stanton, as the only surviving member of the family he killed gave evidence against him.

Fourteen-year-old Katie Mayes survived because she was hiding in the pantry of the kitchen in her family's home. Her mother, father and younger brother had been tied to chairs around the kitchen table before being brutally tortured and murdered.

Today the evil murders finally caught up with Stanton and he was sentenced to life without parole.

The 28-year-old unemployed builder had gained access to the family home by agreeing to carry out some alterations to the kitchen. He had presented himself that evening on the pretext of needing to view the property in order to provide a quote for the building work.

Once he had gained entry he subdued the family by grabbing 39-year-old Emma Mayes by the throat and threatening to strangle her if the other members of the family did not do as he said.

He ordered them into the kitchen, where he instructed 42-year-old David Mayes to tie his family to the chairs around the kitchen table. David Mayes was then forced to watch as his wife and six-year-old son endured hours of torture with various building tools and implements before he killed all three of them by cutting their throats.

Forensic evidence and the testimony of two forensic experts showed that Alfie was the first to die.

Katie was in the kitchen, making a sandwich as an after-school snack for herself and Alfie, when she heard screams from the hall. Crouching beneath a shelf in the dark pantry, she witnessed the torture and eventual deaths of her entire family.

Lord Chief Justice Evans commended Katie for her testimony in court, which was given via a video link, commenting that she had remained calm and had given her evidence clearly.

After the jury's verdict today, Detective Chief Inspector Annie West said, *'To kill the family was despicable enough, but to torture them in the way he did shows how wicked wand contemptible that man is.'*

Stanton was branded a man who *'lacks any remorse and empathy'* by Counsel for the Prosecution George White.

Stanton's hollow final words in court must be ringing in his ears as he begins his first night of a life sentence without parole in Her Majesty's Prison Wakefield, the largest high-security prison in the United Kingdom.

Katie

The first few months had been a blur. Her days seemed to consist of brief hours of daylight that provided a short relief from the endless nights of dreams.

The dreams always started out calmly enough.

She was in the pantry gathering the bread and peanut butter to make an after school-snack for herself and Alfie, just like she had so many times before. Katie felt the cool glass of the heavy peanut butter jar in her hand as she struggled to keep a grip on the slippery plastic of the bag that held the sliced loaf.

As she turned towards the open louvre doors, they shut with a sharp crack and she heard the click of the light switch just before her world went dark. It would be Alfie, playing an old trick with his sister.

'Alf . . . ' she started to say, but the words died in her throat as she heard Dad shouting. He was really shouting, with a desperate edge to his voice she had never heard before.

'Please, please just stop! No-one needs to get hurt! Please!'

Then another voice, one Katie didn't recognise. So obviously angry and yet calm and deliberate, laced with menace. 'Where's the girl?'

'She's not here. She went to a friend's house after school. She won't be back tonight,' she heard Dad tell the angry man.

Katie realised she needed to be quiet. If Dad said she wasn't there, she couldn't afford to make a sound. She placed the jar of peanut butter and the loaf on the floor and knelt down beside them. She peered tentatively between the slats in the door and caught sight of the man who would take her family from her.

He was tall and slim with a shaven head, his eyes bright and feverish. He seemed to vibrate with anger, a cruel smile of satisfaction twisted his lips.

Katie could do nothing but watch as he forced her father to tie her mother and brother to the kitchen chairs that were arranged around the table in the centre of the room.

Her eyes were drawn to Dad who was now seated directly opposite her hiding place. She felt him catch her eye and shake his head ever so slightly. His last message to her seemed to be to stay hidden.

She couldn't look away, hypnotised by the wicked looking blade grasped in the man's right hand. As he raised his hand to her mother's face and made his first slice into the flesh she squeezed her eyes shut and held her hands tight over her ears as she tried to hide from the agonising screams.

She stayed that way, on her knees hiding inside the gloom of the pantry, surrounded by the familiar shapes of tins and packets as she tried to drown out their screams as they echoed inside her head.

Suddenly she was awake and staring out of the gloom into the light that lay just beyond the doors, the doors of her wardrobe, where she had hidden herself away from the dream. But it didn't change the fact that she could still hear their screams. It always took her a moment to realise that the screams were coming from her own throat.

Daily News

12 April 2011
By Alison Bryant

Tragedy of the mummified bodies found in a disused factory by Parkour Club

The Tuesday afternoon run began, like any other club meeting, with the usual stretching and warm-up exercises. Little did they know that this particular afternoon would hold a horror they are all unlikely to forget.

The club took a different route on this particular Tuesday having gained permission from the owner to use a disused property in North Acton as a site for their run.

Such sites are extremely popular with Parkour [Freerunning] fans. They provide a variety of challenges both inside and outside their buildings, allowing runners the opportunity to move over, under and along obstructions as they run and jump their route.

Adrian Freeth was the runner who reached the abandoned air-conditioning unit located on the roof before any of his companions. The eerie tableau which met his eyes is a sight that will remain with him for the rest of his life.

'It was so chilling to see them, sitting round a table like they were about to enjoy a family meal.'

The four mummified bodies were sitting round a family sized dining table. Each body was tied to a chair with electrical cable. The position of their limbs and their various wounds suggested they had been tortured before their throats were slit.

Detective Chief Inspector Annie West has been tasked with investigating this appalling crime.

It is anticipated that she will question Patrick Stanton, the notorious 'Kitchen Killer' who is currently serving life without parole for the murder of the Mayes family.

There are a number of similarities between the murder and placement of these new victims and the Mayes family murders.

Detective Chief Inspector West has so far made no comment on her strategy, however these similarities cannot be denied. It is clear that any investigation will take Stanton's crimes into consideration.

The whereabouts of his only surviving victim is currently unknown. Following the traumatic trial and threats from Stanton, Katie Mayes was issued with a new identity by the Home Office. Wherever she is we wish her well and hope the discovery of these new victims does not cause her more pain and suffering.

WHAT IS MUMMIFICATION?

Professor Ronald Ware, Director of the Institute of Medicine at the University of Budapest, explained to the *Daily News* how mummification can occur 'naturally'.

'The most famous examples of mummification are the mummies created by the Egyptians who used it as way of preparing their dead for burial; however, it is possible for mummification to happen naturally providing the environmental conditions are right,' he said. 'In general the dead tissue becomes dehydrated and this causes the cells to shrink, which can be seen in the effect on the skin. The environmental conditions include temperature, level of humidity and the amount of bacteria present in both the environment and the body. The final factor that can lead to mummification is the amount of air flowing around the corpse.

'Once the process of mummification is complete, the process of decomposition stops and a mummified corpse can last almost indefinitely, its hair and nails intact.'

Katie

Her eyes sprang open as she realised she had done it again. For the first time in years she had woken up inside her wardrobe, the screams of her family ringing in her ears once more.

As always, it took her a minute to slow her breathing and wipe away her tears before she attempted to use her unsteady legs to step out into the soft light of her bedroom.

Katie made her way over to her bed and sat down, it was understandable that she was feeling nervous on the eve of her entry back into the world.

She had been given all the support and help anyone in her position could want or need. It had been hard at first, she didn't want to talk about it. The seemingly endless need to go over and over it, first for the police and then in the weekly therapy sessions. No-one seemed to understand that talking about that night meant reliving it repeatedly in her mind.

Then she had met Dr Jones. He was older than the other therapists she had seen so far. He radiated calm, nothing ever seemed to bother him. When she cried hysterically about the unfairness of it all or when she had refused to say anything at all, he had just looked her straight in the eye, and smiled kindly.

He hadn't been like the others, encouraging her to talk about it. He had asked her one simple question, 'What do you want now?'

Katie smiled as she remembered how shocked she had been by the question, she hadn't dare think about anything other than getting through a night without waking up screaming.

Every week she would go along to his clinic and he would ask her the same question. Once she began to think about her answer, she really started to think about what she wanted and that's when she decided she wanted her own life, a life that wasn't defined by what had happened.

She could have let that night colour her whole life, cripple her with the inability to move forward and make something of herself.

Once she knew Stanton had been caught and locked away forever, she knew he could never hurt her again. That was the point when she made her decision and really started to think about the kind of life she wanted. Dr Jones had helped her to see that hiding away from what had happened wouldn't help, instead he helped her to acknowledge that she had suffered a terribly traumatic experience that was now over. It was time for her to decide what she wanted and then work out how she was going to achieve it.

Her main goal had been to finish her education and, tomorrow, she would graduate from Manchester University with a degree in Business Administration. Other people looking at her situation would say that she had achieved a great deal to complete her education.

Yet, despite how hard she worked or how much she tried to move on, that man was always there in the background. It was almost as if she needed him to be there to spur her on, to motivate her to prove that she can cope and lead a normal life.

Tomorrow was her chance to step out into the world and start her life properly, away from the shadow of Patrick Stanton.

Daily News

25 February 2012
By Alison Bryant

Mummified bodies finally identified as investigation continues

The mummified bodies that were found in North Acton in 2008 have finally been identified as John and Karen Holmes and their two children Sarah and Ian.

The condition of the bodies meant that forensic evidence was able to provide a clear picture of their deaths but it has taken until now to confirm their identities.

The family disappeared from their home in North Acton in 1999 and what happened to them has been a mystery until now.

The Holmes family were due to leave for Australia in June 1999 where John Holmes had secured a job as a Project Manager.

Their impending departure delayed any investigation into their disappearance, as it was assumed they had travelled to Australia and begun their new life.

It was only when

they failed to contact friends and family that they were considered to be missing.

A ten-year wait for news of their whereabouts has finally resulted in an answer, albeit the answer no-one – least of all their friends and family – wanted to hear.

'I have always known that something bad had happened. They just wouldn't have left and never contacted us again. We were too close as a family for that.'

James Holmes, John Holmes's brother, has kept a ten-year vigil in his search for answers. He explained that, while this is the worst news anyone could possibly have, at least now he knows their fate and he looks forward to the day when they will rest in peace.

This is currently unlikely as the investigation into the horrific murders continues, with Detective Chief Inspector Annie West at the helm.

Her current line of inquiry must surely include the notorious 'Kitchen Killer', Patrick Stanton, who was convicted of the Mayes family murders which took place in 2002.

It has been suggested that the Holmes family may have been Stanton's first victims, which would make him one of the very few British serial killers alive today.

The police have issued a statement which makes it clear that the investigation is ongoing as more evidence is gathered.

What is known is that Detective Chief Inspector West has visited Wakefield high-security prison on several occasions in recent months.

Although we can only speculate at this stage, it is reasonable to assume that Stanton is a prime suspect in this case.

The similarities between these crimes are striking.

- Both murders targeted families.
- Both sets of victims were tied to dining chairs using electrical cable.
- Both sets of victims were seated around a dining table, as if about to eat a family meal.
- Both sets of victims were tortured before their deaths.
- The victims in both cases died as a result of having their throats slit.

Despite these similarities, the police have not yet been able to find any evidence linking Stanton to the Holmes's murders.

Leading forensic experts told the *Daily News* that the mummification of the Holmes's bodies should provide a wealth of DNA evidence which could then be linked to any possible murder weapon.

The whereabouts of Katie, the only surviving member of the Mayes family, is currently unknown. She is, therefore, unavailable for comment.

Ruby

The leather of the battered brown couch creaked as I sat down and breathed in the cool dark air of the small artist's studio which was optimistically called The Gallery by the sign on the shiny polished door.

The small space was lit by shafts of light that bled through the glass panels set in the high ceiling. As usual, I was alone.

I looked up at the familiar painting, so different from the beautiful landscapes and portraits that lined the walls. I liked to think of it as the artist's self-portrait, but I wasn't really sure who the subject was.

The central figure is a tall, dark-haired man, standing with his back to the artist, staring out of a window. His long hair rests on his broad shoulders, the sleeves of his dingy white shirt rolled up to his elbows to reveal powerful forearms. There are paint stains on his dark trousers that are held up with a pair of red braces. His right fist is curled tightly around the handle of a sharp knife that glints brightly from the canvas. The tension in his hunched shoulders is obvious, the white-knuckled grip of his left hand on the sill as he stares out of the window underlines his frustration or maybe anger.

The view from the window is the same as the view from his room, a view of the rose garden. A carpet of white and red roses that stretches out to meet the velvet lawns beyond.

To his left stands an easel that holds a large canvas with a single slash that splits the canvas in two, a diagonal gash that lets the light from the window shine through.

There is a power about the picture as if the artist had poured his feelings into the paint before putting it on the canvas. All I know is it holds a fascination that draws me to this couch each lunchtime. The peace and quiet of the small room; an oasis away from the busy stressful office where I work as a recruitment consultant. I would stare up at the painting, eating my boring sandwich while ideas about the cause of his frustration and anger skittered through my brain.

Was he angry at his own talent, frustrated that he couldn't replicate the picture in his own mind on to the canvas? Was he angry with the person he was painting? Were they an unfaithful lover? Was the person who commissioned the painting no longer interested in owning it?

'It's a real shame, isn't it?' said the soft, deep voice that interrupted my thoughts.

'I'm sorry, I . . . ' I turned away from the painting and found myself looking into the intelligent brown eyes of a dark-haired man who was sitting next to me. My stomach churned as I realised I had been so focused on the painting that I hadn't heard him approach, let alone sit down.

'It's a shame,' he repeated, 'that we are closing down.'

'Oh yes, I know. That's why I came today, to get one last look at the painting,' I babbled. 'I mean, I just find it fascinating . . .' My voice trailed off.

I felt my cheeks begin to burn as I looked at the man sitting next me on the creaky old couch. His long dark hair touched his shoulders, providing a sleek background for his handsome features and deep, brown eyes.

'I'm Will, by the way,' he said as he offered his hand.

I placed my hand in his and felt his strong fingers curl around mine in a firm grip.

'Ruby,' I finally squeaked, my blush deepening as I realised I had held on to his fingers for slightly longer than was necessary. I hurriedly pulled my hand away as if my fingers were on fire.

'If we had more regular visitors like you, we might not be closing. But there you go – the house has been sold and will be converted into a conference centre by the winter,' Will continued, kindly. It was obvious he was pretending not to notice my bizarre behaviour.

'I come here to eat my lunch and take a break from the office, clear my head, that kind of thing,' I replied.

'I'm glad you have enjoyed it here. I'm just here to oversee the packing and the clear-out before the handover.'

'How sad,' I said before I could stop myself.

'Yes it is... Look, these painting aren't worth anything – if they were they would have been sold off long ago. They will probably all be destroyed or left to mould in a storage unit somewhere. Why don't you take this one? As a gift from the artist's great-great-grandson.'

'I couldn't possibly, it must be worth a fortune!' I protested.

'Not at all! As I said, if it was worth anything it would have been sold a long time ago. Please take it. I like the idea of it going to someone who will appreciate it,' he replied.

It was then that he smiled at me, and I knew I was going to take the painting.

Daily News

20 February 2016
By Alison Bryant

Notorious 'Kitchen Killer' Patrick Stanton is charged with murder in connection with the Holmes family

At a press conference held yesterday, Detective Chief Inspector Annie West announced that Patrick Stanton had been charged in connection with the murder of the Holmes family.

All but one member of the Holmes family was murdered in 1999. The location of their bodies was unknown until they were discovered at a disused factory in North Acton in 2008.

The bodies were completely mummified, which meant they were an excellent source of forensic evidence.

Despite Stanton being the main suspect in an investigation that has taken eight years to complete, he remained uncharged until now.

The breakthrough came when a van, once owned and used by Stanton for his building business, was taken to a breaker's yard. The subsequent break-up of the vehicle yielded a number of tools and implements which were shown to bear traces of the DNA of members of the Holmes family as well as Stanton.

'It has been a long road and, although we may have known in our hearts who was responsible, it has taken a number of years to gather enough evidence to charge Stanton with this awful crime.'

Detective Chief Inspector West issued a short statement in which she praised the dedication of the officers and investigators who have persevered and eventually secured the vital evidence that will allow Stanton to be brought to justice once more.

Stanton denies the charges and our sources tell us he will appear at the Old Bailey in June 2016.

Despite Stanton's denial, there appears to be a wealth of evidence that points to his guilt. We understand that he has declined legal representation and will represent himself in court, a rarely used but legal option within the English legal system.

Whatever happens during Stanton's trial, it is difficult to see how he will be able to defend himself against such strong DNA evidence.

Daily News

12 June 2016
By Alison Bryant

'Kitchen Killer' Patrick Stanton escapes custody

At approximately 3:15pm yesterday, the secure vehicle which was taking Patrick Stanton from Wakefield Prison to stand trial at the Old Bailey was involved in an accident.

A lorry purported to be transporting toxic chemicals hit the secure vehicle side-on, causing it to somersault and land on its roof.

In the minutes immediately following the accident the rear doors were removed with an oxyacetylene torch.

Stanton and his accomplices then escaped the scene of the accident using two waiting motorcycles.

The protocol surrounding the treatment of accidents involving toxic chemicals gave these criminals the precious minutes they needed to get as far from the site of the accident as possible.

Police have issued a description of Stanton, whose appearance has changed dramatically since his last trial.

He is said to be approximately 6ft in height with an athletic build. In direct contrast to his court appearance when his hair was shaved closely to his skull, his dark brown hair is now shoulder length. He has a substantial beard and wears spectacles on occasion.

Police have issued a warning that Stanton is highly dangerous and should not be approached under any circumstances.

A hotline has been set up for members of the public to report sightings.

One school of thought says that Stanton will probably change his appearance and leave the country as soon as possible, heading for a country that does not have an extradition treaty with the UK. However, a search of his cell has revealed evidence of his frustration at having failed to kill the entire Mayes family. It would appear that he has spent the intervening years writing diaries and letters addressed to Katie Mayes, the only survivor, in which he complains of her lucky escape from him providing graphic and detailed descriptions of his intentions towards her if they should meet again. It is thought he could be heading for London.

Detective Chief Inspector Annie West has assured the public that Katie's safety is a priority and called the recapture of Stanton *'an inevitability'*.

Anyone who sees Patrick Stanton or someone who resembles his appearance should contact Crimestoppers in confidence on 0800 555 111.

Ruby

The early evening sun bounced off the white roof of the old-fashioned Land Rover that was parked on my drive as I turned the corner of Shakespeare Street and my little house came into view.

As I parked my tiny Mini behind the huge rusted hulk of the Land Rover, I saw Will leap from behind its steering wheel.

'Hello! I hope you don't mind, but I thought I would deliver the painting this evening. Is that OK?' Will seemed nervous, as if wondering whether I would turn him away.

'Not at all! I was just surprised to see you. I thought you would send it with DHL or someone like that. I didn't expect you to deliver it yourself. Please come in,' I offered. I fiddled with the locks, trying to remember if I had tidied away my breakfast things before rushing off to the office this morning.

'Great. Just let me get the painting and I'll bring it in for you.' Will stepped round to the back of the Land Rover, giving me time to step inside and check that the kitchen was tidy.

I rushed back to the front door to see Will manoeuvring the substantial parcel into the small hallway.

'Where would like me to put it?' he asked.

'Well, just by the door is fine. I'll move it later,' I replied.

'OK but, if you would like me to help you hang it, I have my tools on the car. It's quite a big job for one person. The painting is a lot bigger than it looked hanging in the studio.'

'That would be really helpful, but I don't want to put you to any trouble . . . ' I wavered because, while I would need some help to hang the painting, it seemed like I was taking advantage of Will. Especially as he had delivered it himself.

'Please, it's no trouble. Just tell me where you would like me to hang it for you,' came his reply.

'OK. I think it would be perfect in the dining room that runs along the back of the kitchen. It would be like having a view again, like the studio which looks out on to the rose garden, although my view isn't as grand as yours,' I babbled, realising once more that I sounded ridiculous. I led him through the kitchen and showed him the blank space at the head of the dining table that gave a wide view of my garden.

Will turned to me and smiled. 'I think that's a perfect idea. Just let me get my toolbox.' He turned and I felt my stomach turn over as I watched the man who could have stepped from the painting walk towards my front door.

He was soon delving into the box, pulling out some very professional-looking tools before measuring the wall and working out the exact place he would fix the hooks.

'Can I get you a coffee?' I asked, tentatively.

'That would be great. Black with one sugar, if that's OK?' he asked.

'Sure, no problem.' I retreated to the kitchen to make coffee, asking myself why I had invited him. He was my very first guest here in Shakespeare Street, the first stranger I had ever allowed inside my home.

By the time I had returned with a tray of coffee and a plate of biscuits, Will had hung the picture and had taken a step back to admire his handiwork.

'Do you think it sits square?' he asked, as I balanced the tray in my hands.

'Perfect. Thank you so much. I am so pleased that you have given it to me,' I replied.

Seeing the familiar painting in this unfamiliar environment was a bit disconcerting but it still fascinated me and I could still feel its power. I pulled my eyes away from the picture that held me in its thrall and turned my attention to my unexpected guest, who was busily packing his tools away.

'Please come and sit down and have your coffee,' I said.

'So, what do you do that means you need to clear your head at lunchtime?' He asked after he had settled himself on the sofa that sat in front of the dining table.

'It's very boring really. I'm a recruitment consultant. Nothing very important, but it's busy and pressured. We basically sell people to employers and, unlike products, people have minds of their own and they don't always do what you expect. Makes it interesting sometimes, but the pressure is always there to make the sale. I surprised myself with my honest answer. I normally trotted out the usual line about helping people find jobs but there was something about Will that made me want to tell the truth, however bizarre I seemed to sound.

'That's interesting. I wouldn't have thought about it like that. Did you always want to be a recruitment consultant?' Will asked.

'Not really. I started out in sales and moved into recruitment because I thought it would be a kinder environment somehow but, however you look at it, it's still sales.'

'What would you do if you could do anything you liked?' he asked.

'Like an astronaut or a movie star?' I teased.

'Maybe, if that's what you would like to do. I've always wanted to be a vampire hunter or a Victorian explorer, but you don't get much call for those nowadays.'

'I don't know, you might be surprised. Perhaps you should advertise your services on a job board and see if you get any responses?'

'I might, you never know, but until then I'll stick with the teaching.'

'So you're a teacher, what subject?' I asked.

'Unsurprisingly, I lecture in history and anthropology. You know, the way people lived, their cultures and religions, that kind of thing.' He seemed to want to gloss over what must have been a significant achievement, lecturing at his age. In my head, lecturers where all old men and women who had spent a lifetime locked in libraries reading large dusty old books.

'That sounds fascinating, how did you get into that?' I asked.

'Nothing exciting really. I did my degree and then never ventured outside the academic world. Not very adventurous at all, I am afraid. Hardly the stuff vampire hunters and explorers are made of, but I like it, so there you go.'

'Well you could always make a change. Maybe I could help you with that?' The words popped out of my mouth before I realised how flirty they sounded. I felt my cheeks begin to burn once again as I dropped my eyes to my coffee mug.

When I found the courage to look at Will again, I saw that he was watching me closely with a slight smile to his lips. 'I will bear that in mind,' was all he said.

'Well, I should be going,' he announced as he placed his now-empty coffee mug back on to the tray and stood up.

'Thanks again for the painting it really is a fantastic gift, especially giving it to someone you don't really know,' I blurted out. What was it about him that seemed to turn me into a complete idiot every time I opened my mouth?

'As I said, it's fine. I'm really glad it's with someone who appreciates it,' he replied.

'I'll show you out,' I said, as I led him back through the house to the front door.

He turned back to face me as he stood on the doorstep.

'Do you have a business card, just in case I need to contact you again – you know about the possibility of me becoming a vampire hunter?'

'Of course.' I bent down and dived into the huge handbag I had dropped by the front door on my way in. 'There you go.'

'I'll be in touch,' he said. And with those words walked away to his Land Rover.

The dramatic effect of his exit was somewhat marred by his need to return to ask me to move my car so he could leave. After bumbling around for two or three minutes to find my keys, I finally moved my car and, as he drove away with a cheery wave, I watched him through my rear-view mirror.

Will

I found myself whistling brightly as I drove away from Ruby. Somehow I knew she was watching me. It gave me a sense of satisfaction, that tiny signal that she liked me.

I thought back to the first time that I had seen her, sitting staring at the painting of my great-great-grandfather, the *almost*-famous painter who left his estate to the family on condition that The Gallery was opened to the public for the next one hundred years.

I never understood why; he was technically a good painter, but he had never really made a living at it. His inherited wealth gave him the opportunity to indulge in his art. He had exhibited a number of times, even sold a few paintings, but somehow had never reached the heights of fame of some of his contemporaries like Whistler or Korovin. He was a notoriously difficult man, who felt slighted by his lack of fame and commercial success. I remember thinking how he would have enjoyed seeing someone so fascinated by his painting.

The second time I saw Ruby I recognised her glossy dark hair, falling over the back of the sofa as she tipped back her head to look up. Her whole attention was focused on the painting, her lips parted in a shy smile, her cheeks faintly flushed as she stared upwards. She didn't seem to notice as I sat down on the sofa next to her.

For some reason I felt drawn to her. She was exceptionally pretty but she seemed lonely and I guessed she was a little shy, a guess which proved so obviously correct at the start of our first conversation.

Before I knew what I was doing I had offered the painting to her as a gift. I could say it was because she seemed to like it so much and the painting would otherwise be stored or destroyed, but I knew it was because it gave me the chance to see her again.

Ruby

The sharp rapping of someone knocking on my front door, broke through the fog that seemed to have settled in my head. I looked down at my phone, still gripped in my hand and the text message that had arrived three hours earlier.

Your parcel will be delivered today between
3pm and 5pm. This parcel requires a signature.
Please make sure you are available to sign for it.

The words stared back at me from the screen, telling me what I feared to be true. Something had gone horribly wrong and I was no longer safe. Someone was coming for me. I could only hope it wasn't him.

As soon as I heard the knock on the front door, I knew it was going to be her. Bile rose in my throat and my hands shook as I undid the locks and pulled the door open.

I was right, it was Annie. There could be only one reason for her visit. My mouth dried up and I gasped, trying to get some air in my lungs. Nothing was happening and I couldn't breathe. The edges of vision began to darken and I sank to the floor as the world faded away into darkness.

The weight of the wet flannel on my forehead pulled me back to reality and I heard Annie moving about my kitchen, obviously making a cup of tea.

I took a deep breath and, fighting the wave of nausea that was threatening to overwhelm me, I sat up and looked across at my only friend.

The years had not been kind to Annie, her bright red hair was threaded with grey and her forehead was marred by thick furrows of worry. But her eyes were still the same, bright and shiny, she seemed able to see everything about me in just one appraising look. She had always appeared capable and in control but now she had a weary air and she looked smaller, somehow, as if her tiredness had diminished her frame, worn her away.

One thing was still the same: she was my friend, and I trusted her.

'Hello, Annie,' I said.

'Hello, Katie,' she replied.

Annie had called me by my name, my *real* name. She never did that, and it could only mean one thing.

'So, is he free? Is that what you've come to tell me?' My voice shook as I finally allowed myself to speak my greatest fear aloud.

'I'm so sorry, Katie. He has escaped, but please understand that we will do everything we can to catch him again. Please focus on that.'

'Does he know where I am? Does he know who I am now?' My voice rose as it dawned on me that he was going to become a very real shadow in my life once again.

'Please try to stay calm. I know how difficult this is for you, but you need to know.' Annie's tone was soothing and I knew she meant what she was saying. But that didn't mean I was at any less of a risk.

Annie sat down on the sofa next to me and turned to look me in the eye. 'We have no reason to believe he knows your new name or where you live now. However, we do think he is heading to the London area, and that is a concern.'

Her simple words struck me hard, as if she had slapped me.

'What should I do? Should I go away for a while, somewhere quieter, somewhere no-one knows me at all?'

'Well, that is one option, but I would be concerned that isolating yourself like that would make you easier to find. You are safe here and you have a job where people see you every day, and there is a security in that. You have never told anyone who you really are and, again, that adds to your security. I think you should stay and carry on as usual, at least for the time being,' Annie said firmly. 'Let's just make sure that we look closely at any new friends or strangers who approach you?'

New friends or strangers who approach me . . . My thoughts immediately turned to Will. He had been so kind, and I didn't want to believe he had a sinister motive.

'What is it, Katie? Has someone new turned up in your life?' Annie ran her hands through her short red hair, pulling it upwards as if she was trying to make room in her brain for my answer.

'I have met someone, recently. He gave me a painting and came in for coffee, but I haven't heard from him since so he can't be involved . . . can he? It can't be him, surely. I would have recognised him!'

'OK. He escaped today and you met this guy before today, but I would say we still need to check him out, just to be careful.' Annie reached into her jacket pocket and pulled out her notebook.

'But if it was him, he would have hurt me by now, wouldn't he . . . ?' My voice trailed off as my mind started to fill with the terrible thoughts of what he would or could do to me.

'Katie . . . Katie . . . Look at me, just at me. I promise you that if I thought that there was a real threat, I would move you now, tonight. Let's just be more vigilant from now on, raise the security level a little. I'm going to give you a mobile phone that has just two numbers in it, mine and the number of my Sergeant. I want you to phone us twice a day, every day, until this situation is over. If you don't call us by nine in the morning and again by ten at night we will come looking for you.'

She made it all sound so reasonable and sensible, and I found myself nodding my head in agreement.

Ruby

The sun was blisteringly hot as I walked through the rose garden. The warmth seemed to soak into my skin and heat me up from the inside. With the heady scent of the blooms in my nose and with my eyes squinting against the bright sunlight that bounced off the glass of the windows, I walked steadily towards the house and the French windows of the artist's studio.

Once I had left the rose garden behind me, I stopped and watched as the doors creaked open and a familiar figure stepped outside.

He walked towards me, holding out his left hand in invitation.

Without thinking I raised my hand and he grabbed it with his large calloused grip. Before I knew it we were turning away from the house and gliding back towards the rose garden, hand in hand.

I looked up into his face, but all I could see was the heat haze created by the sun, although his hands, his strong forearms and his muscled chest were all clearly in view.

My steps faltered and he took the opportunity to stop, bending down to cut a rose from the closest bush with the sharp knife he still clutched in his right hand, a deep-red rose with silken petals.

'This is for you, my love. My Beloved, I knew that you would come to me eventually.' I heard the words in my ear in the same deep gruff voice.

I looked down and realised that I was gripping the rose tightly in my hand, the sharp thorns tearing into my flesh, coating my hand with slick red blood.

My head began to spin with a sudden wave of dizziness and I felt the world fall away into darkness as I lost consciousness.

I woke up in the safety of my own bed, breathless and relieved to be awake after such a vivid dream. I grinned to myself, feeling ridiculous. I had such a colourful imagination.

I stretched, raising my arms above my head. Something didn't feel right. I felt a scream begin to rise in my chest as I saw petals begin to fall, followed by drops of bright red blood as I tried to shake free the rose stem that was attached to my hand by the thorns digging into my flesh.

Ruby

I close the door firmly behind me, locking all three of the locks definitively, checking each one three times to be sure that the front entrance is secure. Dropping my briefcase and enormous handbag on to the hall table with a loud thud, I move into the main body of the house and begin the nightly routine of securing the perimeter. Now more than ever I need to stay safe, confident that I am alone.

The next step in my routine is to move to each window in turn, ensuring that the venetian blinds are tightly shut and that the heavy curtains are drawn. Once satisfied that there is no gap that would allow anyone to see in, I move from room to room repeating the procedure until I know that the ground floor is secure.

Step three. I check each of the three locks on the back door and move to the first floor, feeling my way up the staircase. My outstretched fingers feel the familiar bumps on the uneven walls and I use them as a guide to move forward in the darkness.

At the top of the stairs I move around from bedroom to bedroom, securing the windows from any outside light. Finally, I turn on the lights, bathing the rooms in a faint soft glow and ensuring I don't cast a shadow that can be seen from outside.

Step four. I pull the step ladder from the alcove conveniently set in the wall alongside the stairs. I set them directly below the ceiling hatch that leads to the large attic running from one end of the detached house to the other. Once there, I lift the heavy rubber-encased torch I keep with the steps and climb to the top, flipping the hatch open quickly and decisively.

I deliberately keep the attic empty so that there can be no place for an intruder to hide. The emptiness also makes it easier to swing the beam of light in a single wide arc to confirm that the large space is indeed empty.

Once confident that there is no-one there, I move backwards down the steps as swiftly and as smoothly as I can. I feel the familiar panic rising in my chest as I realise, once again, how vulnerable I am while moving backwards down the steps. It would take very little force to unbalance me entirely. I grip the torch more tightly, take a deep breath and move slowly and resolutely until I reach the solid familiar carpeted surface of the landing.

At this point I always stand still for a few seconds, listening to the sound of the comforting silence before folding up the steps and replacing them in the alcove along with the torch.

I can now move to the bathroom and start to run a warm bath

while I check that the walk-in wardrobe running the length of the wall in my bedroom contains only my clothes.

Leaning down to the two mattresses I use as a bed to avoid any gap between the bed and the floor, I change into my bathrobe and, checking that my mobile phone is in my pocket, I move into the bathroom to soak in the soothing water. It is tempting to stay floating in the water and, even though I know that my house is secure, I can't bring myself to stay naked and vulnerable for too long.

Finally, I set the security alarm and phone Annie to let her know I have stayed safe for another day. Just one more day but to me it is still a victory, however small it seems.

This is my life, a constant round of security procedures so that I can feel safe.

Before long I am dressed in pyjamas and crawling into my soft bed, where I begin the final task of checking my Go Bag. I empty the bag on to the covers and sort through the items as I lay them out, ticking each one off my mental checklist as I repack the bag neatly and methodically. The simple soft dark jersey trousers, two dark long sleeved t-shirts, two changes of underwear, a cap to hide my dark hair, a short blonde wig, a small make-up kit that would help me to change my appearance, identification, cash and a set of keys.

The angry bang of a car door breaks into my thoughts and I freeze. I hear voices, a man and a woman, right outside in the street. I take a deep breath and crawl over to the window. My hand shakes as I reach up and pull a small corner of the curtain aside and poke my head above the windowsill. I finally breathe out when I recognise the couple, Simon and Laura I think they are called, and it looks like they are having a row. I watch as she stops and turns at her front door, her footsteps ringing out loudly in the quiet of the night as she walks to the car and climbs back inside. Maybe she is going to apologise? Either way it doesn't matter. They aren't here for me and I can go to bed.

I put the bag by the side of the bed next to my boots and lie back on the soft pillows, turning on my side and watching for any shadow that could appear in the strip of light between my bedroom door and the landing before I finally drift off to sleep.

That night, as I had finished my ritual of checking all the doors and windows before going to bed, I had stopped in the dining room to look once again at the painting. It really was a striking image that reached out to my imagination and held my attention. I couldn't understand why the painter hadn't been more famous or successful. Taking one last look I turned and went through the doorway. I felt a shiver ripple through me as I heard a gruff voice in my ear utter the words *Thank you.*

* * *

Ruby

'I work well within a team, but can also work alone very effectively,' proclaimed the very earnest man sitting across the table from me.

He paused, and I realised he expected a response. The silence lengthened as I continued to stare across the table.

'Right, OK, thank you,' I heard myself say.

I had been listening to the middle-aged man sitting opposite me for about twenty minutes and I hadn't really heard anything he had said.

'Well, I think I have a pretty good picture of your skills and experience, so let's leave it there for now and we will be in touch,' I said, bringing the interview to a close.

'Are you sure?' he asked. 'I haven't even started to tell you about my full experience yet. I can give you lots of examples of projects I have worked on and show you my portfolio . . . I haven't shown you my portfolio yet . . . '

'I don't think that will be necessary at this stage. Why don't we save that for our next meeting?' I rose to my feet to signal the end of the interview.

'OK. That's great news. Thank you. I look forward to hearing from you then.'

I reached out my hand for the traditional handshake and realised that it had begun to bleed again, bright drops of crimson that fell heavily on to the table between us.

'I'm so sorry, I seem to have cut my hand. Please check out with reception as you leave and, as I said, we will be in touch.'

Not stopping to see if he had left, I turned and fled the room. I ran straight into the Ladies' where I tore off the large sticking plaster, now damp and slick with more blood. I felt the cool porcelain against the back of my hand as I ran the cold tap – hard and fast – on to the offending palm.

I leant forward and took a deep breath, and thought back over the last five days. Each night had been the same: the dream of the rose garden, and waking up with a bleeding palm, a red rose clutched in my hand.

At first I tried to convince myself that the dream was a product of an overactive imagination, that I had been sleepwalking and had collected the roses from the garden myself.

After last night, when the dream returned once more, as terrifyingly vivid as each previous occasion, I was sure I didn't ever want to fall asleep again.

Worst of all was the voice that invaded my thoughts. It was like he was standing at my shoulder, whispering words of encouragement, urging me to join him in the rose garden. Where we would walk amongst the flowers and talk together, my small hand secured firmly in his grip.

Coming into the office today had been a mistake. I lifted my head and met the gaze of the woman who stared back at me.

My dirty hair was scraped back into a pony tail, my make-up was unfinished so it looked as if one half of my face was naked. My eyes were the worst, they seemed to have sunk back into their sockets with black shadows underneath that were so dark they looked like bruises.

I realised with shock that I was still wearing the T shirt I had worn to bed last night, the dried blood stains stark against the white of the shirt, not quite hidden by the lapel of my black jacket.

As I leant my forehead against the cold surface of the mirror I heard the deep voice in my ear once again, 'Come home to me, my Beloved.'

'No, no, no!' I stifled the scream rising in my throat and pushed my forehead harder against the glass as his words continued, over and over again, in my ear.

I heard a sharp crack and realised I had pushed so hard against the mirror that it had fractured and as I pulled my forehead away in horror, the sharp shards fell into the sink. There was a small cut on my forehead and a bright crimson drop of blood dripped on to the shattered glass. It took a moment before I realised that the voice in my ear was gone. There was nothing but blessed silence, and I could think clearly once more.

I had found a way to make him stop, a way to silence his voice in my ear.

So that was how it all began; I found I could control the dreams and silence his voice by expanding my nightly ritual. Now I not only checked that all the doors and windows were closed and that the painting was still hanging in the dining room and cleaned my teeth. I also used my nail scissors to make a tiny cut on my forearm. Nothing too big, just enough to let a drop of blood fall into the sink, a little sacrifice that put me back in control. It gave me a feeling of power and satisfaction that I could banish his voice. I felt almost proud that I had found a way to handle the situation, a way to deal with what was happening to me.

Every day, I would wake up and plan to get rid of the painting. The simplest plan was to donate it to a museum. In my braver moments, I thought about burning it and destroying the voice once and for all. Then a small doubt would creep into my thoughts. Maybe it was nothing to do with the painting at all? Maybe it was a product of my over active imagination? Maybe I was ill, having some kind of a breakdown?

It had been two weeks now, and my arms were covered in tiny nicks and cuts. Whilst I had managed to keep his voice from my ear and his presence from my dreams, it was becoming harder and harder to keep him away.

In those moments when my control slipped and his voice broke through, he seemed angry that I was trying to keep him away. At other times he seemed to encourage me to spill more of my blood, enough for me to lose consciousness and be able to walk in the rose garden with him once more.

Since the incident in the Ladies' when I had discovered my power, I had taken some time out of the office, pleading a violent migraine that had laid me low. It had explained my pale complexion and sunken eyes when I returned to work and, as long as I concentrated, I could function relatively well. If I felt his voice invading my thoughts, I had only to take a trip to the Ladies' and make a small cut, a small drop of blood and I was back in control.

Will

I couldn't believe my luck when I walked into the coffee shop and saw Ruby, sat at a small table in the corner. She had obviously found somewhere else to escape from her busy job, now that The Gallery had closed.

I had wanted to call her, to hear her voice again, every day since I had met her. But fate – or rather the closing of The Gallery and my busy teaching commitments – had conspired against me. Long days of conversations with removal and storage companies, solicitors and the National Gallery, to which my great-great-grandfather had grandly left one small self-portrait. Days filled with the packing, cleaning and emptying of each room left me with little free time, and that had been filled supporting my students with their studies.

It had been only a few days since we had actually met, but she had stayed in my mind and somehow I had missed her. During all my conversations I wondered what *she* would say to the student begging for more time to complete their assignment, or to the removal company who had decided to increase their charges at the last minute.

She was staring out of the window with a vacant look in her eyes and didn't seem to have noticed me enter the coffee shop.

'Hello again.' I stood right in front of her but she still didn't notice me. Her attention was clearly elsewhere.

'Ruby . . . It's me, Will. We met at The Gallery . . .'

'Oh yes, I remember . . . Sorry, I was miles away,' she replied, with a lopsided smile that didn't quite reach her eyes.

'Do you mind if I join you?'

Now I could see her properly, she didn't look right. She was still the same Ruby but her eyes looked bruised, her bright red lipstick a stark contrast to her pale face. Her once-glossy hair was dull and dirty, the collar of her shirt grubby and creased.

'Of course. Please sit down. How are you, all done with The

Gallery?' she asked quickly.

'Almost, just a few things left to do. You know how it is, there's always more to do than you think. How have you been?' I paused to take a bite out of my peanut butter on toast.

'I'm fine, apart from a migraine and I've been having a bit of trouble sleeping lately,' Ruby replied. I watched as she fiddled with the sleeve of her jacket, my eyes drawn to the chipped polish of her nails. She kept pulling at her sleeve trying to hide the large sticking plaster on her palm.

Suddenly she was on her feet. 'It's been lovely to see you, but I have to go . . . Maybe we can meet up for coffee again when we both have a bit more time?'

'Sure I would love to . . . 'I began, only to realise she had left the coffee shop and was climbing into her car. I watched from the window as she sped away, narrowly missing the kerb.

Ruby

Meeting Will again in the coffee shop helped me make up my mind. He was too kind to say so, but he must have noticed how badly I had let myself go. I felt embarrassed and ashamed of my appearance.

My stomach had heaved as the sweet smell of his peanut butter reached my nostrils. What must he have thought of me, I couldn't string a coherent sentence together. I know that it hadn't been long since we met, but what he thought of me mattered for some reason and I was filled with a determination to resolve my situation and show him a better version of me, the real me.

I drove home as fast as I could and skidded to a stop on the drive with a squeal of brakes.

I let myself into the garden by the side gate, I grabbed the heavy barbecue and pulled and pushed it to the centre of the lawn, as far away from the house as I could.

I unlocked the shed and pulled out the can of paraffin, the box of firelighters and the long matches. *Always best for a barbecue, the long matches,* I thought.

Splashes of paraffin flew at my hair and clothes as I poured the entire contents on to the heap of coals and firelighters. I took a step back, and threw three lit matches on to the coals. There was a hiss and a whoosh as the flames took hold and the fire began to burn.

Now for the hard part, I thought. I walked back to the front of the house and let myself in through the front door and crept carefully into the kitchen. Once there I went to a drawer and pulled out the largest carving knife, the one I kept for carving the Christmas turkey.

I took a deep breath. 'It's the only way. It's the only way . . .' I repeated the words over and over, as if concentrating on them would give me the strength I would need to end it once and for all.

I stepped into the dining room and stood before him. I raised my arm and almost daring him to stop me, I slashed at the canvas. A wide gash appeared across its centre and I screamed as rivulets of dark scarlet immediately started pouring from the canvas.

At the same time I heard his voice in my ear once again. 'How could you hurt me so, my Beloved? You know what you must do to make this right. Now is the time.'

'No, no! No!' I heard myself scream. *Not this time,* I thought, as my eyes fell on the remote control of the stereo sitting on the coffee table. I grabbed the remote control, my hands now slick with blood and soon the room was filled with loud angry rock music. I turned it up defiantly. If I could drown him out I could finish the job and soon this would all be over.

I turned back to the painting and began to slash at its surface once more, tearing and pulling great pieces of torn canvas from the wall. Once I had an armful I stumbled out to the garden, to the now-blazing fire, and threw them into the heart of the flames.

Now that I was outside, away from the insulating effect of the music, I could hear his voice once more and he was angry. He was screaming at me over and over again. I covered my ears and staggered unsteadily back to the safety of the music. There was still more of the painting to be destroyed and I could not stop now. I had to finish what I had started.

Will

I don't know why I followed her home. I can only say I was worried about her. She seemed so uncoordinated and unlike herself in the coffee shop.

Something was definitely off kilter, even the way she had taken so long to answer me, as if she was having a conversation with herself in her head, rehearsing her replies. Then to suddenly run away like that . . . It just didn't seem right.

When I turned the corner on to Shakespeare Street, I saw her car parked on the drive, the door wide open as if she had left it in a hurry. I was most disturbed by the sound of loud rock music that pounded out of the house and the plume of black smoke that rose from the back garden.

I leapt out of my car and ran into the back garden, where I found Ruby sitting on the lawn staring into the flames of a large fire on a barbecue. She was just sitting there, a big carving knife clutched in her right hand with blood pouring copiously from a wound on her left arm.

I knelt down and reached out to her, pulling her into my arms as I loosened the grip of her fingers and pulled the slippery handle of the knife from her grasp.

She turned her head and looked straight into my eyes. 'It was the only way to make him stop. You do understand that, don't you?'

Daily News

18 September 2016
By Alison Bryant

'Kitchen Killer' Patrick Stanton dies in stand-off with police

In a dramatic turn of events, worthy of a Hollywood movie, Patrick Stanton the notorious Kitchen Killer was killed in a fall from the window of the hotel room where he was hiding.

The police were alerted by Stacy Wheeler a hotel receptionist who recognised Stanton from a news report.

'He went into his room with long hair and came out a couple of hours later with a shaved head. It seemed so suspicious that I took a closer look at him than I would have normally.'

The observant hotel worker didn't hesitate to call Crimestoppers immediately.

Her prompt actions enabled police to evacuate the hotel before armed officers approached Stanton's room.

Unsurprisingly, Stanton refused to open the door, at which point armed officers broke down the door to find that

Stanton had climbed out of the window on to the balcony.

In an attempt to reach the roof he had climbed on to a guard rail and in trying to reach the floor above, overbalanced and fell four storeys to the pavement below.

Stanton was declared dead at the scene.

Detective Chief Inspector Annie West made the following statement.

'Whilst we still need to examine the details, we can say for certain that Patrick Stanton is dead. He cannot harm anyone ever again.'

A full investigation into his escape and his dramatic end will be conducted before Stanton and his horrific crimes can finally be laid to rest.

Stanton had remained at large for the best part of three months by moving between hotels, boarding houses and on some occasions it is thought that he broke into private homes whilst their owners were away.

Police will now investigate Stanton's journey to freedom in detail, searching for any individual who may have assisted in his escape.

Detective Chief Inspector West has made her intentions clear. Charges will be made against any individual who helped Stanton in his bid for freedom, however small a part they may have played.

Regardless of any future charges, the citizens of Great Britain, in particular Katie Mayes, can now rest easy knowing that Stanton no longer represents a threat.

Will

I leant against the doorframe, my eyes searching for her, my Ruby. I finally found her curled up in a large rocking chair on the terrace, looking out on to the beautiful rose garden.

Her dark glossy hair stood out against the pale blue of her pyjamas, a tartan blanket around her knees.

I looked down at the bunch of wild flowers I clutched in my hand, their stems bent by my grip. I remembered the first time I came to see her, I had brought her roses.

She had stared at them for a few minutes before tearing them from my grasp and ripping them to pieces with her hands, all the while staring at me in silent reproach. Once she had destroyed every leaf, stem and petal she began to scream, long howls of anguish that tore at my heart.

She had been sedated and, as I sat by her bed watching her sleep, I realised I couldn't leave her. We had never kissed or even held hands, but the thought of not being with her was unthinkable.

So, I had visited her every day. Every day she had sat in silence, staring out at the rose garden seemingly oblivious to my chatter.

The first time I had reached out and touched her hand she flinched, but she didn't scream and that began the pattern of our afternoons. I would arrive and chat for a while and then I would take her hand and we would sit in silence until it was time for me to leave.

That was six long months ago and I was starting to give up hope she would ever return to me, but I wouldn't desert her.

I realised I had been standing in the doorway just watching for a while, so I conjured up a bright smile and prepared to step out on to the terrace.

Please let today be the day. I sent up a silent prayer in the hope that today would be the day she would come back to me and I could finally take her home.

As I stepped out on to the terrace, her head turned and for the first time she smiled at me. 'Hello Will,' she said.

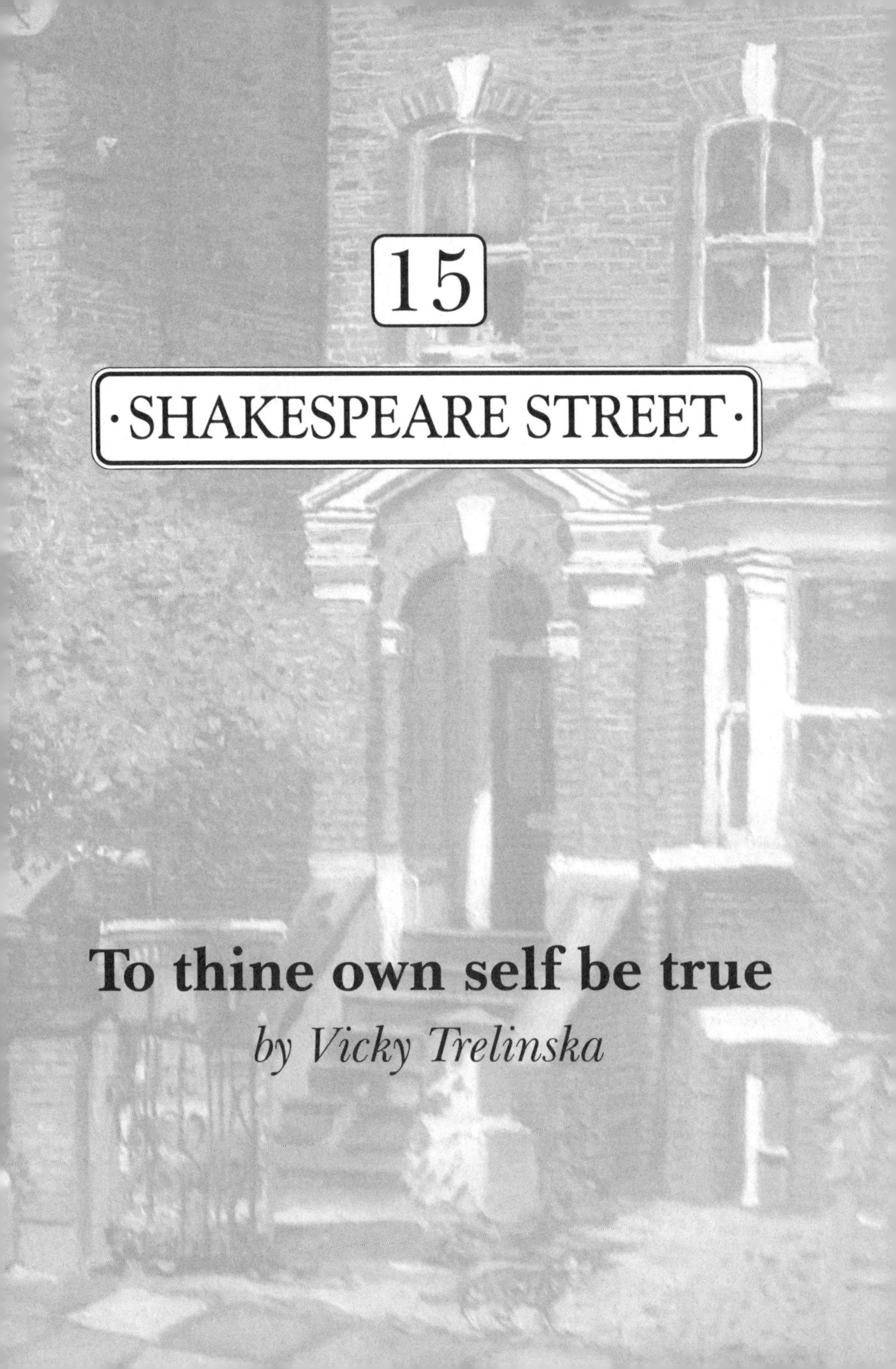

15 · SHAKESPEARE STREET ·

To thine own self be true

by Vicky Trelinska

To thine own self be true

Hamlet, Act 1, Scene 3

Sybil sat alone at the breakfast table.

'I won't get up today dear,' her mother, Dorothy, had said when Sybil had gone to wake her with the usual cup of tea. 'I have one of my headaches.'

The headaches had started in 1914, over three years ago, and been a constant theme ever since. Along with 'It's all the worry, dear' and 'If only your father was still alive. I'm not able to cope on my own.'

The only fear of her mother's that Sybil had sympathy with was 'Any moment a telegram could arrive saying one of your brothers has gone down with his ship.' It was at the back of Sybil's mind, but she'd rather keep it there and not have it brought to the forefront at least once a day by Dorothy.

Sybil buttered her toast and thought about the coming day. She had not envisaged such an aimless existence when she graduated from King's College for Women in the summer. Before the war Sybil had high hopes of working after she had gained a degree. Her father had increasingly relied on her to help him with the research and writing for his books on naval history. She loved doing his research and writing up his notes. He had married her mother late in life and was more like a grandfather than a father. Her older brothers were more interested in mathematics and engineering than history.

'You've a good brain, my dear,' she remembered her father telling her just before he died in the summer of 1914. 'You are more than equal to your brothers. When you've got your degree you can take over my work. You will make a fine historian.'

Now her mornings were taken up with tedious household duties. There was no time for reading, or going to the library and working, as she had to help Nellie, their last remaining servant.

Servants, or the lack of them, were another of her mother's worries. 'It's so difficult to find servants these days.' Sybil could not make her mother understand that the faithful Nellie was unlikely to leave. She was too old and too infirm – with her corns, bunions, veins and rheumatics – to earn better money working in a factory and, with no close relatives, she had nowhere else to go. She had been with the family so long Nellie knew they would look after her when she could no longer work.

'But helping me with the house is so useful,' Dorothy had tried to soothe Sybil one day. 'A daughter should be at home until she marries.' But her daughter marched up and down the sitting room talking of friends who were training to be doctors and how useless she felt and how if she'd been good at science she would have applied to study medicine. King's College for Women had started to train female doctors earlier in the year.

'I could not have allowed that,' said the horrified Dorothy. 'It was bad enough when you wanted to be a VAD.'

When Sybil had suggested joining the VAD and training as a nurse, Dorothy's pronouncement – from astride her high horse – had been devastating. 'No daughter of mine will do such work.' In vain Sybil had listed the titled women who were working in France as VADs, or driving ambulances or working with the Red Cross. 'The nobility are different,' countered Dorothy. 'They can get away with anything. We're not aristocracy. Anyway, you'd see the most appalling things, helping with operations and nursing men in dreadful conditions. From what I've heard the regular nurses look down on the volunteer nurses and treat them like skivvies. No. It's quite out of the question.'

If only father was still alive, thought Sybil. He would have let me join the VADs and be a nurse. He would have thought it a good occupation and would have known I could cope. He had overridden Dorothy when she objected to Sybil studying history. 'But who will marry a blue stocking?' Dorothy had asked. 'Men don't want to marry women with brains.'

Her father had specifically left money in his will for Sybil's education so there was nothing Dorothy could do except to carry on worrying about her daughter's marriage prospects.

The war and Sybil's father's death had changed everything. She desperately wanted to do something to help the war effort that wasn't just knitting or visiting the badly injured in hospital, although she agreed that was worthy work. She just felt that she had more to offer with all the exciting new opportunities that were opening up for women.

Sybil knew marriage opportunities after the war would be limited for her generation. Most of the young men she knew had been killed. How was she to convince Dorothy that life would not return to what it had been in 1910 and that, for her, marriage was not the only way of life to which she could aspire? Sybil wanted more than sitting quietly at home looking after her mother as she decayed into old age. She was certain she was capable of doing just as much as the men she knew.

She sighed, sipped her tea and turned to *The Times*. Thankfully, today there were no names she recognized on the paper's opening pages. Sibyl hated reading the lists of the men who had been killed in action or who had died of their wounds, but she felt it was her duty. Even the lists of the men mentioned in dispatches filled her with dread.

Flicking through the pages, an advertisement on page nine caught her eye.

WOMEN FOR THE NAVY
New shore service to be formed

Had Sybil been a man she would have joined the Royal Navy with her brothers at the start of the war. She had given up hope they would ever take women. She skimmed through the notice about the new service.

> . . . employment of women on various duties on shore hitherto performed by men . . . distinctive uniform . . . take on duties directly connected with the Royal Navy . . . further announcements will be made . . .

Surely her mother would not object to her joining the Navy? It wouldn't be like the Women's Army Auxiliary Corps, which Sybil had wanted to join earlier in the year. 'I cannot understand why you want to be like a man,' Dorothy had complained. 'Leave these things to the men. This is not a role for women. You'll be wanting to wear trousers next.'

The advertisement clearly said the duties would be ashore, and Sybil supposed it was most likely to be office work. What could her mother object to with that? Plenty of girls from good backgrounds worked in offices these days.

Sybil made up her mind. That's what she would do. She would go today. She couldn't wait for *further announcements*. She was not going to miss this opportunity.

* * *

'No-one is being interviewed yet.' An unsmiling woman faced Sybil from behind a typewriter on a desk covered with papers.

'Could you take my name and address and tell someone I'm interested in joining?'

'I've no instructions to take names and addresses. You will have to wait for a further announcement.' The woman busied herself putting paper in the typewriter.

'Then I'll wait until someone can see me,' said Sybil, sitting down very firmly on a chair near the door.

'I have no idea when anyone will be back.'

'I'm in no hurry.'

'As you wish.' The woman started typing hitting the keys, hard and fast.

It wasn't long before Sybil heard quick footsteps in the corridor. The door was flung open.

'Sorry I've been so long, Miss Jordan. I couldn't get away from the Admiral. Hello, who's this?'

A tall, slim, dark-haired woman smiled down at Sybil. Sybil

immediately stood up. The woman had as much authority as the Admirals Sybil had met at her brothers' passing out parades, although Sybil thought she saw kindness in the clear, intelligent eyes.

'I'm Sybil Young. I saw the announcement in *The Times* today about the new naval service for women. I want to join.'

'Well, we weren't expecting anyone to come along yet. There will be further announcements about recruiting.' The woman handed her hat and coat to Miss Jordan. 'But, as you're here, we might as well have a chat. Miss Jordan, will you see if Mrs Crane and Miss Crowdy can join us? And would you please take Miss Young's coat?'

'Yes, Dame Katharine.' Miss Jordan took Sybil's coat and went to the telephone.

Gosh, thought Sybil. This must be Dame Katharine Furse, the Director of the new service. For the first time, Sybil wondered at her nerve in ignoring the instructions in the newspaper. Of course she'd heard of Dame Katharine, everybody had. She had first gone to France in 1914 and had recently been made a Dame of the British Empire for her work with the Red Cross, training VADs. No wonder she had the air of an Admiral. Sybil felt like turning and running out of the building but showing such fear would surely sink her chances of being accepted into the new service. There was nothing for it but to follow Dame Katharine into her office. Sybil hoped her hair was tidy and there were no smuts on her face. At least she'd cleaned her shoes before coming.

Dame Katharine sat in an armchair near the fire and indicated that Sybil should take the one opposite.

'So, why are you so keen to join you cannot wait, as instructed, until further announcements? The Navy needs people who obey orders, you know.'

I hope, thought Sybil, *they also need people with initiative.*

* * *

Sybil walked home thinking about her interview. When Mrs Crane and Miss Crowdy joined them, their questions about her background and education had been easy to answer. Apart from 'What experience do you have of administration?' That was trickier, though they seemed to think that being captain of the college hockey team counted. She tried to convince them she wanted to work and was capable of hard work. They said they would write to her.

Sybil liked all three women and enjoyed talking to them. They were lively, intelligent, energetic and good company. It had made her more determined than ever to get into the new service, even if it meant starting as the lowest junior rating.

* * *

For the next two weeks Sybil made sure she was the first to get to the post when it arrived. As the weeks passed and nothing came, Sybil began to wonder whether they had forgotten about her or were just not going to accept her. Should she go and see them again or would she be better to obey orders and wait for another announcement?

Returning home late one afternoon, her mother called her into the drawing room.

'There's a letter for you.' Dorothy handed it to Sybil. 'It looks rather official.'

Sybil tried not to snatch the envelope and rip it open. Supposing they said she was unsuitable, not the right type? She held her breath and opened the letter.

'I'm in.' Sybil waved the letter and danced round the room nearly knocking over a vase of flowers on the table.

'In what? Do stand still, dear, you're making me dizzy.'

'The new naval service for women. That's what I'm in – or rather *going* to be in. They want me to join as an officer in the New Year for initial training.'

'Oh, my goodness… ' Dorothy sat down on the sofa. 'I feel quite faint. I thought you'd given up all that nonsense about joining a service.'

Sybil sat down and took her mother's hand.

'It's alright, Mother,' said Sybil scanning the letter quickly. 'They say I have to report to Crystal Palace. That's not far away and I can come home often. I'll still be around to help.'

'It's too much. I can't be on my own. I need you more than they do.'

'Things are different now for women. We're expected to help the war effort.'

'Why can't you do some charity work? You could visit wounded officers in hospital. There must be something else you could do, something genteel and more suitable for a girl.'

'I want to join the Navy.'

'You simply cannot go.' Dorothy banged her fist of the arm of her chair. 'I forbid it.'

'You can't stop me.' Sybil had inherited some of her mother's obstinacy. 'I'm over twenty-one and I have my own inheritance.' Sybil raised her voice. 'I have to do this. They are desperate for women to relieve the men who are doing shore duties so they can send them to sea . . .'

'So you'd have your brothers spend more time at sea, giving them more chance of being sunk and left to drown?'

'You know I didn't mean-' Sybil's protest was interrupted by loud knocking at the front door. 'Who can that be?'

They heard Nellie open the front door and cry out, 'Oh Sirs!' followed by men's voices.

'George! Albert!' the two women exclaimed. They rushed into the hall, Dorothy having quite forgotten that she was feeling faint. Two men in naval uniform were hugging Nellie, who was laughing and crying.

'Why didn't you let us know you were coming?' asked Dorothy, while trying to hug and kiss both of them at the same time.

'The last time I sent a telegram,' said George, the elder of the two and a Commander, 'Sybil told me you fainted because you thought it would say I'd been killed in action.'

'Albert! What *have* you done to your arm?' Sybil noticed it was in a sling.

'I fell down a gangway in rough seas and broke it. It's not healing well, so I'm home on sick leave.'

Nellie was sent to get refreshments while Dorothy and Sybil took the men into the drawing room, keen to hear all their news. George would also at be home for several months. He'd been drafted to the Admiralty.

'So I'll be able to live at home, Mother.'

'Just as well. Sybil is deserting me.'

'Sybil what are you up to?' asked Albert.

'I'm joining the new women's naval service in the New Year.'

'Smashing,' said Albert.

'Good for you, old bird,' said George.

'It's not good at all,' said Dorothy. 'I shall be on my own. As if I didn't have enough to worry about with you boys at sea,' said Dorothy.

'But Mother, Albert and I will be at home,' said George. 'We'll all be together for Christmas.'

'It'll be the best Christmas since 1913,' said Albert.

* * *

Dorothy was pleased to have the boys at home. Later that evening, the four of them sat round the fire in the drawing room discussing the new naval service and, with her brothers' support, Sybil was able to laugh off her mother's pointed remarks.

'A daughter's place is at home in these times.'

'But you'll have us, Mother,' said Albert.

'It's not the same as having a daughter around. If George is sent back to sea I shall be all on my own.'

'It will be months before I'm drafted to another ship,' said George.

'Sybil won't be far away and it will be her coming home on leave instead of us,' said Albert. 'She deserves to have a chance.'

'Well, if you are all determined to ruin Sybil's future I don't suppose I can stop you.'

Albert winked at Sybil.

'Don't worry about Mother,' George said to Sybil later in the evening when Dorothy had gone to bed and the three siblings were on their own. 'I'll see she's alright. She'll come round, then she'll be just as proud of you as she is of Albert and me.'

'We desperately need women to take over some of the shore jobs,' said Albert. 'I can't think why the Admiralty has taken so long to introduce a women's service. Women are doing everything else these days.'

'I'm so looking forward to it but I do worry about Mother,' said Sybil. 'Is it very selfish of me to want to go? I'm languishing here. I don't feel I was meant to be a stay-at-home, dutiful daughter. I want to be a part of what is going on.'

'You're too intelligent to stay at home knitting,' said George. He stopped pacing round the room like an officer of the watch on the bridge and looked directly at Sybil.

'Look here,' he said as if he were addressing a rating up in front of the Captain. 'We've discussed this enough. Albert and I are both agreed you should go. You must be true to yourself. The world will be very different when the war is over. Mother is just afraid of all the changes that have taken place. But she'll survive, and we're here for a few months at least. By the time we have to leave, she will have become accustomed to it.'

* * *

The day before Sybil was due to leave, Dorothy took to bed with one of her headaches and refused to see anyone except Nellie. Sybil wondered if she should postpone her departure, but George and Albert insisted she go. She'd been given her orders and she must obey them, George told her.

The following day, with the cab waiting outside number 15 Shakespeare Street, Albert, Nellie and George stood at the door ready to say goodbye. Sybil looked up at the stairs, hoping her mother was coming down, but there was no sign of Dorothy. Sybil turned toward the door.

'Cheer up,' said Albert, seeing Sybil's shoulders droop and her head hanging down. 'Worse things happen at sea.' Sybil gave him a watery smile.

'Wait there a minute,' said George, as Nellie was about to open the door. He bounded up the stairs.

'What's he doing?' asked Sybil. 'I can't wait very long. I'll be late.'

As they waited in the hall for George to return, Sybil fiddled with her gloves and hat and checked her bags while Albert paced up and down. After five minutes, when there was still no sign of George, Sybil said to Albert, 'I'll have to go, say goodbye to George and Mother for me.'

At that moment they heard George order, 'Guard of Honour, Ho!'

Albert stood at attention.

George came downstairs with Dorothy on his arm. Sybil would never know how he had persuaded their mother to come and say goodbye, but she would forever be grateful to him. In that moment, her enjoyment and excitement were restored.

Dorothy kissed Sybil. 'George says you must go, dear,' she said.

'Pipe the side,' ordered George. Albert took a bosun's whistle out of his jacket pocket and blew the pipe for a senior officer going ashore. George and Albert saluted. Sybil returned the salute. Dorothy took out her handkerchief.

'By the left, quick march,' ordered Albert.

Laughing, Sybil picked up her bags.

18

·SHAKESPEARE STREET·

A very ecstasy

by Chris Payne

This is the very ecstasy of love, Whose
violent property fordoes itself And
leads the will to desperate undertakings
As oft as any passion under heaven
That does afflict our natures

Hamlet, Act 2, Scene 1

It was Adrian's idea to place the advertisement.

When Tania heard his key in the lock on Friday night, after his usual visit to the pub, she rose from where she'd been waiting with her glass of wine for his return. They'd long ago agreed on different ways to slough off the working week. For Adrian, it was to go to the local pub and catch up with the neighbours; for Tania, it was to stay at home and play the piano, finally allowing herself full expression of the pieces she'd been patiently drilling into her students' fumbling teenage fingers all week.

Adrian slammed the door and called out, 'Tania!'

'Just coming,' she called back. Tania pulled the curtains shut. She'd been sitting in the dark after she finished playing, gazing out of the window to the quiet street. She loved to watch people walking by in the glow of the street lamps as their Friday evening finished and the weekend began. No-one ever gave the house a glance as they went by; no-one noticed the silent watcher.

Tania joined Adrian in the kitchen and could see he was bursting to make an announcement. She gazed at him fondly. His cheeks were flushed red from the cold night air and the pints, his auburn hair dishevelled from where he'd run his hands through it in excitement. His ocean-coloured eyes were alight as he sat down at the kitchen table and said, 'You'll never guess what I found out tonight.'

'What? Big news at the local?'

'Harry from number twelve told me that they're only going to go and open their place as a bed-and-breakfast! Can you believe it? They've put washbasins in all the rooms, and will start letting out in a couple of months. They're already taking bookings for the summer and they aren't even properly open yet. They're going to make an absolute fortune.'

'That is news,' agreed Tania, turning to the sink to wash her glass. Over the sound of the running water she almost missed Adrian's next words. 'I thought we could do the same.'

Tania shut off the water and turned to face him. 'Open a bed-and-breakfast? Are you mad? I'm already a teacher. Now you want me to be a landlady too?'

Adrian folded his hands and looked down at the table. 'No, not a bed-and-breakfast. That wouldn't work for us. But I did think we could take in a lodger, in the spare room.'

Tania turned back to the sink and gripped its edge. Adrian knew that she didn't consider the back bedroom in any way a 'spare room'. It was the room they had planned as the nursery, and the first room Tania had decorated when they moved in. As soon as she had seen it, she had mentally peopled it with a baby and had soon turned it into the perfect space to welcome one.

But no baby came.

It was five years now since the doctor had shaken his head definitively and said that there was no hope. 'There's nothing wrong, medically, with either of you,' he'd explained. 'It just sometimes works out like this, that the combination of two people isn't right for making a baby. There's no reason why you couldn't have a baby; but I would be being unprofessional if I said I thought that you would.'

They had come home from the doctor's that evening and separated silently at the door. Adrian had walked through to the kitchen and, as she slowly climbed the stairs, Tania had heard the sound of a bottle cap being prised off as Adrian sought, as usual, to blur unpleasantness with beer. Tania had stepped, dreamlike, to the door of the nursery and pushed it open. The primrose-yellow walls with the cheery fairy watercolours she'd painted had seemed to mock her. The cot was in the corner, its soft white blanket never ruffled with a baby's breath. Tania had paused in the middle of the room for a moment, breathing in the scent of laundered bed linen and talcum powder that already seemed to have a stale and unnecessary edge. Then she had collapsed into the nursing chair and sobbed as if her heart would break. Tania never remembered falling asleep that night, but when she had woken hours later, cold and stiff, she had found Adrian curled on the floor by her side, deep in his own dreams away from their shared grief.

They had tried everything. Every piece of advice Tania could glean – from doctors, nurses, strangers on the bus – was worth a gamble. She'd even found her thoughts turning to a higher power. Each lunchtime, before her students began to arrive, she'd leave the house and cross furtively to the church for the noon service, sitting silently at the back and letting her desire wash over her and up to where she thought Someone might be listening. These interludes brought her calm but no joy. Each time she left the service she'd cross over to the stone angel at the entrance gate and lay her hand on the stiff folds of its gown, the chill of the stone meeting the chill in her heart. 'Please, make it happen,' she'd whisper under her breath.

Over the years, it became the one thing she and Adrian couldn't speak about. After the doctor's verdict, Adrian never went into the back bedroom again whereas Tania couldn't keep away. Each morning, Adrian would bring her a cup of tea in bed before he left for work. As soon as she heard the front door click shut, Tania would steal from her bed, cross the landing and push open the door. She would sit in the nursing chair, cradling her cup and reaching out her warmed hand to stroke the silken edges of the baby blanket. If she closed her eyes, she could pretend its satin finish was the soft down of her baby's head.

At night it was worse. Tania would wake as if to a cry, and be pulled across the landing by its silver thread. She'd check the cot and stand at the window in the moonlight, looking out between the houses and listening to the hushed sounds of sleeping London. In her mind she'd cradle her wakeful infant to her chest and croon to it as, together, they gazed out to the world it would never inhabit.

Tania left the house less and less often, drawing her interactions back to her piano students and pouring her passion for a child into her passion for her students. When their parents rang the doorbell she would look anywhere but into their eyes, wanting to avoid showing what lay inside her own. She feared her pain was clearly visible in her pale gaze, like looking through blue water to a riverbed of razor-sharp stones.

Adrian's voice brought her back to the present.

'I went in there the other day, Tania, for the first time in ages. We can't just ignore it, keeping the room like that. I know you've been in there, it's spotless. But it's like some kind of shrine, it doesn't make sense. It's not healthy, keeping the baby furniture in there when we know . . . ' His voice trailed off.

'Know what?' Tania asked, quietly.

Adrian matched her tone. 'When we *know* there's no hope,' he finished. He pushed back his chair and crossed the floor to her, wrapping her in his arms. 'We know. We've been told and told. It just can't work for us. I know we tried, but it just can't happen. It's just going to be us. Let's do this, Tan. Let's admit it. Let's clear out that room and move on.'

Tania turned towards him, leaning into his shoulder and breathing in his familiar smell, overlaid with beer and cigarettes. Adrian whispered into her hair, 'We have to be enough for each other, Tan. Are you with me?'

They stood entwined for a few moments, their breaths aligned. Finally Tania brought her head back and looked up at his dear, familiar face. She laid a hand on his ruddy cheek and saw the bright glimmer of tears in his blue eyes. Matching tears stood in her own as she nodded and took a deep breath. From the back of her throat down to the pit of her stomach she felt a tense mass, as if something heavy had landed on her chest. Her voice came, with an effort. 'You're right. It's time to change. But don't ask me to do anything in the room. I can't bear it.'

She turned away from him and gripped the edge of the sink again. *So this is what it feels like for a heart to break,* she thought as she heard Adrian leave the room.

That night, once again, Tania slipped from beneath the covers and went to the nursery for the last time, to say goodbye to her babies. Already the room felt different, colder, as if they knew. This time their unborn spirits didn't nestle to her breast. She felt them looking at her accusingly, as if she had turned her back on them. As she stood by the window and looked to the cold, glittering lights of the city she could see their soft, formless faces reflected in the glass, their hollow eyes boring into her in betrayal.

It was as if Adrian had had an army of painters and decorators standing in the wings, waiting for her assent. The first weeks of the new year were marked by the sounds of workmen's boots tramping up and down the stairs as Tania gave piano lessons. When Adrian declared himself satisfied, he gently escorted Tania to the room to look inside. She stood outside the closed, freshly painted door, looking at its gleaming new keyhole. Adrian unlocked the door and allowed her to step inside first.

Her magic fairyland had been washed away. The room was now plain white, with a simple iron bedstead and serviceable blue coverlet. The washbasin in the corner was coyly shaded by a screen, and a wooden wardrobe squatted severely against the other wall. No-one could ever mistake this for a child's room. Tania stroked the smooth surface of the wall and breathed in the smell of fresh paint. She knew Adrian had been right, and perhaps this didn't have to be the death of hope. Maybe it could be the birth of a new beginning.

Tania wrote out the card in her neat schoolmistress's hand, and Adrian had it placed on the community noticeboard outside the church. It hadn't been up for more than a day when the calls started coming. Adrian had been right; people were desperate to live in Shakespeare Street. The telephone would shrill in the middle of Tania's piano lessons, forcing her to abandon her students to lift the receiver. Adrian interviewed each candidate, but no-one seemed quite right for what they needed.

One weekend, Tania was polishing the door brasses when she heard a gentle cough behind her. She swung round, shielding her eyes. A tall, thin silhouette stood before her, its outline haloed by the low winter sun.

'I hope I don't disturb you,' said a softly accented voice.

'Can I help you?'

'The people in the newsagent's told me this was the house with a room to let. Am I correct?' the man continued.

'Yes, but you'll have to speak to my husband. Adrian!' Tania called. The dazzle had faded and she could see a slight young man with the blackest hair and darkest eyes she'd ever seen. Adrian joined them on the step and soon offered to show the man the room. Tania bent close to the brass and rubbed hard at her watery reflection.

Feeling strangely unsettled, she came back inside. This was the first candidate she'd seen who looked like he might fit the bill. She went into the living room and sat at the piano. On the music stand was the piece she'd been working on most recently. Her fingers caressed the keys while she waited. Soon Adrian came back down, closely followed by the slender shadow. After he introduced himself to Tania – his name was Vik – Adrian gestured him to sit and began asking their rehearsed questions. Vik sat upright at the edge of the couch and answered them calmly, in measured tones, producing written references and offering a month's rent in advance. He had come to England, he explained, to save up enough money to attend college by working at his cousin's restaurant. The family did not have room for him to live with them, but were able to pay him a wage and to feed him a meal each night.

Tania and Adrian exchanged glances and Tania gave a minuscule nod. The decision was made.

If it had been difficult to get used to the idea of someone living in the house with them, it was less difficult to get used to the reality.

Adrian and Tania hardly saw Vik at first. He would rise late and stay in his room until the early afternoon, when he would let himself softly out of the house to go to work. He returned home just after midnight. Sometimes Tania would start awake at the click of the latch and reach the landing before remembering that the room no longer called to her in the same way.

Over the weeks, the three of them fell into a regular pattern. Tania relaxed into a routine, spending the mornings on housework and mindful of the sleeping tenant upstairs. Her youngest students began arriving soon after lunch and she would hear Vik come downstairs, moving around the kitchen as she worked patiently through their piano scales and simple pieces.

Through the afternoon the students gradually progressed from hesitant pre-school steps through the scales all the way up to sixth-formers whose ability would refresh her faith in the joys of music. Now and then she would see Vik's slim figure passing the frosted glass of the living room door. As Adrian arrived home, Vik would be leaving for work. Only on Fridays did the routine alter; on those evenings, Adrian went straight to the pub from work and, after Vik left the house, Tania had the evening to herself.

Winter was giving way to spring when, one day, Tania closed the front door behind her last student and pressed her head briefly to the cool glass panels. This week, every student had seemed to have lead weights attached to their fingers. She had been hard pressed to control her exasperation as she listened to them fumble their way through pieces they ought to have known by heart. Years of experience had taught Tania to keep her frustration to herself, so she continued to encourage and advise while inside she longed to push the child from the piano stool and take their place.

Now it *was* her turn. She returned to the living room and seated herself at the keys. Drawing in a breath, she closed her eyes and lost herself in her favourite concerto. As she played she felt the anger leave her, to be replaced by waves of warmth as she poured out her feelings through her fingers and filled the house with liquid joy. She came to the cadenza and threw the full force of her heart into the final phrases, listening as the last chord rang through the silent house. She remained that way, her fingers still above the keys and her eyes shut, allowing the passion to leave her body as the echo of the music died away. As she sat at the piano, she became aware of an aroma nearby. The smell of tea. Puzzled, she opened her eyes and there, on top of the piano, was a mug of steaming freshly poured tea.

Tania reached up to take the mug. She turned slowly around on the piano stool, holding the steaming brew to her lips. A gasp escaped her as, across the darkening room, she saw Vik sitting upright on the edge of the couch, his body held stiffly as if not sure of his welcome.

'I'm sorry.' He spoke gently. 'I couldn't resist. I've never heard playing like that before. I had to see it for myself. I hope you will forgive the intrusion.'

He crossed to the door, obviously intending to go back upstairs.

Tania collected herself just as he opened the door. 'It's OK, Vik. You just startled me. I thought you were working. Thank you for the tea. I'm glad you enjoy my playing.'

Vik turned back to her, his face alight. '*Enjoy* is not the word, Mrs Jensen. Really, it was beautiful. I have never heard the piano played like that except in a concert hall.'

Tania blushed. 'It has been a long time since I performed. Fridays are the evenings when I get the chance to play for myself. I hadn't realised you were at home.'

'My cousin doesn't need me on Fridays for a while. I really hope you do not mind that I came in. I loved to hear you play.'

The next week, Tania again said goodbye to her final student on Friday evening and returned to the piano. She hadn't seen Vik go out so she paused a moment, listening for any sounds of movement in the house. All was quiet.

She began to play, this time warming up with some scales and finger exercises before launching in to her favourite piece. As she played, she found herself in part playing not only for herself but for her unseen listener. Knowing that Vik was upstairs and paying attention to her lent a different dimension to the music. It had been a long time since she'd had an audience. Again she became lost in the music and heard nothing but, when she opened her eyes at the end, a mug of hot tea sat on top of the piano. When she turned on the stool, no-one was there.

Gradually over the weeks Tania found she was changing her selection. Instead of focusing only on her favourite concerto she began to bring in pieces from her past, playing music that she hadn't touched in years but that she found she could still call to her fingertips. She strained her ears before beginning to play, trying to discern if Vik was really there. She never heard a sound but, at the end of each set of pieces she would lift her eyes with surprise to see that Vik had silently joined her in the room again. She began to leave the door slightly ajar so that he could slip in soundlessly. For the first time, she began to look forward to sharing her Friday evenings.

Throughout that spring, Tania would perform their private concert. As spring slipped into summer, her playing would be followed by a quiet chat with her audience. She and Vik would sit and talk about the music, and about his life before he came to England. She didn't mention this new routine to Adrian, feeling the new friendship sat shell-fragile in her hands. Describing it would somehow shatter it. When Adrian joked that they had the perfect lodger – never seen, never heard – her absent, outward smile of agreement masked an inner, secret smile for the music they had shared.

With the midpoint of the year came time for Adrian's annual weekend trip to the coast with his pub mates. Their annual *Lads on Tour* holiday took them to a different seaside resort each year to play golf and drink like the youths they no longer were. This tradition had started when they first moved to the area, when Adrian had joked it was the only time he'd be free with his friends without the responsibilities of being a parent. The responsibilities hadn't appeared but the tradition continued.

'Are you going to be OK on your own with the Silent Lodger?' Adrian asked the night before he left.

'Yes, of course. Vik's no trouble. I hardly know he's here. Makes me feel safer, actually,' Tania lied.

After Adrian had gathered up his duffel bag and departed that Friday evening, Tania shut the door behind him and let the silence of the house wash over her. She became conscious of a deep hum within her body, like an electrical charge, each nerve stretching out in consciousness of Vik waiting upstairs, thinking that he, too, had heard the door shut. Tania walked back to the kitchen and filled the kettle, her hands moving distractedly. She opened the back door to let in a burst of warm summer air. *This is no good,* she thought. *I have to go out.*

Her steps took her, unthinkingly, to the churchyard and the feet of the stone angel. She reached out her hand to stroke the cold folds of the robes, looking up to the sightless eyes.

'Help me,' she mouthed. 'I don't know if I can do this.'

She didn't know how long she stood there, hearing nothing, feeling only her heart pounding as the chill stone warmed beneath her touch. Her thoughts pulled her back to her house where once again, one room seemed to be calling to her with a need only she could hear.

* * *

Tania took her seat at the piano. Knowing that Adrian would not be back made the evening feel different from every other Friday. Even before she pressed a key, the instrument seemed to thrum with the pounding of her heart. Tania took a deep breath and began to play.

After the final notes echoed in the room, Tania opened her eyes. A new aroma rose from the top of the piano. Where she had expected to see the usual mug of tea, this time she saw a small, silver shot glass. She turned round and her eyes met Vik's. He inclined his head, silently indicating she should taste what was in the glass. Cautiously she lifted it down and peered inside, seeing a honey-coloured liquid from which arose a sweet and spicy scent.

'It's a liqueur from my home,' Vik said. 'Last week, the piece you played made me think of home so I wanted to share this with you.'

Tania saw that there was another, similar glass beside him on a small, mirrored tray. He raised it to her in a silent toast, and sipped. She did the same, keeping her eyes on his. Blue gaze held black as the liquid's power warmed her heart with a taste as clean and bright as metal.

Vik slowly set his glass back on the tray then crossed the floor and held out his hand for her glass. Their fingers brushed and a jolt shuddered through Tania. She looked at him, uncertain. Slowly she rose from the piano stool to stand by him, their bodies close, her eyes never leaving his. Tania couldn't say who moved first but she was in his arms, his lips crushing against hers as the heat continued to flow through her, lost in his kiss.

They broke apart, breathing heavily. Vik stammered, 'I'm sorry, I'm sorry!' and turned to flee from the room, but Tania held out a hand to stop him.

'Vik, no. Wait. It's me. It's all right. Just wait a moment.' She paused, repeating distractedly 'It's all right. It's all right. It's . . . '

But as she came close to him again she couldn't help it – she had to touch him. She put her hands on his face and drew him closer, gazing again into the dark eyes that pulled her in. Their lips pressed together, and Tania felt a lightness inside her. She had to have more of him. She drew back and slid her hands down to his, gently leading him towards the stairs.

Tania pushed away all thoughts but this moment. A force stronger than anything she'd felt before seemed to propel her to fulfil the need she'd had for years.

Outside Vik's door she paused, turning her face to his. The kiss began again and she felt she was kissing him not just with her lips but with every part of her body, her mind, even her soul. It was almost too much. Together they pushed the door open and went into the room, their hands reaching for one another, urgently pushing aside clothes and pulling at each other more strongly, both feeling the need to become part of the other. Tania couldn't remember ever feeling like this before, her hands slipping over Vik's smooth brown chest and feeling heat flowing through her like a shaman, not knowing where her body ended and his began. As she knelt on the bed above him she looked down into his eyes and knew that this had to happen. Adrian could have been in the next room and she wouldn't care. This was the moment she had needed all her life.

The night passed like a dream, with Tania sliding into sleep then waking and turning her head to see Vik's eyes gleaming in the moonlight as he gazed at her. Tania's whole body would flood with desire and she'd reach for him again.

In that weekend, Tania felt she became a different person. Her entire body, her entire being was focused on a single objective and nothing could stand in her way. She pushed thoughts of Adrian into a separate room in her mind and closed the door, firmly. All she could think about was Vik and what this time meant to her.

On Sunday night, Tania lay in bed and gazed around the white walls of the room. It was hard to imagine that this was the same space where she had spent so much time with her unborn babies. It seemed an entirely different life. She sighed, feeling tears in her eyes for the missed opportunities.

Turning her head on the pillow, she saw Vik's dark eyes on hers.

'You know Adrian is back tomorrow,' she began softly.

'Do we need to talk about that?'

'I think so.'

'Is that all this is? An interlude while he's away?'

'You know it's not.' Tania stroked Vik's cheek. 'I don't know what this is yet. But there *is* Adrian. What I have with him, it's... Well, it's not what we're having now. I don't *know* what we're having now, but it seems separate from *anything* to do with Adrian.'

'I don't like to betray him. He's a good man.'

Tania gazed at Vik, continuing to stroke his cheek. 'You're right. Let's not talk about that now. Let's just make the most of this last night together.'

Adrian arrived home the next evening, flinging open the front door and dropping his bag like a schoolboy as he shouted, 'I'm home!'

'In the kitchen,' Tania replied, hastily drying her hands and smoothing back her hair. Adrian pulled her to him in a warm embrace. His face buried in her hair, he whispered against her ear, 'Everything all right?' Tania pulled back from him to look into his eyes, nodding. 'Yes, darling. I think everything's fine.'

The next morning, after Adrian had left for work, Tania stood in the kitchen, her nerves as taut as piano strings. No sound came from upstairs. Could Vik be asleep? Tania moved restlessly from the counter to the table and then the window before returning to the counter. Finally she went to the living room, opened the piano and began to press the keys, gently at first then more angrily until, with a discordant cry, she crashed all her fingers down at once. She pushed back from the piano and approached Vik's room, laying her hand flat on the door for a moment then forming her fist to knock. Before she struck, the door opened and Vik pulled her to him again.

There was a kind of madness to life throughout that summer. The hours of Adrian's absence became time for her and Vik. Duplicity was easier than Tania had ever thought possible. When Adrian remarked again on their 'perfect lodger' Tania nodded and agreed, all the while stilling her body from the shudder that ran through her at the sound of Vik's name. Those few hours each Friday night, when previously she had poured out her passion on the piano, were now given over to her and Vik. Throughout that summer, her role changed from landlady to lover. During the rest of the week, Tania continued with her students in the daytime and cooked for Adrian each evening, her chrysalis firmly intact. Only on Friday evenings did it split and allow a new creature to emerge. Surely Adrian would notice a difference, would see that the ravaged stones beneath her gaze were finally being overlaid with something softer?

It was the hottest summer anyone could remember, with days shimmering into humid nights and air so still you could touch it. Her students listlessly pumped the keys and Tania turned sheets of music as if underwater.

It was on a Friday in late August that the heat finally broke and a new, fresh breeze heralded the start of autumn. Tania had woken that morning knowing something was different. She sat up in bed and reached for the mug of tea Adrian had brought her. She took a sip then rested the mug on the mound of covers over her belly, feeling the warmth spread through her. She turned her face to the window, to the scudding clouds arguing above the rooftops. Setting down the mug on the bedside table, she lifted the telephone receiver and dialled a number she knew by heart.

* * *

Tania returned from her errand and let herself into the silent house. She leaned back against the door and finally allowed the smile that had been held inside throughout her journey home to fix upon her face. She opened her handbag and gazed again at the slip of paper inside it then looked up the stairs, her expression hardening.

In the evening, Tania stayed at the piano and waited for Vik to join her. She picked out a brief melody on the highest keys as she waited. Finally his puzzled face appeared around the door; it was the first Friday since their new routine began that she had not come to him. Tania kept her face fixed on the sheets of her music as she spoke.

'Vik, we need to talk.'

He lowered himself gently to the couch. 'Is something the matter?'

Tania spoke to the orderly staves of music before her. 'Vik, these few months with you have been wonderful but I can't do this any more. I have to be loyal to my husband and my marriage. I can't keep up this deception.'

Stiffening her shoulders, Tania twisted slowly on the piano stool to face him. She lifted her head and met his dark gaze forthrightly. Vik's eyes searched hers. 'May I ask what has changed?'

'Nothing, Vik. Well, everything. Inside me. I just can't do this any more. I am going to have to ask you to leave, to give me a chance to rebuild.'

'What will Adrian say to that? I am the perfect lodger, after all,' Vik said bitterly. 'I pay my rent on time, I make no noise, I cause no trouble. Aside from what you and I have, he is not bothered by me at all. And he doesn't know about us. Why do we have to do things differently? Tania, you don't understand. This isn't a casual thing for me. I think I am in love with you.'

Tania took a breath to speak, but Vik carried on.

'It started with your playing. Your music drew me in like it was a spell. And when you turned to me that evening, when Adrian was away, I felt that what we had was special. It's not just sex to me, Tania. We have a connection. We *work* together, surely you feel it too? How can it be wrong?

'I am not afraid of Adrian. He's a sympathetic man, he'll understand that we couldn't help ourselves. Come away with me, Tania. We can find somewhere else to live, far away from Shakespeare Street. We can be together forever. Please, give me a chance!'

Vik had tears running down his face as he moved from the couch to kneel at Tania's side, burying his face in her lap. She sat rigid on the piano stool but, unwittingly, her hands rose to stroke his sleek black hair, feeling its texture, so stiff and yet so smooth, so different to her own. For a moment she paused, feeling the urge to slide her hands further, below his collar to the smooth warm skin of his back, but she resisted. A core deep inside her stirred, reminding her of her resolve.

'I'm sorry, Vik. It's over. It has to be over. I think it's best that you leave as soon as possible.'

She rose, pushing back the piano stool and stepping away from his kneeling form. Tania swiftly stepped to the kitchen where she sat at the table, her hands twisting as she listened to the sobs from the other room. After what seemed like a lifetime the sound ceased, and she heard Vik's footsteps ascend.

As soon as Adrian left the house the next day, Vik came to her again. Tania sat at the kitchen table, her hands clasped in front of her as Vik begged, even falling to his knees again in front of her. Still she remained obdurate and, throughout the week, Vik's pain and disbelief gradually turned to anger.

On the next Friday, Tania waited in the living room in front of the piano, not touching the keys. Vik pushed open the door.

'What if I tell?' he demanded.

'Vik,' she began wearily.

'No really,' he broke in. 'What if I tell? What if I tell Adrian what we've been doing? Then what? That would change everything, wouldn't it?'

Tania lifted her head to look at him. His thin frame was almost skeletal and she felt pity for how his emotion had drained him. His hands shook and his eyes were glowing with an almost evangelical fervour.

'Vik please, sit down,' she said gently. He sank to the couch and buried his face in his hands. Tania moved to sit beside him and lifted her hand to his shoulder. His body shook at her touch.

'Vik, I can't explain it. You know I've tried. It was crazy, what we were doing. It was beautiful, but I can't keep living in a dream. It's not fair on Adrian, it's not fair on you . . . And it's not fair on me. I didn't have the resolve before to stop myself, but something changed inside me. I still care for you. I care for you very much, and I'll always keep something of you with me. But I can't carry on living a lie. And telling Adrian . . . Well, it wouldn't make any difference. You and I are never going to continue as we were.'

She put her hand beneath his chin and raised his head till their faces were level. At first his eyes darted round the room and refused to focus on hers then, finally, reluctantly, they settled to her like a butterfly landing on a flower petal. Gradually Tania saw a kernel deep within Vik's eyes change as he focused on her implacable resolve.

'You really, really mean it, don't you Tania?' he whispered.

'I really, really mean it. I'm so sorry, Vik. Please forgive me.'

The next morning, Tania was woken by Adrian gently shaking her shoulder. 'Wake up, Tan. Vik's gone!'

Tania rubbed her eyes and looked blearily at her husband. 'What do you mean, gone?'

'His door was standing open when I got up and I peeked inside. The bed is stripped, the wardrobe is standing open and empty, and there's a note with some cash on the bed.'

Tania sat up. 'A note? What did it say?'

Adrian looked at the piece of paper in his hand. *'Circumstances call me away and here's a month's rent in lieu of notice*. Did you notice anything strange about him lately? Do you have any idea why he's gone?'

Tania shook her head. 'No, he's been the same as ever. I wonder what could have happened.'

She lay back on the pillow and allowed herself to feel relief that Vik had taken her advice to heart and had left as quickly as he could. Now it was time for her to focus on the future. She lifted the cup of tea Adrian had brought her and looked at him over the rim. 'You know, darling, I am not sure that having a lodger is such a great idea. I think we should do something different with that room now. Let me talk to you about my ideas . . . '

* * *

The first buds of spring were just bursting into blossom when Tania and Adrian decided that the weather was right for a walk. They meandered slowly along the high street, pausing to look in shop windows as they went. As they approached the newsagent's Adrian said, 'I'm just going to nip in and get a paper, love. Won't be a tick. You wait out here.'

Tania smiled and agreed. 'I'll be in the churchyard,' she said.

She strolled through the churchyard until she reached the stone angel. Looking up in to its eyes she placed her hand on the stiff folds of stone as she had done so many times before. The spring sunshine had warmed the stone and she closed her eyes, remembering. Then she heard a voice say her name.

Startled, she turned quickly and, for a moment, was dazzled by the sun. A figure stood before her, a long, shadowed shape ringed with the glow of the sun, just as Vik had been all that time ago. As her vision cleared, she realised it *was* Vik.

'Vik! I thought you must be gone for good!' she exclaimed.

'I know, Tania. I'm sorry. I . . . I had to leave suddenly. I should have said a proper goodbye to you but I couldn't bear to talk about it any more. I wasn't thinking very clearly at the time and, by the time I had thought how I could do it differently, it was too late. But I should not have run away. I should have tried harder. So many times I nearly came back to see you, and I nearly wrote you a letter . . . But, in the end, I couldn't bring myself to contact you.'

Vik bit his lip and drew a ragged breath. 'It's nearly a year since I left Shakespeare Street. I thought it was time I tried to come back. I hoped I might see you, but I didn't have the nerve to come to the house.'

'Vik, I'm sorry too. I know it was so hard. It was hard for me too. I shouldn't have broken it to you so suddenly but I had . . . I can only call it an awakening. I just realised that I had to do things differently. It was a beautiful time, but it was madness and I had to bring it to an end.'

'And Adrian? How is he?'

'He's fine. In fact, we . . . We're all fine.' As she said this, Tania moved slightly to one side to allow Vik to see what was behind her. In the shadow of the stone angel stood a gleaming pram and, within it, nestled beneath soft white blankets, Vik could see a cap of wispy, dark hair.

Vik looked at Tania in bewilderment. Her voice was soft. 'What you and I had made me realise that I needed to try again with my husband. And this was the result! Adrian and I are thrilled. We'd just about given up hope,' Tania said firmly.

Vik stepped closer to peer at the sleeping baby. Before he could speak, a whistle heralded Adrian's approach. 'Vik! Long time no see, mate! Are you admiring our new addition? Gorgeous, isn't she?'

As he spoke, the baby stirred, yawned, and opened her eyes. Vik bent closer to look. The baby blinked and gazed at this new face, her limpid eyes pools of shiny black ink.

Vik raised his head to meet Adrian and Tania's blank blue gazes. 'But . . . ' he began.

Adrian forestalled him by holding out his hand. Automatically, Vik raised his to meet Adrian's and the two men shook hands. 'It's great to see you, Vik. You'll never know what a difference you made to us. We just can't thank you enough. Come on now, Tania; we'd better get madam here back home before she starts demanding something to eat.'

With a last look at Vik, Tania turned away and put her arm through Adrian's, the other hand pushing the pram. Vik stood rooted to the pavement, watching their shapes get smaller as they drew further away.

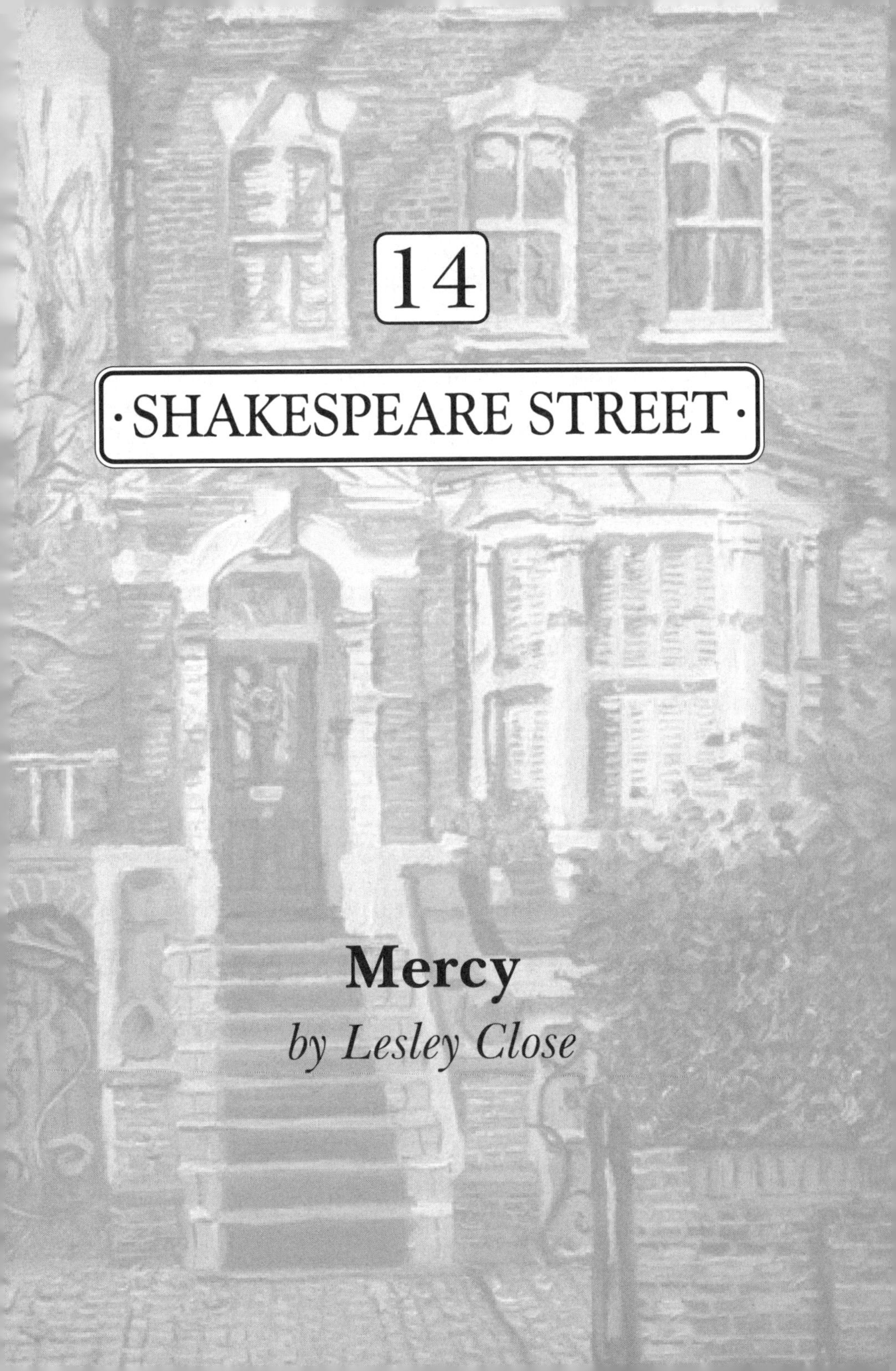

14 SHAKESPEARE STREET

Mercy

by Lesley Close

Ay me, I see the downfall of our house!
The tiger now hath seized the gentle hind;
Insulting tyranny begins to jet Upon the innocent and aweless throne: Welcome, destruction, death, and massacre!
I see, as in a map, the end of all.

Richard III, Act 2, Scene 4

The introduction

I'm far from enthusiastic about writing this but I'm told it might assuage my guilt, so here goes. *What guilt?* I hear you ask. We'll come to that later. For the moment all you need to know is that it was Lil, that most unwelcome – and thankfully short-term – house-guest, who started this particular ball rolling. Having declined to accept all the blame for what happened with Alison and her husband (Alison's husband, that is – you have to be so careful when writing things down . . .) Lil, quite rightly, blamed me. And then, quite understandably, Lil's niece declined to believe her. 'A ghost told you to do that?' It does sound ridiculous when you say it aloud, doesn't it?

Lil tried various methods to get rid of me, most of which were smelly. She burned incense and sprinkled salt and rice about. When that failed, she turned to a foul combination of garlic and cabbage water. After I got the stench of her *very* creative attempts to get rid of me out of my nostrils, I wanted to tell her how many others had tried and failed. I had hoped it would work this time, and Lil seemed to know whereof she spoke. You see I'm tired of my 'life' and could do with a break, as people say these days. I could go all democratic and say that it's time for me to step aside and give a younger ghost a chance, but that's not how I feel. I'm just *tired*.

Amongst all the gobbledegook, Lil said something astonishingly profound: *What someone leaves behind is what people remember of them.* That idea stayed with – and troubled – me. While it is over a hundred years since there was anybody alive to remember me, if James and my lodgers inhabit this street as ghosts they will remember me just as clearly as I can recall them. I cannot see or interact with other 'ethereal beings' but my newly acquired conscience hates the thought of being remembered as unpleasant, even by the dead. We all deserve peace after death, however disruptive we were in life.

Even though I am unable to simply give up being 'alive', it looks like I am in charge of this situation so I have decided to try exorcising myself. Technically, I will be attempting to clear myself – getting rid of a ghost from a building is 'clearance' while exorcism removes a spirit from a person. Or so the faithful would have you believe. I was never a believer in any of this spiritual stuff until 'it' happened to me, at which point – well, I had no choice in the matter.

I chose this exorcism method – the punster in me wants to call it a 'novel' approach – following Lil's final attempt. While she waited for the taxi, she burned one of the parrot's feathers in the hall. My, how that woman loved creating an awful smell. She horrified her poor niece by attempting to elevate a simple item of bird's plumage to the status of Shakespeare's quill via some arcane ritual involving fire. As the blue barbs burned, she intoned something about using the quill to inscribe my sins on my heart before examining my woes, repenting and expunging my guilt so I can move on to the next level – or words to that effect. What level I'm on now and where I'm going next Lil didn't make clear, but something I once heard someone say about 'laying a ghost' by writing about it came back to me so strongly when I heard Lil's dramatic incantation that I decided to try her idea. Frankly, I'm so tired I'll try anything.

If you listen to the psychologically informed mediums (of whom quite a few have visited the house over the last hundred or so years), it would appear that I am in some form of purgatory because of the wickedness of my life (and I do mean while I was alive). And, apparently, it is the resulting feeling of being trapped on

Shakespeare Street that has made me behave so wickedly towards other its residents after my death.

Living on Shakespeare Street for so long, I have seen all sorts of people come and go. More interestingly, I have seen all sorts of relationship grow, flourish and be fruitful or else wither and die. I can take very little credit for any of the successes, but I have played a role in many of the failures. I am the very opposite of a matchmaker, you see. I suppose you could call me a matchbreaker, although I'm not sure that any such job title has ever existed. Calling it a 'job' is a bit grand of me, to be honest. It's just what I do, what I've always done, and ghosts don't really have jobs do they? But I'm tired now. Tired of, by and because of my occupation.

Just like me, you probably find it surprising that ghosts get tired but, believe me, that's definitely how I feel. Maybe it's the burden of the guilt, weighing me down; maybe I'll feel more spritely when the guilt is gone. (Did you get the joke? It wasn't a spelling mistake but another attempt at a pun. Okay, I never said I was going to be any good at this writing thing . . .) Here's hoping for one or the other outcome, either I vanish or I feel reinvigorated. I simply know that things can't go on as they are for much longer.

So, to the task in hand. They say a good story needs a beginning, a middle and an end. Mine starts many years ago and will, I hope, end when I complete this writing task and have told my story in full.

The beginning

I've lived in this house since it was built in 1795 and, until very recently, I had no intention of moving out whatever anyone said or did. I mentioned exorcism earlier and, inspired by a popular horror film, in 1975 the owner tried the full ritual but sold up after it failed, spectacularly, to shift me. The vicar who agreed to do the job sprinkled holy water everywhere and prayed all over the place in a fashionable and expensive – but completely ineffectual – attempt to cure what he referred to as *the haunting*. I enjoyed the experience, though, and I was able to display all the tricks in my arsenal to good effect, from tilting tables (which – excuse the pun – is dead easy when you are invisible) to making 'ectoplasm' appear (it was really a piece of much-used muslin, but don't tell the people from television's *Most Haunted*). Another couple thought they could get rid of me by Morris Dancing and invited the whole troupe – or is it clan? – to practise in the house in the hope that I'd give up and move out. Not me – it takes a lot more than a bit of hocus-pocus or bell-jingling to scare me.

My name is not important – nobody but me knows it now, after all – but, for what it's worth, I became Mercy Scudder when I married in 1792. Mercy is singularly inapt – I'm heartless – but Scudder is good. It means a spy. I choose my victims carefully, then watch and listen and observe and record until I have enough material before I set to my self-appointed task.

Why did I choose this line of work? Because of that rogue James Scudder, my thankfully dead husband. He of the wandering hands and silver tongue who persuaded me into his bed then left me there, ignorant of his whereabouts, while he went off in search of another innocent to seduce. To quote and misquote Charlotte Brontë in *Jane Eyre,* published twelve years after my death, 'Reader, I married – then murdered – him'.

Which reminds me – there's another reason why I chose writing as my self-help therapy, as I started to hear people call things like this in the late twentieth century. I adored reading – and being read to – while I was alive. One of my favourite activities, even now, is to sit with someone while they read. I promise you that I don't do anything other than to read along with them and there's absolutely nothing sinister in it. But, while silent reading is fast and efficient, it is so much better if they are reading aloud. The sound of the human voice is one of the few things that allows me to relax, especially if the reader is a fluent speaker who puts feeling and expression in to their diction. I close my eyes, letting their spoken words tell the story, and the story takes me to another place. Which reminds me, I must get back to telling my own tale!

It was only after the wedding that I discovered how loathsome James really was. So I poisoned him. But that was a long time ago, 1798 to be precise. He had behaved in a particularly vexatious manner at Christmas and New Year of 1797 and my resolution for 1798 was to stop his philandering ways by whatever means it took. In my innocence, my intention was to reignite the flame of our love (a phrase I remember, word-for-word, from a Barbara Cartland book that I read much later) but that idea failed to get off the ground because he always came home drunk, if and when he came home at all. In my next attempt at healing the physical and emotional rift between us (more romantic fiction, I'm afraid) I tried to talk to him about my feelings, but he just laughed and made a rude joke about 'feeling' that I could not possibly relate here.

So I visited several different apothecaries, obtaining a few grains of arsenic from each after telling them I needed to poison some rats. It was ludicrously easy to buy arsenic and I ended up with enough to poison everyone in Shakespeare Street. I don't mind admitting that that idea had its appeal but, despite some of our neighbours being deeply unpleasant people, mass-murder was never my serious intention. Anyway, that would have aroused more than a little suspicion when all I wanted was to murder James.

Having obtained the means of solving my problem I toyed with the idea of slowly poisoning James. I liked the notion that the distress and discomfort he would suffer over a period of months would mirror and amplify the distress and anxiety he had inflicted on me over a period of years. But I rejected that thought as he was a vain and silly man would probably seek the opinion of a doctor. My worry was that, if the practitioner was up to snuff, James might be diagnosed with slow poisoning. No – much as I would have enjoyed seeing James's suffering lead to a slow and painful death, I decided that one fatal dose was the most reliable route. I added it to a small cup of hot chocolate which he accepted from my hands, without a word of thanks, late one bitterly cold night in February 1798. I deliberately made the drink rich and creamy, using the taste of cardamom and cinnamon to mask any unpleasant flavour the arsenic might impart. Unluckily, he took the untasted drink with him when he went to sleep in the second bedroom so I didn't have the pleasure of witnessing his end.

The following morning I knocked on his door long before dawn. I received no shouted 'Go away!' so felt free to enter his chamber. He was on the bed, the almost-empty cup clutched in his hand. Some of the remaining chocolate had spilled on to the bed sheet beneath and beside him and, ominously, the dark mark resembled an old blood stain. After prising the cup from his cold, rigid fingers, I took the vessel downstairs and poured what remained of the drink down the drain.

Back in the bedroom, I carefully washed James's body before removing the soiled bedlinen, dressing him in a clean nightgown and remaking the bed. I'm not prepared to elaborate on why I needed to give him a bed bath, but it wasn't an office I enjoyed performing. None of those tasks was easy as his corpse was stiff and twisted, but they were necessary.

Just one hour after knocking on James's bedroom door, I was satisfied with the way he looked. His corpse was clean and lying under clean covers, although his twisted convolutions gave the impression that he was mid-way through leaping out of bed in surprise.

Over the next hour or so, I paced the kitchen floor. Had I forgotten anything in my attempt to hide my murderous actions? I left the house as early as was respectable in the hope that, if I left him alone all day, the stiffness in his body would pass. I had no intention of calling for the doctor, of course, but if anyone should call to see him I wanted them to think that he had died during a fit of apoplexy. Luckily, when I got back after spending a very pleasant day in the Vauxhall Pleasure Gardens, not somewhere I would ever be seen after dark, the worst of the rigor had loosened. I knew I would be able to manipulate his body into its hiding place but there was no hurry. The bedroom – indeed the whole house – was cold and I wasn't expecting visitors.

Early in the morning of the second day I visited the builder who had erected some of the houses in Shakespeare Street, including mine. He owed me a favour but it would be best if you didn't know the precise nature of his debt. I can tell you that his miserable, violent wife had recently vanished and the cause of her disappearance was unknown, except to me and him . . . He agreed to come to Shakespeare Street the following day, on his own, to assess the scale of the task I outlined.

As with all the houses in this short terrace there was a corridor, along the party wall, between the withdrawing and dining rooms. It was as long as the back-to-back chimney breasts were deep, about eight feet, and only a little wider than the door at either end. Over the next two days my friendly builder bricked up both doorways after helping me to install the secret chamber's sole occupant. It was a warm and dry place, rather like the environment in the pyramids discovered over one hundred years later by Howard Carter, and James's body simply dried out after being sealed in. The alterations included extending the wainscoting to cover the new bricks.

If anyone enquired after James my cover story (if you'll forgive the pun) was that he had arranged for the building work to be done. Shortly after it started, the two of us had an almighty argument about the mess and the expense and he had left home in a huff. I fully expected him to return from his bolt hole when the work was complete. The builder agreed to that story – the hold I had over him meant he had no choice in the matter.

The location of James's body is one – in fact the only – reason the Morris Dancers gave me such joy. James 'the rapscallion' Scudder would have hated all that prancing about, and he would have detested the steel band which was invited to play there by another owner keen to get rid of me. Hooray for would-be exorcists with a vivid imagination, I say!

Do forgive me – I've this awful tendency to get ahead of myself. It's probably the result of spending so much time in this house. I assume everyone knows the whole story of my life as well as I do, and I forget to fill in the background.

Where was I? I don't think I'd finished the beginning of the story, so let me start again. For three years after I married James and before we moved to this house, we lived with his mother in the house his father's will provided for her lifetime use. As far as James was concerned, the most logical step was for his mother to sell the house and give James the money that would otherwise only come to him after her death. He didn't put it like that, of course, instead asking whether she would like to enjoy the benefits of moving to the much nicer Shakespeare Street house with us. As it was, it seemed that James wouldn't have had to wait long for his inheritance as Mrs Scudder senior died when we had only been living here for two years. I say seemed because her death was, let's say, unexpected and it didn't cause James a great deal of distress. It simply meant she no longer cost him anything to feed and clothe. I didn't miss her at all as she was an annoying woman, not least for thinking the sun shone out of her beloved son's – well, I won't use her word, but it was pretty fundamental.

Robert, James's younger brother, didn't get a look in on their mother's estate, such as it was, further souring the relationship between them which had deteriorated since their father's death. Robert's lack of an inheritance may also explain why he was so keen to reclaim James's estate later . . . But I'm skipping bits again – so sorry.

James was always too busy gallivanting to earn a proper living, although his mother didn't know anything about that. She thought her ne'er-do-well son was doing very well as the result of working very hard. To justify the handouts she willingly gave him, he claimed to have his fingers in many 'investment' pies. I know where his fingers really were, at least some of the time. They were dipping into other people's pockets, literally and metaphorically, to appropriate their wealth for himself.

After poisoning James and having his body walled up, I lived here on my own for a long time. I'm glad we didn't have children – they would have used up James's money much more quickly. As it was, I didn't empty the coffers for about ten years. After that I took in the occasional single, male lodger when my finances got particularly tight. They were, without exception, unpleasant and demanding men who had experienced some difficulty finding lodgings. As a result, they were grateful that I was willing, for a price, to provide them with food and a bed. I also provided some of wealthiest and most friendless of them with a single dose of arsenic in one of the breakfasts or dinners we shared.

By being a respectable landlady who charged a high rent I obtained enough cash to see me through lean times between lodgers. That, and by making sure I knew where in the house the cash-rich lodgers kept their wealth. Oh, and by getting the guilt-laden builder back in to remove a section of wainscoting and wall then putting everything back to 'normal' around what remained of the most vile of them. So, as I said, I lived here on my own –

apart, that is, from James and his 'cell-mates', the missing lodgers who nobody else missed. And then . . .

The middle

. . . And then, on 28th June 1838, I was almost home after travelling into The City to celebrate the young Queen Victoria's coronation when I got into an argument with a woman on top of the knifeboard bus. Ladies normally sat downstairs, inside the bus, but there were a great many ladies and very few men that day. With the conductor's permission, and in the company of other ladies, I sat 'up top' for the first – and last – time.

When my stop was near I stood up to disembark, making my way towards the stairs. I was trying to get round one particular lady (not a title I would choose to bestow on her) when I accidentally stood on her foot. Well, maybe not accidentally. In her inebriated condition, I thought she was making too much noise and taking up far too much room. Her overreaction to the small pain I inflicted on her was to push me away very hard and my reaction to her shove was overly dramatic, a combination which led to me slipping over the handrail and falling on to the cobbles. That wouldn't have been so bad but a passing brewery dray, whose driver had sampled a bit too much of his master's wares in celebration of the Great Day, ran me over just after I hit the ground. Even though the cart was empty, having unloaded its cargo to slake the thirsts of the new Queen's Londoners, as soon as I stood up I knew I was dead. I could see my fatally damaged body lying beneath me although I wasn't aware of floating above my corporeal self, like some people claim in near-death experiences. I was just standing there, staring at my corpse and hearing the screams. Not my screams, though. I felt remarkably calm and, besides, my mouth was shut forever.

James's drip of a brother Robert took charge of 'my' estate. His wife was one of the most appalling women I have ever met. She and I were introduced when Robert brought her to my wedding breakfast. The mere fact that he had the gall to invite a stranger into the bosom of his family on such a special day says a lot about him. That she accepted his invitation said a lot about her and, as I got to know her, I realised that my first impression of her wasn't nearly bad enough. In character she was vain, arrogant, conceited and selfish while in appearance she was very tall and painfully thin.

For her wedding to Robert, which took place eighteen months after mine to James, she wore a dress which had been especially made for the occasion. It was a fashionable gown of white silk trimmed with lace. That kind of lavish expense may be the norm in twenty-first century, but most late-eighteenth century brides wore a coloured dress that they could re-use for balls. And only the wealthiest wore silk.

It was typical of her to demand the best, and typical of her indulgent father to virtually bankrupt himself to provide the best for his only child. But he had always encouraged her to feel superior to everyone else, starting with her very name. She was christened Jemima Postlethwaite in honour of the great explorer James Cook who her father had known when he lived in Whitby. Mr and Mrs Postlethwaite had been hoping their first child would be a boy and Mr P hoped all his life for a boy, but no other children came along. Externally Jemima remained resolutely feminine and frilly but underneath the frippery was an iron constitution, a heart of stone and acidic blood.

After her marriage to Robert, she was definitely in charge of their household. Robert simply did as he was told, calling her his 'Princess' at her request. This was partly a reaction to her father calling her 'pet', which wouldn't have been out of place in his native north east but didn't sound right in suburban London.

Robert and Princess Poison-pen Peacock (don't get me started on her nasty letter-writing skills – oh my word!) claimed the house and its contents on the grounds that nobody knew whether or not James was still alive so, as his next of kin, they had the right to take over his possessions (which were only mine to 'enjoy' during my lifetime by virtue of being his widow). There was no lodger to evict at that time but – and I like to think they were following my example – they decided to rent the house out to get a steady income. They could always sell it later if they needed the cash. The first tenant was a young man who had moved to the city to start a civil engineering business. They didn't tell him about me, James or Mrs Scudder senior, claiming that they had lived in the house for many years. He – I'll call him William – was pleased to take on such a charming home (to use my poisonous sister-in-law's for-once accurate words), and he moved in just before Christmas 1838.

To set the scene for his arrival (you see how much better I'm getting at this story-telling lark?), I need to step back a bit to the earliest days of living here as a ghost – if it can be called living. I found it really difficult to adapt to my new status, if that's the right word. The first time I walked up to the front door, while my bleeding corpse still lay on the cobbles, I grasped the handle to open it and found that my incorporeal fingers went straight through the metal and wood. Stepping forward I experienced no sensations, pleasant or otherwise, as I crossed the apparently formless threshold into the hallway. Nothing had changed to look at, but the black and white tiles on the floor no longer felt cold beneath my feet. (Later I discovered that, by choosing the right 'mind-set', as they started saying in the late twentieth century, I could decide whether or not to feel and interact with things around the house and, at times, it was a useful choice to be able to make.)

I'm getting distracted again. Sorry. That first day of my death, after walking the length of the tiled hall, I entered the kitchen to pick up the gin bottle for a much-needed slug. Disaster! I saw my hand appear in the longed-for slightly greasy-looking fluid behind the green glass. A thought crossed my mind – *Whose gin is this if I am dead?* – and, in that instant of acknowledging that I no longer owned it, I felt the cool, smooth surface of the bottle beneath my hand. I smelled juniper as the cork came out but, as I tilted the bottle to my lips to take a swig, the precious botanically scented liquid hit the floor at my feet. I realised that not having a corporeal throat meant no drinking and that the gin had, literally, gone straight through me.

In ordinary circumstances, that realisation would have made me feel like weeping but no feelings stirred in my breast nor did any tears come to my eyes. I realised that, unlike my interaction with objects, it appeared that I could neither feel nor express emotions. You may consider the resulting emotional deprivation to be the most terrible thing about being a ghost, but I enjoyed being liberated from feelings over which I had previously had little or no control.

It turned out that I could still feel anger towards people to whom I had been close, albeit unwillingly. Much, much later I discovered that guilt could still be real to me in some circumstances, hence this story, but those annoyingly unpredictable feelings – sadness, happiness, love, hatred – were lost to me forever.

This lack of the ability to feel things on the inside of my body, at least – meaning that I didn't need to eat or perform ablutions either – was a huge blessing. I hated everything associated with the stone-floored kitchen and that dreadful, smelly outside privy and I was delighted that I would no longer feel the biting cold on my exposed skin when I was in those places. I soon discovered that I could walk through furniture and walls if I thought of the building and its contents as mine, but if I acknowledged that James was the new owner, those same walls and items became solid. After practising for a while, I later developed the ability to flip between the two modes of thinking. Eventually I was able to apply my ability to 'pass-through – or not' – to everything in the house, whether it had been 'mine' or belonged to other people, and it became a useful part of my armoury of tricks to play on the living.

Despite the problems I was bound to encounter as a ghost, I decided I would stay in the house that had been my home for over forty years. What choice did I have? I was sixty-five, I had lived in Shakespeare Street longer than I'd lived anywhere else and I had nowhere else to go. In fact, it turned out that I probably couldn't go anywhere else. During the post-funeral tea, which was held in 'my' house, cousin Kathleen said, "Once you're dead you stay where you lived." Mind you, she's from Ireland and they have all sorts of funny ideas about life and death there.

I worked out how useful it was going to be to have a choice about being able to make contact with things – as well as controlling whether I was visible and audible to people – the day after my death. Robert and his spouse came to the house and, not being in possession of a key, they brought with them a lout whose sole job was to apply his shoulder to the door and force it open. I was lying on my bed, wondering what would happen next in my new life as a ghost, when I was suddenly aware of a lot of banging at the front of the house. With gravity no longer having a hold over me

I (literally) hovered at the top of the stairs, looking down into the entrance hall. After a particularly loud crash, the lout appeared. He was followed through the now unlocked and un-lockable door by Robert and Princess Poison-pen Peacock. While Robert paid the lout, she started looking round haughtily, proprietarily. I really resented that, and resolved there and then to try changing her mind about taking ownership of my house and my possessions.

As she rooted through the cupboards and drawers in my bedroom, putting some small things in her pocket and placing some larger items in a wooden box she had brought for the purpose, she kept calling out lies, utter falsehoods, for Robert's benefit. 'This may all be ours now, but there's nothing here that's worth having,' she said as she pocketed an ivory-handled fan that James and Robert's mother had been given by an uncle who worked in Africa in the 1740s. 'It's just a load of old rubbish,' she trilled as the tortoiseshell and silver hairbrush, comb and mirror set my mother had given me as a wedding present went in the box. 'We can leave the least-awful items of furniture for the tenant to use,' she said as, running her hand down the door of the beautiful wardrobe James's father had bought on a visit to The Netherlands, she cooed, 'Tell you what, I'll get my brother to take away the worst of it.' He, Jack, was yet another ne'er-do-well, a younger and even less handsome version of my late and not-much-missed husband. Under his dreadful sister's direction, Jack would take all the best things to the nearest pawn shop, I was sure, and split the proceeds with her. I simply couldn't allow that to happen. Not only did I want to stop Jack and the sister-in-law from Hell profiting at my expense, but I also wanted some of my favourite things to remain in the house with me. Or, at least, not to be anywhere near her for too long.

As I followed her from room to room, apparently invisible, I wondered whether the light level might have an influence on her ability to see me. First I stood directly in front of her as she used the light from the window to allow her to admire – and then discard – a set of table runners I had embroidered during my engagement to James. No reaction to my presence. I flitted to and fro in front of the glass while she looked at the various prints hanging from the picture rail but I didn't cast a shadow so her reverie was undisturbed. I wondered whether she would be able to see and feel me if I touched her so I crossed the room and caught up with her as she started to root through my chest of drawers. I was just considering how best to make contact with her when she made contact with some of my most intimate items. Her behaviour was atrocious. She picked up my delicate undergarments between her fingertips and threw them to the floor, her lips pursed in distaste. And then, as she was about to hit what I would later learn could be called 'paydirt', she called out, 'Nobody's going to want all this filthy junk.'

She had found the box of diaries I kept hidden in my bottom drawer. As she opened the volume dated 1798, her voice faded to a whisper. I recoiled in horror as she mis-spoke my confessional language but, recovering enough common sense to understand that I needed to act quickly, I grasped her hand to take the book back. As I touched her warm skin, the colour faded from her face. The look in her eyes told me she could see as well as feel me, and the scream echoing around the bedroom clearly wasn't just her reaction to reading what I'd written at the time I murdered James. She reached out her free hand, trying to push me away, maybe even to scratch my face, and I knew I needed to take radical action if I was to get my diary back. Pulling her with me, I crossed the room towards the wardrobe. The solid wooden doors were still open and, as I pushed her inside, the change in its centre of gravity made it fall over. As the heavy item of furniture landed on top of her, the diary flew out of her hand. In a sequence of moves I like to think of as the 'saving my bacon' dance – which started with the quick thought *Even my diaries belong to James now, I suppose* – I caught the book, put it back in the box with the other volumes and scurried away to hide the whole lot in the attic.

Robert, hearing a scream followed by the sound of falling furniture, dashed up the stairs to rescue his beloved. After he had manfully lifted the wardrobe off her, she started raving about murder. He soothed her, mopped her brow with his handkerchief, saying 'Hush, my darling,' and carried her long, limp form downstairs. The medicinal brandy he gave her perked her up, but she carried on raving. She was adamant she had seen a ghost and it had pushed her into the wardrobe in an attempt to kill her. Robert felt certain that she'd suffered a blow to the head and was simply confused.

Princess Poison-pen Peacock could not be persuaded to forget what she had seen in that room. She insisted that she had read my account of James's murder, but no diaries could be found anywhere in the house (I made sure of that). With no way to back up her story that I had murdered James – thankfully she hadn't reached the section of my 'confession' dealing with how I disposed of his body – and absolutely no evidence that I was living in the house as a ghost, she was compelled to drop the matter.

Who would be interested in hearing that kind of story, anyway? Robert was about to benefit financially from the house and raising the spectre of murder – and, even worse, of a ghost – might reduce the rent he could obtain for it. Despite his execrable taste in women, he was an eminently sensible man, in some ways . . .

They decided to leave my furniture in the house, after emptying all the cupboards and drawers. The kitchen contained only very basic equipment, and they left all that too. I didn't mind that they threw away all my clothes and bed linen, but I was pleased that they left the paintings and prints hanging from the rails.

A lot changed when the first tenant moved in to 21 Shakespeare Street. He was a practical, modern man. He used the attic to store many of the less attractive items which Robert and my thankfully now ex-sister-in-law had left behind and brought in his own furniture. Initially that new stuff, which clearly belonged to him, caused me some difficulty. Not having previously been mine, to start with it was as real an obstacle to my progress around the house as mine had been when I was alive. I worked it out soon enough, though, and was able to 'flip' through his ugly modern stuff just as easily as my own elegant early Georgian items.

But I digress. I was telling you about the bumpy road to love and the joy I get from making it as rocky as possible. I'd ruined quite a few 'love lives' when I was alive, even before James disappeared. As a young woman I got great pleasure from watching another young woman's happiness dissolve in her tears when I innocently told her how I had recently seen her beau at the theatre with an outrageous tart. After moving to Shakespeare Street I enjoyed seeing a happily married man who lived across from this house become incandescent with rage when I mentioned that his wife had admitted a well-dressed man to the house shortly after her husband left for work, and that the handsome visitor hadn't left until late afternoon. I worked on my lies, making up bigger and better stories at every opportunity and becoming more adept at generating utterly believable untruths. And of course, without the ubiquitous mobile phones that now mean everyone knows – or can find out – where everyone else is at all times, there was plenty of room for unfounded suspicion. You must understand that Georgian ladies knew their place in life and that respectable women did not answer back when their husbands challenged them. In those days, Shakespeare Street had only well-to-do, respectable residents. Nowadays? Don't get me started!

Robert and Princess Poison-pen Peacock's first tenant was also my first victim as a ghost. Don't get the wrong idea – I don't mean like James and some of the lodgers were victims. Not at all – it is simply not possible for someone in my position to end the life of a living being, as I discovered when, soon after that first visit, I dealt what I thought would be a fatal blow to my detested sister-in-law. Enough said: it didn't work, so why waste time telling you about it?

My torture of William started when he brought a young woman to the house one Sunday afternoon. It was all quite decorous, boringly respectable in fact. The young woman, Anne, was accompanied by her sister Jane. The two women giggled and tittered their way through afternoon tea while William blushed and stammered and tried to hide his awkwardness. After they left, William moped around the house for hours. When alone, he normally bustled and drew and measured and recorded and thought but here he was, with the sun still shining late on a Sunday afternoon in May, behaving like some of the teenage girls who lived in the house in later years.

Where had I got to? Ah yes. William invited the two women to tea every other Sunday for a while until, one day, they brought a woman who was clearly Mama to both of them. Poor man – did he realize that his beloved might one day look like that? It was clear that he was really smitten with this young woman who could never be his intellectual equal. She, in turn, needed to be saved from a lifetime of boredom as she watched him drawing, measuring and recording – she needed the theatre, gaiety, fun.

I had been thinking this whilst hidden in the one-time corridor. Naturally, I was sharing the space with James and the lodgers but they were of no concern to me. I decided to flip my thinking and become visible to the tea-party guests but I flipped a moment too soon and found myself colliding with the back of the wall. The resulting thumps startled the quartet and I heard matronly cries and girlish screams underlain by a deeper voice attempting to be sensible. 'It's probably the water supply,' I heard the pragmatic William say as I flipped back and prepared to have another go at making a dramatic appearance. I had not previously appeared in front of William, partly for lack of opportunity but mainly because I was still perfecting the flip (as you can tell . . .).

I paused to gather my thoughts and to compose myself, adopting what I hoped was a suitably ghoulish expression. I looked down at the dress I had worn since the day I died and realized, with a degree of pleasure that was unexpected, that it was dirty and torn as was appropriate to a ghost. Steeling myself to make the flip at the right moment, I stepped through the wall. Flipping back I was standing exactly where I had hoped, behind a new floor-to-ceiling drape. It was a copy of a Gobelins tapestry that William had installed as a draught-proof barrier and, when I discovered that William felt the need for the cloth, all sorts of questions arose, like 'Is my builder's work showing signs of its age?' and 'Is there any danger of the bodies being discovered?' There was nothing I could do to correct any defects in the brickwork and no way I could be punished if the corpses were found, but I still felt anxious.

But this was no time for reflecting on my anxieties – I wanted to induce anxiety in the potentially happy couple. Reaching out with both hands, I lifted the heavy fabric in two places then let it drop. I did this a couple of times without having a noticeable effect on anyone's equilibrium. Disappointing, but this was my first attempt. I lifted it again: this time I splayed my elbows more widely and caught the edge of an unseen – and presumably quite tall – jardinière at the top of the swing. I heard a crash and a scream before the girls' mother spoke.

'I say, William. That plant just fell over. Is there a draught blowing the curtain about? Have you left the front door open?' The girls were being annoying, their fright having turned to tittering and simpering. William approached the curtain, sweeping it to one side. It didn't matter that he uncovered me as I had chosen to be invisible. I made my way into the room and decided to sit next to William's beloved Anne on William's green leather-covered settee. Sitting down should have produced a visible 'dent' on the seat, but nobody appeared to notice. That was disappointing too, but it was a substantial horsehair-stuffed item of furniture. I'd have to find something else on which to make an impression. Or someone.

Mama had a small plate on her lap containing a half-eaten Madeleine. I decided to remove the uneaten portion and see how long it would take her to notice. Waiting until her attention was absorbed in Jane's attempt to make polite conversation, I picked up the moist confection with its distinctive ridges and hurled it across the room. Or, rather, that had been my intention: the slight greasiness of the cake let it slip through my fingers and it landed on the rug at Mama's feet. 'Oh dear,' she said. 'I'm so sorry, William. I don't know how that happened.'

William picked up the crumbling Madeleine and, considerate gentleman and competent home-maker that he was, put it on his own plate. 'Never mind,' he soothed. 'Have another.' He handed round the plate of mixed cakes he had bought the previous afternoon, and Jane took the last of them. When William went to the pantry to get more, I decided to take advantage of his absence to do something more dramatic.

After I tipped Anne's hat off her head, she shrieked and stood up. 'What was that? I felt something!' Her face was pale and her eyes were wide so I chose this moment to appear before the ladies. I may have faded in a bit too slowly as I was still perfecting the slow fade to visibility. Lewis Carol got it absolutely right with his description of the Cheshire Cat some fifty years later, although his was a more effective slow fade to invisibility. Suffice to say, Jane, Anne and Mama were startled to see a pair of feet appear on the carpet near where the Madeleine had fallen. My legs soon followed, or rather the lower part of my ragged dress, before my hands, the tattered long sleeves covering my arms, my torso and, finally, my hatless head – with a birds' nest of hair – completed the picture. (It was the reverse of the intended effect, and it took me several days to work out that I needed to focus on the first-to-appear part before starting the fade-in. This first time I'd been thinking about the Madeleine lying on the carpet, you see.) Above the noise of three women almost collapsing with hysteria, I heard William's footsteps speeding along the hall, and I disappeared again (quickly and completely, this time) before he entered the room.

'Whatever is the matter?' he asked, although his question could hardly be heard over the hubbub. He looked around for a mouse or rat which might have caused such an upset, but there was nothing to see. I watched as he gently tried to persuade his beloved to sit down again, to take one of the cakes that had survived that speedy journey from the kitchen.

'William.' Mama's tone was stern. 'Is there a ghost in this house? My daughters and I saw something and we will not stay here a moment longer if you cannot explain it.' William's face was the very embodiment of confusion, his eyes flicking from woman to woman and his mouth opening and closing with no meaningful sounds issuing forth.

'I . . . ' When he tried to speak, Anne was having none of it.

'No excuses, William. Mama, Jane and I have had the most awful fright. We are going now and, if you want us to come back, you must investigate and ensure that that thing goes away. I don't care what you have to do: if you want to see me again in this house, you will do something.' William knew that look – she meant what she said. What else could he do but help them into their coats and see them safely off the premises? He then set about investigating the cause of the disturbance and apparent haunting and I stayed out of the way – I didn't want to be measured and recorded. I just wanted him to give up seeing that simple woman.

Later that week, having found nothing and having lost hope that he would be able to persuade Anne to re-enter the house, he wrote to James, telling him that he would be moving out at the end of the month. I never saw Anne, Jane or Mama again, and William soon became but a memory. I missed him, but at least my old furniture was restored to its rightful places in the house when his was removed. As for the romance, who knows? I feel I failed in my self-appointed 'duty' as far as William and Anne were concerned. Did they marry, despite my best efforts? Who knows? From time to time, I allow myself to speculate on the two scenarios – what difference might it have made to the world whether or not they brought up children together?

One thing I forgot to mention is that I can leave this house, but every day, wherever I have been during the day or evening, I am returned to it as midnight starts to chime. (I know there are far fewer church bells chiming midnight these days than was the case in my day, but you will understand what I mean.) A medium who was brought in to investigate the haunting claimed to be able to explain the phenomenon: apparently it's because a cursed object has kept me bound to the earthly plane. If she is right (and who's to say one way or the other? There is no rule book for ghostly behaviour, after all . . .) I cannot imagine what that cursed object might be other than the bodies I hid in the house. What I do know is that it can be very disturbing to lose track of time at night: I'll be doing a bit of window-rattling at the back of one of the houses across the road when – whoosh! – I find myself back in my own hall.

Those bodies – and it grieves me to tell you this – were discovered in the early twenty-first century. The next-door neighbour, Phillip, was partly to blame. He attended the new owners' house-warming party and, as he stood admiring what estate agents love to call 'the period features' of the virtually unimproved dining room at the front of the house, he realised that the short corridor between that room and the room at the back of the house was missing. He had a casual look at the panelling but couldn't see any evidence of new work. That's hardly surprising, as it had been almost two hundred years since my tame builder last walled up a body there and the house was virtually new when he did the work. Before he left, Phillip introduced himself to the new owners and told them that he was interested in their house from an architectural point of view. They invited him to return, soon, as they were planning to have some work done and, as he clearly knew a lot about the structure, they would appreciate his advice.

It was a while before the mutually convenient date arrived, and Phillip had forgotten the reason for his interest until he walked into the dining room. 'Ah yes,' he murmured as he made his way to the corner furthest from both the door and the window. 'This corridor. It's a curious anomaly. I'm sure it must have been bricked up.' The new owners watched, transfixed, as Phillip knocked on panels and measured them by eye. Eventually the woman spoke.

'We were thinking of knocking this wall down to make one big room. What do you think? Have many people done that on the street?' Phillip's shocked expression told her she had transgressed some unwritten rule of talking to an architect, perhaps the one that says *I'm here to talk, and you must simply listen. Maybe later I'll ask you questions – that's when you can talk.*

'This is a supporting wall built with a great thickness of bricks,' Phillip said. 'In the other houses of this age and plan it contains a short corridor, here,' – he waved his arm at the corner – 'which runs along the party wall to the room behind. I'd like to look in that room next, please.'

The three of them left the dining room and walked through the entrance hall, still floored in black and white like the tiles I had floated over in 1838 (replacements now, of course) to the drawing room at the back. Here my pet builder had been less meticulous in his work and it was obvious to Phillip, with his trained eye, that changes had been made in the corner. (That lack of care was why William felt a draught, of course.) Phillip turned to face the couple and said the words I'd been hoping I'd never hear. 'Look here, carefully, and you'll see evidence of that corridor I mentioned. Look at that vertical section of panelling, how it's slightly more narrow that the others. And see here – this panel has some marks on its edge, like it has been prised out. You could probably re-open the corridor – so much nicer than knocking down the wall and putting up RSJs to support the floor above.'

To my great horror, they agreed to investigate. Naturally, the bodies were found. When the artefacts found with them showed that they had been walled up for about two hundred years, the reason they had been hidden was of no further interest to the police. The forensic archaeology team which recovered the bodies appreciated the relics I had unintentionally interred with them. One chap had a beautiful hunter watch I'd missed when I emptied his pockets. I don't know which chap it was (and the investigators didn't identify any of the bodies, not even my husband) but I kicked myself when I watched them untangle the gold chain from his ribs, although I was unable to feel the self-inflicted blow. In the places where the men's trouser pockets, long since turned to dust, had been were found a few coins. These helped the dating process, and some of them were uncommon examples of Georgian currency.

I was disappointed to realise that, although the bodies had been removed, I was still being returned to the house at midnight every day. It obviously wasn't just their physical presence which was making me stay here. At the time I wondered whether it was the house itself and the number of people I had hurt and upset while alive that drew me back in. Or maybe the bad behaviour I had encouraged in some of the people who had lived here after me was acting as a magnet, keeping me stuck to the site of my sins. I have recently begun to recognise that my unacknowledged guilt kept me tied to this building.

But I had been living with this curfew for a long time and it was a very small inconvenience, far less problematic than being stuck in this ghostly state way beyond my expiry date. Anyway, where would I go if I was given the chance to spend longer away from the house? I had no friends or family to visit, of course, and I definitely had no descendants. Although this address was linked with me through legal documents, nobody had ever turned up at the house saying, 'I'm investigating my family history and have discovered that my great great aunt Mercy Scudder lived here in the 1830s. Can I come in?' Maybe the Scudder line had simply died out, like they do. My future, if you see what I mean, was a bit dull after all.

Much of my past has also been dull, despite the hauntings. Many of them have been dull affairs, the pedestrian and predictable stuff beloved by novelists. On occasion, I have even decided that an individual's situation militates against my tormenting them. That was the case when that new vicar arrived during the Second World War. After arguing with myself about it for several days, I decided not to trouble him as he seemed to be haunted by his own troubles. Normally, adding to someone's woes wasn't grounds for coming over all conscientious but he was a man of the cloth and I a mere spirit. Ironically, given my current quest, my biggest concern was that he might have an effective means of getting rid of me.

The end (I hope)

The people who live here at the time I am writing this are pleasant enough. Lil, the mad old woman who came to stay and taxed everyone's patience, is sensitive (to use her word) and knew that I am here. As I mentioned in The Introduction, she tried to exorcise me. Like the others, she failed, but I think she had fun on the way.

Lil's niece said that she should feel guilty for the way she has behaved, encouraging Alison to take revenge on her husband. In fact Lil got all her best ideas from me so it's me who should feel guilty and, for the first time since – well, for the first time ever – I think I do. It's weird to feel what amounts to an emotion after nearly two hundred years. Is there a possibility that I'm getting soft in my old age?

As well as feeling bad about showing Lil how to 'help' Alison, I am amazed to find myself stricken with guilt for some of the many times I have hurt people by appearing in front of them or taking away things – and/or people – that they value. I don't regret James or the bricked-up lodgers – they were odious to a fault – but I do regret that episode during the First World War when I hid those fascinating letters at number 37.

After I restored the letters to their rightful place and the old man was reunited with them, his obvious joy at seeing them for the first time made me think about the other awful things I have done to people over the years. For the first time in my life – or since my death – they were guilt-laden thoughts. Yes, guilt, the strange feeling I mentioned at the start of this story

* * *

All this writing and thinking about my life has had a profound effect on me. Believe it or not, I have come to realise that my attitude towards love and other people's happiness is hurting me more than anyone else. I now understand that it is holding me back in that I am unable to leave this mortal coil and move on unless and until I truly repent of my evil ways. Throughout my existence, both while I lived and since I died, I have ruined lives and destroyed relationships without gaining anything myself, except a twisted satisfaction. And so twisted. I am ashamed of the harm I have done, and I deeply regret that the vast majority of what I've done cannot now be undone. Much as I wish I could make proper amends, all I can do is say three little words I have never used before in this – or any other – context.

I – am – sorry.

Oh! I can feel the end of the story starting. I can feel a weight lifting from my shoulders, and my heart becoming lighter. I can feel – oh my word! I can feel the quill pen between my fingers and the paper beneath my hand. I can feel the warmth of the sun on my face and the touch of the breeze on my shoulders. And, for the first time since I died, I feel sadness, regret, remorse at my despicable behaviour.

As those sentiments settle over me the world starts to fade before my eyes, breaking up as if it has been hit by an earthquake. Is it my vision or my existence that is faulty? I hope it is the latter but my failing ability to see clearly enough to write means I must stop soon, before I have time to decide and commit the answer to paper. Perhaps I really have laid my own ghost by writing with the quill that grew out of the feather you burned, Lil. If that's what's happening, I will be eternally grateful to you for showing me the way to get rid of my own demons. I wonder whether you were right about me moving on to the second level? I can feel something changing in me, so I hope to find out soon. Thank you, and farewell . . .

42

SHAKESPEARE STREET

Careering

by Phil Tysoe

The fault, dear Brutus, is not in our stars But in ourselves.

Julius Caesar, Act 1, Scene 2

Sunday

The terrace was the reason they'd taken the house originally. It had been further from the tube than they'd wanted and the only pub in spitting distance was the Three Feathers, stubbornly untouched by the estate agent's claims for the area's gentrification, but the little roof space had woven a spell on all of them. It was just a flat space, maybe four feet square fringed with a low wall and adorned with a battered old deck chair, a couple of stools and a plant pot, now *sans* plant. The house had taken a direct hit in the Blitz and, when the money for renovations had run dry, a flat roof had proven a cheap short cut to making it habitable again. They were unaware of this happy accident arising from the house's unhappy past and had simply fallen in love with the views it afforded down and across Islington and, more importantly, up and out, over the London skies.

There was usually an hour in the evening when the light was still good enough for Sarah to paint but when the first hint of the muted constellations above had begun to glow, it would tempt Alex out to join her on the roof. He would name the stars as they appeared while Sarah and Rob, if he was back from work, would gently tease him by picking out planes in the stack over Heathrow and asking whether they were comets or UFOs. Or they'd pretend to forget that he'd told them that the brightest point they could see, one of the few celestial bodies that did cut through the London light pollution, was Venus and not a star at all. Alex would patiently explain it to them again.

Sarah was cleaning her brushes, watching paint leach from the tips into the water in her jam jar, a swirling blue blur. It reminded her of a Japanese print she'd had in her room as a student, back when all futures seemed possible. She glanced over at Alex. He was slouched in the deck chair, a pair of binoculars resting on his stomach.

'You know what happened last time you looked through those . . . ' said Sarah.

'They are strictly for star gazing,' replied Alex. 'That incident with the couple on Woodfall Road was not entirely my fault.'

Rob's head appeared in the hatch at the top of the steep stairs that served as the route up to the terrace.

'The One With The Naked Neighbours And The Surprising Things You Can Do With Fruit,' he announced. 'Still can't believe they called the police.'

'It wasn't an episode of *Friends,* Rob.'

'No, it was funnier,' said Rob. 'Although if it was, I'd be Joey, right? The good looking one.'

'It's not much of a choice. The funny one, the good looking one and the . . . The other one. What was the point of Ross anyway?' asked Alex.

'He was the nice one, wasn't he?' said Sarah, still idly stirring her brush in the jar, the water now a murky grey. 'You'd be Ross, Alex.'

'Thanks a lot,' he replied. 'So I'm the dull, wet guy who's so lacking in character that he gets given a pet monkey just to make him more interesting.'

'Well I didn't mean it quite like that,' smiled Sarah. 'Anyway, you don't need the monkey. You've got that whole neighbourhood Peeping Tom thing going on as a character quirk . . . '

'I was star gazing.'

As dusk fell, the natural light faded fast and was gradually replaced by the soft, artificial glow of the city. Sarah finished cleaning her brushes and sat down on one of the stools, accepting a quick swig of the beer that Rob had brought up with him and was offering round. He stood looking at the picture Sarah had left drying on her makeshift easel. It was an abstract series of blue and grey circles, bold and well-defined in the centre and then progressively distorted and smudged towards the periphery of the page. He liked it although, if he was honest, he preferred her pencil drawings, preferred things rooted more directly in reality. Sarah caught him looking at the picture and raised a quizzical eyebrow. He smiled and nodded approvingly but knew better than to offer more; too many well-intentioned observations about her painting had ended with the critiqued picture in pieces. He pulled up the other stool, took his beer back from Sarah and offered it to Alex who was now peering up towards the sky through his binoculars.

'What are you looking for up there?' asked Rob. 'Trying to see our destinies?'

'God, no. Nothing like that. There's no glimpse of the future up there, just lights from the past,' replied Alex.

'That's deep.'

'It's just physics.' Alex adjusted the focusing ring on the binoculars, trying to get a better view of the Moon. It was only a quarter full but still one of the few things bright enough to cut through the light-sodden sky. *It's just physics.* He remembered saying something similar three years ago as his justification for jacking in the PhD, walking away from all that conceptual stuff about gravity and relativity to take up a graduate place with Deloitte. Swapping Lorentz transformations for double-entry bookkeeping. It paid better, but it was a mental downshift and he still felt the nagging, gravitational pull of his old studies.

'I didn't expect it to be like this,' interrupted Sarah suddenly.

'Like what?'

'This . . . This . . . I don't know. This scratching out our days.' She pushed her hand through her hair and frowned. 'What happened to what we wanted to do?'

'You mean you didn't want to design towers for video games?' It was Alex's usual tease.

'Hey, those games need a lot of towers . . . And my correct title is *Concept Artist*, as you well know.' Sarah straightened on her stool and extended her arm with a flourish. 'Concept Artist responsible for initial design of 'player-climbable' structures. Should I continue to impress with my sketched portfolio of traversable in-game terrain, then I have a very decent shot at being *Lead* Concept Artist in two to three years' time'.

'It's something to dream about.'

'Every day on the 153, believe me.'

'Maybe this is just a phase,' said Rob. He drained the last of his beer. 'Maybe we need to go through this while we figure it out.'

'But we had it figured out,' protested Sarah. 'When I met you . . . At that talk, what was it?'

'NGO roles in provision of public services,' said Rob.

'Sounds like quite the party,' said Alex from behind the binoculars. Sarah ignored him.

'Yeah, that. When we met, you knew exactly what you wanted to do. It was the thing that struck me about you. The passion. You were absolutely going to work in the public sector, or the third sector or whatever it's called, and you were going to help people.'

'And hopefully I still will,' said Rob. 'The social media thing's just temporary, just to get some money behind me early on. It's not forever.' They all fell silent, feeling slightly awkward. Sarah tentatively touched the paint to see if it was dry and rolled up her picture. Alex put down his binoculars and tried to lighten the mood.

'What were you doing at that talk anyway, Sarah? Doesn't strike me as your sort of thing.'

'What makes you think I'm not interested in social enterprise?'

'She was in the wrong room,' said Rob.

'You promised you wouldn't tell anyone that,' smirked Sarah. They all laughed and Alex wagged a finger in admonishment.

'Alright, alright. It was at the Barbican and I'd gone to see a Murakami exhibition but I was running late, got a bit lost, and ended up in a room full of earnest liberals listening to someone talk about co-operatives and sustainable funding. They all seemed so nice that I thought it'd be impolite to just walk out.'

'Just imagine the vicious tut-tutting you could have been subjected to . . . ' said Alex.

'We could be quite scathing in our shows of mild disapproval,' agreed Rob. 'Some poor guy turned up to another talk one time with a coffee from Starbucks, it was just after the whole tax avoidance thing, and I think we briefly created a vacuum in the auditorium when everyone took a simultaneous sharp intake of breath.'

'Well it wouldn't have technically been a vacuum – ' started Alex before being drowned out under a mock chorus of tut-tuts from his flatmates.

The early evening dusk was giving itself up to the beginnings of night now and the last of the sun's warmth that had baked itself into the terrace was fading. Sarah rubbed her bare arms with her hands before gathering up her painting equipment.

'I think I'm going to head in,' she said. 'Early start tomorrow.'

The other two didn't move. She knew they liked to sit out for longer, eke out the weekend and delay the onset of Monday morning. Alex would usually be last to come back downstairs, pulling the hatch behind him. Sometimes he'd sit and try to wait until all of the lights across the surrounding streets winked out, hoping that the progressive darkening of the neighbourhood would allow more illumination from above. Once there'd been a power cut and he'd been able to just pick out Mars, seemingly tucked away behind Venus, just a trick of their relative positions and rotational orbits. The others teased him about how scientific, how clinical, he was about it all but he saw the beauty in it too. When he told Rob he wasn't looking for destiny up there it was true, but he was perhaps looking for something. Perspective? He wasn't sure anymore.

'Good night,' said Rob. 'Don't forget our guest arrives tomorrow.'

'Guest?' asked Sarah, pausing at the head of the stairs.

'God, Sarah. Do you read anything the landlord sends us? We talked about this last week. He's offered up the spare room on Airbnb.

We're splitting the money, remember? He'll take half and then take the other half off the rent. Said we can stop it anytime we want if it doesn't work out.'

'Vaguely,' said Sarah. 'Might be nice to have someone else around anyway. And I could definitely use the cash.'

'Tell me about it,' said Rob.

Monday

It was already dark by the time Alex returned from work. He walked down Shakespeare Street under the orange-white glow of its street lights, his shadow lengthening as he got further away from each one then shortening as he approached the next. He paused at the mid-point between two of them and briefly tried to remember the maths. Why would his shadow grow? He figured it was just triangles. He used to know this stuff. As he continued along the street the light closest to his destination, number 42, faded and winked out. That'll save the Council about 27p tonight then. He'd just finished a project reviewing potential infrastructure savings for all the London Boroughs, something the Mayor's office had commissioned. That was the stuff he knew now. Next door's cat, a tabby with white feet, watched him from the wall outside the house, both of them now in darkness.

'Alright Schrodinger? Still alive then. Bet you've had a better day than me,' he said to the cat, cracking his usual physicist's joke. The cat began to lick its paw. 'I guess you'll only answer to Socks, eh?' Socks remained silent and Alex, shaking his head at himself, let himself into the house.

He could hear voices coming from up on the terrace as he stepped into the hallway, almost tripping over a large, flower-patterned carpetbag that had been left behind the door next to a propped-up umbrella. Rob and Sarah and a woman's voice he didn't recognise. They seemed to be laughing a lot. Slowly he put the pieces together. The unfamiliar bag and brolly. Their guest. Airbnb. Somewhat reluctantly he headed up to join them.

'. . . So then Rob moved in a few months after we'd met at some event.' Sarah was just finishing the story about how they'd ended up in the house as Alex emerged on to the roof. She was sitting forward in the deckchair, talking to a small, immaculately dressed lady. Late sixties? Alex was terrible at gauging ages. The first time he'd met Sarah he'd guessed she was thirty-five, largely on the basis that she had been wearing a cardigan and had just told him that she was a big fan of *Countdown*. She'd been twenty-five at the time. Their guest had short, grey hair, pushed back on one side with an ornate mother-of-pearl clip, a bright white flower design, above her left ear. She was looking at Sarah intently, and smiling. She sat straight, upright, and there was something immediately confident and calm about her. Sarah described it later as like that moment when a passer-by intervenes at an accident you've witnessed and announces 'Don't worry, I'm a doctor'.

'Hey, Alex, you're back,' said Sarah jumping up from her chair. 'You must meet Maria.'

'Hello, part-timers,' replied Alex, before more formally turning towards their guest and extending his hand. 'Hi, Maria, lovely to meet you. I'm Alex.'

She stood and took his hand, her grip firmer than he'd expected. They held eye contact for a few seconds before she closed her other hand on top of their handshake and squeezed, smiling. 'It's lovely to meet you too, Alex.' She spoke softly and slowly, drawing out her vowels.

'Was your journey OK? Did you have far to come?' he asked, now curious about her accent.

'I'm over from Kansas. It's been a fun trip so far.'

'We've done the Wizard of Oz joke,' interrupted Rob, before Alex could reply.

'All you London folk do sound a little like Munchkins to me, though,' said Maria, eyes twinkling. She sat back down smoothing her skirt on her lap before folding her hands together. She was precise and graceful in her movements. 'I was saying to Rob and Sarah how much I adore your roof terrace. It's the reason I booked the room.'

'It's the reason we took the house,' said Alex. 'It's just a shame we get more light from the streets than we do from the sky. You must have more luck at home?'

'Oh sure. Out in the countryside it's glorious. And if you ever get a chance to get over to Bryce Canyon then it feels like the stars are laid out across the sky like diamonds that you could just pluck down and claim as your own.' She paused, briefly, and looked down at a ring on her left hand, turned it on her finger, rubbed its single stone. 'But it's good to see a different view of it all once in a while.'

'Maybe we should swap,' laughed Alex. 'I don't seem to be able to make out what I want to see up there.' He gestured up and out at the night sky.

'When things get dark you'll see what you need to see,' she replied.

The four of them contemplated the London sky for a few minutes, lost in their own thoughts. Sarah broke the silence, insisting that they were being terrible hosts and rushing downstairs to fetch glasses and a bottle of wine. Maria sat and had a drink with them for half an hour or so before declaring that jet lag had defeated her and that she ought to retire to be fresh for her planned tour of London's galleries in the morning. She asked Sarah if she'd like to accompany her. Alex filled in the blanks and realised they must have been talking about her painting before he'd arrived home. Impulsively Sarah agreed, shushing her house mates' queries about work. Looking quietly pleased, Maria left them and went downstairs to her room.

'How are you going to get out of work?' asked Rob after Maria had gone.

'I'll chuck a sickie or something,' said Sarah. 'It'll be okay. Besides, there's a game set in London in the production schedule for next year so it'll double as research if I take my sketch book with me.'

'Really? Are you sure? We hardly know her . . . ?' questioned Alex.

'And yet we're perfectly happy to have her stay in our house,' said Sarah. 'That's kind of how Airbnb works.'

'I think what Alex is saying is that it's not AirbnbnTourGuide,' said Rob, trying and failing to enunciate each 'n' clearly.

'Don't talk with your mouth full,' said Sarah. Rob faked a silent laugh, sarcastically, by way of reply. 'It'll be nice. She's over here on her own, doesn't know the city. Why not show her that Londoners don't deserve their less-than-legendary reputation for hospitality? What do you think, Alex?'

'I guess it'll be fine,' he said. 'I don't know. There's something about her that I can't really describe though. Like she's got a . . . '

'An aura?' asked Sarah. 'Really? Coming from you, Alex?'

'Not an aura,' sighed Alex.

'A dark and mysterious past that haunts her?' said Rob, affecting a fake film voice over.

'Not that either. I don't know. A presence. There's something assured about her. She just seems utterly and completely *herself,* if that makes sense. And, no, Sarah. I haven't started believing in auras.'

'Sounds a bit like it to me,' teased Sarah. 'I think I know what you mean. That's why I'd like to spend the day with her.'

'I'm going to bed,' said Rob. 'One thing's for sure, none of us is in Kansas anymore. He theatrically clicked his heels together, muttered 'there's no place like home' and left Alex and Sarah sat out on the terrace looking up at the night. Out of habit Alex looked for Polaris but there was too much light. It seemed rare that he could find it these days.

Tuesday

The late morning sun was struggling to break through the clouds over Trafalgar Square as Sarah and Maria emerged from the National Gallery. Making their way down the steps they linked arms, like old school friends, and Sarah felt her companion lean into her slightly as she took the stairs. It was almost imperceptible but there was just a sense that Maria wanted, or needed, some support. *Well she's not a young woman. Probably mid sixties?* Sarah hoped Alex hadn't made any observations about their guest's age at breakfast. He was hopeless at things like that. Could tell you how old Saturn's moons were, but ask him to judge something, someone, staring him in the face and he'd be off by eons. She patted Maria's arm and suggested that they stop for a bit, told her that she really needed to make some sketches of the square.

They perched on the bottom step in silence for a few minutes as Sarah swiftly pencilled the grey, granite lines of Nelson's Column in her notebook. Feeling vaguely guilty at her absence from work she started to embellish the drawing a little, adding details that might be useful as hand holds or points that someone could hook a rope around. She started to pencil in Nelson's details but couldn't get the angles of his bicorn right so she gave him a makeshift fez instead. Nelson continued to stare stoically in the opposite direction, seemingly untroubled by her alterations. Maria had spent the minutes gazing at the square, watching fellow tourists idling past, but now she looked over at Sarah's sketch, curious.

'That's great but what are those extra bits sticking out? And what's with the hat?'

Sarah flipped her notebook closed. 'I thought he might fancy a change. The extra bits are for work. When they take my drawings and use them in games they often need to change them so they'll work for the player.' She sensed Maria wasn't entirely following. 'So in this game there'll probably be lots of things to do in London, lots of things they want the player to explore and find. I was just making the column easier to climb up. They always like things you can climb.'

'Why'd they make them like that?'

'Oh I don't know. It gives the player something to do. They call it goal-oriented game design or something. Lots of little, achievable tasks. Apparently you get a hit of . . . What's that brain chemical that makes you happy?'

'Dopamine?' suggested Maria.

'Yeah, you get a hit of dopamine every time you complete one of these little tasks and that keeps you playing.'

'Sounds like life, wouldn't you say?' asked Maria, looking at Sarah intently. Sarah hadn't really noticed how green her eyes were before. She had a slight cloudy patch in her left pupil, a smattering of blurred white dots. It reminded Sarah a little of the view from their terrace at night. Like stars fighting to break through the haze.

'Well it depends on the tasks,' answered Sarah finally. 'Put it this way, I'm not sure how much dopamine I've been getting lately.'

'Perhaps you need to go and climb up that,' said Maria pointing up at Nelson's Column and laughing.

'Well, assuming I didn't break my neck, then it would certainly give me a hit of something.'

'And a great view.'

'And a great view,' agreed Sarah. 'That's the other reason they make them like that – the games I mean, why I spend my life drawing towers. In the game, whenever you get to the top of something tall, it opens up the world to you. Shows you new things to do and places to go.'

'So your art shows people where they are and where they might go?'

Sarah shook her head. 'I hadn't thought of it like that but . . . At a stretch, maybe. I used to think my painting *outside* of work was trying to do that. Or at least, that it was trying to show where I was and where I might go and that would resonate with some people.'

'You shouldn't distinguish between the two,' said Maria. 'What you call your work and what you call your painting *outside* of work. It all comes from you. It's all how you spend your days.' She patted Sarah's arm and smiled. 'Anyway, would you listen to me, doling out advice to a talented young artist. I have to say that, personally, I liked the flowers. Back in the gallery. The Monet and the Van Gogh.' She sounded out the Gogh to rhyme with dough, extending the 'o' sound, and caught Sarah frowning at her. 'What'd I say? Van Gogh? How'd you say it? Goff?' They both laughed. 'You prefer the abstract work, don't you?'

'I do,' said Sarah. 'And thank you for the advice. It's nice to hear.' She wrinkled her brow, her nose crinkling in concentration, lost momentarily in thought. 'I like the flowers too but there's always something slightly sad about them to me. Something so beautiful, yet so fragile. Those paintings are just a snapshot of something fleeting, something that's going to disappear.'

'Oh my dear. That's not sad. That's the very definition of joy. Come on, I sense you need something more modern. Take me to the Tate and I'll buy you lunch on the South Bank.'

Inside the Tate, Sarah felt a deep feeling of calm as the peace and vastness of the canopy above seemed to absorb her anxieties. Gave them room to lift and dissolve. They walked in with nothing but the echo of their footsteps for company. Outside the South Bank bustled; in here it was still. For a long time they just walked the floor, absorbed in the space, watching dust motes dance in the slats of light falling across the concrete from the high, vertical windows above. Eventually Maria pointed out that there was an exhibition running. Yayoi Kusama. They bought tickets and ventured into a world of coloured dots and circles and impressionistic shapes, endless patterns repeating, forms stretched and mutating. Another room filled with nothing but giant, monochrome canvasses on each wall, monolithic blank tranquillity. And then, at the end, a darkened room with mirrored floors, walls and ceiling. They cautiously ventured in, eyes adjusting, and a myriad of LED lights overhead began to blink on and off, pulses of colour reflecting back from the surfaces and into infinity, flashes there, everywhere, and then they were gone. Sarah felt like she was standing in the centre of the universe watching its evolution on fast forward. The flash of the Big Bang, stars exploding into life, collapsing in on themselves, and then darkness. Or like she was a single neuron firing inside her own mind, watching the millions of other chemical reactions trigger and blaze in her cerebral cortex. It was dizzying and euphoric. They both sat down and lost themselves in the ineffable dazzle of lights.

Later they ate lunch on the roof garden of the Queen Elizabeth Hall, a green oasis atop a brutal concrete slab of a building. The sun had won its struggle with the clouds and they sat watching a faint shimmer of heat haze dance across the Thames.

Wednesday

It was still dark as Rob and Maria left the house. The early start had been her idea; jet lag had her on American time and she said she'd sooner go out first thing rather than in the evening. Rob thought she must have been up for a full hour or so before they left because she was as perfectly elegant as she'd been the day before. There was a precision and neatness about her that he thought must require serious time. He looked like he'd rolled straight out of bed, planted his feet in his trainers, and pulled on whichever coat he'd passed *en route* to the front door. From under the duvet to the porch in thirty seconds flat. It was cold. The heat from yesterday's late autumn sun had faded fast, up and out as evening cooled to night with no cloud cover to cap its escape. They'd all sat on the terrace and watched it sink over Highgate. They were up too early to see it reappear.

'This better be good,' said Rob.

'Well, good morning to you too,' replied Maria brightly. 'It's nice to see you made an effort for me.'

'Believe me. Being up at this time is an effort.'

'I can't believe you've never seen the dawn before, Rob?' smiled Maria. 'Open your eyes, it's beautiful.'

Rob glanced up and mentally conceded that there was something magical about the half-light and quiet of this hour. He *had* seen it, many times. It's just that he usually saw it woozily, soft-filtered through the alcohol of the previous night before he found his way to bed. The idea for this morning's early start had germinated the previous evening. They'd been on the roof, listening to Sarah rave about the Kusama installation at the Tate, none of them wanting to point out the smudge of paint on her cheek that lifted and fell each time she smiled. She'd spent the late afternoon absorbed in a fresh canvas. Rob couldn't remember seeing her so passionate since the day they'd met, back when she insisted on dragging him round the Murakami exhibition that she'd missed after he insisted that she stay and listen to the talk from Vision Housing and the various other social enterprises speaking that evening. They'd both been so certain then. Both fit to burst with ideas and energy. For a while he'd mistaken their mutual passion as a spark between them, a shared attraction, but as they spent longer together they settled into an easy friendship. There was a drunken kiss one night, shortly after they moved into the house, but it had marked the end of any romance rather than the beginning. They'd both laughed it off: you can't fake chemistry. Alex had told them that the mutual attraction of objects into each other's orbit was actually more of a physics thing. This story had come up during the previous evening when Maria asked how they'd all wound up together in the house. In turn, that had led to a conversation about how Rob had fallen into his current job rather than pursuing the idiosyncrasies of London's housing policies. He'd told her how those things had happened, but he hadn't really told her why. He wasn't sure if he knew why. He knew the lines he said out loud when people asked him – it's just a stop gap, I'm just getting some money behind me, it's just a temporary thing – but he couldn't remember now whether they were true.

Maria had insisted that she wanted to see London's homeless crisis (Rob's words) for herself. The others, surprised, had listed a host of alternative ways to spend a morning in the city but she wouldn't budge. She said she wanted to experience the place as it was, not as its people presented it for visitors. After he'd first moved into the house Rob had done some volunteering at the various homeless shelters round Islington so he'd offered to take her to one of them. He hadn't been for about a year but if the circuit hadn't changed then breakfast would need serving at Union Chapel. They took the tube from Finsbury Park to Highbury and Islington, sitting quietly in half-empty carriages with early-rising, suited commuters and late-returning nightshift workers, stifled yawns marking the beginnings and endings of days.

There were soft slashes of pink in the dawn sky, sunrise's forward scouts, as they approached the church. The Union Chapel spire was bathed in the early morning glow, red brick framing high vaulted windows and gothic revival details. A pair of magpies took flight from a perch near the top of the tower, squabbling in their rattling, staccato voices. Rob was halfway up Compton Terrace, almost at the church, before he realised that Maria wasn't with him. Turning back he saw her standing beneath the overhang of a spreading oak, leaning on an iron railing, just gazing at the building. He was about to urge her to hurry up but something in her reaction gave him pause. He walked back to her and together they stood for a few minutes and watched as the rising sun slowly warmed the russet tones of the old spire, watched it come to life in the light.

'Do you believe in God?' asked Maria, relinquishing her hand on the railing and taking Rob's arm instead.

'No, I don't I'm afraid, Maria,' he answered. 'But it's kind of magical at this time of the day though, I'll give you that. I can see why people see something bigger.'.

'Oh no, don't misunderstand,' said Maria. 'I don't believe either. Not any more at least. Not since my late husband passed away. There's nobody and nothing controlling our futures. There's just here and now. Come on, you promised you'd show me the shelter.'

They ended up working the morning shift, changing bedding, washing up, serving London's lost bacon and eggs and endless cups of tea. The centre manager, Jenny, remembered Rob and had set them straight to helping out. Maria was a novelty for the patrons of the shelter and she spent most of her time sitting quietly talking with each of them individually, laughter following her around the room. She was deep in conversation with an older man when their shift finished. He had a grey flecked beard and a nasty scar, running between his right ear and the corner of his eye, gave him an intimidating look. The smell of stale alcohol and tobacco clung to him. Maria was sitting opposite him, holding his upturned hands in her own, gently massaging his fingers with her thumbs. Rob stood, arms folded, and watched them from across the room.

'He's in a bad way.' Jenny had noticed Rob watching the odd couple. 'He shouldn't be here, to be honest. He's got stomach cancer. Late stages. They've told him it's incurable so every time he's admitted to hospital he just checks himself out again. Says he'd rather live out his last days on the street than lie down in a ward.'

'Hasn't he got anybody?' asked Rob. He knew what the answer would be. He'd had this conversation so many times before in the early days of his volunteering. Surely everyone has someone. The truth was that everyone didn't have someone. This was a community to pick up the pieces for people without a community.

'He had a wife. From what he's told me, after she died he lost his way, took to drinking too much, lost his job. You know the story. You're only ever-'

'You're only ever six bad months away from the street,' interrupted Rob. 'I remember.'

They went over to join Maria and the scarred man. She was whispering something to him and, in response, the man reached up to touch her hair clip. He had started to cry. As his fingers found the carved flower in her hair, Maria quickly reached for his hand, removing it and pressing it to her cheek instead. Eventually she released his hand and said her goodbyes.

'Come on,' said Rob. 'Let me show you inside the church. It's quite something.'

Maria shook her head. 'I've seen the church,' she replied. 'I've seen your church. It's all here, in this room, in the bedrooms we cleaned and the pots we washed up. Sarah showed me the Tate, I don't need to see another grand and imposing space.'

Rob smiled at her. 'Let me buy you a coffee then. There's a kiosk in the foyer that does a great cappuccino and all the money comes back into the shelter. You don't have to look at the stained glass windows or the chandeliers or the balustrades. Just have a drink with me. You've reminded me of something today and I wanted to say thank you.'

'Alright, it's a deal,' said Maria. 'And just what have I reminded you of today young man?'

'You've reminded me of who I used to be,' said Rob.

'No, no, no,' replied Maria gently. 'Not who you used to be. Who you are.'

Thursday

'Explain it to me again,' insisted Maria. Alex leaned forward in his seat, elbows on knees, to narrow the gap between them across the tube carriage. He didn't want to raise his voice. Around them people examined their phones.

'Are you just humouring me now?' he asked. 'I'm sure there'll be things that explain it all when we get there.'

'No, I really want to try to understand it,' she replied. 'And I like hearing you talk about it. I want you to humour me, not the other way round.'

The train slowed into its next station. Alex watched the blur through the window resolve itself into a platform, waiting people, a name. Camden Town. He always thought it was like watching a film slowing down into a series of still photographs and, finally, a single, framed shot. There was a moment, even if it was just a fraction of a second, a heartbeat, when everything stopped before the train doors slid open and exhaled its passengers on to the platform. Mind the gap.

'OK. Imagine the world and imagine a big line drawn all the way around the equator,' started Alex.

'I think I have this part,' said Maria. 'I'm imagining parallel lines horizontally stacked on top of each other . . . '

'And underneath each other . . . '

'And underneath each other,' she continued, 'reaching to the North and South Poles. If you take the equator as your start point, you can measure how far north or south you are. Degrees of latitude. Seems straightforward enough.'

'Well, allowing for a certain degree of latitude in your explanation, you're right,' acknowledged Alex with a smile. 'But latitude was always the easy part because it works from a fixed physical point – the lines you draw north and south around the earth don't move relative to the equator. And if you know your stars and a bit of maths then you can work it out by looking at the sky. Longitude was where it got messy because all those imaginary lines are now running vertically and without a natural reference point.'

'This is where I lost you last time,' said Maria. 'What do you mean there's no natural reference point?'

'Because the Earth is spinning. Longitude is a distance in the planet's daily rotation. Unless you agree an arbitrary fixed point to measure against, no-one will ever agree on where they are. The Earth is always moving. One degree every four minutes.'

'Well I never did like to sit still anyway,' laughed Maria. 'So the good folks at Greenwich offered to be the fixed point of reference for measuring how far east or west you were?'

'We've missed out a bunch of stuff about how they standardised solar time for everyone first so that you could always know what time it was wherever you were but, yes, I guess you have it about right.'

'Not bad for an amateur,' smiled Maria with a satisfied nod of her head. 'We can't all be . . . what was it again?'

'A physicist. Technically an astrophysicist, I guess, although I never finished my thesis.'

'Well, I don't know about physics but I do know that you'll never find your way to where you want to go unless you know where you are now.'

The Tannoy on the train interrupted them, announcing that there were suspensions on the Northern Line from the next stop in a tone that Alex recognised as more apologetic than Maria did. They changed at King's Cross with a plan to follow part of the circumference of the Circle Line and then take a boat up the Thames. It would take longer, but Alex figured that spending time on the river would allow Maria to see some of the sights and might give him a better chance to explain the intricacies of a system of navigation that had, after all, arisen to guide people lost on the waves. He wasn't altogether sure why he'd agreed to the trip but Maria had suggested it and had been roundly supported by Sarah and Rob, the three of them nagging him through yesterday evening until he'd agreed to show her the Observatory at Greenwich. Despite himself, the idea of it had got under his skin, sparked something of the curiosity he'd often felt in his post-grad days. He wasn't booked out to a specific client this week so he'd taken a couple of days leave. He was long overdue a holiday anyway. It was a standing joke in the house that he had so much time off in lieu stacked up that he could spend all of next year in Cornwall. It had taken Rob some time to explain this to Maria. *Looe. It's a place in Cornwall. In lieu. Oh never mind.*

The disruption that had forced the change of route seemed to be causing problems across the network. They made halting progress on the Circle Line before the train stopped at Liverpool Street. Alex felt his phone vibrate in his pocket as it picked up the station Wi-Fi and he reflexively pulled it out to check his messages. Maria watched his expression change as he stared at the screen, the frown, the slight slump in his shoulders. He looked up and took a deep breath. She saved them both the awkwardness.

'Do you need to be somewhere else?'

'I'm sorry. *Really* sorry. It's a work thing. There's a client audit that's over running. They need an extra pair of hands to get it over the line by this evening. I don't want to leave you in the lurch but . . .'

'Don't worry about me,' said Maria. 'I will find Greenwich just fine. Fifty one degrees north and zero degrees west, right?'

'You were just humouring me,' said Alex. 'How did you know that?'

'I like to know where I am and where I'm going. Now, go on, go do whatever it is that your job needs you to do. I'm a grown woman. Go count things. Just promise you'll let me tell you all about it tonight.'

'OK, that sounds good. Just stay on this train to Tower Hill and then you should be able to pick up the boat service.'

Alex left the train, left Maria, just as the doors slid shut again. He turned to wave and she lifted her arm in response, a brief flash of white as her watch caught the glare of an overhead light. Somewhere in the back of his mind he remembered Professor Miller testily explaining relativity to them again, three of them sitting in his dusty study in Oxford, listening to the rain outside. He remembered listening for patterns and order in the rhythmic fall of water on pavement. Remembered debating the apparent randomness of rain with colleagues who went on to help discover gravitational waves. Discovered the universe's pulse. Remembered letting his mind roam, untethered, to fathom the smallest particles and the largest spaces and the longest times. He knew, dimly, that he and Maria would observe that light on the train differently. Her from inside the carriage. Him watching her move with the train from the platform. They would see the light relative to their perspectives. The train cleared the platform and, buffeted by the sudden back draught, Alex turned and headed for work.

Maria closed her eyes. The contrast was a little too bright when the carriage was plunged into the darkness of the tunnel. She felt the familiar, nagging tingle in her hands and rubbed them together until it faded.

Friday

Maria had blacked out somewhere between Mars and Jupiter. She'd woken up in the University Hospital at Lewisham. They told her that she'd passed out in the planetarium at the Royal Observatory but in the darkness of the auditorium nobody had realised until the audience was returned from its tour of the solar system and the lights came back on. She remembered seeing the sun. Distended solar flares erupting across its writhing, fiery surface. It looked, to her, like an angry, malignant tumour seen in detail through a microscope. She remembered the perspective pulling away from the sun and the sensation of spinning, facing out towards the neighbourhood of planets. Accelerating past Mercury and Venus and Earth. Fragments of the commentary stuck in her memory. Not the scientific facts but the more human attributions. Mercury, named for the messenger of the gods. Blake writing in tribute to Venus. *Speak silence with thy glimmering eyes, And wash the dusk with silver.* She remembered Mars. Another angry, red circle.

Remembered it growing on the screen above her until it filled her vision, seeming to throb and pulse, bringer of war, until she slipped from consciousness.

She was sitting up in bed when they arrived.

'God, we were so worried,' said Sarah. 'When you didn't come back, we just didn't know what to think.'

'Are you OK?' asked Rob. 'They won't tell us anything because we're not family or anything. We tried to tell them that you're our guest and that you don't know anyone here but they said they can't disclose information.'

Alex was silent. He hovered at the end of the bed, head down, shifting his weight between his feet.

'What happened?' said Sarah.

Maria closed her eyes. The telling was the thing she had found hardest in the last few months. The shock she had felt on being told was something she felt again each time she passed on the news. She resented it. Resented seeing herself reduced to the victim of something random, an object of sympathy, in the eyes of those with whom she shared the shock. There were many things she had chosen to be in life and she wanted to be remembered for them. Not for this. Not this arbitrary act of war that her own body had declared on itself.

As she opened her eyes she pulled the delicately carved hair clip from its position above her left ear and laid it on the sheet in front of her. Tipping her head forward she lifted her hair deftly from her scalp and placed it next to the clip, dark grey strands spread across the crisp whiteness of the bed. The exposed skin was smooth and pale save for a blotchy, swollen lump, crimson stained behind her right ear, the size of a dollar coin. *It used to be the size of a dime. Look after the dimes and the dollars will look after themselves. That's what Mom always used to say.* She looked up at the three of them. Sarah had covered her mouth with her hand, eyes pricking with tears. Rob was shaking his head. Alex had pulled his arms across his chest, colour drained from his face. And then Sarah's arms were round her and they were both crying.

In the aftermath, with the three of them perched on the edge of her bed, Sarah closest, Alex furthest away, she told them all of it.

She told them that she had been diagnosed nine months ago, had been told the chemo wasn't working three months ago, and that she'd taken the decision to abandon the treatment and live what time she had left. Maybe six months. They didn't really know. It had brought a certain clarity to her thinking. Not peace exactly, she felt restless for life rather than reconciled to death. She told them that she'd lost her husband ten years ago. That they'd never had children – she paused as she recounted this, an unspoken regret – and she'd found herself alone. Initially, she admitted, she'd felt lost and had only really made sense of her new circumstances when she'd moved away from Wichita and deeper into the country where, eventually, she'd found a new sense of perspective under the broad and sweeping Midwestern skies. Found enrichment in the amplified solitude of a small town rather than the isolation she'd felt in a bustling, busy city.

They listened in silence, letting her talk. Sarah held her hand. Rob poured a glass of water.

Alex grew increasingly agitated, rising from the bed and pacing the floor. When she seemed to have finished speaking he started to rock backwards and forwards on his heels. He spoke quietly and urgently.

'It's unforgivable. I'm sorry. To leave you like that.' Words tumbled from him in a torrent, addressed as much to himself as to Maria. 'How could I have done that? Someone should have been with you. I should have been with you. I was with you. And then I left. For an overdue audit. Left to count things when you were counting on me. I'm sorry. I'm sorry. I'm sorry.' He was shaking his head, fists clenching and unclenching until Rob put his hand on his shoulder.

'Hey, hey, Alex. It's alright. This wasn't your fault. You didn't know. None of us knew.'

'Rob's right,' said Maria softly. 'Don't blame yourself for this. I chose to take the trip and I don't regret it. Whilst I still have choices I'm damned if I'm not going to use them. Please, please don't blame yourself.'

'But I should have been there,' said Alex.

Maria stared at him until he met her gaze. He noticed the

cataract in her eye, the smudged white dots, stars through an unfocused telescope.

'Not for me,' she said. 'You shouldn't have been there for me. I made my choice and don't need looking after, Alex. You need to make your choices. Trust me. Make them before they get made for you.'

Saturday

It was late by the time Rob and Sarah arrived back at the house with Maria. She'd stayed at the hospital for twenty-four hours, reluctantly agreeing that she might need the rest but impatient to be away from the array of medical equipment and drugs and professionals that could do nothing for her. She'd joked with the nurses that she was like a diabetic with a sweet tooth in a candy store. *You got nothing I can have but boy do I want it all.* Sarah had insisted on organising a taxi, worried about the hustle and bustle of the tube on Saturday evening. Maria had agreed on condition that she paid, they use a black cab, and that they make the driver cross the Thames via Tower Bridge. She told Sarah that it'd be another landmark she could sketch for her game, another little source of dopamine for people playing, another marker to help them navigate. Sarah thought there was more of the tourist in Maria than she cared to admit and that she probably just wanted to see the strange castle on the river.

They crossed the Thames as the sun was going down, the towers on the bridge short and squat against the skyline in comparison to the jagged thrust of the Shard which dominated the view to the west. London was a city of silhouettes in the dusk, the fading light leaving just familiar shapes, the impression of places. Rob pointed out the sights as they appeared, sometimes just a momentary glimpse between office blocks and flats, and then a broader sweep of buildings as they crossed the bridge. A jumble of shapes and styles from the past and from the future. St Paul's. The Gherkin. The Tower of London. City Hall. Traffic was unusually light and they didn't get stuck as they crossed. Rob had hoped that perhaps they would so Maria would have more time to admire the view but she had to absorb it in less than a minute before they plunged into Whitechapel and everything closed in around them again.

When they stopped outside their house it was dark. The street light hadn't been fixed and all of the lights inside were off. Rob let them in and called for Alex. There was no reply but it was then that they heard the shouts from outside.

* * *

Alex hadn't gone back to the hospital. The others knew he blamed himself for what had happened but didn't realise how hard it had hit him. He'd said he wanted a bit of time on his own and they'd respected that. In the time they'd lived together it was something they'd become used to. Rob teased him for being grumpy and they knew he'd never really settled into corporate life but neither of them thought there was more to it than that. If he was honest with himself he knew that the way he felt had a name. Depression. He should have been more clinical about it, more scientific, but he found it hard to apply his usual, objective mode of thinking to his own internal emotional landscape.

He knew it had been getting worse and he could trace some of it to the small sets of decisions that had taken him further and further from the things that he'd thought of as making up who he was. He remembered the genuine disappointment that Professor Miller had expressed when he'd told him that he was giving it up. He hadn't been angry and he'd even understood it – no-one's getting rich mapping the universe – but there was almost a resignation to it. A sense that another bright talent was about to be eclipsed by the need to pay the rent.

There had been occasional rational moments when he realised that he could just jack it all in, walk away from the office and start again. Lately those moments had come less often. The sane and reasonable voice in his head drowned out by a chorus of anxiety, regret and sadness.

Seeing Maria in the hospital had shattered what was left of his fragile inner peace. It wasn't just the guilt, on some level he knew that it wasn't his fault, but the stark confrontation with mortality that had shaken him. There seemed to him to be a pointlessness to it. He'd always valued order and structure, causality and consequences, and whilst he could understand the facts of her disease he couldn't explain why it was happening anymore than he could explain his own illness.

He put on his suit, straightened his tie, and headed up to the terrace.

* * *

Up on the roof Alex had his back to them. There was a small wall that ran round the sides of the terrace at knee height, there as a gentle reminder if someone got too close to the edge. You could perch on it and dangle your legs over the side of the house if you didn't mind the guttering. None of them had ever thought of it as particularly dangerous. Early on the landlord had offered to put up a taller set of railings but they thought it would obstruct the view and had told him not to bother. Alex was standing on the wall, seemingly oblivious to the shouts from people in the flats in the adjacent street telling him to get down.

'What are you doing, Alex?' Rob spoke quietly, holding his arms out, palms down, trying to signal a sense of calm that he didn't feel to Sarah and Maria.

'Alex, please,' said Sarah. 'Just step down and let's talk.'

Alex didn't reply and didn't move. It had been a cloudless day and the temperature was dropping now that the sun had gone, and the air was still. Alex didn't feel the cold through his suit. Pure wool. He vaguely remembered that fact had been important at work, they'd all been given pointers on personal presentation in the first year on the graduate scheme. A couple of the partners, knowing his background, had joked that he'd have to leave the cords and the elbow patches behind now that he was a professional. There'd been no malice in it. He hadn't been offended. It wasn't until later that he'd begun to reflect on his decision and wonder whether he'd got it badly wrong. It was Maria who broke the impasse.

'Where are you Alex?' He didn't turn but this time he did reply.

'I don't know. I honestly don't know.'

'Latitude. Start with that. Tell me our latitude,' nudged Maria.

'I don't know,' said Alex. 'How would I know that?'

'We're not so far from Greenwich. I bet it's roughly fifty one degrees north and a touch over zero degrees west. How would you know if I hadn't told you? You taught me this Alex.'

'A fixed reference point. You need a fixed reference point and then you can work it out.'

Across Islington the lights went out. Later it was reported as a power cut, some problem with a sudden surge on the National Grid causing fail safes to kick in and the electricity to switch off. Around them, shining rectangular frames, the windows of the surrounding flats and houses, winked out. The street lights snapped off. Shakespeare Street went dark. As their eyes adjusted to the absence of light Maria walked across the terrace, reached up, and took Alex's hand.

'Tell me what you see,' she said.

'You can never see much here,' he replied. 'Usually just Venus and some of the brighter stars. The moon obviously, when it's out.'

Rob and Sarah cautiously crossed the terrace and stood beside Alex. Sarah took his other hand.

'I saw Mars at the planetarium,' said Maria. 'It's the last thing I remember before I fainted. Where would it be if we could see it now?'

Alex described its position relative to Venus and slowly began to tell them what he could remember about the positions of the distant objects they could see and the ones that they couldn't. He was a little rusty but none of them would have known if he got anything wrong. He showed them Orion's Belt, the three stars in a line that they could usually see above them, bright enough even when London wasn't dimmed, and then he noticed the slightly skewed rectangle of Ursa Major. It was just visible now that the glare from the ground had been subdued and, just a slight turn of the head on from that if he followed an imagined line from its two pointer stars, he could make out Polaris. The North Star. He described it to the others.

'So you know where you are now,' said Maria squeezing his hand.

'It's a start,' said Alex. 'I could work out the latitude but you know longitude is always trickier than that.'

'Because we're always spinning, always moving,' said Maria.

'Yes. Yes, we are. I just wanted to make it stop.'

'You can't make it stop, Alex,' she answered. 'Not like this. It'll stop for you, sure, but everything else keeps on spinning. You've got your fixed point up there,' she gestured at the sky, 'and maybe you just need to pick your own fixed point down here. Your own Greenwich.'

'I think I had it,' said Alex. 'I think I used to have it. Maybe I just need to find my way back to it again.' He stepped down from the wall and quietly accepted Maria's embrace. Rob and Sarah clutched at his back and the four of them stood on the roof holding him as he wept.

They stayed out on the terrace until the power came back on about an hour later. Sarah had made them all tea and they'd sat staring across the rooftops, hands wrapped round warm mugs, steam rising into the night air. When the lights returned the stars overhead faded but all of them swore they could still see the North Star, unwavering, the sky rotating around it.

Sunday (one year later)

They had promised Maria that they'd watch the sun rise over Bryce Canyon and remember her. She had died in the spring, the emails and Skype calls that they'd all maintained after she returned home from London becoming steadily less frequent as her illness took hold. They'd all wanted to fly out but she had insisted that they shouldn't.

I am well cared for. Come and remember me when I'm gone, she'd told them. *Come and pick me out a diamond from the sky. Don't let Alex tell you that stars and diamonds aren't the same things either. I've been reading a lot now I'm stuck in bed and all the carbon in our solar system might just be the scattered dust from a dying star. Some of it must be diamonds and some of it must be us. I kinda like the idea that I'm built from a supernova. Don't spoil it for me.*

Alex, back now at Oxford, had called in a favour from one of the professors in the Chemistry department and persuaded him to send Maria a letter, on very official looking University headed paper, confirming that essentially, yes, she *was* made from stardust.

They had travelled to Kansas for the funeral. Sarah flew in from Montreal, Rob and Alex from Heathrow. Sarah's design work from her sketches around London had picked up positive critical notices when the game had shipped and she'd taken a larger role in the Canadian office. She'd held firm on a flexible arrangement that left her enough time to paint and she'd just exhibited for the first time in a small downtown gallery. The others teased her when they met up – Lead Concept Artist putting on shows at Station 16, get you – but she could see how pleased they were for her. Despite them all leaving the house they were closer now than when they'd lived together. Rob had stayed in London but had needed to move a bit further out, his new job at the housing association didn't pay well but he knew why he was doing it. Alex, in Oxford, was picking up the thread of his unfinished thesis, looking again for order in the chaos.

The three of them sat in silence as the first light of dawn stole over the jagged formations of the canyon, orange rocks warming into life, shadows extending. The last of the visible stars overhead slowly faded from view but they knew they were still there. Sarah had brought a flask and shared out paper cups of hot coffee to ward off the last of the night's chill. It was a long time before anyone spoke.

'Thirty-seven degrees north. One hundred and twelve degrees west,' said Alex.

'What's that?' said Rob.

'It's where we are, isn't it?' asked Sarah. 'Co-ordinates.' Alex nodded.

'You'll never find where you want to go unless you know where you are now,' he said softly.

'You're getting all deep on us again,' said Rob. 'Who said that?'

'Someone who always knew where she was. Someone who'll be missed.' He raised his coffee in salute and the others held their cups up in a quiet toast as the sun began its steady ascent marking the new day.

The End

Linda Cohen was born in Leicestershire. She has lived in various places, but has been settled in Little Chalfont for the last ten years. After leaving school at a very young age – and regretting it ever since – she joined Sally Norton's writing class in 2014. It was wonderful at last to be able to let her imagination go wherever it wanted, sometimes in most surprising directions. Linda retired after working for many years as a Social Work Assistant on a Spinal Injuries Unit as well as in many other roles. A mum to two very old children and grandmother to five, she finds that going to the writing group has at least kept her off the streets!

Liz Losty was born in Belfast and graduated with an Honours Degree in Political Science from Queens University, Belfast. Liz travelled after graduating, before settling in London and pursuing the well-worn path to a career in the City where she worked for Reuters. She continued her career as a Project Management and Business Consultant and is involved in a number of charities, including Young Enterprise. Liz lives in Buckinghamshire with her three children, who teach her every day how to see the world through their eyes. They all dote on the family dog, who rules the roost!

Richard Hopgood was born in 1952 in South East London, the son of a policeman and a nurse and one of five children. After boarding school in Sussex he studied English at Oxford and London. His childhood ambition was to be a naturalist and a poet, neither of which transpired. His favourite short story writer is John McGahern.

Debbie Hunter was born in Berkshire. At the age of sixteen she emigrated with her family to South Africa where she lived for thirty years. She now lives in Amersham where she enjoys both the beautiful countryside and the close proximity to London. She is married with two grown up children and a brand new grandson.

A native of Sussex, **Angela Haward** has lived in Amersham for twenty-eight years. She is married with three adult children and two grandchildren. Following retirement, she is reinventing herself in her original incarnation as a writer. After university, she worked as an industrial journalist and did a bit of freelance work on the side. She has had a few articles published and produced a French teaching aid for primary school children. In between, she has done a lot of other things – worked in school business management and in PR for a charity, travelled in her motorhome and cared for elderly family members. Angela is privileged to have been part of Just Write who produced the award-winning anthology Spilling the Beans as well as Delayed Reaction, in which she experimented with the thriller genre. In Shakespeare Street, she tries her hand at a historical mystery. The group has raised her faltering literary ambition into second gear!

Emma Dark, born in 1948, previously lived in Dorset and Surrey and spent some years in Central America where she taught English. Emma comes from an artistic and literary family. Her father, aunt and cousin are published authors and her late brother and eldest daughter are accomplished artists. Her husband is a wonderful photographer and her youngest daughter is an aspiring writer. Emma has lived in Amersham for 25 years. After retiring, Emma decided to follow her love of writing and is currently trying to cope with her first novel, with which she has a love-hate relationship. She has found the help and support of her fellow writers very helpful when her drive to keep writing flags.

For her story in this book, Emma found inspiration in some of the correspondence sent by WW1 soldiers at the front to their friends and family. The only characters based on real people are Dr Sophie Bryant and Miss Buss. Frances Mary Buss (1827 – 1894) founded the North London Collegiate School, in 1850, and the Camden School for Girls, in 1871. Dr Sophie Bryant (1850 – 1922) was the first woman to be awarded a DSc by London University and she succeeded Miss Buss in 1885, remaining Headmistress of the North London Collegiate School until 1918. Dr Bryant supported women's suffrage but thought it should be delayed until women were better educated: a little literary licence has been taken with her character.

A native of The Potteries, **Carol Hall** left the cups and saucers behind to settle in sunny Chalfont St Giles, Buckinghamshire, in 1985. She always wanted to be a writer but could never find the time or the energy to write until she retired, aged 58, in 2013. Carol had worked full-time for 40 years, most of it in social housing management. Her last job before retirement was Director of Housing and Customer Services at a large Housing Association in Dunstable, where she had the daunting task of keeping 10,000 families happy in their homes. Carol lives with Jeff, her husband of 42 years, and their cocker spaniel, Ted. When she's not writing, she tries to keep fit with tap dancing and yoga.

Nicki Kelland learnt to read before she went to school and learnt to speed read at the age of five. As a result she grew up reading Alan Garner, Tolkien, Margery Allingham and Agatha Christie. She moved on to Robin Jarvis, Phil Rickman, Stephen King and Lee Child. Her favourite book will always be one of the first ever detective novels The Moonstone by Wilkie Collins. She soon began writing her own stories and her great ambition is to write a thrilling mystery. By day, Nicki works in Learning and Development and spends her spare time writing, and was awarded Runner-Up Prize in the Swansea and District Writers' Circle 2015 Short Story Competition. Nicki has previously been published in Garage 64 and Dark Gathering Tales of Horror and Mystery. Nicki lives in Loudwater, Buckinghamshire, home of the Midsomer Murders . . .

Now that she has retired from careers as diverse as a freelance musician and an officer in the Royal Naval Reserve, **Vicky Trelinska** has the time to concentrate on writing. Originally from Sussex, she was educated at St Swithun's School, Winchester, and trained as a pianist at the Royal Academy of Music, London. So far her writing successes include an article published in Yours magazine, a story shortlisted in a Writers' News competition and another shortlisted in Writing Magazine's subscribers' competition as well as letters and press releases printed in local papers. She is married to a retired GP and has a step-son.

Chris Payne moved to England from Vancouver, Canada in 1989 for one year's work experience and never went back. She lives in Amersham with her British husband and their three children, who encouraged her to take practical steps with Just Write towards her dream of being an author. She works in employee engagement in the healthcare industry and is a digital communications geek. Her story in this collection is dedicated to the memory of her proudest advocate, her father.

Lesley Close, the youngest of three children, was born in Oxford in 1956 and went to school in Buckingham. A voracious reader from an early age, she managed to avoid reading any of the English language literary classics until middle age! Her favourite writers include Ruth Rendell, Phillip Pullman, William Trevor and Alice Munro among (many) others. Lesley learned tap dancing and singing as an adult, and is a keen cyclist, walker and photographer. She has two non-fiction books in print and her third title, an e-publication, hit the 'shelves' in May 2013.

Phil Tysoe was born in Nottinghamshire in the 1970s, graduated from Leicester University in the 1990s and now lives in Amersham with his wife and daughter. By day he works in the field of retail consumer insights and by night he indulges his weakness for red wine, playing the guitar, and Bruce Springsteen. He writes and publishes short stories on his blog at: www.42at42.wordpress.com Careering is his third story with Just Write and is dedicated to his mum: his best and most loyal reader.